GODDESS LEGACY

M.W. Muse

Edited by Lacey Thacker
Cover art by Letitia Hasser | RBA Designs © May 2014
Formatting by JTLW Design © July 2014

Mandolin Park Publishing
Penning Princess Publishing
P.O. Box 13188 Maumelle, AR 72113
www.penningprincess.com

ISBN: 978-0-9882130-4-3

Dedication

To JT Lacy for all the hard work you did (and still do) behind the scenes to ensure this new endeavor became a reality. Branching out on my own is very scary and exciting, but I wouldn't have been able to take this leap without your love and support. To fellow author Parker Kincade for, among so many things, being my writing rock. I honestly don't know how I published books before you came into my life. You are truly awesome.

And to all my fans who followed me over to this new facet of my writing career and giving M.W. Muse the same love and support you have on my works in other genres.

This book is for you.

Chapter 1

"Surprise!"

Legacy jumped and nearly dropped the new shoes her friend Calli had just bought at the mall. She'd been dragged there after school with dubious taunts of makeup and bling-bling, but had spent the majority of the time feeding Calli's shoe fetish. And now they were at Legacy's house, in the doorway, staring at a living room full of her friends and some people who worked with her guardian, Lissa. Great. A surprise birthday party. Legacy should've known she couldn't sneak by the not-so-big-one-seven with just a nod from her non-traditional family and a night with her BFF.

Especially when she'd told Lissa she didn't want

a birthday party. But she'd learned long ago that Lissa did whatever she wanted anyway. She'd been Legacy's guardian since the night her parents had died when she was just a baby, and the woman had always been there for her, even on silly celebratory days like this one. Lissa and her mom, Dora, had been friends when Legacy was a baby, so she usually told her stories to help her feel close to her mom on occasions like this. Legacy feared today would be no different. Only now she'd be donning a party hat for trips down memory lane.

Legacy smiled as she turned to Calli. "You must be in on this. I can't believe it." She was shocked her friend had kept the secret, since discretion was not one of Calli's strong suits.

Calli Rhodes was her best friend, and had been for many years. She was one of those girls that came from money and lots of it. Being the fashionista she was, she regularly wore the latest fashions and rarely wore the same outfit the same way twice. Even though Calli came from money and would probably never work a day in her life, she never seemed to let that go to her head. Of course, she usually made comments about other people's clothing, but that was really the extent of her snobbery.

"Guilty." She fluttered her eyelashes with false innocence.

Legacy hugged her and then turned around to gaze at the room, which had been decorated perfectly. There were streamers draped across the ceiling, and balloons gathered in bunches and disbursed throughout the room. A large, personalized sign hung on the far wall that read *Happy Seventeenth Birthday Legacy Kore!* Everyone was grinning. Some already had plates full of finger foods while others had plastic cups with red punch. It was definitely a party in full swing.

Lissa had one table set up with several gifts, a different table with all kinds of snacks, and another table in the middle of the room with two birthday cakes. One was obviously a homemade chocolate cake, probably the one Lissa had mentioned making this morning as a ruse to throw Legacy off any party trail. The other cake looked like no ordinary cake. In fact, it didn't look like a cake at all. If it weren't for the icing, it would have just looked like a centerpiece as it was made into the shape of a beautifully wrapped present with a billowing bow atop it.

Wow. Legacy felt tears form in the corners of her eyes as she fully took in the grand scene. Lissa had gone through a lot of trouble. Just for her. The woman in question stepped over and threw her arms around Legacy, hugging her tightly.

"Happy birthday, Legacy."

Olive squealed next to her. "Are you surprised?"

Olive Borne was Lissa's other ward. But unlike Legacy, Lissa had adopted her. There had been talk about Olive's mother putting her up for adoption before she was born, but no specifics were ever discussed. As far as the family was concerned, Lissa was Olive's mother, though Lissa had been very open about the fact Olive was adopted. Olive was a couple of years younger than Legacy, and the three of them made up their happy home.

"Totally," Legacy said, smiling at Olive while blinking in an effort to keep the tears from falling to her cheeks.

Truth was, she'd been very surprised. Lissa usually made her feel special on important occasions, but she had never done anything like this before. Legacy had always thought she didn't like surprises, but she had to admit to herself this felt pretty nice.

"How long have you been planning this?" she was finally able to ask Lissa, knowing her voice wouldn't crack.

"A few weeks. Calli called me. It was her idea. Olive

and I wanted to do something special, but Calli didn't think you'd willingly agree to a party, so she figured a surprise party would be just what you needed."

Legacy glanced over at Calli. "You plotted this," she accused teasingly, and several people in the room laughed.

"I didn't plot. I just planned," she said angelically.

"So the trip to the mall. The shoes. The makeup." *The speech about how I should make a pass at Adin,* Legacy added in her head. "That was all just a setup?"

With a wink and a nod, Legacy got her answer.

She turned toward the few people who were standing the closest and thanked them for coming. Several of the other people in the room got more snacks and talked amongst themselves in small groups. She started to feel a little more relaxed as the previously undivided attention she'd held turned to a more suitable level of interest. She continued to scan the room as small talk commenced.

And then whipped her head around to double-check what she thought she'd just seen.

Legacy gasped at the confirmation and then coughed to cover it as she quickly turned away, barely remembering her manners to excuse herself from the recently started conversation. But it was hard because she couldn't pretend she hadn't just seen who was here. At her house. Celebrating her birthday.

Adin Sheppard.

Gods, ever since she was little, she'd had it bad for the guy, and the fact that his grandma lived next door caused a few mini heart attacks for Legacy over the years—the only thing hotter than Adin was Adin *shirtless* doing yard work for his sweet grandma. Yum.

Legacy had wondered when she'd get to see him again since today wasn't only her birthday but the last day of school … and Adin had been a senior who graduated a couple of weeks ago. He'd returned today with the rest of the graduating class for the annual parade and float competition between the leaving senior classmen and the rising seniors. She'd put on her favorite outfit—a green dress with just the right accessories. Her official eye color was blue, but her eyes tended to change colors from blue to green depending on what she was wearing. *Hopefully,* her eyes had cooperated and had gotten on board with the color scheme when she'd seen Adin.

And see him she did. But she hadn't been the only girl in school eager to ogle one last time. Ellen and Kate had been fawning all over him and his new Camaro like they didn't already have boyfriends. Yeah, it had bothered her in a way she didn't want to analyze. It wasn't like he and Legacy had ever been an item. He was just outgoing and charming in such a way that it seemed like second nature to him, making her insides melt every time he gave her any attention. Not to mention the fact that he was unbelievably gorgeous. Not that looks mattered to her … *much.* But the way he looked should be considered a sin. He was tall with dark blond hair and piercing blue eyes. He didn't even look like a senior because none of the other seniors looked anything like him. It was as if he'd stepped out of her personal fairytale.

Thankfully, Calli had mentioned to the crowd this morning that it was Legacy's birthday, and Adin had overheard. Even though it had just happened, the events would forever be burned into her brain…

"It's Legacy's birthday." Calli looked over at Legacy. "It's a day for celebration."

"It sure is," she heard, coming from behind her in an unmistakable masculine voice. "Happy birthday, Legacy."

She turned around to look at the guy who'd just wished her a happy birthday, but she already knew who had said it. She could hone into that voice from several feet away and still go weak in the knees.

"Thanks, Adin." She smiled as their eyes met, hoping she didn't look like a star-struck idiot. "Nice car."

"Thanks. My parents promised me a new car when I graduated, but since I decided to go to college close by, they used the extra money to surprise me with something nicer. You know, now that there's no room and board to worry about." He swayed onto his toes. "So …do you have any plans for your birthday?"

"Um, not really. I mean, Calli and I are going shopping after school, and Lissa is baking me a cake for tonight."

"Well, you look stunning," he said as he took in her green dress. "That color really brings out the color of your eyes. They're so beautiful."

"*Thank you.*" Don't think anything of it. He's nice to everyone, *she reminded herself. "Er, you look nice today, too."*

"You look nice every day, but thank you."

"Legacy," Calli interrupted. "We need to get ready for the parade."

"Oh, okay." Thank heavens she didn't have time to process what Adin just said and make more out of it than what it truly was.

Adin smiled at her and took a step closer. Her heart tried to break free from her chest, and she felt blood rushing to her face.

"I hope you have a wonderful birthday, Legacy," Adin whispered to her in such a sincere manner that it made her feel like they were the only two people in the parking lot. He stroked her arm as he stepped even closer in a move that she was sure to end in an embrace.

She was silently screaming in anticipation. Sure, Adin had hugged her before, but she never got used to it.

He held her tightly for a brief couple of seconds, and, somehow, she managed to move her numb arms from her sides to around his back before he stepped away.

"Good luck on your float," Legacy said to Adin to try to distract herself from the wonderful smell of his skin. *"You'll need it. Ours is really cool."*

"You too." He laughed and winked at her as she turned and walked...

Oh yeah, she'd never forget that brief conversation or the way he'd made her feel. And now Prince Charming was standing in her living room.

Since everyone seemed to be comfortable mingling with each other, Legacy figured she wouldn't be missed or gawked at if she tried to have a private discussion. She walked toward Calli who was still talking to one of the other guests, but she excused herself and walked over when she saw Legacy with a frown.

"What is it?" she asked with concern in her voice. "You look constipated or something."

"Did you, er, invite everyone here?" Legacy asked, ignoring the constipation comment.

"I invited some of our friends from school, but Lissa talked to the people in your neighborhood and at her office and invited them. Why?"

"Oh, I'm just surprised to see some of these people."

Calli started to turn around to scan the room. Legacy grabbed her arm. "Don't."

"Huh? What's with you?"

She knew Adin's grandmother lived next door, so he probably found out about the party through her. Legacy didn't want her friend to make it obvious they were talking about him. Even though she apparently hadn't figured that out yet herself.

"Act natural. Look around the room *casually*. I'll meet you at the buffet table." Legacy couldn't even say his name out loud to explain.

"Er, okay ... um, are you going to explain this to me

when we get over there?"

"Uh-huh, just act natural."

Legacy left her side and walked over to the closest group of people that were engaged in their own conversation. She joined in — they were talking about an upcoming storm. At least it wasn't a topic she had to be fully involved in, so she could participate lightly in the conversation while watching Calli take in the room.

Then Calli looked in Adin's direction. Luckily, he wasn't looking at her because she looked utterly shocked. She composed herself quickly and made her way to the buffet table. Legacy politely excused herself and walked over to the table, grabbing a plate for snacks as she walked to the end where Calli stood.

"I take it you didn't invite him?" Legacy asked as she grabbed a pair of tongs to get some food.

"No."

"I figured that much when I saw you look at him."

"Are you okay?" she asked in a timid whisper.

"Yeah, just shocked. His grandma probably told him about the party since you said Lissa invited the neighbors." How he found out about the party was quickly taking a backseat to another issue, though. "Did you see who was standing next to him?"

"Yep. Ellen and Kate." Ellen Battles and Kate Travis were best friends who attached themselves to whomever they felt was popular at any given moment. Considering this was a small school and they really didn't have cliques, Ellen and Kate tried their best to form them. Legacy liked them just fine, but didn't trust either of them. They were both the type of girl who would stab you in the back to get ahead — Ellen more so than Kate. Since Calli was obviously the richest girl in school, they tended to gravitate toward her. Legacy was just an unfortunate aspect of that vanity they had to endure, but she pretended she was oblivious just the same.

"Uh-huh."

"Don't worry about them. Just be happy he's here." Calli put her hand on her hip and smirked. "You know, there's nothing wrong with liking someone, Legacy. I've liked lots of guys."

"Yeah, but you usually date the guys you like."

Calli chuckled. "True, girl. But maybe now you can make a move on Adin like I suggested earlier."

Legacy felt herself blanching as she shook her head frantically.

Calli sighed. "Okay. Take it easy. I won't press it anymore tonight. But don't worry about Ellen or Kate either. They both have boyfriends."

"Like that matters..."

"I know you don't like either of them, but really, I don't think they mean any harm."

"They are fully capable of causing any amount of harm they want."

"True. But they don't know you like Adin. He's the best looking guy in school, or at least he was before he graduated. They're probably just enjoying the eye candy."

"You know they have to be wondering what *he* is doing at *my* party."

"Which is something else you don't need to worry about. Jeez, you could stroke out from the stress. I'll go figure out what's been said and make sure they understand his grandma is your neighbor."

"If you bring it up, it'll look like I'm hiding something from them."

"No, it won't. I'll be really casual about it. "Calli grabbed her arm. "C'mon, we need to keep walking around so it doesn't seem like I'm hogging your attention. People will think it's rude if you don't personally thank everyone for coming tonight."

"I know. Just give me a sec." She took a deep breath and then nodded.

Calli threw on a quick smile to remind her she was supposed to be sporting a happy face, and then they disbanded. Legacy approached the closest group to chat. This conversation started out better as it wasn't about the weather, but then it turned to her, and she had to put on her game face. These were people Lissa worked with. Legacy usually saw them a few times a year, every year, at picnics, holiday parties, and other office functions that family members were invited to. They asked her about school, plans for the summer, and the types of classes she was taking next school year. They commented on how much she'd grown since the last time they all saw her, and she was the gracious hostess, answering all their questions attentively and blushing at the comments about her growth spurt.

When Lissa and Olive walked over to Calli and they walked over to the cake, Legacy turned to face them.

"It's time for Legacy to blow out her candles," Lissa announced as the crowd quieted down.

Legacy quickly popped the last of the chocolate covered strawberries she'd retrieved from the buffet table into her mouth and made her way over to the cake.

Calli took pictures of her behind the two cakes while Lissa lit the seventeen candles on the chocolate cake. She smiled as she scanned the room, locking eyes with several of the guests. She saw Ellen's forced smile and Kate's more natural one.

She saved Adin's face for last because she knew when she saw him looking at her, it would be difficult to keep her composure. When she allowed herself to look at him, he looked incredible. His hair slightly was disheveled. As she glanced from his hair to his face, his piercing blue eyes locked onto hers. She couldn't go any further. He could have been nude for all she knew. His face lit up like they were long lost friends seeing each other for the first time in too many years. Her heart pounded in her chest, and she forced herself to keep breathing regularly. She tried to feign a little shock, pretending this was the first time she saw him and really feigning for the benefit of Ellen and Kate since she didn't know what they were thinking about Adin being here. She then returned his smile. Even though she knew she needed to speak to everyone here, she definitely knew now that she would have to go talk to him as soon as she could.

Luckily, Lissa finished with the candles and turned to her, getting her attention. She was able to unlock her gaze with Adin to watch Lissa as she started the crowd with the birthday song.

She laughed appreciatively, and once they were finished singing — some shouting — the rendition, she bowed her head and held her hair back while she extinguished the candles with her shaky breath. Flashes blinded her while she rose back to a full standing position, and she kept cheesing while the cameras finished clicking in her direction.

Lissa quickly removed the hot candles and started cutting the cake. She handed Legacy the first piece, and she took it with her away from the table. Calli grabbed a piece and came over to the wall she was leaning against while the rest of the crowd lined up to get their pieces.

"What did you find out from Ellen and Kate?" Legacy asked through her teeth while she kept a smile on her face.

Calli turned her back to the crowd so she could face her and speak without anyone seeing her expression.

"Nothing we didn't already expect. He told them he found out from his grandma."

"Do they suspect anything else?"

"I don't think so."

"Did you talk to him?"

"Yes. He thanked me for taking the initiative on the surprise party and said I did a wonderful job."

"Did he compliment you? *Personally*, I mean?" She didn't know why, but she just had to know.

"Um … I don't think so. Well, he did say he liked my dress."

"Okay." She was only slightly appeased that Adin hadn't compliment her friend like he had her earlier, but she was really happy Ellen and Kate seemed as if they weren't expecting anything out of the ordinary, even after seeing Adin here tonight.

"I know you don't want to hear this now, but maybe … it'll give you a little courage."

"Ugh. What?" She looked away, irritated.

"You assumed Adin's grandma invited him, and he apparently confirmed that assumption to Ellen and Kate."

"And?" She knew those things, so she couldn't see Calli's point.

"And … I don't see his grandma here."

Her eyes shot back to Calli. "What?"

"I looked around the room, and I do admit there are some people I don't recognize from Lissa's office, but as much as I've been over here, I know I've seen his grandma a few times. Unless she's grown about twenty years *younger*, she's not here. It looks like Adin heard about the party … and came here alone."

"I don't want to hear your theories as to why he would do that."

"Fine. But you know you have to speak to him before he leaves. You've already spoken to just about everyone else."

"I haven't talked to Ellen or Kate yet," she defended

herself.

"Because they've been talking to Adin. I'll get them away from him, so you can have a moment alone."

"No! I mean, you don't have to do that."

"Legacy, you *have* to talk to him. Besides, I know you want to talk."

"I do," she confessed, looking back down again.

"Don't worry about it. Just keep telling yourself he's just a friend, and that's all he'll ever be." Calli couldn't help but smirk at her own sarcasm as she spoke.

"Fine. But I want to talk to Ellen and Kate first."

Calli nodded as she stepped away from her to help Lissa and Olive with the cake.

Legacy walked over to Ellen and Kate while she played with the icing on her piece. "Hey, girls. Thanks for coming tonight. I really appreciate it."

"Oh, we wouldn't have missed this for the world," Kate said with a genuine smile on her face.

"Yeah, Calli asked us if we would come," Ellen responded, a little less enthused.

"Where's Thad and Seth?" she asked, trying to keep the conversation flowing.

Thad was Ellen's boyfriend. He was a typical jock. He was a better athlete than any other guy in school, but he was still a jerk.

Seth was Kate's boyfriend. He was more likable. He was also an athlete, but was nicer to people than Thad was. He and Seth were pretty close, so she guessed it made sense they would date two girls who were already best friends.

"They're out destroying the senior float with Alex and Laos, and I don't even understand why those two are there. They can't stand each other," Ellen said in a bored manner.

"Some of the juniors didn't like the fact that they lost, so they're taking out their frustration on the senior float," Kate said, slightly embarrassed.

"Well, we're the seniors now. I guess they can get rid of that monstrosity if they want to," she teased, keeping the conversation light.

Ellen perked up and nodded. "I see Adin Sheppard made it to your party."

Uh-oh. "Yeah, his grandma lives next door."

"That's what we heard," Kate said, slashing her gaze to Ellen, trying to diffuse her friend's intent.

"Hey, girlies. What are you talking about?" Calli interrupted, coming to Legacy's rescue.

"Oh, nothing. Just school. They told me about the juniors demolishing the senior float," she added with a wicked laugh, hoping to divert Ellen from the conversation she knew she'd rather have.

"I heard about that," Calli responded, giggling and then turning to Ellen and Kate. "Hey, why don't you come over here and look at this cake. Cake Bake did a fabulous job on the fondant bow."

Calli easily got their attention away from her. Ellen was all about Calli, and Kate hung on every word Ellen said, so it wasn't as difficult as she thought it would've been to drag away Ellen and Kate from the side of the room that Adin stayed in.

She glanced in Adin's direction. He was by himself against a wall finishing his piece of cake. She took a deep breath, psyching herself up as she walked toward him, but then she saw he had on a different shirt from this morning. He had been wearing a fitted blue, button-down shirt with the top few buttons unfastened. Gods, he'd looked so hot as he casually leaned against his new dark blue Camaro. Blue car, blue shirt, blue eyes, against a clear blue sky. He'd blended in perfectly with the beautiful day.

But this shirt wasn't blue. She hadn't noticed before

because when their gazes locked, she hadn't been able to look away from his eyes. No, this one was green—a beautiful emerald green that matched her green dress. They were matching! *It must be a coincidence.* She tried to keep herself from shaking as she neared. It was already too late to keep her hands from sweating, assuming she could even keep that from happening anyway.

His eyes flashed up and locked onto her once again. She forcefully kept her composure and smiled at him.

"Happy birthday." He smiled as he took his free hand and wrapped his arm around her shoulder in a sideways hug.

"Thanks." She stepped back out of his embrace.

He took her empty plate with his and set them aside. "You have a little icing on your lip," he said as he gently took his index finger and wiped it away.

She couldn't breathe. He was touching her lips, and his skin smelled so good. And then to her utter disbelief, he took that same index finger and put it in his mouth to taste the icing. She laughed nervously, glanced away from him, and then looked back into his eyes.

"Have you had a nice day today?" he asked as he stepped closer and took not one, but both her hands into his, holding them at their sides.

"Er, yes. Calli and I did some shopping after school." She didn't know what to say. The hugs she could *try* to get used to, but him touching her lips and holding her hands — these were a first in all their years of their friendship.

"How about the party? Are you enjoying yourself?" he asked, his head cocked to the side, eyes opened wide.

"Absolutely. This was a wonderful surprise." Maybe she was feeling brave. Maybe she just knew she needed to thank him for coming. Either way, she knew she was going to have to keep her composure as she continued. "I'm really happy that you came tonight. That, too, was a wonderful surprise."

"I wouldn't want to be any other place," he said, smiling and gazing into her eyes. "You look so radiant. Everyone has been commenting on how beautiful you are. You should see yourself. You're positively glowing."

"Oh, it's just my party face." She shrugged, trying to lighten the conversation. "I'm actually horrified at all this attention. If I let my real emotions show, everyone will think I'm some ungrateful brat." She laughed.

"I doubt that." He gave a half-smile.

She continued to stare at him, not knowing what to say. He was still holding her hands. His hands felt so strong, even though he was holding hers gingerly.

"Did your grandma not come tonight?" There, that was a good question.

"No, tonight's her bunko night. I'll probably have to pick her up. It was her night to bring the wine, and she got an early start." Adin chuckled.

So she hadn't shown up because she had other plans. Not because Adin had told her to stay away so he could come to Legacy's party and seduce her with his charm. And it would be so easy for him, what with his sincere personality, piercing eyes, delectable scent, strong arms... *Stop it!*

"Um ... that sounds like fun." Great, now she sounded like a babbling idiot.

"I wouldn't know. I've never played."

"Does she play often?" Why were they still talking about his grandma?

"Yeah, once a week." He nodded as he answered.

"That's good. I mean, it's nice she has a hobby." Oh for the love of...

He took in a deep breath and exhaled sharply. She assumed he wanted to steer this conversation back away from his grandma just about as much as she did.

"Can I ask you a question?"

He could do whatever he wanted. "Sure."

"Well, it seems like whenever I give you a compliment, you don't seem to believe me. I was wondering why that is?"

"What?" Her hands started trembling.

"Do I make you uncomfortable?" he asked with sincere confusion.

"No, of course not." *Get yourself together!* "Um, I think I'm not used to getting compliments from anyone. It's not you."

"It's just that I say things sometimes without thinking them through, and I've noticed that … um …usually happens when I'm around you."

"Oh." Huh? What was he trying to say?

"Legacy, it's time to open your presents," she heard Calli say as she walked toward them.

Adin kept hold of her hands as Calli approached. She looked over at Legacy, and she glanced at Adin. Then she peered at Legacy's hands in Adin's hands and stared back at her.

"Um, whenever you're ready," she modified.

"I'm ready," Legacy said in a slow, flat tone.

Adin slipped his hands away from hers while she was still looking at Calli. She faced Adin, and he was watching at Calli with a pleasant expression on his face.

So this was it. Her moment with Adin Sheppard was about to be over, and she wasn't sure when she'd see him again. "In case I don't get to see you before you leave," Legacy started to say, and he flashed his gaze back over to her, "thanks again for coming tonight."

He had a strange look on his face. Almost sad, but he was smiling and nodding at her. He then abruptly put his arms around her waist, and she put her arms around his neck for what she assumed was a goodbye hug. He held her tightly like this morning, but for several seconds longer. He turned his head so his face was buried in her hair. If she wasn't in complete and total shock at how close he was, feeling his breath on her, she probably would've been squealing internally.

"Happy birthday," he whispered to her one more time.

She couldn't help herself—she stroked the back of his neck at the bottom of his hairline with her slick palm as they pulled away from each other.

"Thanks," she whispered back to him.

She walked off in a daze at Calli's side, sat at the table with a frozen smile on her face, and opened her gifts in a fog of surrealism. After the first couple of gifts, she was able to focus better, and she remembered to thank everyone individually. She got a lot of cash and gift cards. Lissa's co-workers had chipped in and gotten her an iPad mini, so she couldn't wait to download her Kindle and Nook apps. Lissa had gotten her a beautiful silk red dress. It had brought Legacy to tears because she knew it was much more than Lissa could afford, but she couldn't wait to find an occasion to wear it. Adin had given her a watch that had a sun with crystals that reflected the sun's rays during the daytime and a moon with those crystals turning to stars during the nighttime. She had never seen anything like it. She tried not to act too shocked at his gift, but she wasn't sure if she fooled anybody. The funniest surprise gift was from Calli because Legacy hadn't seen it coming. The trip to the mall this afternoon hadn't been a distraction after all. The red shoes were for Legacy, not Calli. Her BFF knew what Lissa had gotten her and figured she'd use that as a reason to buy her expensive shoes. Calli and her accessories.

After Legacy finished unwrapping her presents,

everyone said their goodbyes and left. Adin had sneaked out shortly after she'd opened his gift. Calli stayed to help clean up the remnants of the party, so she'd been the last to leave. Once the house was empty, Legacy kicked off her shoes and plopped onto the couch. Lissa sat down beside her, but when Legacy looked at her, she frowned. Lissa seemed somber, which didn't jive after throwing a party. She was being eerily quiet.

"What's wrong?" Legacy asked as she sat up.

"I have something to tell you, and I can't figure out the right way to do it."

"Why don't you just come out and say it? I'm sure whatever it is it'll be okay."

"It's about your mother."

What? Was Lissa about to tell her another story about her mom? If so, she surely didn't sound as if she were about to regurgitate one of those trivial, generic ones. She sounded like she had something meaningful to say.

Lissa sighed, and an ominous feeling crept up Legacy's spine. "Your mom didn't die when you were a baby." Legacy gaped at her, and Lissa cupped her hand. "She had to leave. She left you in my care because she was worried about your safety."

"So she's still alive?" Legacy barely breathed. Could this really be true?

"It's not that simple. Your mom was a powerful woman. There were people who tried to hurt her. She knew she couldn't keep you safe with her, so she trusted me to look after you."

"I'm not following." She could feel the tears forming in her eyes.

"It's time you learned the truth. What I'm about to tell you will change your life forever."

Chapter 2

Legacy sat there reeling, waiting for Lissa to explain.

"What do you know about Greek mythology?"

"Um, not much. Why? What does that have to do with my mother?"

"According to the myths, Gaia is the goddess of earth, the great mother of all. All gods and goddess were born of her. One such goddess is Demeter, the goddess of harvest and the circle of life and death. She gave birth to a daughter named Persephone." Lissa looked at her pointedly. "But some refer to her as Kore."

Legacy gasped. "That's my last name."

"That's because *you* are Kore. Well, one version of her

anyway."

"What?" Legacy screeched.

"Greek mythology is not the story of legends. There are actual gods and goddesses on Mount Olympus to this day. Some go way back to the beginning of time, others are newly created. But gods don't always descend the way people normally do, giving birth to children who then give birth to their own children and so on in a vertical fashion. They also descend horizontally. The original gods and goddess created by Gaia continue to create offspring. They're just not always offspring in the sense that you think they are. What I mean is they can also create a likeness of themselves with other gods."

Legacy was too confused and too shocked to say anything. It was hard enough keeping up with what Lissa was trying to tell her, much less grasp the point of this conversation.

"The path to ascension for a new god begins on the first day of the seventeenth year of birth and culminates on his or her eighteenth birthday."

Did the air suddenly leave the room? That had to be why Legacy couldn't breathe. She shook her head, refusing to wrap said head around this information.

Lissa nodded. "Yes. Sweetie, your mom, Dora, is a goddess. Whether she descended after several generations that originated from Demeter or if Demeter created Dora directly from herself, doesn't matter. Either way, you are her offspring with the legacy to one day be a goddess."

Legacy busted out laughing. "O-M-G, you really had me going there for a minute." She stood as she continued to laugh. "Not cool that you brought up my dead mother, but I'll give you props for creativity. Goddess? Right." She chuckled as she walked into the kitchen to grab a soda.

Lissa followed her. "I know this is a lot to take in. Your

mom didn't want me to tell you yet, but I felt it was for the best."

Legacy slammed the refrigerator door shut. "Stop talking like my mother isn't dead."

Lissa pursed her lips. "You can get mad at me all you want. It's not like I can tell you much more anyway. I'm on a need to know basis, and apparently, I don't need to know all the specifics. It'll be on you to learn what you can about your change."

"My change?" Legacy asked mockingly. "Like what? Am I going to grow wings now? Is that it?"

"You're thinking of angels."

Legacy scoffed as she opened her can of soda. She wasn't going to listen to this crap anymore.

"When you're ready to talk, you know where to find me. I can't promise I can answer all your questions. I have no idea if you were created for a reason, to accomplish some goal, or if Dora just wanted a daughter and then realized you'd be safer away from her until you ascended. But I'm here to help you in any way I can. The sooner you accept what is happening to you, the safer we'll all be."

Safer? Whatever. Legacy stormed up to her room and slammed the door. Happy freakin' birthday to her.

* * * * *

With a faint image of a dream still lingering, Legacy suddenly awoke to the sound of thunder. Her head was foggy, but she managed to sit up and stare out her window. She saw nothing. In the seconds that passed, the rest of her body adjusted to the sound of the thunder and rain in what seemed to be a start to a gloomy day. She tried to think back to the dream she'd just had, but just as she stared out her window and saw nothing, she saw nothing of the lingering images left in her head.

She glanced over at her clock out of habit and slowly slid out of the bed. After slipping on her house shoes, she carefully walked over to the window to watch the rain pouring from the clouds. As she stepped up to the window, a flash of lightning illuminated the dark morning sky, and a crash of thunder erupted in an ominous sound. She stared a few seconds longer in awe. For those living in this part of the country, storms were a common occurrence, but their power never ceased to amaze her. Storms never bothered her like they did some people. Maybe she just enjoyed the distraction that storms provided. Distractions from the mundane processes of regular life. This one was definitely a distraction now. She wasn't actually studying the swirls of the clouds, the angle of the rain, or the distances between the sounds of thunder. She was mulling over the events that transpired yesterday. The storm just gave her something to focus on externally.

She could have stayed at this window and continued to stare all day. Staring at the storm developing was easier than understanding what Lissa told her last night. At least the storm made sense.

As she stood, still staring out the window, questions flew in her mind at the same speed lightning flashed across the sky. Too many questions and not a single answer. She didn't even know how to begin to comprehend all the questions she had about her mom. Or whether to believe anything Lissa had told her. If her mom was really alive, why had she left for Legacy's protection? And if Legacy suspended reality for, like, a second, what *changes* had Lissa been talking about?

She sighed and turned away from the window. She didn't have time to dwell on this. She had to get dressed and go back to the mall because she'd totally forgotten about filling out job applications while she was there yesterday. Fantasies could wait. She got dressed and headed downstairs. Reality was more important right now.

When she neared the kitchen, she smelled blueberry pancakes. Her favorite.

"Why are you cooking breakfast? We have a ton of leftovers," Legacy asked Lissa as she pulled out a chair and sat at the table.

"I wanted to use these blueberries before they spoiled."

Legacy looked at her in disbelief.

"Fine. I wanted to do something nice for you. I didn't know what kind of mood you'd be in when you got up this morning, so I figured I'd take the initiative to try and avert any negative feelings."

"And you thought blueberry pancakes would do the job?"

"I put the blueberries in the shape of happy faces," Lissa said with a timid laugh while handing Legacy a plateful. "I'm really sorry about last night. I think I probably shouldn't have said anything."

"Why?" Was she going to confess it was all a big joke?

"Because now you'll be worried about it."

"Worried? What do you mean by that?"

"I meant wondering, not worried," Lissa said as she put her plate on the table and sat down.

"Of course I'll be wondering about it. How could I not? You told me my mother is alive, that she's a goddess, and that I'm going to turn into one too."

"You're not *turning* into one. You're changing. It's different. And you must learn to accept this because your life is at stake. *Other* lives are at stake."

"So you're really going to stick with this story? You know, they make pills you can take for craziness."

"Legacy, being upset and confused isn't going to change

the truth. You have a year to get ready. That's not a lot of time."

"And what exactly is the truth here? That my mother is a goddess, and I'll be *changing* into one by my eighteenth birthday? Is that it? Or is a ghost going to come guide me to the mother ship where legions of trolls will dance in my honor?" Lissa opened her mouth, but Legacy stood and raised her hand. "Save it. I don't have time to deal with this nonsense right now."

Legacy stormed out of the kitchen, grabbed her purse, and left the house, slamming the door behind her. Lissa had some nerve. Legacy was so furious she was shaking. She could barely put on her seatbelt or get the key in the ignition. When she managed to get the car started, she tore out of the driveway and headed straight to Calli's house. She knew she had to get started on her job hunt, but she was in no condition to tout her assets and abilities to a hiring manager. She needed to talk to someone, and Calli would get a kick out of this.

Legacy's mind reeled as she drove to her best friend's house. When she got into the ritzy neighborhood, she couldn't help but be a little distracted by all the opulence. It never seemed to get any easier seeing how the other half lived. To say Calli's house was big would be a huge understatement. She lived in the most lavish neighborhood around, which had been developed by her real estate guru parents. She said they had picked this land because they were inspired by the beautiful pond at the back of the property. Even though the land wasn't developed at that end, the area that *was* developed had lot sizes of at least five acres. The road into her neighborhood was lined with Bradford pear trees in the median and manicured shrubs along the sides. All the houses — or rather, estates — had gated entrances. There weren't many kids in this posh community, but of them, Calli was the only one who attended Oak Grove, a public school in the Pulaski County system. Her parents attended the same schools, and they obviously turned out well. Legacy was sure they also believed that attending public schools would help keep Calli grounded in reality. But her black American Express Card helped her realize what reality she belonged to.

Legacy entered the code at the gate and parked in the circle drive out front. Calli opened the door as she jogged up the big stairs.

"Hey, what are you doing here?"

"I just felt like visiting before I start begging people for a summer job."

"Did you have fun last night?" Calli asked, ignoring her comment. "I thought it was a great turnout. Everyone commented on how beautiful you were, and it seems like you really raked in the goodies!" Legacy didn't miss the glance to her wrist as they made their way inside the house and to Calli's bedroom.

"Yeah, the party was great. I did have a wonderful time."

"Adin seemed really happy to see you."

"It was nice seeing him there last night."

"Wow." Calli stared at her with obvious shock on her face.

"What?"

"I didn't expect you to respond so easily to me bringing up Adin. I figured I'd have to talk some sense into you about how serious his attraction is to you."

She grimaced and looked away. "It *was* really weird having him there last night," she admitted.

"But you're not going to deny that something is going on … I mean, on his side too."

"You know nothing is going on."

"After last night, it's pretty obvious he has feelings for

you."

"I think you might be right."

"I can't believe you're not denying this!" Calli sat down on the edge of her bed, and Legacy followed. She sat quietly for a moment and looked down at her hands as she spoke.

"It's not like it matters now. He's out of high school. Going to college."

"Like that matters! Girl, there's nothing sexier than a hot college guy for a boyfriend," she said with a giggle.

"The only thing sexier than a hot college guy as a boyfriend is if that hot college guy were Adin." She looked back at Calli with a crooked smile.

"At least you've accepted the fact you two like each other more than just as friends."

"I said I think you might be right about that, not that I believed it completely." She looked at Calli more seriously.

"I saw him holding your hands. I've *never* seen him do that with anyone, not even those anorexic skanks he brought to all those dances. How are you able to have a coherent conversation about him after last night? I figured you'd be screaming at the top of your lungs all morning while I tried fruitlessly to calm you down."

It was true, Adin had come to all the school dances with beautiful girls that looked as if they belonged in his league, and he never brought the same girl twice. He obviously had a stash of ladies on the side ripe for his picking. And Calli was just as aware of these facts as she was. But talking about Adin cooled her frustrations with Lissa and her silly story about goddesses and myths.

Legacy smiled. "Okay, so it was totally squeal-worthy."

"So what did he say? I want all the deets!"

"He told me I was radiant," she said as her grin got bigger.

"Aw, that was very nice."

"And, um, he asked me if he made me uncomfortable."

"What?" Calli's eyes grew wider in sudden disbelief.

"Yeah, he said something about complimenting me and mentioned that he sometimes says things to me without thinking." She fidgeted and strained to maintain eye contact with her friend.

"So when he compliments you, he's speaking without thinking first?"

"I think so, but I don't think he was just talking about the words he said. I think he also meant his actions."

"Why do you think that?"

She knew she had to be honest with her. "Because after you interrupted, he pulled me into a hug and *whispered* in my ear."

"No way!"

"Uh-huh. And right after I walked over to him, he told me I had some icing on my lip, and er, he wiped it off with his finger and then put that finger in his mouth."

"He touched your lips?" Calli screeched as she jumped up off her bed.

"Yes."

"So he touched your lips, hugged you twice, held your hands the entire time, and whispered in your ear? Did I miss anything?"

"Nope, I think that's pretty much it."

"So why are you so calm? He's apparently into you. And I know that's what you've always wanted."

"Well, besides the fact that he's still just a friend —" Calli started to interrupt, but Legacy put her hand up to stop her. "Something else happened last night to trump that."

"What could possibly have happened that would've topped that?"

There was no easy way to buffer this. "Lissa told me some crazy story about my mom being alive."

Calli stared at her in total astonishment. "I'm sorry, what?" she said as she sat on the bed again.

Legacy told her everything, right down to the changes and the goddess crap. Gods, she felt ridiculous even talking about this.

"Seriously, I'm not sure if I should get her some mental help or scream at her for using my mom this way."

"Hmm, okay, hear me out here. I wonder if there's some truth to your mom being alive, and Lissa is covering it up with the silly story so you won't be totally shocked when you see her again. Maybe your mom is in some kind of Witness Protection Program or something if she left you for your protection. That happens."

"In the movies." Legacy rolled her eyes.

"Well, I think we should try to figure this out. There has to be a valid reason Lissa told you this story. Maybe she needs you to read between the lines or something."

"I wouldn't know where to begin. Besides, I really need to find a job before the summer comes to an end," Legacy said sarcastically.

"I might actually be able to help you with that. This morning, I heard my mom talking to the new neighbor. She owns that new alternative medicine shop on Main Street, and she has a son our age." Calli wagged her eyebrows before continuing. "Anyway, she said something about hiring seasonal help to get the store up and running. Apparently, she's opening a bunch of other stores across the state, so she's going to be out of town a lot."

"I know where it is. That would be perfect, actually."

"Let me grab my purse, and I'll go with you. It couldn't hurt to drop my mom's name in the conversation. Maybe she'd hire you as a favor to her new neighbors." Calli shrugged as they both got up. Once Calli grabbed her purse, they took her BMW to the store. Even though the storm had subsided, the rain was relentless. Legacy looked out into the rain while Calli drove, and she thought about some clever responses to possible questions the owner might ask her.

"I see the only gift you're wearing today is the watch Adin gave you," Calli mentioned, distracting her from her previous train of thought.

"Mm-hmm. I need a special occasion to wear the red dress that Lissa gave me and the red shoes that you gave me," she said, trying to make light of the fact that she was wearing Adin's beautiful gift.

"Can I see it? I didn't really get a good look at it last night. I assumed you didn't want me calling too much attention to it."

"I'm glad you showed some restraint," Legacy said, laughing. She took off the watch and handed it to Calli.

"Wow. This is really something. I've never seen anything like it before. It's very pretty," she said, handing it back to Legacy.

The rain eased as they pulled into the parking lot of the store. They hurried inside and went straight to the cashier working the front register.

"I'm Calli Rhodes," Calli began. "Is Ms. Gorgos in? My friend Legacy would like to fill out an application."

"She's in the office. Go down aisle two and you'll run right into the door."

"Thanks," Calli said, and then she turned to her. "Let's go."

They walked down the aisle, and her palms started sweating. She tried to maintain some level of composure, but was having extreme difficulty. She'd never had a job before. Well, not one that didn't include babysitting, chores, or yard work.

Calli knocked on the door to the office while she stood patiently by her side.

"Come in." She heard a quiet voice respond.

They walked into the office, and Ms. Gorgos stood up from behind a desk covered with papers. She was strikingly beautiful, except for the 80s style perm she was sporting. But even her unruly curls couldn't distract from her other features.

"May I help you?" she asked.

"Yes, ma'am. I'm Calli Rhodes. You met my mom, Beth, this morning."

"Yes, of course. Your mother was very gracious and inviting. I'm Petra Gorgos. It's a pleasure to meet you."

"I heard you tell her you'll be hiring seasonal help, and my friend Legacy is currently looking for a summer job." Calli nodded her head in her direction, and she smiled at Ms. Gorgos.

"Well, Legacy, do you have any experience?"

Ugh. "No, ma'am, but I'm a quick learner."

"That's good. You'll need to be. How soon can you start?"

A shock ran through her body as she realized she was giving her the job. "I can start whenever you need me."

"How about Monday? Can you be here at nine o'clock?"

"Sure."

Ms. Gorgos rummaged around her desk and found a stack of papers. "Take this paperwork and fill it out. You can bring it back with you on Monday."

"Okay. Thanks, Ms. Gorgos; I really appreciate this opportunity," she said graciously as she shook her hand.

They left her office and had started for the front door when a guy caught them both by surprise.

He was tall with dark hair and green eyes. He looked to be about their age, but Legacy knew she had never seen him before. Judging from Calli's reaction, it was apparent she'd never seen him before either. He was strikingly handsome and built like an athlete. She'd only seen one guy better looking than him in this town, but this guy could definitely hold his own. Calli and she stood, both dazed, while he carried what looked to be heavy boxes with ease into the front door of the store.

He glanced over at them. Legacy knew she was still staring, and Calli's mouth was still open in shock. He cocked his head to the side and flashed a quick, beautiful smile as he put the boxes on the counter.

"Yale," he said to the girl at the counter, "can you tell my mom I'm bringing in the supplies she ordered?"

"Okay," she said eagerly, gazing at him. Apparently, Yale enjoyed the view too.

He glanced back over at them and started walking in their direction. She collected herself, but Calli hadn't found her composure yet.

"Hi. I'm River Rysaor," he said, waiting for a response from either one of them.

Calli must have checked out because she wasn't quick to engage him. She usually had no difficulty with conversation, regardless of how absurdly handsome the guy was.

"Hi, River. I'm Legacy, Legacy Kore. This is my friend, Calli Rhodes."

The way River looked at her while she spoke actually gave her butterflies in her stomach. Reflex reaction, she guessed.

"It's a pleasure to meet you, Legacy. You too, Calli," he said as he stuck his hand out toward each of them for a quick handshake. She shook his with ease. Calli had a little more difficulty feigning nonchalance.

"What can I do for you?" he continued as he glanced back and forth from each of them.

Calli giggled a short laugh that she quickly suppressed.

"Er, nothing, thanks. Ms. Gorgos just gave me a job,"

she offered to get the attention off Calli while her friend pulled herself together.

"Really? That's great. We need a lot of help around here." He smiled, locking his eyes with hers once again before glancing back at Calli.

"So, will you be working here, too?" he asked her.

"No. I came here for moral support," Calli was finally able to comment.

"That's too bad," he said, and he actually sounded like he meant that.

"Don't worry. You'll still see me around. Legacy's my best friend, and apparently, you and I are now neighbors." Calli had finally slipped back into her regular, flirtatious personality.

"Well, that's nice to know. Maybe I'll come borrow a cup of sugar sometime," he said, responding to her coy demeanor.

"You can come borrow anything you want." Calli flashed a sly smile at him.

Okay, now Legacy was beginning to feel uncomfortable for a different reason.

River just laughed at her response and turned back to the counter to pick up the boxes.

"It was a pleasure to meet you both," he said, but his eyes—though they lingered on Legacy's a little longer—seemed almost confused.

Calli smiled and shot her eyebrows up and back down. Legacy's smile was somewhat more casual as they turned to leave, assuming the chilly breeze she just felt was the air kicking on.

Once they were in the car, they weren't even out of the parking lot before Calli started. "Oh my! Have you ever seen anything more beautiful than that?"

"Yes," Legacy said matter-of-factly.

"Well, Adin certainly is hot, but River is fire!"

"River is definitely a looker, and he seems really nice too. At least, I hope he is if I'm going to be working with him."

"Maybe I should get a summer job too!" Calli was still too excited.

"Nobody will believe that *you* need a summer job. If you get a job up here, everyone will know why you did it," she tried to rationalize with her.

"True. I don't want to come off too obvious."

"I think it's a little late to worry about not looking like you're interested," she teased.

"At least he knows he has an option," she responded.

"Calli, he might have a girlfriend."

"I'm not worried about that. I have a girl on the inside."

"What are you talking about?" she asked, not liking the look in her eyes.

"You're going to find out everything about him." And Legacy knew there'd be no getting out of that.

"Only because you're my best friend and you *did* just help me get a job."

"And don't you forget it."

Once they got back to Calli's, Legacy headed back home. Calli had some family stuff she needed to do today, and Legacy didn't want to be in the way. When she got home, she noticed Lissa's car wasn't there. She went into the house and called out to both Lissa and Olive, but there were no answers. She figured they'd gone to the store and would be back shortly. But as she stood in the empty house and stared at the couch where Lissa had made that crazy confession, Legacy wondered if there were any clues around here that'd help shed some light on things. Calli had suggested they get to the bottom of the story, and Legacy didn't see any reason why she couldn't begin their little investigation. Starting with Lissa's room.

Legacy walked through Lissa's doorway, turning on the light as she scanned the room. She knew she was home alone, but she still felt like she was being watched. She shut the door behind her and looked over at her dresser. It was an old, hand-carved mahogany dresser with brass knobs and little apothecary-style drawers that lined the top row. None of Lissa's furniture matched. She had several pieces from various periods that created her own eclectic style.

Legacy moved toward the behemoth dresser and started rummaging through the drawers. Jewelry was in the small drawers at the top. She recognized some of the pieces, but a lot of them looked to be antiques. She didn't know what she was looking for, so she examined some of the old items. There was a gold comb with jewels encrusted at the top in the shape of a butterfly, a silver-colored broach in the shape of a ladybug with rubies and other gemstones, and several other ornate pieces that looked to be worth a lot of money. As much as Lissa struggled financially to ensure Olive and she had a good life, the jewelry felt out of place. Each of the eight drawers was full of it, and none of it looked to be costume. Not exactly what she thought she would find, but not exactly what she was looking for either.

Legacy pawed through the rest of her drawers looking for something, anything that might be a clue. When that proved fruitless, she turned to her nightstand, then to her closet. Nothing stood out. As she was about to leave the room in defeat, she glanced at her bed, and then lunged herself to the floor to look under it.

Underneath the bed was a wooden box. It, too, looked very old. She tried to slide it out with one hand, but it was too heavy. She squeezed herself under the bed and grabbed the box with both hands and yanked it toward her. It seemed to be stuck to the floor, but with some effort, it finally dislodged and slid in the direction she coaxed it. Once out from under the bed, she tried to lift the lid. It did not budge. She examined the box closely, but could not find the proper way to open it. Then she found a spot that looked like some kind of keyhole, but she couldn't be sure. If that was a keyhole, it seemed too small for such a big, heavy box. She jumped up and ran to Lissa's bathroom to grab a bobby pin. She figured she could try to pick the lock—it looked easy enough in the movies. But when she tried to unlock it, nothing happened. Frustrated, she walked back to the bathroom to put the pin back in its place.

She walked back toward the box on the floor. She stood staring at it, wondering how she could open it, and then considered that the box might not be anything either. She started to realize she was being silly. Lissa was making her act crazy with the ridiculous story. She was just getting back to her senses when the phone rang. She ran to her room to answer it since it was the closest.

"Hello?"

"Legacy?"

She gasped. She knew this voice better than her own, even though she had no right to. "Yes," she responded, trying to stay calm.

"It's me, Adin. I ... um..."

Not that she was used to talking to him, but when she did, he usually articulated himself fairly well. "I was up taking care of some stuff around the house since Lissa is out," she said to get the conversation going.

"Oh, are you home alone?" He sounded concerned.

"Yeah, but it's okay."

"Are you sure? I could come over if you need me to."

What? Was he for real? Her heart tried to jump out of her chest. "Oh, I'm fine, really." She knew it would take too long for her to make herself presentable. She probably reeked and knew she was covered with dust bunnies from crawling around on the floor like an idiot. Served her right for being nosey!

"I, er, wanted to ask you something," he continued. Adin took a deep breath, drawing out his exhale. He had difficulty with whatever he was going to ask, and this reminded her of how he'd acted at her party. She waited quietly, eagerly while the blood raced in her veins just from the sound of his voice. "I was wondering if you'd like to go out with me?"

Shock took over her system. She couldn't believe her ears. Even after how he acted yesterday, she still could not comprehend what he just asked her. Adin, beautiful, magnificent, Adin just asked her out. Her brain could not make sense of the words as she thought them over. She was at a complete loss. Then her heart pounded so loudly in her head that she was sure he could hear it on the other end of the phone. She had to say something, but she was trying her best not to freak out and scare him away by screaming.

"I'd love to." She was only able to whisper to him because she did not trust her voice to stay even.

His sigh of relief thrilled her even more. He *sighed!* He wasn't just asking her out to be nice. He *wanted* to go out with her!

"Good," he said, and it sounded like there was true joy in his voice. "I'm leaving early on Monday to go to Florida with my family for the week, so I was thinking about tomorrow night if you're free."

Tomorrow? Holy crap! "Er, sure."

"Awesome. I wanted to take you to a botanical garden, but that'd be better for a day trip. How about we just go out to eat? Do you like Japanese food?"

"Yes. I *love* sushi."

"Great. I'll pick you up at seven tomorrow night. We can

do the botanical garden Saturday after I get back, if you'd like."

He was already making plans with her for another date? *Yay!*

"Sounds good. I'll see you then."

She couldn't believe it. She'd get to go out on a date with him tomorrow and *again* on Saturday. This just kept getting better and better!

After exchanging cell phone numbers, she hung up the phone and stared at it. She couldn't believe what just happened. She started to call Calli, but she knew she needed to get herself back together before she told her the news. Calli thought she would be screaming over Adin just holding her hands. She had to prepare herself not to scream about him asking her out. The last thing she wanted was Calli to be right about her not being able to have a coherent conversation about him. But if she opened her mouth now, she was sure she would start screaming.

She made her way back to Lissa's room in a blissful fog. She examined the room to make sure it didn't look like she had been in there. She then got back down on her knees to push the box back under the bed. When her hands grasped the bottom corners of the box, the corner pieces shoved inward and the lid popped up a few inches.

Why, when she had been resolved to let this go, was the box opening now? She stared at it as she lifted the lid open all the way.

A chill overtook her, a draft that wasn't actually there, as she stared into the box. The empty box. The only markings inside were a carving at the bottom that read *Elpis*.

The uncomfortable feeling stayed with her as she closed the box, slid it back into place, and left the room.

Chapter

3

Legacy stood at the edge of a forest on a dirt road. This was no place she had ever seen before, just random woods. While looking into the dense forest, she turned in the opposite direction to stare at a field. The sky was black over the field, and a tornado formed overhead. She watched the tornado as it edged toward her. In the forest, she heard voices screaming for her to take cover. She started to walk into the woods, but stopped when a black snake slithered out from the edge. She had an uneasy feeling watching the snake come toward her. She realized she would rather take her chances with the tornado than go into the woods. It somehow felt safer in the open. When she didn't come into the woods, the voices stopped screaming and started speaking in a soothing tone, trying to lure her into the darkness. The snake continued to watch her hesitation, and when she didn't walk into the forest, it moved very quickly toward her. She turned and started running down the dirt road, turning onto another dirt road, and then another, looking back frequently to watch the snake gaining on her. The tornado changed course and was headed right for her too. On the last dirt road stood a tiny house. The house was so small it was really the size of a small closet. She ran for it, closing the door behind her, not wanting the snake or the tornado to find her. Even though the house was small and in the direct path of the tornado, she felt completely safe.

Once inside, she was shocked to see she wasn't alone. Standing in the corner next to her was a little girl with long, blonde curly hair and blue eyes. She stared at her in horror. Suddenly, she felt she needed to protect this girl as if she were her child. She'd never had a mothering instinct before, but this instinct felt natural, strong. She had no other choice but to protect this girl; her own life meant nothing. The girl stepped over to her with fear in her eyes and smiled, but the fearful expression stayed. It was mocking.

She could hear the tornado right outside. It was about to hit them. The girl stepped one step closer. Legacy felt an uneasy tremble slide down her spine as she stared at her. The girl lifted her index finger and touched her face in the middle of her eyebrows.

"See," she whispered, dragging out the word.

As she released her finger, Legacy fell back in slow motion. A peaceful feeling covered her entire body as she slowly fell to the floor. She couldn't help herself; she was smiling. In the instant that the girl touched her forehead, she knew the answers to everything. Everything made sense. She was at peace with herself.

As she was about it hit the floor of the tiny shelter in her dream, her eyes opened.

Legacy had been dreaming.

She lay in bed looking at the ceiling fan, not wanting to move. A feeling of peace still covered her. She couldn't explain it. It had definitely been a dream, but for some reason, she felt better having experienced it. She stayed there, enjoying the afterglow of her dream for several minutes until she begin to wonder why she'd dreamed it in the first place. She thought back over the last couple of days, feeling as if maybe her brain was just trying to make sense of something that couldn't be explained. That or the dream was just a coincidence.

"Nothing is ever a coincidence," a soft, feminine voice whispered through the air.

Legacy shot up and looked around. No one was there. Her window wasn't open. No air was coming from the vents. And she surely wasn't still dreaming. What was happening? She cautiously eased back down, clutching the covers to her.

Maybe Lissa was being honest about her mother being alive. The story had been that her parents died in a car accident after they'd gone out to dinner in the city to celebrate a job promotion with some friends. It had been storming that night, a horrible electrical storm. Lightning had flashed across the sky all night. It had rained so much that the storm flooded the roads. When her parents had turned onto a street that was under water, it was too dark to notice until it was too late. Lissa had been babysitting her when it happened.

Legacy had been too young to remember her parents. The things she knew about them included generic details like her mom's wavy blonde hair and her dad's frizzy black hair. Legacy ended up with frizzy dark blonde hair, inheriting traits from both. She also knew her parents were not the business type. Her mom was an artist, her dad a musician.

But it wouldn't be hard to fake their deaths. They had been self-employed, so there would've been less people to answer to when they had allegedly died. If it wasn't for that conversation with Lissa, Legacy wouldn't even be questioning it now.

And what about the other stuff? The goddess story? If Legacy were to believe any of that and that her life really was at stake, then she could die by her next birthday. Heck, on her next birthday for all she knew. Dead at eighteen. It hardly seemed fair. Whether she actually died then or not, apparently, it was something she needed to consider—her life ending before she had time to fall in love, go to college, get married, have children. What would she do differently if she knew she only had one more year left to live? She didn't know the answer to that. Not at first. But as she lay there, she realized she would live her life to the fullest.

And then she had her answer. She wasn't going to let Lissa's news about her mother get her down. She didn't want to worry about it anymore. She wanted to live each day like it was her last and enjoy whatever life handed her. And what life was handing her right now was Adin.

Who she had a date with tonight. *Yay!*

Legacy jumped out of bed and threw on some clothes. She needed to be happy about her date, and she was ready to shout it from the rooftops. She was tired of Lissa's story overshadowing what was happening with Adin. She grabbed her keys and bolted out the door. This was the kind of news she had to tell Calli in person.

Calli was already at the door since Legacy called her just before she pulled in.

"What's up? Why didn't you tell me on the phone? You

know I hate waiting on gossip," she said with a huge smile on her face.

"You'll never guess who called me last night."

"Adin?"

"Okay, so you guessed!" She laughed, jumped up while clapping her hands, and squealed in delight.

Calli grabbed her arm, and they ran up the grand staircase to her bedroom.

They both sat on her bed and stared at each other with huge grins on their faces. Legacy took a deep breath, calming the excitement she was now able to really feel for the first time.

"So," Calli started with a smirk on her face, "what did he say?"

"He asked me out!"

"No way! How did he ask you? What did you say?"

"He was a little nervous, I think, because he struggled with the question. He asked me if I'd like to go out to eat tonight!"

"Oh, Legacy, this is wonderful! I *told* you he liked you more than just a friend. I told you! After all these years of never asking a girl out from school, you're the one he asks out!"

"I know. I'm really excited. He even asked if I wanted to go to a botanical garden after he gets back from vacation!"

"Shut up!"

"I know, right? I was so shocked I had goose bumps. He and his family are leaving for the beach Monday, so we're doing date number two on Saturday."

Calli squealed again. "What are you going to wear tonight?"

"Um, I haven't really thought about it. I may need your help with that," she said, smiling angelically at her.

"Of course," Calli said, winking at her. "Let me show

you some ideas."

They got off her bed and walked over to her closet, which was really a dressing room. All her clothing was hidden in built-in drawers and behind cabinet doors along every wall. There was a large island in the middle of the room with drawers that held her accessories and a built-in vanity at the opposite wall set up like a makeup station. This would be considered a dream closet for a master suite, but she knew the real master suite in this house contained a closet that put this one to shame. Not that Calli was complaining.

Calli pulled out sundresses, nice dresses, and pants outfits. She explained the differences between the dresses and other ensembles—why one would be better over the other in particular scenarios. Luckily, they were the same size, so Legacy knew she could rely on her to provide the best possible outfit for the evening.

"You know, if he takes you someplace really nice, you could wear your new red dress and shoes that you got for your birthday."

"Yeah, I already thought about that. When I got them, I tried to think about the perfect occasion to wear them. I would love for that to be a date with Adin."

"You never know," she said, smiling.

"Well, I don't think he'll take me somewhere that nice for a first date. He was pretty nervous, so I figure he'll start out taking me somewhere casual."

"Start out?" Calli asked with an even bigger smile. "Do you think this is the beginning of a relationship?"

Legacy tried to reign herself in. Even though she loved the idea of being involved with Adin and was trying to embrace her new lease on life, she didn't want to get her hopes up too much. She would live each day to the fullest, not make more out of them than what they actually were.

"I'm not sure, Calli. Let's just see how tonight goes."

"I can do that," she said as they walked back out of her closet.

That makes one of us.

* * * * *

Three soft knocks on the door that afternoon sent Legacy's heart racing. She took a deep breath and exhaled slowly through her smiling lips. She got off the couch with her purse in hand and glided to the door. She took another deep breath while she put her hand on the doorknob.

This was it. Her date with Adin.

When she opened the door, there stood the best-looking man in the world. And he was a man, technically. Even though he was eighteen, he could easily pass for a guy in his early twenties.

His hair was tousled and gelled into place. He wore a white, fitted, button-down shirt with a cotton T-shirt underneath peeking out from the two unfastened buttons at the top. The bright white of his shirt made his blue eyes glow more than she had ever seen. How was that possible? His jeans were faded but still dark and loose with a brown belt that matched his brown shoes. Even in her four-inch heels, she was still the shorter of the two.

As she appraised him, he certainly was getting his own assessment of her. He wasn't hiding that. His smile grew wider as he looked at her, starting from the opposite direction she'd gone. From her shoes to her hair, it was obvious he didn't find one thing not to his liking.

"You," he hesitated, "are absolutely breathtaking."

"Thanks." If she started blushing now, she wouldn't be able to stop. "You look very handsome yourself."

"Thank you," he said, still smiling at her, and then he pulled his right hand out from his back and into view.

In his hand were a dozen long-stem red roses wrapped delicately in floral paper.

She gasped, and the grin on his face turned into a gleam. He stepped closer and handed her the flowers. "These are for you," he said, glowing.

"Thank you," she whispered. "They're beautiful." She didn't know what else to say or if she would be able to get anything else out without her voice cracking.

"They match perfectly," he said.

And he was right. With the red roses against her red blouse, she looked picture perfect.

She quickly put the flowers in some water and returned to him. He reached his hand out to take hers. "Shall we?"

She nodded and pulled the locked door shut behind her.

Adin held her hand and walked beside her as they made their way to his car—never once taking his gaze off her. She looked down, feeling shier than normal, but kept a soft smile on her face. Once they reached the passenger door of his car, she looked up at him.

"Your eyes are more blue than green today," he murmured. "They look like the ocean. Just as powerful and deep. Beautiful…"

She smiled appreciatively, not knowing if she could speak. He then let go of her hand to open the door for her. Being the gentleman that he was, he placed his other hand on the small of her back to guide her into the seat, and then softly shut the door before getting in on his side.

He pulled out of her driveway, watching the road. She wondered if he would speak first or if she should. She knew exactly what she wanted to ask, but wasn't sure if she should start off with a question like the one she was thinking of. After a few seconds of silence, she decided to give it whirl.

"So, what brought this on?" she asked, looking down at her hands and hoping they wouldn't start sweating.

His eyebrows came together as if he were thinking of a way to respond. "I … er… I've liked you for a long time," he said slowly, nodding to himself as if that answer would suffice.

She smiled at him when he made eye contact with her. She really had no way to respond to that. Of course she wanted to ask him a million questions about what he'd just said, but she didn't want to interrogate him.

"Why did you agree to go out with me?" he asked softly.

Oh no. How did she answer? Better keep it simple. "I've liked you for a long time." There. He should be able to understand his own words, and she didn't have to think of a different way of phrasing her answer without giving too much away.

"I was hoping you'd say that."

"Why?"

"Because if you just agreed to go out with me because I put you on the spot last night, then I'd have my work cut out for me."

"What do you mean?"

"Well," he said, reaching over and placing his hand into hers, intertwining their fingers, "I'd have to find a way … umm … I'd have to work at making you like me. Now I don't have to do that."

"How long have you wanted to ask me out?" She had to know.

"Awhile. But I didn't know how to go about it."

"I haven't seen you date much," she offered.

"No, I'm not one to date. Not unless I'm spending time with someone I really want to be with."

He really wanted to be with her. Even though he was giving some insight into his feelings, she still had a hard time believing him. Not that she didn't want to and not that she didn't smile from ear-to-ear while he was speaking, but it was just so unbelievable. As she thought about that, her smile began to fade.

"What's wrong?" he asked.

She looked at him. "It's just kinda surreal."

"Why?"

"Because I've liked you for a really long time. I've tried not to show it, so now that we are actually on a date and you've told me you like me too, it just doesn't seem real."

He began stroking her hand with his thumb. "That's just because this is new for us."

"I know," she breathed, looking down because her heart started racing when he'd said *us*.

She was so involved in their conversation that she didn't notice, at first, they had arrived at the restaurant.

"Wait here. I want to get the door for you."

"Okay." She giggled.

He walked around and opened her door. He took her hand and helped her out of the car, and then put his hand on the small of her back to guide her away from the car so he could shut the door. He kept his hand on her back, leading her into the restaurant and to their seat.

They sat in a booth by the sushi bar, and both of them ordered sushi and fried rice. Once they got settled in, she felt more at ease and ready to talk about some trivial things. Anything could be considered trivial if it wasn't related to feelings.

"So tell me about your family," she started as she opened up her chopsticks. "I know your grandmother lives next door, but that's about all I really know. Well, that, and the fact she loves bunko." Legacy laughed.

"It's not so much the bunko as it is the wine," he said, laughing with her. "Well, let's see ... my parents work in information technology. My dad's a programmer. My mom builds websites. They're divorced. I don't really live with either of them. It seems more like I go back and forth visiting while they're in town. They both travel, but try to coordinate with each other so neither of them is out of town while the other is. I guess that's why I spend so much time at my grandma's house—she's my mom's mom, and she's always there. Except for bunko night, of course."

"Of course," Legacy said with a smile.

"Tell me about your family," Adin said as they both finished their rice and were now waiting on the sushi.

"Well, I live with Lissa. She's my guardian. Then there's Olive. Lissa adopted her when I was two." She wasn't sure how much she should tell him, but she wanted to be honest.

"What happened to your parents?" he asked softly. "I mean, I heard they'd died, but you never really talked about it while we were growing up, and I didn't ever feel comfortable asking."

"The story is they died in a car accident when I was a baby. Apparently, my parents were friends with Lissa, so Lissa stayed home and babysat while they'd gone out with some friends to celebrate a job promotion."

"I'm sorry." And she could see that he meant it.

"It's no big deal. It was a long time ago. I've had a great life with Lissa."

"That's good. Something you said, though, doesn't make sense."

"What's that?" She was truly curious what he could've picked up out of that short answer.

He shook his head. "I don't want to pry, and I don't want to take the chance of saying something that might hurt your feelings."

"It's okay, really. I don't even remember my parents." She tried to sound casual, but she was eager to hear his thoughts.

"Well, if Lissa was friends with your parents and it was

a night for celebration, then why hadn't Lissa gone with them? I'm sure they could've found another babysitter."

Oh my. He was right! She'd heard the story a thousand times and had never really thought about it that way. She guessed her parents didn't want to leave her with a stranger, but surely they had other less important friends they could trust with her for one night. Hmm... She'd definitely have to revisit this later. "That's an interesting take on it. I've never really thought about that," she said, trying to keep her voice light.

Luckily, the sushi arrived, so she grabbed a piece of her California roll and put it in her mouth. Then, remembering who she was eating in front of, she realized she probably should have picked a place that didn't require her to put huge pieces of food in her mouth. It wasn't as if she could cut her sushi in half. Ugh! She covered her mouth while she quickly chewed.

"You look very cute with your mouth full." He laughed.

She swallowed what she could and dropped her hand while she finished chewing the rest. "Yeah, they never seem to cut the pieces small enough for me," she was finally able to say.

"I can have the waitress send it back. I'm sure they won't mind cutting it into smaller pieces," he teased, but he was seriously offering to do so.

"That won't be necessary." She smirked, and he laughed again.

They continued eating and talking. They talked about her birthday party, his upcoming trip to the beach, and memories they had of each other growing up.

"You know, you were the first girl I ever kissed," Adin whispered as he flashed his gaze up to her, looking at her through his light lashes.

"What are you talking about?" she asked with a wide

smile on her face. She really didn't have a clue. If she had ever kissed Adin, she was sure she would've remembered.

"It was on my third birthday. My parents threw me a party at the zoo, and you were there. I kissed you on the cheek in front of the tiger exhibit." Adin chuckled.

"No wonder I don't remember that." She laughed. "I'm surprised you do."

"Well, I don't, actually. My grandma took a picture of me kissing you. She wrote on the back that it was my first kiss. She still has the picture."

They both laughed and continued reminiscing. The conversation flowed casually, naturally. Not only did it feel normal, it felt right.

They finished their sushi fairly quickly, but the night was still young.

He paid their ticket, and they left the restaurant. Every door they encountered, he opened for her and guided her through with his hand on her back.

She felt like she was floating. She liked him, and he liked her, and this date was perfect. He was attentive, funny, and charming. He said and did everything right. She wondered how he could even consider the alternative that she only accepted his invitation because he put her on the spot, but then curiously wondered what more he would have done to make her fall for him. He was already doing everything just right.

They drove around town, but he didn't say much. He just held her hand and smiled. It seemed as if they were heading somewhere, but she wasn't sure. He hadn't asked her if she wanted to do anything else or that he'd had something else planned.

"Where are we going?" she finally asked, and the smile that was already on his face got a little bigger.

"I have a surprise for you. I hope you like it."

After the night they'd had so far, that was a pretty safe bet. But there was nothing he could do at this point to top the evening.

She was sure of it.

Oh, how she'd been wrong.

Chapter

4

Adin started driving up a hill. The trees grew right up to the narrow road on both sides with the leaves providing a canopy overhead, blocking the sun.

As they made it to the top of the hill, the road turned into a narrow dirt path in a field. The hill wasn't too tall, but it felt as if they were on the highest peak in town. He stopped the car and got out. After he opened her door, he took her hand, and they walked in the field. He didn't say anything. He just walked her over to a huge tree near the edge of the hill. As they got closer, she noticed something over by the tall oak and gasped.

A blanket was spread out over the flattest part of the

grass under the shade of the tree. On the blanket was a short wooden tray — it looked like it were one of those trays people use when eating breakfast in bed. Beside the blanket sat a picnic basket and more red roses. She was in complete and total shock. She had to bring her free hand to her throat to keep the lump down.

Adin pulled her over to the blanket. "Have a seat," he said, smiling.

"This is so…" She was at a loss for words, so she settled for the first word that popped into her head. "Unbelievable."

"I wanted to do something different for our first date. I figured starting off in a restaurant would help us ease into the evening. But you're very special to me, so a regular date wasn't going to be enough. This is a place where I like to come and just think, so I wanted to share it with you."

She felt the lump rise again, so she put her hand back to her throat and grinned as she sat down. She crossed her legs in front of her and watched Adin open the basket. It was wicker, but the inside was actually a cooler.

Adin dropped to his knees beside it. He pulled out a small platter that held chocolate covered strawberries in the middle with chocolate mints lining the outside, a bottle of sparkling water, and two crystal glasses. He put the items on the tray and opened the bottle. He poured a glass for each of them and then put the bottle back in the basket before closing the lid. He reached for the roses and shifted so he was sitting crossed-legged beside her, their sides touching.

"These are for you," he whispered, repeating the same line from before.

"Thank you," she said as she took them out of his hand, examining the roses. This was a smaller bouquet than what he had given her earlier. She assumed these were only half a dozen, until she counted them and realized there were only five roses.

"Five?" she murmured. Not that she cared there were only five, but she didn't see the logic behind it.

"Not exactly." Adin smiled. "Um, I wanted to give you one rose for every year we've known each other. Since we've known each other seventeen years, I gave you seventeen roses." He hesitated and glanced away from her timidly before training his gaze on her again. "I didn't want to show up at your house on our first date without *any* flowers, but I was worried giving you all seventeen at the beginning would've been too much." He shrugged and looked away. She couldn't tell, but it almost looked as if he were blushing.

She felt her body trembling when she realized how much thought Adin had put into the flowers. "You really shouldn't have."

"Why? Don't you like flowers?" he asked, teasing her.

"That's not what I meant," she murmured.

"What did you mean then?" he asked, whispering again with a concerned look in his eyes.

"I just meant that you didn't have to go through all this trouble for me."

"I disagree," he said as he gently reached up and moved a strand of her hair out of her face.

She looked over at him in awe. If there were any doubts about his feelings before, those doubts were now gone.

"Flowers are unique, don't you think?" he asked, looking into her eyes.

"Why do you say that?" Flowers weren't really unique. People received flowers every day. Although she absolutely loved the flowers he had given her, she didn't consider the gesture a unique one, or two, since he had given them to her twice now.

"Because if you think about it, the sole purpose of a flower's life is to live and die for someone's enjoyment. These flowers are uniquely special because the sole purpose in their lives was to live and die for *your* enjoyment."

"I never thought of it that way," she breathed.

Adin continued to stare into her eyes. Legacy could tell there was more he wanted to say in that moment, but didn't. Instead, he laughed a small, nervous laugh and looked away. "Would you like a strawberry? They're really good."

"Sure." Her smile was stuck on her face. She knew her cheeks would probably hurt tomorrow, but she really didn't care about that now.

He reached over, picked up two strawberries, and handed her one. She was glad he didn't try to feed it to her. That would have been too much for her heart to take.

"When I was planning our date, I remembered you eating a couple of these at your birthday party, so I figured they were a safe choice." He laughed again.

She remembered back to her party. She was pretty sure she had her back to Adin when she'd gotten her plate of food that night and had been with Lissa's co-workers when she ate. The only way he could've noticed was if he were really paying attention to her. That thought sent a shiver up her spine—in a very good way.

She ate her strawberry, which was delicious, and reached for her water—the perfect complement to the strawberry. He'd definitely planned this well. He finished his strawberry and slipped his hand into hers. They both looked out over the horizon, and then she suddenly realized why he'd picked out this perfect spot.

"The sunset is beautiful," she murmured. And it was. From their angle, the sun was centered over the horizon and falling behind the distant hills. It wasn't hot in the shade and the wind was all but forgotten. She could have sat there with him forever.

"It is," he responded. Not taking his eyes off the sun, he took their joined hands and put them into his lap. He then took his free hand and molded it over their hands, holding her one hand tightly between the two of his. "That's why I like to come up here. No matter what I may be going through, I can watch the day end and know another is coming tomorrow. A new day brings with it new hope."

Ironic, that this was the place he came to when he wanted to put a day behind him and welcome a new day, but in this moment, she didn't want this day to end. "Do you come here often?" she wondered, pulling him out of his reverie.

"Hmm … yes and no. I didn't used to, but I've found myself coming here a lot lately."

"What have you been struggling with?" she whispered, not wanting to pry, but concerned.

"What?" He looked back at her with wide eyes.

"You said you come here when you want to see the end of a day because each new day brings new hope. If you're coming here more often," she guessed, "then, you're seeking a lot of hope."

"Insightful," he breathed, and looked back down.

"Why is that?" she persisted.

"Because of you." He was barely audible when he spoke.

Her heart started racing, and she could feel the blood rushing up to her face. Her breathing became heavy, and she wasn't sure how to control it, nor was she sure if she wanted to.

Adin looked at her with gentle eyes. "Legacy, I care about you … a lot. And that … that scares me."

"Why?" she asked automatically, still reeling over how much he felt for her.

"Legacy…" he said slowly, shook his head, and looked away. He didn't want to answer. He was obviously uncomfortable talking about his feelings.

"I'm sorry," she said, and looked down at her lap — wanting to look at his lap instead since that was where he was holding onto her hand. The one part of her body he was squeezing as if he were trying to get strength from her.

He took his hand off the top of their joined ones and gently lifted her chin with his finger until she met his gaze. "Don't be sorry," he said with a smile. "It's just that part of me feels like I've waited too long. If I'd approached you sooner, we would have had so much more time together. Yet, now that I have you here, with me, like this," he said as he trailed off and shook his head again, looking for the right words. "I'm terrified."

She looked at him. Even though his words seemed so unbelievable, she was relieved he felt about her the way she did about him. But she couldn't trust her voice enough to speak yet.

"I'm terrified," he continued, "of a lot of things. Things like knowing the right thing to do, knowing how I feel about you, wondering how you feel about me, and not knowing what to do about all those things and many other things. I don't know what the answers are—what really is the right thing."

"We don't have to know all the answers," she whispered, looking at the setting sun.

"No, we don't," he agreed, and turned to watch the sun fall completely below the horizon.

It was beautiful. She had never watched a sunset before, so it thrilled her that she got to experience this for the first time with Adin. They were both quiet for several minutes after the sun had set. Her thoughts were drowning in this moment, which was beyond perfect. As she thought about how happy she was just sitting here beside Adin, she began to wonder what he could be thinking. If his thoughts were the same as hers. But she didn't want to ask. She was happy sitting here not speaking.

"Would you like another strawberry?" Adin asked after

several more minutes had gone by.

"Sure," she said, smiling at him. He held her gaze longer than necessary before retrieving two more strawberries from the platter.

As she ate, she knew her personality had shifted over the course of the evening. Before, she had been shy and didn't allow herself to think of the possibilities with Adin. Now, she was happy embracing all those forbidden possibilities.

Now that the sun had set, it started to get dark. Adin sighed, and she assumed it was because he realized they'd have to go soon.

He looked back into her eyes. He took his free hand and delicately brushed her cheek with trembling fingers. His touch on her face was indescribable. He sighed again and put his hand down onto his lap without taking his eyes off her. "I'm not sure how to do this," he confessed, and she realized that *this* was one of the *things* that terrified him. He didn't know how to be with her. "We've been friends for so long," he continued, "and I'm scared that I—I mean, we— might do something that will hurt that friendship."

"Why don't we just play everything by ear?" Then she couldn't help herself; she reached up with her free hand to stroke his cheek. She wanted to comfort him. She wanted to touch him. Her hand was cold against his warm cheek, and with *her* trembling fingers, she could feel how soft his face was.

Adin's breath caught, and his eyes bored into hers at her touch. He reached up with his free hand and placed it over hers on his face. Her hand curved around his features, and she could feel his hot breath on her cold palm. He shut his eyes and leaned slightly into their hands. Even though only several seconds had passed without either of them moving, it felt like an eternity.

He opened his eyes and shifted his head back up. He

seemed unwilling to, but eventually, let his hand fall from hers. She slowly slid her hand down his cheek until the tips of her fingernails grazed his jaw and then dropped her hand back into her lap.

"That sounds good to me," he whispered.

What was he talking about? She had to quickly think back to what she had just said. *Right, playing it by ear*, she remembered.

She smiled at him and nodded.

He reached back up and stroked her cheek again while he spoke. "But I think we should take things slowly."

She started marveling in how strongly her reactions were to him. She wanted to put her hand on top of his like he'd just done to her. Then she remembered the night of her birthday party when he'd hugged her and she couldn't stop herself from caressing his neck, just as she couldn't stop herself from caressing his cheek a few minutes ago. The bond of their friendship had grown much stronger. She knew she'd have to be more aware of her reactions if they were going to be taking things slowly.

"Slowly works for me," she said with a half-smile, keeping her hand in her lap.

He moved his hand across her cheek to beside her ear and then slowly slid it down her jaw before dropping it from her face. He finally unlocked her from his gaze, looking down at her hand that he'd been holding all evening. "Slowly," he murmured, but it seemed as if he were directing that to himself rather than to her. He looked back at her eyes and smiled. "We should probably get going."

He released her hand after she nodded and picked up the platter to put it in the basket. Then he hesitated and put it right in front of her. "Would you like some more before I put this away?"

Knowing she was already beyond stuffed, she took a

couple of the small mints and said, "Thank you."

"You're welcome," he said smiling, a little more relaxed.

He put the platter in the basket, and she picked up the glasses and handed them to him. Partly because she wanted to help, but mostly because she knew she wouldn't be able to drink more if he offered.

They both stood up, and he folded the blanket and placed it over his arm. He picked up the basket with the same hand, and placed his free hand on the small of her back. They walked over to his car, and he opened the door for her before putting the items in his trunk. After he started the car and got on the main road, he reached over to hold her hand again.

The ride to her house was pleasant. She glanced at him often, and she could feel him doing the same. They were both smiling. Every now and then, he'd rub his thumb on the side of her hand. But neither of them said much, so she spent the time going back over the evening in her head. She never wanted to forget even one detail.

Suddenly, she considered what might happen once they got back to her house. She was surprised she hadn't thought about this possibility when she was thinking about all those previously forbidden possibilities. Was Adin going to kiss her tonight? She felt new nerves in the pit of her stomach. She tried not to think about it but then felt Adin rub his thumb on her hand again. It was as if he were trying to soothe her worries. Maybe he'd been thinking about this already and that was why he'd been rubbing her hand periodically. Maybe he was trying to soothe his worries too. Regardless, she was immediately pleased she had eaten a couple of the mints before he'd put the platter away.

Adin pulled into her driveway and walked around to her side to open her door. He guided her while they walked to her porch. This walk seemed to take forever, yet it was over *way* too quickly.

Once they were standing in front of the door, she looked at him. His eyes were gentle, and she feared hers were panicked. Luckily, she didn't see that reflection in his.

"I've had a lovely time with you this evening," he whispered.

"Thank you. It was better than I could have ever imagined," she said as she felt her body trembling.

"Me too." He looked down.

She was lost in her own thoughts and trying to read his. She couldn't help but wonder if he'd decided which way he was going to go. Kiss or no kiss? She knew she would soon find out.

Unable to speak, she smiled shyly and placed her hand gently on his chest. That was a mistake. Now she could feel how hard his heart was beating, and it was beating much faster than hers. It was crashing into her hand, and she watched as his gentle eyes turned intense at her touch. Realizing she was holding her breath, she exhaled slowly, but was unable to remove her hand or look away from him. He slid one hand onto her cheek, and she took an unsteady breath. Her heart was now beating just as fast and as hard as his.

Adin took a step closer so their bodies were touching—just barely touching—and tilted her head up in his direction. He placed his arm around her lower back, pulling her tighter against him while he leaned his head down toward her. He slowly placed his cheek against hers, holding her face against his. She no longer needed her hand on his chest to know his heart was racing. They were so close to each other that they could both hear and feel each other's hearts beating.

"I can do this slowly," he breathed.

Her breathing came much too fast and shallow. She

started to feel faint. She put her free hand around his back to stabilize herself. She didn't want anything embarrassing to ruin the moment. Although, he was holding her so tightly that he probably wouldn't have noticed.

She slid her other hand up from his chest to the side of his neck. His breathing became ragged, and she started to feel weak. She didn't want him to let go of her, but she didn't know how much longer her heart could stand this.

"Legacy," he breathed as if he were in disbelief she was actually in his arms. Then he shifted his head and slowly brushed his lips down her cheekbone. A shiver went up her spine, and she felt his knees buckle slightly — she wasn't the only one fighting weakness. He stopped in the middle of her cheek and kissed her there, pressing his lips gently against her skin and then pulling away to lean his forehead against hers.

They stood there for several seconds feeling each other's heart beating and listening to their breaths slowing. And she knew he was trying to maintain his hold on the whole *going slowly* concept.

Then he let go of her face and put that arm around her neck to hug her. Her hand went from the side of his neck to around the back of it, caressing it slowly at his hairline. They held their embrace for several more seconds, and then with a final squeeze, he released her. After he stepped back and they slowly slid their hands off each other, he took both her hands in his.

"I'll see you when I get back," he said with a soft smile, and leaned in to kiss her forehead before meeting her gaze again.

"Have fun."

He let go of one hand first as his body turned away from her. He kept his gaze on her as long as he could, then turned his head and slipped his other hand free as he walked away.

She stood on the porch watching him leave. Once he was in his car, she could see his face again. He had a glow she'd never seen before tonight, a glow she was sure she shared.

She turned to walk into the house, inhaling his lingering scent, and knew this was a night she'd never forget.

* * * * *

The wind had howled all night. Legacy had tossed and turned, but luckily, no dreams had plagued her. After the strange dream she'd woken up to yesterday, she was pleasantly surprised that this morning wasn't a repeat. She didn't need that kind of drama before starting her new job.

She got up and put on some khaki pants, a short-sleeved white blouse, and some comfy slip-on shoes. She figured she needed to dress up, but the light colors and breathable material would keep her cool and comfortable since she really had no idea what her work would entail.

She walked down the stairs and into the kitchen. Lissa had already left for work, but she left a note on the refrigerator stating she would be working late and Legacy would have to fend for herself at dinner. This happened often, so it wasn't going to be problem. She quickly ate some cereal and cleaned up her dishes, so she wouldn't have to do it when she got back home. She grabbed her purse, keys, and paperwork and headed to her new job.

When she got there, she walked in and saw River standing against the counter.

With everything that had happened, she'd sort of forgotten about him. Calli must not be too obsessed with him since she hadn't brought him up after they left here Saturday. Maybe she was just being the true friend she was by letting Legacy talk about her own problems and squeal about Adin without any other distractions. Calli had even been forced into an hours-long conversation about her date as soon as she'd gotten home last night. Legacy would need to make sure she made this up to her friend by getting the skinny on River.

And as for the guy in question, he still looked gorgeous. On Saturday, he'd been wearing casual clothes. Today he wore slacks and a fitted collared shirt, which made her feel better about her own clothing choices.

"Good morning." He smiled at her as she walked toward him.

"Good morning to you too."

He looked at her with a strange expression. It reminded her of when she saw him as she was leaving here on Saturday. He had a similar expression then. Odd.

"How was your weekend?" he asked, his face returning to a smile.

"Interesting, and yours?"

"Interesting works for mine too," he responded cryptically.

He just stood there staring at her. She wasn't sure what to make of his demeanor. Then she laughed nervously and looked away from his gazing eyes.

"Interesting, indeed," he whispered, but it seemed like he was whispering to himself.

She tossed her hair over her shoulder and casually looked back at him. He continued to stare at her with a polite smile on his face, but his eyes were intense and full of questions. She didn't understand his behavior, but for some reason, he rubbed her the wrong way. Part of her felt like snapping at him, asking him what his deal was, but he was the boss's son and all. That would not be appropriate behavior on her first day. Not if she wanted to keep this job. Besides, she needed him to confide in her for Calli's benefit. She couldn't scare him off with a tirade, no matter how justified she felt it was at this moment.

Or maybe he was just shy and didn't know how to articulate himself.

Legacy needed to focus. She couldn't stand here and let him stare at her all day. She figured Ms. Gorgos wouldn't think too kindly of her if she continued to stand here like an idiot on the clock.

"Er, where is Ms. Gorgos? I need to turn in my paperwork and find out what she needs me to do."

River continued to stare at her, saying nothing. His gaze—before irritating—was now intimidating her.

"I-I'll take these to her office," she said as an excuse to walk away from him.

He wasn't having that. "I'll take those. She's not here, and the office is locked," he said as he reached his hand out to take the papers without releasing her from his stare.

"Okay," she said as she handed him the paperwork. "What do I need to do?"

Again, he just stared at her. His eyes were hard, cold. Their emerald green color from Saturday seemed more forest green today.

"Are you going to answer me, or are we just going to stand here all day?" She tried to sound rude, but sounded more like a scared child.

He shifted his weight to his left leg and looked down. His features relaxed. He shot his gaze up at her again with a soft, apologetic look on his face. He looked back down to the floor before he started speaking. "I'm sorry. I just didn't..." he trailed off. His gaze shot back to her and was penetrating, his smile fading.

"What?" she asked, hoping to avoid a repeat of his silent gazing.

He shook his head as if he were trying to clear it and smiled at her again. "I'm sorry, really. I'm just surprised. I didn't expect," he said, shaking his head again. "You look just like her."

His reply caught her by surprise. He looked away from her because now she was the one staring, but her eyes were not cold, they were wide.

"Who?" she murmured, trying to meet his gaze.

He slowly looked at her again, but this time, his eyes were as confused as hers. "Dora," he whispered.

She felt her knees wobble. They stood there looking at each other, both with a ton of questions in each other's eyes. He was the first one to speak. "Are you all right?"

She couldn't remember how to speak. She needed to think about what he just told her. She felt a wave of emotions come over her, and she knew she would have to remember how to move her tongue.

"How," she started, still in shock and not really knowing what to say to him or how to get it out. "How do you know my mom?" She stepped closer to River. His body seemed frozen, but his confused eyes traced her every move. He took a deep breath and looked as if he were preparing to answer her question, but ignored it and asked her one instead.

"What are you talking about?"

"You said I look just like Dora. How do you know her?"

"I don't." He was being evasive.

"You know something," she insisted as she stepped closer.

He stumbled as he took a step back, still staring, unable to speak.

"Say something!"

"Umm ... I ... don't understand." And she realized he truly meant that.

"Tell me what you know."

River looked at her beseechingly. Then he shook his head. "I'm sorry. I honestly didn't know you were her daughter."

Her spine tingled. Why did this new guy know anything about her mother? "What do you know?"

"Everything," he whispered. "I know you'll be a goddess. And you're going to hate me for the truth."

Chapter
5

"No," Legacy breathed. *No freakin' way. No way!*

"Yes," River said, nodding. "I don't know how much you already know—"

Yale walked hurriedly through the front door.

"Sorry I'm late. I overslept," Yale said as she quickly put on her nametag and unlocked her cash register.

River looked at her. "No problem, my mom's not here yet, but you should probably hurry up and count your drawer. I think she'll be here any minute."

"Sure. Thanks!" she responded as she quickly counted the money and entered the information on a form she pulled out from underneath the register.

River looked back at Legacy. "We should get your nametag," he said as he led the way to the break area. If he thought this was the end of their conversation, he was sorely mistaken.

He fumbled around in a drawer and pulled out a readymade nametag. "Here, put this on." His hands were shaking. She took the nametag and put it on her shirt. He was watching out the window on the door of the break room and spoke through hurried whispers. "I know you want answers, but now's not the time. My mom will be here any minute."

"No, tell me what you know," she whispered heatedly.

Just then, the front door of the store opened and Ms. Gorgos walked in.

"Later," he said, and walked back into the lobby. She followed behind, reluctant to drop this conversation for now, but determined to get all the information she could out of him later as he'd promised.

"Ah, Legacy, you're here. Good. I hope River has been helpful," Ms. Gorgos said as she walked in their direction.

"Very," she responded, trying to put a pleasant smile on her face.

"Good. I need to take care of some things before we get started. River, why don't you get the boxes out of my car? Legacy, you can sit with Yale at the register."

Ms. Gorgos walked toward her office with her keys in hand. River walked out of the store and into the parking lot to retrieve the boxes from his mom's car. She obediently walked over to Yale and sat on the stool next to her.

Yale showed her how to work the register and explained how things were done around the store. Legacy tried concentrating on what she was showing her, but she had some difficulty paying attention. She tried to keep her brain on the tasks at hand, but her thoughts were elsewhere. Like what the hell River had to do with her mom and just what he knew about this whole *goddess* business.

After watching Yale with the first few customers, she had Legacy work the register. It did not require her undivided attention, so she hadn't missed that after River had taken the boxes into his mom's office, he hadn't come back out. He was hiding from her. That tactic would only work for so long.

"What year are you?" Yale asked.

"I'm gonna be a senior."

"Oh, that's cool. I loved being a senior in high school. Well, up until my dad realized I was going to a state college and not Yale like he had. Boy, was he hot." She rolled her eyes. "You won't believe the pressure he put on me all my life to go there. If I were going to go to an Ivy League school, I'd go to Harvard just to piss him off. Couldn't you imagine … a lady named Yale going to Harvard? Priceless." She laughed.

Legacy smiled at her, but was too caught up in her own musings to pay too much attention to Yale's ramblings.

"Do you have a boyfriend?" Yale asked.

"No." Did she? One date didn't actually equal a boyfriend. And they were taking things slowly. Did that mean it'd be a while before they reached the boyfriend and girlfriend labels status? She didn't know.

"Well, I'm not sure if River has a girlfriend. Too bad he's too young for me," Yale said with a giggle. "He seemed really helpful to you this morning. When I first met him, it took him several days before he approached me."

"He was the only one here when I arrived. I assumed he was just filling in for his mom until she got here."

"Once you get to know him, I think you might like him," she offered in an amusing tone.

"I get along well with just about everybody." Legacy

shrugged and looked away from her.

"I didn't mean anything by that. I tend to blurt out things without thinking."

Obviously. "It's okay." Then it hit her. Maybe Yale knew some things about the family they worked for. Maybe she could make the chick ramble about stuff that might be useful to her. "What do you know about the Gorgos family?" she asked, a little too eagerly.

"Not much. Probably the same things you know. They're ridiculously rich. Stores all over the place. Houses everywhere. They travel around a lot. River has been in boarding school overseas for several years, but since his dad is still in Greece, I heard him mention he'd be attending school here to help out his mom."

"Greece?"

"Yes. I'm not sure what he does there. I mean, they're all from around here, but I think their ancestors came here from Greece. They go back several times a year, but I've never met his dad. Any time his name comes up, Ms. Gorgos says he's working in Greece. They might even be divorced." Yale shrugged.

Legacy looked out the window, absorbing this information and wondering if it was relevant to the information about her mother. She looked at the sky and saw clouds rolling in. These were not the soft, fluffy clouds of a pleasant summer day. No, these clouds were dark and menacing.

"Is it supposed to storm today?" she asked as she turned back to Yale.

"Oh, yeah. Didn't you watch the weather? There's a front moving in and we're supposed to have bad weather all week. They're also talking about a tropical storm in the Gulf of Mexico, but it *is* hurricane season."

"Tropical storm? Where?" Adin's family was at the

beach this week, but he hadn't mentioned where, and she'd been too awestruck to think clearly when he mentioned that fact.

"I'm not sure, but I think they mentioned something about it making landfall in the Florida panhandle."

Forceful thunder rocked the building.

"Maybe I should go to the break room and see if there's anything about the weather on the news," Yale said anxiously. "Will you be okay here by yourself until I get back?"

Legacy nodded, and Yale slipped off the stool beside her, quickly making her way to the back of the store. Legacy turned to watch the clouds rolling in. She didn't share Yale's anxiety — storms never bothered her. But as she watched the trees across the street sway forcefully with the wind, she began to feel somewhat uneasy. She didn't understand the emotion, but for some reason, she felt compelled to go outside.

Without conscious effort, she silkily stood up and stepped to the door. She couldn't take her eyes off the trees. With forceful determination, it seemed as if they were beckoning her. It reminded her of her dream, and then she saw something slide out from the edge of the trees. A snake? She couldn't tell. She reached for the door and then jumped at the touch of someone's hand on her shoulder.

She turned around to see who it was just as a piercing alarm sounded outside.

"Where are you going?" River asked, his hand still on her shoulder.

"Er, nowhere. I was just looking at the sky."

"We're under a tornado warning. We need to go down to the basement."

She looked back outside and stared at the sky. River locked the front door and the register before turning back to her.

"C'mon. We need to go," he said as he grabbed her hand and yanked her behind him.

By the time they got into the basement, the others were already there. Ms. Gorgos sat in a chair at the far wall and glared at her as she came into the damp room. As soon as she saw her, she realized River was still holding her hand, so she gently moved her hand away from his. When she let go, Ms. Gorgos' eyes softened. *Overprotective much?* she thought to herself, and then shrugged it off.

She went to sit by Yale who looked like she was on the verge of freaking out. No, not on the verge. She was already freaking out. She jumped at the slightest sound that came in through the walls and ceiling.

"It's okay," Legacy said as she patted her leg, trying to console her.

"Er, I know. Um, I'm sorry I didn't come get you." She jumped again as the thundered crashed. "River came in while I was watching the weather report and told me to take cover. That he'd go get you."

"He did," she said, stating the obvious. She felt like she was talking to a five-year-old.

River took a seat across from her. He leaned in toward her, placing his arms on his knees and clasping his hands together. He looked at the floor like he was uncomfortable being here, but he wasn't scared like Yale was. In fact, no one looked scared except for her.

Ms. Gorgos broke the silence just as it was becoming uncomfortable. "How's everything going, Legacy? I'm sorry I've been too busy to show you things myself."

"That's okay. Yale's doing a great job showing me the ropes."

"Good. If you have any questions, please feel free to knock on my door at any time. Regardless of how busy I am, I will always make time to answer any questions you may have. And River, too. Right, River?" she asked as her eyes flashed at him.

"Of course," River said, looking up at her. He didn't look long, though.

They all sat quietly, listening to the weather radio. Legacy looked over at Yale, and she was still on edge. "It's probably almost over," she whispered. "I'm sure it's already past us by now." Her comments didn't seem to help her, so she looked away. She was surprised to see River staring at her again, but this time, his smile was gentle.

"That's very kind of you, trying to make her feel better," he offered.

She shrugged, but smiled back.

Yale looked over at him and smiled halfheartedly. Then the radio announced the all clear, and Yale sighed in obvious relief.

Ms. Gorgos got up first and led the way out. Yale followed next, and then Legacy. River turned out the lights as he followed her out of the basement.

"Legacy," he murmured, and she turned to look at him. "Would you like to go out with me tonight?"

Oh no! What did he mean by that? Like go out on a date or just get her alone to talk about what he knew?

He saw the confusion on her face and saved her from any embarrassing comment she feared she was about to make. "I would just like to be alone to talk about things."

"Um, sure."

"I'll pick you up at seven. I can get your address off your application."

"Okay," she said as she turned around and walked back toward the lobby.

She finished the rest of her shift in a haze, trying to think of reasons why River would know, or at least know of, her mom. She came up empty. It didn't make any sense, but if she wanted to be honest with herself, *none* of this made any sense. At least she found someone who could corroborate what Lissa had said.

She left work feeling confident that this job would be an easy one for her to do with the added bonus of working with someone who knew her mom. She slipped out without seeing River again, but she was eager to see him that night.

Once she got home, she dashed upstairs and picked out an outfit for her non-date. She selected her favorite jeans and a cute shirt. She took a shower and tried to relax. It didn't work. She was sure the nerves she felt were due to the impending news she would be getting.

She got out and dried her hair before returning to her room. Once in the hallway, she heard some noise from downstairs.

"Is that you, Lissa?" she called down from the top of the stairs.

"Yes, but I'm on my way out."

"I thought you had to work late."

"I still do. Olive is staying with a friend, so I needed to get her some clothes."

"Oh, okay," she said as she started to turn back toward her room.

"Legacy, can you see if you can stay with Calli for a few days?"

"Er, yeah. Why?"

"I have to go out of town. I need to leave in the morning."

"Is everything okay?"

"Yes, I have a conference to attend and want to make sure everything is set up before it starts."

"All right. I'll see you later," she said, and heard Lissa leave.

She closed the door to her room and got dressed. She

played with her hair, but decided to leave it down. She put on some fresh makeup and sat on the corner of her bed, lost in her thoughts again. When Lissa mentioned Calli, she realized she needed to tell about her plans with River and explain. Maybe she could use this casual time to find out about his personal life. She would have to make a conscious effort to do that since she was more worried about finding out what he knew about her mom than she was worried about what he looked for in women. But she knew she needed to tell Calli. *Now.*

She grabbed her cell and tapped Calli's name.

"Hello?"

"Hey, Calli."

"Oh hi, Legacy. How was your first day?"

"Very interesting." Hmm … River and she had used the word *interesting* when they explained their weekend. Amazing how fitting this description really was.

"What was interesting about it?"

"Well, River apparently knows my mom. Or he knows of her."

"What?"

"Yeah, he didn't realize she was my mother at first."

"How does he know her?"

"I don't know. We're going out tonight so he can explain. He didn't want to talk about it at work, and he knew I wasn't going to let it go."

"Where are you going?" she asked, sounding a little sad.

"I'm not sure, but he'll be here in a few minutes, so I need to go. I'll call you when I get back."

"Okay."

"Oh, Calli?"

"Yes?"

"Lissa has to go out of town for a few days, so she asked me to ask you about staying over at your house until she gets back."

"No prob. You know my parents won't care," she said with more pep in her tone.

"Thanks. I'll talk to you later."

The knock at the door caused her stomach to flip. She casually went downstairs to answer it.

River was standing under the porch light when she opened the door. He was wearing jeans and a cotton v-neck shirt with a short-sleeved, buttoned-down shirt layered on top. He looked and smelled like he just got out of the shower. His hair was still slightly wet with fresh gel scrunched through it. He looked great. If she weren't head-over-hills for Adin, she would definitely have some serious butterflies in her stomach.

It took her half a second too long to respond and he began to smile.

"You're early," she managed to say, keeping her composure.

"I wasn't sure how to get here, so I left a few minutes early."

"That's fine. I'm ready. Just need to get my purse and keys."

She got her things and turned around to follow him to his car. Oh, wow. He was driving a silver Mercedes coup. She should have known he'd have a nice car. He lived in Calli's neighborhood, for crying out loud. But she just hadn't considered that.

River turned around when he heard her audible surprise and gave her a puzzled look. She shrugged and continued walking. He walked to the passenger door to open it for her. Men in the South were taught to be chivalrous, so this really didn't surprise her. She tried, unsuccessfully, not to watch as he walked around to the driver side. He moved gracefully for a guy that looked athletic. Once inside, he started the car and turned down the radio. After they were out of her driveway, he glanced over at her.

"You look very pretty."

What? "Thanks. You look nice too."

"Thank you," he said, fighting a smile.

"So where are we going?"

"I made reservations at the Italian restaurant downtown. It has intimate seating. We should be able to talk freely there. You know, get to know each other without interruptions."

"What's wrong with talking now? We're alone."

He shook his head with a serious look on his face and put his finger to his mouth. "How long have you lived here?" he asked in a casual manner.

"All my life." She wasn't sure what else to say. Was his car bugged or something?

"Do you like living here?"

"Yes. The heat is horrible this time of year, and we get a lot of storms, but they never really bother me."

"I noticed," he said with a short laugh.

"How about you? Do you like living here?" She figured that was a safe question.

"Yes. Things are definitely looking up."

She didn't know what to make of that, nor did she know what else to say.

"I stayed up too late watching baseball last night. What did you do?"

Why was he trying to fill the silence? "I, er, had a date."

"Really? With who?" He tried to sound passive, but his eyes betrayed him.

"A guy I went to school with. We're going out again when he gets back from vacation." She didn't know why she said this.

He was staring at the road, but now his eyebrows were furrowed. River wanted to ask her something, but what?

"So, did you have fun?" He tried to sound causal, but she got a sneaking suspension that *that* wasn't the question he wanted to ask.

"Yes." She wasn't going into any specifics with him about her date.

"So is this guy your boyfriend?" There was the question he wanted to ask.

She avoided the yes or no response. "Last night was our first date," she qualified.

"Oh." He seemed pleased by this, which took her by surprise, though she hid any reaction.

Since he asked her if Adin was her boyfriend, she figured she should use this opportunity to inquire about his personal life, for Calli's sake.

"What about you? Anyone special in your life?" she asked as she leaned back in her seat and folded her arms against her chest.

River chuckled. "As a matter of fact, there is."

She frowned at his response. Calli wouldn't be happy about this.

River let a short laugh slip out before he could compose himself. "You look sad. Were you hoping I was going to say no?" he teased.

She scrambled for a response that would let her off the hook while not betraying Calli in the process. She realized that wouldn't be entirely possible, but she would say what she could. "Well, I have this *friend* who is interested in you."

"You have a lot of friends."

Not really. She figured he knew exactly who she was talking about. "I'm not giving you any more than that. It doesn't matter anyway. You're not available."

He shook his head, and with a smile, said, "No … no, I'm not."

She didn't say anything. She still felt bad for Calli.

Hopefully, she wasn't too invested in any particular fantasy about River. She would just have to wait until he was available. Boys their age tended to change girlfriends more often than they changed their shoes. She would get her chance, eventually.

"So … do you *like* this mystery man who took you out last night?" he said when Legacy didn't comment.

"Yeah," she said, and shrugged her shoulders.

River liked that. He just grinned and said, "Hmm…"

She wanted to get the focus off her. "Do *you* like that special person in your life?" she asked, throwing his question right back at him.

"Of course." He nodded and smiled. No, that wasn't really a smile. It looked more like a smirk. Smirk? What had he meant by that?

Luckily, that was a nonissue since they were pulling into the parking lot of the restaurant. River shut off the engine, and she started to get out. He walked around to her side to get her door, but she had already stepped out of the car.

"You should've let me do that," he chided, but shut her door once she was clear of it. He led the way into the restaurant and approached the hostess. "I have reservations for two."

"Name?" She sounded detached, but her eyes popped when she looked up.

"Rysaor."

"This way," she announced, and they followed her to a table at the end of the restaurant.

Once they were safely seated and had placed their orders, she figured it was time to start. "So what do you know?" she bluntly asked.

"Look, I really don't know how to do this," he stalled.

"Just start at the beginning," she encouraged.

He took a deep breath and leaned toward her. "Okay,

when I saw you on Saturday, I noticed the resemblance. But I didn't understand why."

"Is that why you looked at me funny?"

He laughed. "I didn't realize I had. I apologize if I came off as a jerk."

"You didn't," she lied. "Go on."

"Well, when I saw you, I figured you were probably related to Dora, but I really had no idea she was your mother."

Legacy waited for him to continue. She wanted him to tell her everything he was willing to before she started with specific questions.

"Had I known you were her daughter, I wouldn't have said anything."

"Why?"

"Because I really don't know her."

"But you know of her."

"Yes."

Ugh, this was like pulling teeth. "What do you know?"

"Maybe I should tell you about my family. That may help explain things."

Good idea. She could compare what he told her to what Lissa had told her the other day. "All right." She waited for him to begin again, but he hesitated.

"I'm really not supposed to talk about this," he finally said. "As much as I want to tell you everything I know, I'm not going to be able to. It's not that I don't want to—I want to help. Really, I do, but there are some things that are too private and too involved to tell just anyone. I need to get some things straight myself."

"Jeez. First, Lissa tells me cryptic things, and now you."

"Lissa?"

"My guardian. It's a long story. One I'd be happy to tell you all about *after* you tell me what you know."

River took a deep breath and then started. "What do you know about Greek mythology?"

Apparently not as much as everybody else. "Not much."

"My family came over from Greece, and they still have many connections. My dad still lives there."

"I heard about that," she said in encouragement for him to continue.

"This is going to sound crazy, but the story is my family descends from the Greek gods." River put his elbow on the table and let his head fall into his hand, covering his eyes.

Oh gods, he believed the same things Lissa had told her. "I see."

"No, you don't. The thing is, we have certain *abilities* that the average person does not."

"Abilities?"

"Yes. They seem to be linked to puberty or adolescence and manifest to a complete state by one's eighteenth birthday."

Eighteenth birthday? She felt her face turn white and her breathing accelerated. He heard the change in her breathing and looked up.

"Don't worry. I'm told it's nothing too scary." He misunderstood her expression.

Neither one of them realized how close they were leaning toward each other until the waitress returned with their food. They both sat upright in their chairs and smiled at the server as she put their pasta dishes in front of them. They both began eating, though Legacy really didn't feel like it. She felt a little queasy, actually. Once the waitress was several feet away again, she continued.

"What do you mean exactly by *abilities?*"

"I'm not sure." He shrugged as he placed his fork on his plate and then looked up at her. "I don't turn eighteen until the fall, so I can't speak from personal experience. But if you read up on Greek mythology, you'll learn about the abilities of those gods, or mythical figures, and get a pretty good idea."

"Are you saying that *I* might have some special abilities?"

"No, I'm not saying you *might* — I'm saying you will."

Wow. Just, wow. Hadn't Lissa told her she would be going through changes? Gods, was this what she'd been talking about? Was Legacy going to have some magical abilities? She couldn't even think about that right now. "And what about my mother?"

River sighed. "I saw her in Greece when I was there last year. I didn't speak to her, but she was visiting my dad."

Her brain was churning. River saw her mom? Just last year? She really was alive, but why would she be in Greece? She ignored the obvious answer.

He put his hands in his lap and leaned closer to her like he'd done before the waitress delivered their food. He cocked his head to the side and smiled. He responded as if the questions in her head were clearly displayed on her face.

"I don't know for sure, but I was under the impression they knew each other really well."

"Why do you think that?" She was barely able to speak. Her words came out in a whisper, but somehow, he heard her.

"Because I heard my dad tell her not to worry, not to lose hope, that he'd take care of it. I don't know what they were talking about, but she seemed relieved by his support in whatever it was."

She stared at him in total shock, but was determined to get as much information as she could. She needed to tell him what she knew. Maybe something she said would trigger something for him.

She put down her fork and took a deep breath to prepare

to spill what she knew.

"I just turned seventeen this past Friday. Up until that night, I was under the impression my parents died in a car accident when I was a baby. Lissa told me my mom didn't die back then, that she left to protect me because I was turning, er, *changing*, into a goddess. And now you've told me the same thing." She looked down and shook her head at the strangeness of the whole situation, struggling to find some sense in all this.

"You're ascending," he said matter-of-factly.

Her head flew up to meet his gaze. "How do you know that? Why do you know that? What does that even mean? This is all just so crazy."

"Because I am too. Only my ascension will be happening sooner than yours. October fifteenth to be exact."

"Your eighteenth birthday?" she guessed. She could hardly believe what she was saying, what she was accepting. Her body felt numb, but as she stared at River, his body seemed relaxed.

"Yes."

"Is that all you have to say about it?"

"For now. I think I should take you back home." His mood seemed to shift before her eyes. His relaxed façade transformed to one of concern, if she was reading him correctly.

"I want to hear more about you, about this."

"In time. I've said enough for one night."

"Don't be ridiculous! You've only scratched the surface!"

"Look, Legacy, when I told you earlier that I knew everything, I was being honest. I do know everything. About *me*. Which apparently involves your mother on some level. But I don't know everything about you. What little I did know about you didn't prepare me for how you fit into all of this. I realize now that I know much more than I thought I did, and I'm not ready to tell you."

"That's not fair!" she exploded, and then looked around the restaurant to make sure no one had heard her.

"I didn't say I wasn't going to tell you. I just think this is something that's going to have to come out in stages, and of course, we'll have to be careful where we talk." River smiled as he said this, and she didn't understand why.

"Why didn't you want to talk about this in your car? Is it bugged?" she asked with heavy sarcasm.

"Er, no, my car's not bugged. I didn't want to talk about it then because we were still close to your house."

"What does that have to do with anything?"

"It's too complicated to explain now, but long story short, you're being watched and listened to." He stood and looked down at her. "I will tell you this, though. Lissa was right. You'll be a goddess one day. You need to prepare yourself for that."

She stared at him incredulously, unable to speak.

"And while I'm handing out advice, stay away from my mother. She's evil."

Chapter

6

While Driving to Calli's house after work on Thursday, Legacy thought about her most recent dream. It was similar to the previous one, but there were a few changes.

Instead of a forest, there were two fields. And, technically, she hadn't seen the tornado, but she knew it was coming for her. She could see the black clouds, and she could hear the roar. She'd been standing in one field when she first saw the clouds and looked down into the grass. She had dropped her car keys, so she'd bent down to pick them up before she ran to her car. But as she hunched over, she noticed her keys landed in the field in the middle of three huge snake holes. Frightened, she ran for her car without the keys.

When she got to her car across the street in the second field, she noticed the blonde girl from her last dream sitting in the passenger seat. She opened her eyes wide, scary wide, and screamed for her to go back and get the keys.

"Hurry! Do it now! You must go back!" the girl had screamed frantically at her.

She had turned and ran back to the field where her keys were. But when she got there, she'd woken up.

She still didn't know what to make of the dreams. But she had more important things to digest. Over the last few days, she'd gone to work, but never talked to River about their conversation. His mom had kept him busy. Almost too busy, but she figured she was just being paranoid. Legacy really didn't know what to make of what he said about her being *evil*. She remembered how she'd looked at her that day in the basement and figured that maybe River's comment about her was loosely related to her overprotective nature. Any teenage boy with an overprotective mom probably viewed her as evil—it was all relative.

On the surface, she knew she should probably be asking all kinds of questions, but honestly, as each day passed, she was getting more and more excited about her second date with Adin. That was why she was staying the night with Calli tonight. They were going to talk girl stuff and keep her from jumping out of her skin with excitement.

She pulled in and went straight up to Calli's bedroom. Her friend turned to her with a huge smile.

"I have a date!"

"Really? With who?" The happiness she felt for herself instantly shifted over to happiness for Calli. Legacy sat on the side of the bed and Calli sat beside her.

"This guy named Zach. You don't know him. I went to the park with Ellen while you were at work. I met him there. Of course Ellen was flirting with him like she didn't already have a boyfriend, but he paid her no attention." She giggled.

"Calli, that's great. When are you going out with him?" Legacy had hated telling her River was involved with someone else, so Legacy was thrilled Calli had her eye on someone else now.

"Tomorrow night. He's taking me to dinner and then back to the park where we met. They're playing a movie at the old ball field — it's a classic romantic comedy — so we'll have something to occupy our attention if the date isn't going so well. But it'll be outside and relaxing, so we'll be free to talk and get to know each other if we click."

"That sounds great. Maybe we can double sometime if you two do hit it off."

"Ah, that sounds like fun!" She smirked. "Do you think Adin will kiss you this time?" She was barely able to ask without giggling.

"I don't know. I think it's probably too soon for that. You know he wants to take things slowly, so I think that omits any tongue action. For now." Legacy wagged her eyebrows.

Legacy and Calli spent the next couple of hours theorizing about their impending dates, talking about Legacy's mom, and reminiscing about growing up and how Adin had always been around. Adin and Legacy had been friends since they were little. She remembered playing games with him on the playground in elementary school, hanging out with him and his friends at the skating rink in middle school, and watching him play sports and grow into a very attractive man in high school. Not that he hadn't always been attractive, but as she got older, she appreciated it more. His flawless features were devastatingly beautiful. But his beauty wasn't just skin deep. He was a beautiful person through and through.

"What do you think River is doing tonight?" Calli asked in a nonchalant manner. She wasn't fooling Legacy. It was obvious her best friend wanted to switch gears on their conversation. Not that they hadn't talked about River. His Greek mythology information had dominated about thirty minutes of their conversation.

"Um, I don't know. The store is closed by now, so he might be home," Legacy offered with a shrug.

"Do you want to go for a walk?" Calli perked up and looked at her with hopeful eyes. Yeah, Calli might have a date, but she still appreciated eye candy.

"Sure."

Calli freshened up — touching up her makeup, spraying on her French perfume. They walked down the stairs and out of the house.

"What do you think I should do if Adin doesn't ask me back out again?" Legacy asked in an effort to distract her friend and hoping Callie wasn't getting her hopes up about running into River outside.

Calli looked at her and appraised her expression before responding. "I don't think you have anything to worry about."

"But let's say he doesn't. Should I call him? If so, when? I mean, how soon is too soon to call a guy after a date?"

"Legacy, this isn't the twentieth century. If you want to call him afterward, you should call him. At the very least you could chat with him on Facebook. You did grow up with him. It's not like he's some new guy you hardly know. Besides, he took a big step in calling you and asking you out. Once he gets back in town, you two will probably be inseparable." She giggled.

They were off Calli's property and nearing River's house now. It wasn't as grand as Calli's. It had a more modern flare to it. In fact, it almost had an institutional look. The gray tones made it look cold, and the straight lines of the design were too severe. Even the fence and gate resembled bars in a jail cell rather than an elegant addition to a private estate. But she guessed it went with the décor.

River's car was out front, but Calli didn't notice. Legacy realized then that she had left this detail out of their earlier conversation when Calli had grilled Legacy about her night out with him.

"You see that silver Mercedes?"

"Yeah."

"That's River's car."

"No way!"

"You sound surprised. Why? You drive a luxury car too."

"Um, I know. I just mean that it's a nice car. Very sporty."

Legacy laughed at her response, and they slowed their pace. She felt a little weird spying on his house—she'd never even done that to Adin.

"There's his mother," Calli whispered.

Ms. Gorgos was glaring right at them. Legacy felt a chill as she remembered River's warning about his mother. She did have some kind of cold exterior.

The girls both smiled and waved at her like friendly neighbors would, and her glare softened just before she turned and went back into the house.

"That was weird. Wonder if she was mentally throwing some evil goddess voodoo at us," Calli said with a smirk.

Legacy chuckled at Calli's sarcasm, but she wondered how truthful River was being about his mother. Maybe she needed to talk to him some more, sooner rather than later.

They both stopped walking and turned back around when the gate opened. River was walking toward them.

"Keep your cool," Legacy whispered to Calli while they were still out of earshot.

Calli took a deep breath while he approached.

"Hey, what are you two out doing?" River asked when

he reached them.

"Getting some fresh air," Legacy answered, not waiting on Calli, fearing she'd act like she did the first time she spoke to him.

"What are you doing out here?" Calli asked without skipping a beat this time.

"Getting some fresh air," River said with a half-smile.

"Are you working tomorrow?" she asked River, hoping this conversation would not deviate to that uncomfortable topic about *sugar* like last time.

"Yes, I'll be manning the store. My mom wants us going through a lot of old paperwork."

"Good. Maybe then you'll tell me some more about you know what," Legacy said with a raised eyebrow.

"We'll see. I am doing some of my own research, and I have to tell you, if I'm on the right track, your family is pretty fascinating."

"What do you mean?"

"I'm not going to elaborate just yet. I'm still digging, and I don't want to tell you something that isn't really true."

"But if you've already found out something, how could it not be true?"

"It's complicated." His tone was serene, and she could tell he wasn't going to explain. Fine. She would get it out of him, eventually. She'd rather wait until they were alone anyway. Not that she wouldn't tell Calli everything, but for some reason, River seemed more at ease around her if it was just the two of them.

"I'll get it out of you — one day."

"You won't have to try hard," he whispered back. Suddenly, his expression looked pained.

"River!" Ms. Gorgos called from the front door.

"Sorry, I have to go. She needs help gathering the documents."

"I'll see you tomorrow," she said.

He smiled and nodded. His eyes lingered on her.

"Bye," Calli said softly.

He flashed a brilliant smile at her as he turned to walk back through the gate. "See you later," he finally responded before turning completely around.

Calli and Legacy kept walking in the same direction until they came upon the pond in the undeveloped area and then they turned back. She was glad Calli hadn't turned around and walked right back home after running into River. That would have been too obvious. At least now Calli had the added benefit of walking by his house again. Unfortunately for her, he didn't come back out.

With it being late and Legacy having to work in the morning, they went to bed when they returned. Since it was cool outside, they slept with the windows open in her room. It hadn't taken Legacy long to fall asleep.

Or find herself in another dream.

Instead of being strictly about a tornado, this dream was about the weather in general. She knew a tornado was coming, but as soon as she realized she needed to take cover, the sky turned a vivid pink color. So pink it was blinding. Without the warning of thunder, lightning fell from the sky, but this was no ordinary lightning. Instead of flashing forcefully with an electrical fervor, it glittered and fell like confetti, disappearing before it reached her. Another different characteristic, the strange little girl did not make an appearance. But she was not alone.

As she took cover from the peculiar lightning, Adin was sitting at a patio table under a side porch of a traditional house. She didn't recognize the house, but it was pretty. It looked like a newer house, but built with the cadence of yesteryear. It wasn't the house that stood out, though. The most intriguing aspect of this vision was Adin.

He watched her approach him without getting up. Once she was at the table, he looked at her and handed her a broach. It looked like one of those pieces of jewelry she found in Lissa's room. It was old and very ornate. There wasn't a special design, except it had the numbers 1887 painted in the center of the enamel.

"Be careful," he whispered with a protective look in his eyes.

Then it was over.

She woke to the sound of Calli's dogs barking outside. The window had apparently muffled their barks the previous mornings; it did not shield them now.

Since Calli was still asleep, Legacy gathered her toiletries and took a shower. She stood in there contemplating her dream as the hot water sluiced off her. Why was she having dreams about the weather? The tornado must represent something. She knew dreams usually weren't literal. She learned from Lissa that dreams were usually a manifestation of some subconscious emotion.

She got out of the shower and put on her typical work outfit. She grabbed some Pop Tarts from the kitchen and strolled out of the house. She hadn't burned up enough time in the shower, so she could afford to take her time getting to work.

On the ride there, she watched the sunrise. The sky was pink. The same vivid pink of her dream last night. Weird. But it was still magnificent. The exquisite sunrise was truly mesmerizing. The thin clouds coming up from the south were transparent against the large orange ball, casting a brilliant sheen over the horizon. She kept glancing at the sky while driving to work, watching the thin clouds getting thicker while the comfortable breeze flowing into her car windows picked up. A front must be moving in. She hoped the weather would be beautiful tomorrow for her date to the botanical garden. Her mind went from looking at pretty flowers to fantasizing about Adin pulling her behind one of the rose bushes tomorrow and making out with her. Her face heated as the fantasy continued, which also kicked up her nerves.

She pulled into the parking lot and started for the front door. She tripped twice — once from a pothole, for the second she could find no external culprit. Her nerves were in overdrive. She needed to get into the store and get this day going quickly so tomorrow would get here that much faster.

"Good morning!" she yelled as she walked through the unlocked door.

"Legacy?" River called from the back of the store. "What are you doing here so early?" he asked as he walked into view.

"Calli's dogs woke me up. I decided to come on in so I wouldn't wake her. You?"

"We've already made two trips here." He laughed. "Yale called in sick. She has that *Beautiful Friday Syndrome*," he said with a chuckle.

"I hope she isn't really sick."

"Oh, I'm sure she'll be *all* better come Monday." He smirked. "Mom's closing the store today since Yale won't be here and business has been kinda slow. She really wants us to tackle the paperwork."

She walked to the break room to put up her things and saw all the boxes they'd have to go through. "Ugh. This is going to take forever," she groaned.

"Yep. We'll be going through some stuff we had in storage and throwing out what isn't needed anymore. A lot of this is old documentation that's been scanned and stored on a hard drive. We need to shred the old papers and repack the other stuff. The objective is to store fewer boxes than what was originally packed away."

"Got it."

They spent the morning going through the boxes as needed, but River seemed to be distracted from the menial task. And Legacy couldn't be sure because they hadn't talked much, but it seemed as if he was flirting with her. Every time he handed her a stack of papers to shred, his hand lingered on hers. He would brush his thumb against her thumb, rub her shoulder to get her attention, and once he caught a stray strand of her hair and tucked it behind her ear. She didn't know what to say, so she kept her mouth shut while she worked.

"Are you ready to take a break?" he asked after they'd spent a few hours going through the boxes.

"Sure." She shrugged.

He grabbed a couple of drinks out of the vending machine, and they stayed in the same seats they'd been in all morning.

"I'm glad my mom hasn't come in here to spy on us. She's been in a bad mood since last night."

"Why?"

"Long story," he said cryptically.

"We still have a ton of boxes to go through. I think we have plenty of time for a long story."

He shook his head and glanced at the door, then looked back at her. Right then, Ms. Gorgos walked in.

"I'm going to order some sandwiches from the deli for everyone. Legacy, is turkey okay with you?"

"Yes, thank you."

"River, I'll be back in about an hour. I'm going to run to the bank and make a deposit before I get the sandwiches."

"Okay," he said without looking at her.

He took another drink of his soda while Ms. Gorgos walked out. After a few seconds, he got up and looked out the window of the door. Legacy assumed he was watching his mother leave because when he turned back around he was smiling.

"She didn't seem to be in a bad mood to me," Legacy said matter-of-factly as River sat down.

"Of course not," he said as he raised his eyebrows.

"So what was she mad about?"

"She was mad at me."

"You? Why?"

"It had to do with the things we talked about the other night."

"You mean the stuff you told me about Greek mythology?"

"Yes, but she was really mad I mentioned your mom. I told her about it last night. She was furious."

"Why?"

"Because she doesn't want me talking to you about it."

"Does she know my mom?"

"Legacy," River trailed off, shaking his head.

"Please tell me what you know." It felt as if he wanted to, but was struggling with whether he should.

"I really don't think that's a good idea."

"Please," she tried again, staring into his eyes. "I want to know what you know. I don't care if it doesn't make sense to you. Just please tell me so I can try to make sense of it myself. I'm already taking a huge leap of faith by entertaining any of this."

"Okay," he whispered. He put his arm on the table to rest his head in his hand.

"I'll tell you everything, but please keep in mind that some of this is going to be incomprehensible."

"I'll try."

"And we can never talk about this in front of my mom or Lissa. We can't even talk about it at either of our houses.

I'm not entirely sure if it's safe to talk about it here, so after today, the store is off limits too."

"Okay."

"There are stories today about Greek gods during the mythological times, but those stories eventually came to an end. In reality, the gods created a new generation, and with each new generation, descendants are created from the likeness of the previous generation, but they're different. Not all the special *traits* of their creators are passed to the descendants. Over time, the power given to one god blended with other powers, so instead of a new god with one powerful ability above all others—like the original gods—the new gods created had many, less powerful abilities."

"The abilities you'd mentioned before?"

"Yes. If you think of the thousands of years that have passed, you can see how a gene pool can become a melting pot of abilities. Usually, no one can be certain who has what abilities until each new god reaches adulthood. At which time, those powers are solidified. But since these offspring were created by gods, there are those who know exactly how new gods will turn out. Every once in awhile, a new god is created with a pure ability. The sole ability from the original Greek god. That new god is extremely powerful, and sometimes the other gods become *jealous*. Those who are in the know keep this knowledge to themselves out of safety for the new god, but there are some that know who do not have the best intentions."

"What do you mean?"

"An old god does not die off like a mortal would, which is how they get a horizontal lineage in addition to a vertical lineage."

"Lissa told me about that."

"Okay, so you can see that although new gods are rarely created, over time they would still have too many gods.

Less powerful ones can move up the ranks, so to speak, by preventing a new god from fully developing. If any god prevents the transformation of another, then he assumes the abilities of that would-be god."

He paused to make sure she was grasping everything. She nodded for him to go on.

"There are many different families that descended from the gods. These families are all over the world. Some are extremely powerful and don't even know why. They've been away from the homeland for many generations, and their abilities are so diverse that they haven't made the connection. They don't think of themselves as gods, only magical. But those of us who do know understand the importance of those born of a pure ability."

"What does this have to do with your family or with me?"

"Do you think it was a coincidence that there was a tornado warning when you were here with my mother last week?"

"You think your mom did that?" she asked bleakly.

He nodded. "Like I said, those of us who do understand what they are know the importance of a god being created with a pure ability. I think," he hesitated, "that's why my mom doesn't like your mom. She believes your mom created a god with a pure ability."

"What?" So now it wasn't just some less-powerful abilities … it was a pure ability?

"Legacy, I'm still trying to figure out the specifics of who you are and who exactly your mom is. There are too many variables right now." He sighed, shaking his head. "But I do know mine. I think my mom will stop at nothing to keep you from attaining your full power. She's been emotional lately, and it seems like the weather is connected to her emotional state, but I've never seen it as strong as this before." He sighed. "There's more."

More? She gaped at him.

"There was another reason my mom was mad that I talked to you about this," he said as he looked down to the table.

"What was the other reason?" she asked with an even voice. His qualms didn't matter now—how much weirder could this get?

"She knows that we'll ... er ... be *together*. If—"

"Huh? If what?" she asked as she shook her head. She was wrong, this did get weirder.

"If Adin stays alive," he whispered.

"What does this have to do with Adin, and what do you mean, exactly, that we'll be together?"

"You asked me the other day if there was anyone special in my life, and I told you there was."

"And?" What she really wanted to say was *so what?*

"You're that special someone, Legacy," he said as he looked back up and met her gaze.

She stared back at him in total disbelief.

"I don't know when we'll be together," he continued, "but it has been prophesied that if Adin stays alive, you and I will be together. The three of us are bonded by that. Some action will break it, and I think Adin is that link. I can only guess since I don't know much about him, but if he dies, I think you'll be too distraught to be with me. If you stay with me, then I guess he'll continue to live a long life as any other mortal."

"That is absurd!" she roared.

"Legacy, you asked me to tell you what I know, and that's what I know. You can believe whatever you want. I found out about the prophecy the night before you came in the store and got the job here, so I'm still dealing with all this too."

What? "You found out last Friday night?" she asked, puzzled.

"Yes," he responded, but seemed confused at the change in her tone.

"That's the same night I found out about my mother."

"I know."

"Don't you think it's weird that we both found out things about our lives on the same night?"

"I'm sure it wasn't a coincidence. There are no coincidences."

"I don't understand any of this." And she couldn't. Just when she thought she'd gotten a handle on the goddess stuff, her mind would rebel.

"I'm not sure if I believe it completely myself, but I know when I saw you here that Saturday, I knew there was something special about you. When we went out and you told me about yourself, I realized why. I feel attached to you, like I need to protect you, which is why I don't like my mother's hatred toward you or your mother."

"What do you mean you feel attached to me? We just met!" There went the politeness she was trying to maintain.

"Don't you see? This is why I didn't want to be the one to tell you this. I needed to give you enough time for our relationship to develop naturally. I'm not playing with the same advantages Adin has." He half-smiled and sighed, looking up. "He's known you for years. You've had time to be friends with him first. If he weren't in the picture, then maybe I wouldn't have needed time; I could have just flirted a little and asked you out." He blinked and looked at her with more conviction. "That's why I didn't want to tell you about this just yet. But you pleaded with me, and I can't refuse you," he said shaking his head, watching her eyes. "I already feel like you belong to me. I can only assume Adin feels the same way. He just doesn't understand why he feels so strongly for you now. This is out of all our hands."

She slumped back into her chair. "That's insane," she said, barely a whisper.

"My mom will be back any minute, and I have one more thing I need to say to you before she gets here."

"What?" she asked, her voice distant.

"Legacy, look at me. I need you to pay attention."

She forced her gaze to meet his.

"My mom doesn't like you or your mom, so she's not happy about this prophecy since it's about the two of us being together. I don't know Adin, but I don't have any ill feelings toward him either. I don't think you should talk to him about this because he will not understand, but I think you should watch out for him. If the only thing that keeps us apart is his death, I wouldn't put it past my mother to make sure that *that* happens."

The bell sounded as the front door to the store opened.

"That's her," he said quickly. "Remember, we can't talk about this with her around."

She nodded and picked up a stack of papers to shred, and he dug into another box. Ms. Gorgos walked in with bags of food and put them on the table.

"Did anything happen while I was away?" she asked River.

"Nope," he responded, seeming uninterested while he separated the papers out into different piles.

"I'll be in my office," she said, and turned to walk away.

Legacy ate quickly without another word to River. Once they were finished eating, they went back to the menial task in silence. She caught him staring at her a few times, but he tried to play off those moments as nothing. She wondered what he could be thinking. She already knew what she was thinking.

"Are you okay?" River finally asked.

"Fine," she said without making eye contact.

"I'm really sorry," he whispered. "More than you know."

She took a deep breath and looked at him. "Don't worry about it," she said matching his tone. "I'll be fine." She shrugged and turned back to the shredder.

She heard his chair move, but didn't turn around. Then she felt his hand on her shoulder, which startled her.

"You know you can talk to me about anything," he whispered, being careful not to mention the specifics.

So he felt like she could talk to him about anything, but she didn't think so. To her, he was still someone she hardly knew. But he was right in that he was the only one who'd offered her any explanation. She couldn't deny that. She didn't want to close off this source of information, but she didn't want to encourage him either. He already felt a connection to her, but she didn't feel one for him. She knew who she wanted to be with.

"I know," she said, nodding her head.

He went back to his seat, and they finished going through all the boxes. Ms. Gorgos came in while they were on the last one and was so pleased at their progress that she told her she could go home after they finished. But as she thought of her through River's eyes—with the belief that she didn't like her or want her to be with River—Legacy could see an ulterior motive. Letting her leave when finished meant she wouldn't have to spend any more time with River than what was necessary. But she really didn't know what to think.

As she got up to leave, River stood and stretched. "I'll see you later," he said, stepping over to her.

She nodded at him and left.

With more questions than she had answers.

Chapter

7

Skirt or no skirt? That was the question. Legacy stood in front of her closet wearing a robe, her damp hair still dripping, trying to decide what to wear on her second date with Adin. The weather had been unpredictable lately, and if Legacy were to believe River's theory that his mother had something to do with affecting the weather, then there was no way to know how the weather would be today. Or any day for that matter. So if the wind started howling, wearing a skirt to the botanical garden would be out of the question. She wanted to feel pretty, not pretty embarrassed, which was exactly how she would feel if her skirt flew up and revealed the secret she'd acquired from Victoria.

She opened the window and felt how calm it was. She really wanted to go with a skirt. She'd had on jeans last time, but now she wanted to show some leg.

But definitely no heels if they were to be walking around a garden for who knew how long. She selected a pale, floral-pattern skirt with a nude top and espadrille sandals and set them all aside before heading downstairs to eat breakfast. Adin had sent her a text late last night when he'd gotten in, and they'd arranged for him to be here at ten this morning.

As she grabbed some cereal, she thought back over the night. She'd awoken from a heavenly slumber this morning and hadn't remembered any of her dreams, though she was sure she'd had them. And with how bizarre they'd been lately, there was no telling what they could have been about last night.

Olive came into the kitchen yawning. "Good morning."

"Morning," Legacy said right before she took another bite. Olive retrieved a bowl from the cabinet and a spoon from the drawer before joining her at the table.

"How did you sleep last night?" she asked after swallowing another bite of cereal.

"Fine. You?"

"Fine."

Olive poured milk over her cereal and dug in. "So another big date today, huh?

"Yep."

They sat in silence while eating their cereal. But it didn't last long enough.

"How do you like your new job?"

"Oh, it's great. Kinda slow at times, but it's easy work. Could be worse."

"How well do you get along with the Gorgos family?"

Odd question. "We get along fine."

"When you said you had a date this morning, I thought

maybe you were going to say you went out with that guy River."

"Why would you think that? I didn't even know you knew of River or the Gorgos family."

"Word gets around. The Gorgoses are ridiculously rich."

"But why would you think I'd go out with River?"

"It seemed logical. I assumed you just met him, and you're working with him at his mom's store. Sometimes people who work together play together. Logical."

"Ah, well, no. I mean, we did go out after my first day on the job, but it wasn't like *that*."

Olive perked up. "You did?" she asked, a little too excited.

"I said it wasn't like that." She didn't want to tell her why they'd gone out, not without getting more information from River about his family and maybe more information about her mom. "He's just a friend, and really, he's not even that. He's just a co-worker."

"Well, I'll bet he's a catch," she said as she stood up, rinsed her dishes, and put them in the dishwasher.

"He's definitely good-looking. There's no denying that."

"But you're not interested?" she asked, sounding perplexed.

"Not in that way. I like Adin."

"Right. I hope you have fun today."

"Sure thing," Legacy said as she cleaned her dishes and left the kitchen.

Back upstairs, she stood in the mirror looking at her damp hair. It was already too humid outside for her to straighten her hair today. It'd just end up a frizzy mess before the day was over. She decided to put some pomade in it and scrunch it while drying it. She preferred soft, touchable hair, but she'd have to make due. She'd rather it be hard and nice than soft and a fuzzy mess. The strands that didn't cooperate naturally got a turn around her handy-dandy styling iron. Once she started curling, the naturally curly strands didn't look curly enough, so she ended up curling most of her hair. After she finished, she put some soft finishing spray in it, so the curls would still bounce freely without them all sticking together.

She still had time to kill, so she took her time putting on her makeup. Plus, she didn't want to get any on her clothes. When she got finished, she figured she should change the polish on her toenails. The dark red she'd had on since her first date with him didn't really go with the pale tones of this outfit.

She took off her sandals and changed the polish color to a more earthy shade. After her toenails dried, she put her shoes back on.

She heard the familiar three soft knocks at the door as she walked back downstairs.

"I'll get it," she yelled to Olive, not knowing where she was exactly.

She put her hand on the door, took a deep breath to steady herself, and opened it.

The sight of Adin, now slightly tanned, took her breath away. Just like last time, she appraised him as he appraised her, and it appeared they both liked what they saw. Today he was wearing jeans again, but had a short-sleeved, unbuttoned plaid shirt with a v-neck, fitted, beige T-shirt underneath.

"Come in. I'll be right back."

He walked in, but his eyebrows furrowed.

"Don't worry. I just have to get my purse. I'm coming back." She snickered.

"You'd better," he said, matching her tone.

She walked into the living room to grab her purse and then met him at the door again.

"Are you ready to go?"

"Yes," she said, grinning.

He reached over and took her hand. "Then, let's go," he said with a wink. Adin led her out of the house and into his car. Once they were out of the driveway, he started talking again. "You look very beautiful."

"Thanks, you look nice too."

"Do you remember the last day of school when I was there for the senior parade and you told me that?"

"Yes," she said, but she was puzzled.

"I told you that you looked nice every day," he continued.

"I remember. I dressed up that day."

"It was your birthday," he said, like that was the obvious reason for dressing up.

"Right," she said, knowing that wasn't why she really dressed up, but she didn't have to tell him that.

"Well, I wasn't being truthful when I said that."

Huh? "What do you mean?" Her smile was fading.

"You never look just *nice*," he said, raising his eyebrows and grinning.

"Oh, well, thanks." Her smile returned to her face, but it wasn't the only thing. Now she was blushing.

Adin reached for the hand that was in her lap. His hand grazed her bare leg, and her heart raced. His touch was so soft that she wished he'd forget about her hand and just put his on her knee instead. She glanced at him as he moved their joined hands to the middle of their seats, and as he did, she could see him shift uneasily. He hadn't anticipated touching her bare leg, and it was obvious to her that he enjoyed that touch more than he expected, probably as much as she did. He took a deep breath, but tried concealing his heavy exhale by clearing his throat. He glanced out his side window before turning his eyes back to the road.

He hadn't relaxed his posture yet. She could almost hear

him chanting, *Slowly, slowly, slowly!* to himself as he tried to get the thought of her leg out of his head. Even though he was incredibly handsome, she had to admit his response was adorable. The skirt was an excellent idea.

It was an hour-long ride to the botanical garden, and they still had a good forty-five minutes left. Adin had always been a guy who seemed cool under pressure. Well, except for his initial nervousness around her when he first asked her out. But the leg incident seemed to have penetrated his usual gentlemanly façade. She was surprised that she felt at ease so quickly after it had happened. And the reason, she guessed, was because she was beginning to find his behavior a little funny.

"Is everything okay?" she asked in a teasing tone.

"Er, yeah." He shifted in his seat again.

She pressed her lips together to keep from smiling, not that he would notice—he hadn't made eye contact since he moved their hands away from her leg.

"You seem awfully quiet," she said once she knew she'd be able to get it out without giggling.

"Do I?" he said, still no eye contact.

She shrugged at his response, not that he'd notice.

Legacy would need to take decisive action. After deliberating for a moment, she decided to let go of his hand so she could see his reaction. She would need an excuse, though. If she just let go of it, he'd know something was up. She had a piece of hair that was dangling by her eye, so she could use that. Ladies primped all the time. He shouldn't think anything of her examining herself in the mirror.

She leaned forward, positioned the visor with her right hand, and slipped her left hand out of his grasp simultaneously. She fixed her hair in the mirror but watched his reaction with her peripheral vision.

She heard him catch his breath and saw him turn his

head in her direction. Once he realized what she was doing, he moved his hand from the console between them back to his own lap. Even though he seemed to relax—only slightly—she figured she should help ease his tension even more.

"So, have you ever been to this garden before?" she asked casually while she continued playing with her hair.

"No, I, um, I've heard about it, though. It's supposed to be really beautiful." He struggled to keep going and managed to get only a little more out. "I thought it'd be something you'd like."

She put the visor back into its regular position and leaned back into her seat with her hands in her lap. "If you picked it out, I'm sure I'll love it," she said, looking over at him.

He flashed his gaze at her and smiled quickly, then turned his focus back to the road.

He was still tense, and apparently not going to make a move to get her hand back. Now, she regretted letting go. Even though she enjoyed this more than she should—and why not? She'd liked Adin for a really long time; she should enjoy how she made him feel. She did not like *not* touching him. Her hand ached to be in his again.

She looked over at him, and his wasn't resting gently on his leg. Oh, no. It looked as if he had it clamped down on his thigh. Maybe if she took his hand back, he'd relax.

She sighed, and he blinked his eyes in her direction for a fraction of a second and back to the road. Then she leaned over toward him with her eyes on his face. Because his hand was clamped so tightly, she knew she'd have to brush hers against his jeans to get to his fingers. She slid her hand across his leg and to his hand. She started to gently slip her hand under his with her palm facing down on his leg. Adin looked down and released his grip, realizing what she was doing. His breathing sped up, and he looked back out the windshield.

Touching his leg sent her heart racing. But she wasn't the only one who responded to the sensation. He seemed to enjoy her touching him more than he enjoyed it when he touched her. But now that their hands were on his leg instead of hers, he seemed even tenser.

Adin shifted his hand so that she could wrap her fingers around his, and she turned hers up so that she could grasp his.

She wasn't sure if she should move their hands away, back to the safety of the console. But having them there earlier hadn't seemed to help. She knew they couldn't move them back to her lap. Even though he seemed more worked up when she touched him, apparently that principle didn't apply when touching her bare leg. At least his legs were covered, not that that helped *her*, so she decided to keep their hands on his leg. If it became too much for him, then he could be the one to move them.

They sat quietly with their hands on his leg for the rest of the trip.

Once they arrived at the garden, he released her to turn off the car. Then he got out of the car and walked to her door. She glanced at his face as he took her arm to help her out. She didn't miss his eyes glancing quickly at her legs either.

The garden was beautiful. There were over two hundred acres filled with thousands of rare shrubs, flowers, and trees nestled against a serene lake. Among the varieties were magnolias, camellias, azaleas, Japanese maples, and endless roses.

Adin was back to his regular, charming self. As he guided her around the grounds, he pointed out the antique variety of roses and the rare tree from Burma, which was the only known one of its kind in North America. They continued walking around and easily talking. There were natural bridges over streams, beautifully placed boulders throughout the garden, and several waterfalls that could be heard throughout the grounds. Even though it was hot and sticky outside, the lush trees provided ample shade throughout the park.

For lunch, they visited the restaurant adjacent to the grounds and took their meals out to one of the many picnic tables by the flowing streams.

After eating, they walked one of the several trails that veered off the main grounds and eased into a manicured forest. The forest was thinned, so its natural beauty could be admired. This setting was more private, but Adin didn't seem to care. They talked, laughed, and held hands throughout the rest of the afternoon without the tension that had been there this morning.

Once they made their way back to his car, she felt a little uneasy. She had such a wonderful day that she didn't want a repeat of this morning in the car. Not that she hadn't enjoyed herself then, but she wanted Adin to enjoy himself too.

"Thank you, I've never seen anything so beautiful," she said as they pulled out of the parking lot.

"It *was* beautiful," he said, smirking.

"And all those flowers get to keep living for many people's enjoyment rather than living and dying for one person's," she said, smiling at him.

"True."

She sighed happily and stared out the side window. She was overwhelmed by how peaceful she felt.

"What are you thinking?" Adin asked after a couple of minutes.

She turned to look at him. "I was thinking I've had a

wonderful day with you. And I've never considered myself an outdoorsy type of person, but I was just wondering why that is. Honestly, I really do enjoy being outside and experiencing nature." She looked down at her hands. "It was wonderful to experience it with you."

Adin reached up and stroked her cheek. She turned back to face him and saw his eyes were gentle. She figured the day's activities helped clear his mind of how he'd felt this morning.

"The pleasure was mine," he whispered, and then dropped his hand from her face while he turned to watch the road.

As she continued to watch him, he glanced over at her and then gently took her hand from her lap and put their joined hands on his. She watched his face for any sign of tension, but found none.

"What was the coolest thing you did at the beach?" she asked casually, just wanting to chat. "I need to know if I ever get to go."

"I parasailed. I'd never done that before, and it was awesome."

"Uh-uh! That's not for me. I'm terrified of heights."

"Really? I wouldn't have guessed that," he said calmly.

"Yes. I don't even like thinking about…"

"Your hand is sweating," he interrupted. "Are you okay?" His tone was more urgent.

"Yeah, my hands and feet start tingling and sweating when I think of heights. When I think about being stuck up high, I instinctively want to grab hold of something so I don't fall. Sweaty extremities would make a firm grip impossible, so it just adds to the fear. My stomach gets all knotted up too. It's silly. I know," she said, shaking her head.

"It's not silly," he said, rubbing her hand. "I have fears too."

"What are you afraid of?"

Wrong question. He tensed up again like this morning. "Um, I've told you about my fears," he said, not wanting to revisit his fears about their relationship.

"Is that why you acted *that* way this morning?" She had thought it was cute at first, but she hadn't really thought about it from this perspective.

"Yes," he whispered. "I'm sorry about that. I didn't mean to make you uncomfortable. I don't ever want to make you uncomfortable."

"You didn't. I didn't consider the reason. I was just flattered." She thought it best to go with *flattered* rather than *tickled*.

Adin chuckled and glanced at her. "Flattered?"

"Sure." Hopefully, she could ease his concerns a little. "I've liked you for a long time, and you seemed uneasy at the sudden touch of my bare leg. I figured it was because you liked touching my leg almost as much as I liked you touching it. It was reassuring that your feelings may not be so far off from mine." She shrugged, hoping she didn't cause more damage by being honest.

"Oh," he said, smiling again.

Good. No damage done.

"Do you mind if we stop by my house before I take you home? I brought something back from the beach that I want to give you."

"All right." He brought her back something from the beach? She tried not to squeal.

They pulled into a neighborhood that she could only assume was his since she'd never been to his house before. The houses were nice, and the neighborhood screamed upper-middle class. It was full of young and middle-aged people with kids that varied in ages. It was the kind of neighborhood where most of the residents worked in professional jobs, but probably needed both parents working to afford these types of houses and the cars in the driveways. She knew his parents were divorced, so she wondered how one could afford this on just the one salary.

"Are we going to your mom's house or your dad's?"

"My mom's. I go back and forth between the two, you know, but my mom likes to keep closer tabs on me," he said with a chuckle.

"Did you go with your mom to the beach last week?"

"Yes. We go every year. Sometimes my dad goes and gets his own place nearby, so I can do things with the both of them. But he's been really busy lately." He shrugged. "My mom has been too. She went out of town again."

They turned onto a cul-de-sac, so she knew they were almost there. She looked down at her lap, thinking about what she'd say if Adin asked her in. His mom wasn't home. His house would be empty. What if he wanted to give her a tour of his house? That tour would surely include his bedroom. This morning, he'd been tense being alone in the car with her, and she was still wearing the same skirt. How would he act being alone with her in his bedroom? She tried not to hyperventilate.

"We're here," he said as he turned into a driveway. She was too anxious to look. He got out and came around to her side of the car. Once he opened the door to let her out, she smiled at him, and he took her hand to turn her toward his house.

She looked at his house for the first time and gasped. She yanked her hand away from his and threw it up to cover her mouth. She felt weak in the knees and tears formed in her eyes.

"What's wrong?" Adin asked anxiously, rubbing her arm.

But she couldn't answer him. Something *was* wrong.

Horribly wrong. She was staring at a house she knew she'd never been to before, but she had definitely seen. It wasn't a perfect imitation. It was the real thing.

The house that stood before her was the one that had plagued her dreams.

There was no mistaking it. The traditional feel, the side porch, even the patio table was there. She began to cry. She didn't understand this. It was such a short part of her dream, but why would she dream about a house that actually existed? She couldn't make sense of it or of her reaction.

She stood there staring at it like it was going to disappear or turn into a different house. This couldn't be real. She'd never had dreams that came true before. She knew it was impossible for the rest of that dream to come true. She remembered the lightning wasn't even real lightning. But why this house? And why was Adin at this house in her dream? There was no way this could've been real. But it was.

"Please, Legacy, tell me what's wrong," Adin begged.

"Er, I don't know how to say this..." She continued looking at the house. She stepped closer to it, looking intently. She had to be logical about this. Maybe she *had* seen his house before. She knew she'd never been here, but the two of them had been friends for a long time. She could've seen a picture of it. If so, she was so obsessed with Adin that it could be possible she remembered it on some subconscious level. At least that made more sense than the alternative. An alternative that she didn't even want to consider.

"Legacy," he said again, his tone reproachful.

"I had a dream the other night, and you were in it." She tore her eyes off the house to look at him. "And so was this house," she whispered.

"What do you mean?" His voice was no longer stern; it

was incredulous.

"It was really short, but you were sitting over there." She pointed to the patio table. "Do you know what 1887 means?"

"What are you talking about?" Adin still looked shocked.

"In my dream, I walked over to you, and you handed me a broach, or something, that had the numbers 1887 on it. You said, 'be careful.' Then I woke up."

"I don't know what 1887 means."

"Maybe it doesn't have anything to do with you. I've been having weird dreams lately, so I didn't think much about this one. But now that I see this house…" she trailed off, looking back at it.

"What kind of dreams have you been having?"

"Storms, tornados," she said, shrugging.

"I heard there was a tornado warning last week. Maybe you were just scared about that."

"No, the dreams started before that day."

"When did they start?"

She stared at him, the reality of the truth giving her chills. "The night you asked me out."

Chapter

8

By the gods, that can't be right! Surely, her relationship with Adin didn't have anything to do with her dreams. It had to be because of everything else going on.

Adin's eyes suddenly turned very sad. He let go of her hand and looked down to the ground. "Do you think you're dreaming these dreams because of me?"

"Oh, no," she said, squatting down to force his eyes to meet hers. "No. I don't think that at all."

"Then why?"

She could tell he didn't quite believe her. His eyes lacked any sign of the confidence they normally displayed. She could sense he wanted to look away from her. He would have if she weren't staring so intently at him.

"I don't think that dreams are always literal," she said slowly, thinking about the words she needed to say. "I think the storms represent me dealing with stress or nerves. If they *were* related to you, then I had those dreams to help me get over my nerves."

"But you just said your dreams weren't because of me."

"I meant that they weren't about you literally. I've been dealing with other stress too." She was only trying to make Adin feel better, but then it clicked. "Oh wait," she gasped, looking away from him, but his eyes followed her.

"What?"

"The dreams didn't start Saturday night. They started Friday night. After my party." She thought for a few more seconds. "I woke up Saturday morning to a storm. I remembered I had a dream, but I woke up too quickly and couldn't remember … could not remember," she gasped again, shaking her head.

"Legacy?"

"When I woke up, I tried to think back to the dream I'd just had, but I just stared out my window at the storm, not able to see any lingering images of my dream, and my head was pretty foggy. Then I looked at the alarm clock and got up. I think—"

"What?"

"What if the reason I couldn't remember the dream was because I was still dreaming? It was storming outside, so if I was dreaming about stormy weather, maybe I didn't realize when my dream ended and when I really woke up."

"Was it because I showed up at your party that night?"

"Why would you think that?" His question distracted her from her train of thought.

"Because I'd been out of line."

"What?"

"Legacy, I held your hands, touched your lips, and held you tightly without explanation." Adin closed his eyes and shook his head. "I was supposed to be just a friend, but I couldn't help myself. I couldn't keep my hands off you." He opened his eyes and looked at her again. "I couldn't keep my eyes off you either," he murmured. "I'd been struggling with my feelings for you for so long that my behavior that night caught me by surprise. After you opened your gift," he said, looking down at her wrist where her watch was, "I left. I knew I had to get out of there quickly before I did anything else that was inappropriate."

"You were not being inappropriate."

Adin continued as if she had said nothing. "After I got home, I went over the events of the evening over and over again. I hardly slept. The next day, I thought I should just change colleges so I could get out of town. But that thought, the thought of never seeing you again, I just fought it. I decided that night I would ask you out. I had to know if you'd be willing to go out with me." He paused. "When you said yes, I was elated. But while I was away, I started wondering if you'd just said yes because I put you on the spot."

"I told you that wasn't true."

"I know," he said, his voice still sad.

She reached up to stroke his face and heard him catch his breath, but she didn't stop. "How you acted the night of my party was the best part of my entire day. When you asked me out the next day, I was beyond thrilled. There aren't words to express how I felt in that moment. I've liked you a really, *really* long time, Adin. When I figured out which stress caused my dreams that started Friday night, it had nothing to do with being uncomfortable with you at my party."

Adin smiled at Legacy, but it didn't reach his eyes. She

wanted to do more to help him understand how she felt. She took her hand off his face and put both her arms around his neck. She stepped forward and stretched up on her tiptoes to hug him close to her. He wrapped his arms around her back, and she rested her head against his chest while he squeezed her tightly. He bent his head down and kissed the top of her head, keeping his face buried in her hair.

"Don't worry about my feelings for you. I understand why you're scared. This is new for both of us. This is something we've both wanted. How often does that happen—when two people like each other at the same time?"

"I don't know. This has never happened to me before," he whispered into her hair.

"Me either. Would it have been easier for you if I didn't like you as much as I do? You said something before about getting me to like you if that were the case."

Adin chuckled, and she smiled in his chest at the sound of his laugh. "No, it definitely would not have been easier. I've noticed I have a hard time keeping my manners around you. If you didn't like me as much as you do now, I probably would have just scared you away. You would have thought I was some overbearing prick!"

She laughed at his teasing tone, and he squeezed her harder. She kept one arm around his neck, but slid one hand down to his chest. She rubbed her fingers in circles on his chest in front of her face. She felt the muscles in her body relax into his embrace.

"Maybe we should finish this conversation inside," he suggested. "There's no telling what the neighbors are thinking right now," he teased.

Her heart started pounding against his chest, and she knew he could feel it. He stepped back and removed one of his hands from her back to lift her face up.

"What's wrong?" Adin whispered, staring into her eyes.

Uh-oh. He probably thought she was worried about what they'd been talking about. She couldn't let him believe that. She knew she was freaking out at the thought of being alone with him in his house. How did she tell him she was a chicken?

She grinned widely up at him. His eyebrows came together, but he half-smiled back at her.

"I'm just reacting to the thought of being alone with you in your house," she said, trying to sound teasing, but her voice broke twice, so she sounded nervous.

"Oh, well, then that's an acceptable response." He laughed, and released her face to lead her into his house.

Once inside she, surprisingly, felt more comfortable. She guessed it was because she wasn't staring at the vision of her dream. She didn't see the inside of his house in that dream, so being inside helped make that less real for her.

"It's in my room," he said, and her heart started pounding again. Luckily, her chest wasn't up against his, so he wouldn't notice this time. "Would you like to come up with me?"

Her heart took off in a sprint. She took a deep breath to try to settle it, but that didn't work. "Sure."

"It's this way," he said as he took her hand and led her up the stairs.

His room was right off the stairs, so they didn't have far to go. She wasn't sure how she felt about that. If his room were at the end of the hall, then she could have had more time to steady herself. But she'd probably just use that time to get even more worked up.

Adin opened the door, and they both walked in. He dropped her hand and stepped aside. "Er, it's kinda messy," he said apologetically. It really wasn't.

"This is nothing," she said. "You should see *my* room."

Oh no! Was that an invitation?

Adin laughed a short, nervous laugh and looked down. Then he looked at his desk by the window. "Umm, it's over there."

He walked over to the desk, and she stayed planted by the door.

"It's nothing big," he said as he pulled out a conch shell.

Actually, it was big.

He walked over to her with it in his hands. "I just wanted to get you something to show you I was thinking about you while I was away."

"It's beautiful," she said as she took it from his hands and studied it.

"I picked this one because it has light peach colors, like your skin, and tones of blue and green, like your eyes."

She looked at him, smiling, but he was looking at the shell in her hands.

"What?"

He shrugged. "I like giving you things."

"I like that you like giving me things," she said with a laugh.

"Good," he said, still smiling but now looking in her eyes. "Would you like a tour of the rest of the house?"

"Sure." Maybe if she got out of his bedroom, her heart would return to a healthier pace.

Adin took her hand and showed her the rest of the upstairs first, and when they went downstairs, she put the shell on the living room table. He then showed her the rest of his house, and it was amazing. It had all the latest amenities: waterfall faucets, stainless steel appliances, antique bronze fixtures, copper accessories, travertine floors, custom iron railings. Simply beautiful.

"This door leads out back," he said as he opened the door and they stepped onto a covered patio. It had several ceiling fans, a fireplace, and an outdoor kitchen. They walked to the end of the patio and started to descend the patio stairs when she looked up.

"You have a swimming pool?" She didn't know why, but she was shocked. Though, his house had everything else.

"Yes, you should come take a swim sometime."

They walked down the stairs and around the pool. "You do realize a swimsuit is more revealing than a skirt, don't you?" Was he for real? He had a tough time touching her leg in a skirt. He'd likely have a stroke touching skin exposed in a bikini … skin he wouldn't ordinarily see.

Adin threw back his head in laughter. After he composed himself, somewhat, he looked at her. "I do realize that, yes, but I'll be expecting it then," he said, chuckling.

"True."

Adin led her back up the patio stairs. Once they were back on the patio, he pulled a chair out for her. She sat down, and he sat in the one next to her. He took both her hands in his on top of the table.

"You never did tell me why you're having those dreams. Even though they're not because of me, I still don't like the fact that you're having disturbing dreams."

"It's a long story."

"Will you tell me about it?"

Was she going to? "I'd like to, but it really doesn't make any sense."

"Maybe I can help you figure it out."

"Okay." She could tell him a little. She took a deep breath before beginning. "Do you remember when we were talking about our families, and I told you about my parents?"

"Yes. They died in a car accident."

"Well, what I actually said was that the *story* was they'd died in a car accident."

He waited for her to continue.

"Um, the night of my party, Lissa told me my mom didn't die back then."

He gaped at her. "What happened?"

"I'm not entirely sure. She said she was a powerful woman, but there were people after her, so she had to leave."

"Wow."

"Yeah, but she said she told me this because I'll see my mom again and that I'll be going through changes until my eighteenth birthday."

"What kind of changes?" Adin's face was filled with concern.

"I don't know." She didn't want to get Adin too involved in the mythology stories. "Anyway, I've been thinking a lot about all that, which is why I think I'm having those dreams."

"What have your dreams been about, specifically, I mean?"

She told him all the dreams in detail, ending with the one she had about him.

"It seems like your subconscious thinks you're in danger."

"I think you might be right." She looked down at their hands, thinking over the past week and her conversation with River. She hated not telling Adin everything.

"There's something you're not telling me," he said quickly.

"Yes. There's more," she said, still looking down. A little more wouldn't hurt.

"What?"

"Apparently, the Gorgos family knows my mom. When I met the son, River, he acted weird. Then the next time I saw him, he said I looked just like this lady named 'Dora.' When I told him that was my mom's name, he was shocked.

He said he didn't know I was her daughter. He took me out that night and told me he saw my mom last year in Greece talking to his dad." She looked up at Adin, and his expression was frozen. Even his fingers had stopped soothing the back of her hands.

"How do you know the Gorgoses?"

"I got a summer job at their store in town."

Adin's eyes narrowed slightly, but quickly opened back up. "When?"

"Last Saturday. They live next door to Calli, and she overheard Ms. Gorgos talking to her mom about needing summer help. I was looking for a job anyway, so Calli went with me down there to apply. Ms. Gorgos offered me the job without me even filling out an application."

Adin mumbled something unintelligible under his breath.

"What?"

He ignored that and asked her another question. "How long have they lived next door to Calli?"

"Er, I don't know. I think they just moved here. Where are you going with this?"

"Legacy, my family has never gotten along with the Gorgos family. I don't like the fact that they live next door to your best friend, and I really don't like the fact that you're working for them."

"They seem nice enough."

"Of course they do."

"What's that supposed to mean?"

"The Gorgos family is full of people who do and say whatever they need to get whatever they want."

"I don't understand what you're saying."

"Look, I don't want to scare you, but you should really be careful around them."

His words would have knocked her down if she weren't

already sitting. *Be careful.* Just like he told her in her dream, sitting at a patio table at this house. It wasn't the same porch, but it was close enough.

He immediately noticed the change in her expression. "What's wrong?"

"You just told me to be careful, just like you did in my dream." She stared off into the sky.

"Legacy," Adin said, shaking his head. "I don't know what to say. I didn't mean to say it like that, to use those words. Look at me, please," he said softly. And she did. "It's just that some members of that family are downright evil."

"That's what River said."

"What did he say?"

"He said to watch out for his mom. That she is evil."

"He did?" This clearly caught Adin by surprise. "Why did he say that?"

"I don't know. He didn't elaborate."

"I really don't like this. It seems too convenient that Lissa would give you this news, and the next day you would meet people who may know what's going on. I don't know if you can trust what they have to say about this."

"River is the one who told me, and he is also the one who warned me about his mother. Why would he warn me about her if he's just lying to me anyway?"

"I don't know. Is there anything else?"

"Yeah, there's one more thing." Might as well go for broke where River was concerned. "The night he took me out…" She hesitated, not sure how Adin would take her non-date with River.

"Go on," he said after several seconds had passed.

"He mentioned some things about Greek mythology." She wasn't sure if she should continue. It looked as if Adin was fighting anger. "Um, he also said something about descending from Greek gods and acquiring certain abilities," she said timidly.

Adin's hands ripped away from hers and went straight into his hair. He leaned his head back, shaking it uncontrollably while he stared at the ceiling. "Unbelievable!"

She jumped in her seat at the sound of his tone and waited quietly for him to calm down, but he just kept shaking his head.

"Adin?"

He still didn't look at her.

"Adin, what's wrong?"

He looked at her, but didn't answer that question. "What did you think when he told you this?"

"It seemed pretty farfetched."

He nodded, hands still on his head. He seemed to agree with that assessment.

"But after I thought about it some more," she started slowly, "I realized it matched Lissa's story."

Adin went back to shaking his head.

Great, she'd have to tell him everything Lissa had said. So she did. Adin just gaped at her.

"This is a lot to consider," he finally said. "Maybe you shouldn't think about your mom or any of this other stuff until she contacts you. It's best to get the information straight from the horse's mouth."

"I already considered that, but I'd like to know what River has to say about everything too. Whether or not you think he's lying."

Adin's fist landed on the table. "I don't want you talking about this with him."

"Why?"

"I've *told* you why." Adin looked at her with pleading eyes.

She didn't want to fight with Adin about this. In fact, she didn't want to argue at all. No way was she telling him the prophecy stuff.

She stroked Adin's face, but his eyes were still beseeching. "Let's not talk about this anymore. You're getting mad, and I don't want to upset you."

"You're not upsetting me," he murmured, sliding his hand across the table and taking her free hand in his. "I'm just worried about you, and I don't trust them."

They weren't getting anywhere with this conversation. "It's getting late. Maybe you should take me home."

Adin's face turned sad. "Do you want to go home?"

"No, I didn't mean it that way."

"I'm sorry; I'm being a jerk. I'm not usually so overbearing. I think this falls under that category of not knowing how to react to my feelings. I care about you so much, and I know we need to take things slowly. But going slowly or not, it really doesn't change how I feel about you. I may try to control how I react to those feelings, but it doesn't stop me from having them."

"It doesn't bother me that you have those feelings. I have them too," she said, smiling shyly.

He reached his other hand over to rub her cheek. "Let's go," he whispered.

"Okay," she said, smiling bigger. She grabbed her gift and they left.

On the ride to her house, the conversation about River was dropped, and she realized their relationship had changed. They were still taking things slowly, but now it really felt like they were heading in the right direction. It no longer felt surreal to her. And this made her feel wonderful. It was easy being with Adin, and except for how he felt about his reactions to his feelings for her — good reactions, she thought — it was easy for him to be with her too.

When Adin pulled into her driveway, she looked over at him.

"Would you like to come in?" she asked Adin as he put his car in park.

"I'd love to," he said softly, but smiling exuberantly.

He walked around to her side of the car quickly since it had started to rain. He opened her door and then guided her up to the front door.

As they walked into the house, Adin dropped his hand from the small of her back and kept a couple of paces behind her — out of respect for Lissa, she assumed.

They walked into the living room, but Lissa wasn't in there. She could smell food cooking, so she led the way to the kitchen with Adin right behind her.

Lissa was in there cooking dinner, but she had her back to them. Adin stood right beside her now.

"Hi, Lissa," she said to Lissa, getting her attention.

She turned around with a smile on her face that faded slightly when she saw Legacy wasn't alone.

"Hi, Legacy. Hi, Adin."

She had intended on introducing them, but he had been here on her birthday, and his grandma *did* live next door, so she knew Lissa knew him already. Besides, she really didn't know how to introduce him. She knew what they meant to each other, but since they were going *slowly*, she really didn't know if that entailed formal introductions as boyfriend and girlfriend yet.

"Did you two have a nice time today?"

"Yes, we had a great time," she said calmly. "Do you need any help with dinner?" She thought it best to sidetrack her from the topic of her date.

"No, you should entertain your company. Adin, would you like to stay for dinner?"

"Yes, ma'am," he responded politely with a smile, but quickly glanced at Legacy for approval. She nodded.

They turned to walk out of the kitchen.

"Would you like to see the rest of the house?" she offered nervously. She knew he'd have to see her room on the tour.

"Sure," he murmured.

"Well, you've already seen just about everything downstairs, except for Lissa's office." She pointed to her office door. "And the dining room." She motioned toward that room. "Though we never really use it much."

They walked upstairs, and she pointed out each of the bedrooms, saving hers for last.

"Here's my room," she said as she opened the door. She walked into her bedroom, and he followed behind.

"Hmm," was all he said, smiling.

"What?" she asked as she put her new conch shell on her nightstand.

"Nothing. It's just not what I expected." He shook his head, but seemed amused.

"What did you expect?" She looked across her room, but nothing looked out of the ordinary to her. It was a typical teenage bedroom. She had a modern comforter with matching pillows on her bed, some posters and pictures on her walls, a computer desk with her laptop.

"Honestly, I didn't expect anything. You know when you read a book and visualize how something looks, but when that book is made into a movie, the director's visions aren't always similar to the ones in your head? It's not necessarily a bad thing. It's just different."

"Are you telling me you've visualized what my bedroom looks like?" she asked as she turned to look at him.

"Maybe." He was playing coy. He obviously had thought about it.

She liked that.

"What else have you visualized, besides my bedroom?"

"I've envisioned a lot of things," he said, taking a step forward.

"You have?" She played along, taking a step in his direction.

"Mm-hmm." He took the final step toward her and ran his hand down the length of her arm.

"Legacy, dinner's ready," Olive said as she popped her head into the room.

Legacy jumped, taking a step back, and Adin dropped his hand to his side, smiling.

"Shall we?" she asked.

Adin nodded, his smirk still evident.

Downstairs, Lissa had set the kitchen table for the four of them. While they ate, there was rarely a quiet moment, which was nice. They all seemed to enjoy the conversation, regardless of who it was directed to.

When they were finished eating, Adin walked with her to the living room. "I should go."

She felt a pang of sadness, which was silly. It was probably because of their little tiff, and at this point, they hadn't made any other plans to see each other again.

He frowned at her expression. "Would it be okay with you if I stopped by tomorrow night? I have some things to do tomorrow, but I'd like to see you in the evening if you're free."

Her frown quickly disappeared. "I'd like that a lot."

"Good, then I'll see you tomorrow," he said, and then quickly kissed her forehead.

He started to turn away from her. "I can walk you out," she offered.

"No, it's still raining." He grinned.

"Okay." She smiled back, but followed him to the door.

He turned to face her in the doorway and glanced around to see if they had an audience. They didn't. He leaned toward her, his lips at her ear. "I'll see you tomorrow," he whispered.

Her heart thudded, and she put her hand on his chest to steady herself. "See you tomorrow," she said breathlessly.

He put his hand on her face and slid his lips from her ear to her cheek, where he kissed her. Then he slid his hand down her other cheek as he stepped away from her.

"Tomorrow," he murmured as he turned to walk out the door.

She watched him drive away and then shut the front door. She was tingling from his touch and enjoying the smell of him lingering in the air. When she turned back around with a grin frozen on her face, Lissa was standing there with a confused look on hers.

"Here." Lissa handed her a postal package.

"What's this?" she asked as she took it.

"I don't know, but I think it's from your mother."

Chapter 9

She stared at the box, too nervous to open it. It was wrapped in brown paper and stamped from Greece. Either River was telling the truth about seeing her mom in Greece, or he was a really good liar.

No, she didn't believe he'd lied to her. She would need to get more answers from Adin as to why he didn't trust River's family. In the meantime, she couldn't see why it would hurt to find out what all River knew as long as she stayed objective.

"Aren't you going to open it?" Lissa asked nervously.

She nodded, staring at the package. She turned it around, examining it from all directions, and then ripped the paper off the box. She opened it and sifted through the packing peanuts to find a black, velvet jewelry box. She pulled it out and glanced at Lissa who still looked shocked.

She lifted the lid of the jewelry box and stared at what was inside. It was a silver necklace. It looked very old and beautiful. The pendent was formed out of twisted silver wire. The abstract shape was triangular with rounded edges and the point facing down. It looked as if the silver wire wrapped all around it with diamond chips glittering from exposed crevices beneath the wire. She pulled the necklace out. "It's heavy," she muttered.

"It's platinum," Lissa said.

Platinum? "Wow, it's beautiful." She looked in the package, but didn't see a card. She was so distracted by the beauty of the necklace that she didn't notice, at first, the rain outside had slowly morphed into a storm. "How do you know it's from my mom?"

"She told me she was sending you something."

Legacy was shocked to hear this. "When did you talk to her?"

"This morning."

"What else did she say?"

"That was it."

"Are you going to tell me anything else?"

"I'm sorry, I can't," she said as she turned away from her.

"You are impossible!" she yelled to her, and as she did, thunder crashed.

Lissa turned to stare at her with wary eyes. "You need to calm down."

"I am calm," she said through her teeth while thundered rolled outside.

"Legacy, there's no reason to get worked up over this. Your mom sent you a gift. She's probably going to contact you soon, and when she does, she'll explain everything better."

"Fine," she said, glaring at her while lightning illuminated the room through the windows.

Olive came back down the stairs. "Have you watched the weather report?" she asked Lissa.

"No," Lissa said curtly, not taking her eyes off Legacy.

"There're thunderstorm warnings all over the place," Olive continued.

"You know how unpredictable the weather is here," Legacy said with a smirk.

"True," Olive said.

"I'm going to bed," Legacy announced, and walked up the stairs. She hadn't understood her initial angry response to Lissa not telling her everything her mother had said on the phone, but she was suddenly too tired to deal with it.

But she hardly slept. The storms were relentless. As one would pass, it seemed as if another one fired up without pause. When she did sleep, she dreamed. These dreams weren't really new; they were variations of dreams she'd already had. She dreamed of running from thunderstorms, lightning glittering from the sky, tornados charging for her, the girl she felt the need to protect that always guided her, and snakes. Although, the snakes were a little different. Instead of one snake or just snake holes, there were several snakes. These snakes came at her from several directions, giving her only one course of action to take. Though she felt safe on the path she took because she wasn't running into any more snakes, it felt as if the snakes were guiding her. And she didn't trust that, though she had no other option.

She woke up to a calm morning. She looked outside and saw puddles of water throughout the backyard, and then decided it was time to do some investigating of her own, so she pulled out her laptop and got online.

From what River said, some of these gods were still in existence. She wondered if Zeus was still around. Being the king of gods, she wondered if any other god would try to destroy him to ascend to that throne. She figured he was as good a start as any. But there was just way too much information to digest.

There was a lot of information on Demeter too. All the websites said she was a goddess of earth, harvest, and seasons. Because of the earthly things she was over, she was considered the personification of Mother Nature. She was natural and nurturing. Besides presiding over the harvest and the earth, she also ensured the sanctity of marriage and provided over the circle of life and death.

She had several children, two of which she had with Zeus—Zagreus and Persephone. But other stories about Zagreus's origin conflicted with this account.

Regardless, the story of Zagreus was that the Titans tried to destroy him, so Zeus destroyed the Titans and retrieved Zagreus's heart. His divine flesh mixed with the Titans' ashes, creating humankind, which was why humans had both good and bad tendencies. Interesting twist, but not really relevant. She guessed that, unless the deity who Zeus inserted the heart into was who she descended from, she could rule out Zagreus's line.

Persephone was a different story. There was only one account to her birth, so there was no denying she came from Demeter and Zeus. She married Hades, who presided over the underworld, making her the queen of the underworld. That seemed a little dark, but she continued researching.

She felt the blood rush out of her face when she read about Persephone's abduction. Several gods wanted to be with Persephone, but Demeter kept her hidden from them. Hades abducted her and brought her to the underworld— that was how she became the queen there. Demeter fell into a deep depression, and since she was the goddess of nature, life on earth stopped while she searched for her daughter.

Zeus ordered the return of Persephone, but Hades had tricked her into eating pomegranate seeds because anyone who consumed anything while in the underworld would have to stay. Persephone was eventually allowed to return to her mother, and when reunited with her, the earth flourished. But because she was tricked into eating the seeds in the underworld, Persephone had to return to Hades for part of the year. When she was in the underworld, the earth turned barren. This was how the myths explained the development of the seasons on earth.

Other than her time with Hades, there were other stories that said Persephone spent four months each year with Adonis, and also linked that to the changing seasons, but there wasn't really much about that. The only offspring that she created was Macaria. Persephone created her with Hades, but the only entry on her showed she was the goddess of blissful afterlife. There wasn't any other information on her.

Since she couldn't be sure she descended from Macaria, maybe her line came from one of Demeter's children not created with Zeus. If she created children with him and was a goddess, then maybe he still protected her when it came to her other children. She felt like both Zagreus and Persephone seemed to be dead-ends, Zagreus more so than Persephone.

As she searched, she noticed there were other common names, like Aphrodite and Hercules, besides Zeus. Then there were other names she hadn't heard of before like Artemis and Hermes — though she had heard of the holy grail of handbags, the Hermes Birkin. Calli owned three. But she digressed.

There were some strange stories, like creating offspring

from the earth and swallowing babies that later lived.

Then she thought about River. He said he knew about his family, but didn't know about hers. She wondered which god he'd descended from. He knew. Maybe if she knew where he came from, she could exclude that line. But as she remembered the strange stories, she realized that *that* didn't really matter. It seemed like the gods created offspring with anyone and anything, regardless of whom or what those things were. The typical concept of mating to produce bambinos didn't really seem to apply.

Then she wondered, since mating wasn't necessary, if her parents or River's parents were even really *involved* in the sense that she considered traditional parents. Maybe that was why River stayed with his mom—not his dad—and that was why Lissa always talked about her mom—never her dad. Maybe the parents chose who would be the true parent. In the cases of producing an offspring with an inanimate object, the decision would be fairly obvious, she mused. No tree could raise a child.

Then she felt a roll of nausea. What if one of her parents was not a person? Ugh! That would be so weird. Maybe that was why Lissa never talked about her dad. She could hear her now. "*Legacy, this is your dad, the white oak tree. We planted him here to be close to you. He gave you life. Now try not to hit him with the lawnmower.*" Super weird!

So the one thing that stood out more than any other was that this was all mythology. Myths. Different religions viewed these gods differently. Some even had different names for similar entities. So, if these were myths, how would she know what to believe?

She still had a hard time wrapping her head around everything, but when she tried to stay detached while she thought about it, things started to click. Everything except for what River had said about Adin. She could not, would not, believe that. She felt bonded to Adin, not River. Even though she and Adin were taking things slowly, she still felt their relationship was destined to be something great. She knew it. Adin knew it. Just as she needed air to breathe, she knew through every fiber of her being that Adin was meant for her.

She was slowly discovering there was no way to decipher all this on her own. She needed to talk to someone specific about this. She just hoped River would be open to chatting at work tomorrow. But maybe Calli could provide some insight now. She headed right over to her best friend's house.

When Legacy got there, she was happy to see that Calli was home. Since her mind had gone round and round with information overload, she'd failed to call Calli before coming over. She parked behind the BMW and rang the doorbell. Once Calli answered, Legacy started in, unable to wait. They walked up the stairs to her bedroom and she told her friend everything, about the dreams, her new necklace, what Adin said about the Gorgoses, and everything River had told her. Calli knew some of this already, but spilling everything out also felt therapeutic.

"I believe what River said about his family and my family, but I don't know what he means about Adin. I really like Adin, Calli. I can't conceive of what River said about that."

Calli turned to face her. "If you believe you're actually going to be a god—or is it goddess?—whatever you're going to be, then maybe we should do some research of our own on Greek mythology."

"I've already been looking this morning. The stories are just so out of the realm of what we know of as reality that they are hard to understand."

"Well, fresh eyes won't hurt. Let me grab my iPad."

Legacy breathed deeply, feeling relaxed again. "Thank you so much, Calli. I don't know how I could get through this without you. Adin doesn't understand, so I can't really talk to him about this."

"Yeah, I don't think you should tell him everything River said. Not yet anyway."

"I'm really sorry about River," she said, looking down at her hands in her lap.

She walked back over to her bed and sat beside her. "It's not your fault. Apparently, we're dealing with destiny or some other force."

"I still feel badly about River. I know you like him, and he let me believe he was involved with someone."

"Look, I'm not going to pretend my feelings aren't hurt, but I don't blame you. Heck, I don't even blame him. From what you've said, this is all new to him too. Besides, I really do kinda like Zach."

She'd been so absorbed in her own drama that she'd forgotten to even ask about him. Some friend she was. "How'd your date go?"

"It was great! Oh, Legacy, you should have seen him. He was gorgeous! And charming ... the evening was wonderful."

They talked about her date with Zach and her dates with Adin while they both perused the Internet, looking for more Greek mythology information until Legacy had to leave. Adin had said he was coming over tonight, so she needed to get home and freshen up.

She got home, took a quick shower, and threw on some shorts and a T-shirt. She didn't want it to seem like she was dressing up for Adin, but she did fix her hair and put on some fresh makeup.

She was jogging downstairs when she heard him pull into her driveway. She waited until he knocked before opening the door and smiling at him.

"Hey. How was your day?" he asked as she motioned for him to come in.

"Long." That was the truth without giving too much away.

He turned to look at her and took both her hands in his. His eyes narrowed briefly and then opened back up. "I've missed you all day," he murmured, staring into her eyes. Then he dropped her hands and slid his arms around her back to hug her.

"I've missed you too," she said as she put her arms around his neck.

"Is that Adin?" Lissa called out. "I could use some muscle in here."

They walked into the kitchen where Lissa was trying to move the china cabinet.

"Why are you doing that?" Legacy asked as Adin quickly walked over to grab the other side. He shifted it over effortlessly.

"Something fell from the top." Lissa squeezed behind it and pulled out a doily. All that for a doily?

"Thanks," she said as she righted herself. Adin pushed the china cabinet back into place. "Are you staying for dinner? We're just having burgers."

He glanced at Legacy and she nodded, remembering when he'd done that before. Then he looked at Lissa again.

"Thank you, ma'am. We didn't have anything planned for tonight. So that'd be good."

"Oh, I have something to show you," Legacy said as she grabbed Adin's hand and ran up the stairs to her room. She let go of him and stepped over to her dresser. She pulled out the necklace that her mom had sent her. "My mom sent me this," she said as she showed it to him.

"Hmm, it's very beautiful." Adin spoke truthfully, but

with an unfathomable expression.

"What?"

"Nothing," he said, turning his eyes to her and smiling. "Would you like to join me downstairs? I'm not sure if it's appropriate for me to stay in here with you." His eyes displayed the heat she liked to see, but she didn't want to tempt him into kissing her with Lissa and Olive downstairs.

"Sure."

Adin and she visited in the living room until dark, talking, laughing, eating, and making more plans to be together. When it was time for him to leave, she walked him to his car. They were standing by the driver's side when Adin leaned against the door with his arms crossed.

He looked at her and sighed. "Is there something you're not telling me?"

Uh-oh. There was something she hadn't told him about River, but she wasn't about to jump right into that without an explanation. "What do you mean?" she asked.

"I don't know. I just feel like I need to tell you to be careful."

Then he uncrossed his arms and lightly clutched her waist. He pulled her against him without saying anything else. She put both her arms around his neck and eased her head against his chest, listening to his heart. He leaned his head down against her hair and held her for a long moment. There wasn't anything to be said. Everything they wanted to say was already being communicated.

Adin kissed the top of her head and then let go of her waist to secure his hands on her face. He lifted her head and kissed her forehead. He then leaned his forehead against hers.

"Legacy, please be careful."

"I will," she whispered, trying to reassure whatever unexplainable fear he felt.

Then, leaning over, he buried his face in her neck—where she could feel his hot breath against her skin—wrapped his arms around her back, and lifted her off the ground in a tight hug. She clung to him while he turned his head slightly and kissed her neck.

He put her back down and held her face in his hands. "Goodbye," he whispered.

And then he was gone. She stood outside watching him drive away. As she turned to walk back into the house, she thought of what River had said about Adin. There was no way he could be right about the prophecy. She didn't believe it.

Did she?

* * * * *

"Hi, Legacy," Yale said to her as she set up the register the next morning.

"Hey. Good morning." But she wasn't really paying attention. She was glancing around the store looking for River. She wanted to talk to him about what she'd learned—or rather, what she hadn't learned—yesterday about Greek mythology. Everything had been too confusing, so she just needed him to spell it all out for her. "Have you seen River?"

"Yeah, he's in the back room."

"Cool. Thanks." Legacy walked back there and saw him drinking coffee.

"I didn't know you drank coffee."

"Starbucks. Love the stuff."

She nodded. "Is your mom around?"

"She's in the office. Why?" he asked, sitting up.

"I did some research yesterday, so I have a lot of questions."

He put his coffee down and shook his head. "No. I told

you we couldn't talk about it here," he whispered.

"I want to know everything."

The door opened and River's mother walked in. "Good morning, Legacy. How are you?"

"Good. I'm just putting up my purse. Feeling a little jealous of River since he has Starbucks."

River chuckled. "It's very good. You should be jealous." He sipped it slowly, dramatically, to rub it in.

"I need to see you in my office, son." She turned to leave, but looked over her shoulder just before pushing the door open. "Now."

He nodded and stood.

"Look," he whispered quickly to Legacy. "I can give you my cell number. My mom is going to make it really difficult for us to have any time alone up here. You can call me later about this. Plus, I want you to be able to reach me if you ever need to." He looked at her for several seconds before saying, "For anything."

"Fine." She knew he was right. His mother wasn't going to make it easy on her. Besides, she liked the idea of being able to reach him whenever she had a question. But she didn't want him sitting around waiting for a phone call from her.

After getting his number, she went back out front and continued working. Ms. Gorgos was in and out most of the afternoon, but when she was out, she made sure River was busy and had given Yale tasks so that Legacy would be forced to stay at the register.

The day had been long and Adin was coming over later, so she was ready to bolt at the first opportunity. She grabbed her purse, but had an eerie feeling. As she walked out of the break room, she could feel his eyes on her. She looked around, but didn't see anyone staring. The only person in sight was Yale, who was at the register reading a magazine.

As she passed her co-worker, Yale stopped her.

"Legacy, can you drop these off in the mail on your way out? Ms. Gorgos left them here."

"Sure," she said as she picked up the envelopes.

She glanced at them as she walked out of the building. She wasn't really looking at them; she just needed something to focus her attention on while she made her escape. But she suddenly realized she was studying them intently. They were just bills, but what grabbed her attention was the store's return address. She'd never really paid much attention to the address before. She just knew the store was on Main Street.

She felt the blood fall out of her face by the time she got to the mailbox and had to grip it to keep from falling. The street number to the store was 1887.

She managed to get into her car, but she didn't remember the walk back from the mailbox. She was reeling over this new facet of her dream. Another facet that came true. She tried to rationalize why she dreamed that specific number. She thought about Adin's house and the reason she considered she knew about it. Maybe she did know the address to the store—had seen it on some level and stored it in her memory just like she considered the possibility that she'd done the same with Adin's house.

But why that number? And why did Adin tell her to be careful in that dream when he showed her that number? Even odder, Adin had warned her to be careful around the Gorgos family before she knew what the number meant. Then today, she found out that the number was, in fact, linked to the Gorgos family.

No. That number was just a coincidence.

Coincidence? River told her there were no coincidences, but those words seemed truer now. River was worried about his mom, so maybe some force was telling her to watch out for Ms. Gorgos through her dreams. Then it hit her.

Lissa said her mom would be contacting her. She didn't know when or how. *How?* Could her mom be sending her these messages through her dreams? Was the Gorgos family the people she'd run from all those years ago? If what River said about his family and her family was true, then Legacy could understand why her mom had felt threatened. If his mom wanted to stop Legacy from attaining her full powers, whatever they were, then maybe that was why her mom had left. Lissa said her mom was powerful, so she could have been able to defend herself from the threat. Maybe she separated herself from her daughter so that Legacy could live a normal life in peace without the constant threat of danger.

Her mom had never been in any danger. Legacy was. And now, her mom could become a part of her life once she turned eighteen because the danger would be over. She would no longer be a sitting duck, waiting for her time to go through changes — she would be finished. Legacy would be powerful too.

For the first time, she fully believed that.

She quickly drove home, feeling the certainty of her fate settle into her bones. Okay. She was accepting this. Now, she needed to learn as much as she could. Tonight, she'd enjoy being a teen with no problems as she hung out with Adin, and when the time was right, she'd use that cell number River had given her.

Legacy showered and put on some loose, comfortable clothing. It was really sticky outside, so she wanted to minimize any sweat damage.

When Adin arrived, she yanked opened the door, ready to throw her arms around him. But what was in his hands stopped her.

"I missed you so much," he said as he stepped up to

the threshold, handing her the flowers he was holding. "These are for you. I figured the ones I gave you last week are probably past their usefulness," he teased.

The bouquet was not a dozen red roses like he'd given her at the beginning of their first date. These looked to be much more than a dozen and contained an array of colorful roses that were elegantly arranged. Every color of rose she could imagine was represented and the aroma was simply heavenly. It seemed as if the flowers had an understated feeling, but a clearly defined purpose.

"Thank you. They're beautiful," she said as she took them from his hand, gave him a big hug, and turned into the house.

Adin followed her to the kitchen where he saw that the roses he had given her were dried with petals lying around the vases. He reached for one of the vases to discard the roses.

"What are you doing?" she protested as he pulled the roses out.

"I'm getting rid of these."

"No. I want to keep them."

"Legacy, I plan on giving you flowers all the time. There's no need to keep the dead ones." He chuckled.

"You don't have to give me flowers every time you take me out," she said as she gently took the dead flowers from him.

"I haven't given them to you *every* time we've gone out." He smirked.

"Still, these were the first ones you gave me. They're from our first date, so I want to keep them."

"Okay," he said, smiling. "I won't complain about these dead flowers, but I don't want to see your room covered with dead flowers by the end of summer. Surrounding yourself with all that death isn't healthy." He chuckled.

"I think I know the difference. But fine, I won't save every single flower you give me," she said as she rolled her eyes and laughed. She put the fresh flowers in a new vase and then picked up the two vases of old roses. "I'd better put these somewhere safe," she teased.

Adin waited downstairs in the living room with Lissa while she put the roses safely away in her bedroom. When she came back downstairs, he took her hand and they left for their date.

Like last week, he opened doors and held her hands at all the right moments. They ate pizza, talked, and laughed. It was easy being with Adin. She could hardly remember what it was like when she secretly obsessed about him. She didn't have to be secretive about her feelings anymore.

When they got finished eating, they didn't leave. The restaurant provided a nice place for them to be alone with each other without the need to rush off. They spoke freely about anything that came to their minds. Anything except the goddess stuff. Tonight, she was normal.

When they were in Adin's car, he raised their joined hands and kissed the back of hers.

"My mom will be back in town on Wednesday. I'd like to bring you over to meet her—you know, *formally*."

"Okay," she whispered. So they were taking the next big step in their relationship. But still no kiss.

"Don't worry. You've already met her, and she's still really nice. Besides, I've already told her all about you," he said with a grin.

"What did you say?"

"Well, I told her things like how funny and kind you are and how you've grown into a beautiful woman, though I've always thought you were a beautiful person." Adin's lips quirked into a half-smile, and she knew the last comment wasn't about her looks. "And I told her how I feel about you."

They pulled in her driveway, and Adin turned off the engine without getting out.

"How *do* you feel about me?"

Adin reached over and played with a strand of her hair. "Since we're taking things *slowly*, I think we should save this conversation for a later time," he murmured.

Her heart was pounding, and she blushed. "I can wait," she whispered.

He lifted their joined hands to kiss the back of hers again before letting it go and getting out of the car. He walked her to the door. "Do you mind if I come over tomorrow night after you get off work?" he asked under the glow of the porch light.

"I'd love that."

"Good." He smiled.

Then Adin stepped closer to her, put one arm around her back, and put his other hand on her cheek. He leaned down and kissed her exposed shoulder and then kissed her neck. Finally, he placed his lips at her ear.

"I hope you have a wonderful night's sleep. Dream beautiful dreams. I know I will because I'll be dreaming about you."

He slid his lips down her cheek and kissed her softly at her jaw. Then he started to step back, but she quickly turned her head. Their lips grazed and a strangled groan rumbled in Adin's chest. He quickly kissed her chastely on the lips, then moved his mouth to her cheek and kissed her there again. He squeezed her in a tight hug and then stepped back and took both her hands in his.

"I'll see you tomorrow," he murmured as he licked his lips while staring at hers. He wanted more. She could see it.

Legacy didn't know what to say, feeling her heart pound harder by the second. "Bye," was all she managed to get out, and it sounded strangled.

His jaw clenched and he nodded slowly. "Bye."

He stood there several more seconds before letting her go and walking away.

Chapter
10

After several nights of no dreams, her dreams about weather returned. Most of the elements were the same. She was still being chased by a tornado from one side and snakes from the other. This time, she actually found a storm cellar to take cover in, but as she ran down the steps, she saw the little girl already inside.

"What took you so long?" she asked with narrowed eyes. She seemed to be disgruntled.

"I didn't know what I was looking for," she said, talking about the shelter, but feeling happy she was already safe inside.

The little girl walked over to her. "It's been right in front of you the whole time," she said as she reached out with her index finger extended and touched the middle of her forehead.

For an instant, Legacy felt as if she knew the answers to everything like she did the last time the girl touched her forehead. She gasped in her dream and then woke up with a start, sitting straight up in her bed, clutching her blanket at her chest. But she couldn't remember the revelation at the end.

As she sat in wonder, she considered the fact that if her mom was communicating with her through her dreams, then maybe this girl could give her the answers. She wondered if she could subconsciously make herself ask the girl questions the next time she dreamed about her.

Thunder crashed outside, jerking her out of her thoughts. She looked over at her window and saw the dark clouds hovering in the sky. She got up and walked over to the window. Water was everywhere. It must have rained all night. She guessed her theory about River's mom manipulating the weather was true. She was on the schedule to work today. After all, there were no coincidences.

She got dressed and headed to work. During the ride in, she hydroplaned in several places. She was so tense when she finally got there that she stayed in her car, taking deep breaths. The weather itself never bothered her, but she hated feeling like she was going to skid off the road.

She wrenched her hands out of the death grip she had on her steering wheel and made a run for the front door. Yale was inside mopping up water, and River was up on a ladder taking down waterlogged ceiling tiles. Apparently, the roof had leaked from all the rain. She felt a little smug that Ms. Gorgos's store suffered from the consequences of her actions.

She went to the supply closet and retrieved another

mop to help Yale.

"How bad is the damage?" she asked River with her head down, focused on the floor.

"We're not sure. I'm not going to put in new tiles until the leak is fixed, though. Mom left right after she got here. She's going to get the handyman. Since it's Sunday, he's not in his office."

"I take it she's not in the best of moods," she commented as she glanced up at him.

River stared down at her with a wistful expression. She could see that he wanted to apologize, but he couldn't. Not with Yale around. Besides, he seemed to be a stickler about the no-talking-at-work-about-Greek-stuff rule, so maybe he wouldn't voice anything anyway.

He straightened his face before he spoke. "No. She's not."

She nodded and went back to watching the floor as she mopped.

"Legacy?" River asked as he stepped down the ladder.

She looked at him. "Yes?"

"Will you come with me to the basement? I need to see if it's flooded or if there is any water damage." Then he turned to Yale. "Yale, stay up here and get ready for the store to open. Turn on the sign in five minutes."

Legacy took Yale's mop from her and put both of them back in the closet. Then she followed River down into the basement.

He turned to look at her.

"We're not checking on flood damage, are we?" she asked.

"No. I already checked down here before Yale arrived," he said quickly.

"Then what are we doing?"

"I need to talk to you."

"You said we couldn't talk about *things* here anymore."

"I don't have a choice." He paused. "Are you okay?"

"Yeah, why?"

"Because I know you're aware of the weather connection to my mom. I'm just really sorry," he said, stepping closer to her.

She stepped back, shrugging, and realized she was now up against a wall. He took another casual step in her direction. They were now uncomfortably close — though, she was the only one who was uncomfortable.

"It's not your fault," she said, looking away from him.

"It is partly my fault," he said, looking over at her and forcing her to meet his gaze. "I know my mom has some vendetta against your mom and, more recently, her negative feelings against you have intensified. I know I'm the reason for that," he whispered.

"Don't worry about it."

He sighed and almost smiled. "I don't have a choice. I have to worry about it because I worry about you."

"River," she breathed, and shook her head. She didn't know what to say. She didn't want to hurt his feelings, but she didn't want to give him the wrong impression either.

"Don't," he started, and raised his hand as if he were going to touch her lips to keep her from talking. He stopped himself and put his hand back down. "I understand how you feel. I don't want to put you in a position where you can't stand to be around me. Even if we're not meant to be together *now*."

"Stop," she whispered. "I don't want to think about that." She stepped to the side so she could walk away from the wall. He turned to watch her. "I really do appreciate your honesty, but I'm with Adin." She looked into River's eyes. "I want to be with Adin."

"I know," he whispered, and looked down.

Ugh. Why was this happening? "Look," she said softly, walking back toward River, "I do like you … as a friend. My life changed a few weeks ago, and I feel like you're someone I can really talk to about … about *things* that I can't talk about with other people."

He smiled, but it looked pained.

"I don't want you to be sad about how things are with you and me. I like our friendship, but if you can't handle keeping our relationship as it is, then maybe we shouldn't—"

"No!" River said, panicked. "Don't say that. I … um … you're right. We can keep things strictly on a friendly level. Just don't say you don't want to be friends with me. I get that you want to be with Adin, but I couldn't bear the thought of you not being in my life at all. Friends, I can do."

"*Friends*," she emphasized.

"Friends," he agreed.

She waited a moment to let that sink in. She wanted to be sure he was clear on how she felt about him before they went on. "Can I ask you something?" she asked after several seconds had passed. She'd been wanting to pick his brain since the other night, but hadn't had a moment alone to call him.

"Anything," he whispered. And she was absolutely sure he meant that.

"I had another dream last night about weather. Since Lissa said my mom would be contacting me—but she didn't know when or how—I think that maybe these dreams are my mom's doing. What do you think?"

"Hmm … I'm not entirely sure the dreams are coming from your mom."

"Why not?"

"I think it's more likely that it's your own subconscious trying to work things out." That wasn't the first time she'd considered this alternative.

"But I've received some signs in the dreams that I couldn't have given to myself."

"Are you sure about that?" He was actually curious, but that made her think of the reasons she'd considered when she tried to explain to herself why those images — Adin's house, the store's street address — came to her. She'd thought maybe she'd seen them before but never really noticed.

"I'm not sure about anything," she confessed.

"Well, I guess it's good you're trying to consider all the possibilities."

She gasped. "Do you think it could be your mom's doing?" She hadn't even thought about that until now!

"No," he said calmly. "She can't get into your dreams. We're not descended from Hypnos's line."

"Who's Hypnos?"

"The god of sleep. He had four sons with Pasithea: Ikelos, Morpheus, Phobetor, and Phantasos. Their sons were known as the Oneiroi. But Morpheus is the Greek god of dreams. If one of the gods is involved in manipulating your dreams, I would think that either Morpheus himself or one of his descendants who retained some power over dreams would be the one behind that. We're not part of that lineage, so I know my mom can't do that."

He spoke so freely about his Greek mythology knowledge. She immediately found herself wanting to get more out of him while they had the opportunity.

She stepped quickly over to him and grabbed his arm. "You have to tell me more."

River was startled, but willing. "Um, what do you want to know? There's so much."

"Who did you descend from? Did you ever live here before? Do you know why it's been prophesied that we'll be together?" She tried not to squirm when she asked the last question.

"I came from the line that started with Phorcys and Ceto. They were sea gods who were both created from Gaia, a goddess of nature. They had some monster offspring that paired themselves with more noble mates to produce a better line. But since the monster genes are in my family's gene pool, sometimes new gods can be more monster than noble." He paused and looked down. "Even those of us who are not monsters tend to have *evil* tendencies."

"What does that mean?"

"Well, let's just say my mother's behavior comes naturally."

"What about the rest? Have you ever lived here before?" She didn't want to repeat the *other* question.

"Yes. Well, not in this town. We lived about ten miles out of town when I was a baby."

"So *your* family is why my mom left?" She tried not to shriek, but she wasn't successful.

She still had her hand wrapped firmly around River's arm. He took a deep breath and exhaled slowly. "I don't know for sure, but yes, I think my family was partly to blame. It's not like my mom gives me a play-by-play of her actions, and I could never ask her about what happened back then. Especially not now."

She dropped his arm and folded hers over her chest. "And the prophecy?"

"I don't know anything else about that. Like I said before, I just found out about it a few weeks ago. I already told you everything I know about that," he whispered.

"What else?"

"What?" he asked, clearly puzzled.

"What else don't I know that you know that I should know?" She wondered if her convoluted question made sense to him, but it was obvious that it did.

"Umm," he started, shrugging his shoulders. "I'm

sure you're most curious about your family, but I'm not sure about anything on that. After I found out about the prophecy, I tried to do some research. I haven't really come up with anything yet." But it was obvious he wasn't being completely forthcoming.

"You know something?" she accused.

"I only know pieces. I haven't connected all the pieces yet, so I can't really say what I do know. Believe me, if I did, I would tell you. You know I can't deny you anything."

"Please just tell me," she said as she touched his shoulder. She knew it wasn't fair to persuade him this way, but at this point, she didn't care. "What about my name?"

He stared at her cautiously. She apparently hit a topic he'd already considered.

"Lissa told me Kore is another name for Persephone. And Persephone is Demeter and Zeus's daughter. I also know that Dora is descended from Demeter, either directly of her likeness or generational. But there is no continuation of the line that I can find. Persephone only had one daughter and the line ended. At least in my online research."

River paused before asking, "Why are you concerned with the gods' children?"

"Um, because I'm trying to find exactly who I am."

"You're Legacy. Dora's daughter. *That's* who you are."

"But why am I like this?"

He smiled. "Ahh, now you're thinking the way you should."

"What do you mean?"

"You know gods can create a likeness from themselves with other gods. Demeter could have created Dora directly from herself, and then Dora could've created you. The question is why do this? Why create gods in the likeness of others? That's what I've been digging into. You see, Dora could have created you with Zeus and it not be a sexual creation. They could have tried to recreate a god that was created before."

"Why would they want to create a specific god when they already have that exact one?"

"To allow for a different destiny."

"So if Demeter created Dora and Dora created me, then does that mean I'm an exact replica of Persephone?"

"That's one theory. Another theory is that Dora is actually Demeter and you're actually Persephone, or her likeness created by the original Demeter."

"What?" she yelled. "I can't actually be Persephone. I'm only seventeen!"

"You're in your human form now, and gods don't age the way you're accustomed to. But looking at it from that perspective, *you* could be much older. I could be much older."

"This doesn't make any sense." She shook her head. "If they were already gods, why start over? If every new god must go through changes starting in their seventeenth year of rebirth, why agree to lose that power in the first place, much less run the risk of never attaining it again?"

"To create a new destiny." River had said that once, but she was on information overload. "Whether your mom is actually Demeter or created from her and whether you were created from the original Demeter or from her creation, it really doesn't matter. It matters why you're here now, and me, for that matter. The only thing we need to really focus on is making it to our eighteenth birthdays. If we are original gods or new creations, that doesn't matter now. We'll be powerful *if* we make it through."

"What are your thoughts on why I was created? I know you have to have some theories." She couldn't process anything to come to a conclusion herself.

"I think you were created in the likeness of Persephone,

or are her. Either way, your life is like Persephone. I think you were created—"

"To stop the abduction," she interrupted. Legacy felt the blood fall from her face.

"Yes. Demeter was devastated when Persephone was abducted and that abduction changed the course of her life. She was forced to be with Hades and live part of her life in the underworld. I'm sure she made peace with her course, but Demeter wanted better for her. I think you're the attempt at the better life. The better destiny."

"Where do you fit in with all this?" she asked softly.

River shook his head and looked down. "I'm not really sure. I think I was created in the likeness of one of the many gods that originally pursued Persephone before she was abducted," he whispered.

"Because that god wanted a second chance with Persephone?"

He looked up at her with soft eyes. "Because he wanted a *real* chance with Persephone. What Hades did to her ... that threw us all off course. I'm not saying what's going to happen now is what the right course was to begin with. Maybe what happened to Persephone with Hades would have always happened. Maybe that was the right destiny then. But since gods can create offspring in their likeness, I can only assume one destiny isn't always enough for them—for us."

"But the new gods created aren't always just like the original gods." She remembered what he'd told her before.

"Right, most gods do not know if a new god will have the pure abilities of the original god or if the new god will have a combination of muted powers. It helps to level out the playing field in one respect because it's proof that the new god isn't going to be a clone and repeat the same life as the original god. They may be created in their likeness, but they are their own entities. They don't have to make the same mistakes they did. But that leaves us to make new ones."

"So if my mother left me with Lissa because she was worried about me being abducted like Persephone, then she could have done that to keep me safe from Hades."

River's eyes turned cold. "Yes," he said through gritted teeth. He'd obviously considered this possibility. "Speaking of Lissa, I have one more thing to tell you. Because of Demeter's association with Zeus, she had ladies-in-waiting, priestesses, if you will. They were responsible for taking care of Demeter's needs. Whatever she needed, no matter what, they always took care of her. 'Melissae' was the title given to these women. Since your guardian goes by Lissa, I think it's safe to say she works for your mother."

She shook her head and felt tears glistening in her eyes. Lissa was never really her mother's friend?

River put his arms around her and hugged her gently. "I'm sorry this is so hard for you," he whispered.

She stepped away, but was still dazed.

"Legacy, please ... *please* don't tell anyone this information came from me."

"Why?" she asked, staring past him to the opposite wall.

"Because of my lineage. People who know about us don't trust my family. If they know you found out through me, they'll try to discredit the information."

She nodded and dabbed the tears from her eyes before they could spill over. Then she looked at River. "Thank you for telling me all this. It really does mean a lot to me."

"Whatever you need, whenever you need it, I will always be here for you."

"So, now, do we go back to not talking about this here?"

River scrubbed his face with his palms and looked at her again. "I'd prefer that, but your needs are too important to me. At this point, I don't really care what my mother thinks about us, but I do care what she thinks about you. Your safety is my main concern. If she knew we were talking about this, she'd freak out. But if you need to talk to me," he said, shaking his head, "then I'm going to talk to you. If you need me, then I'm going to be here for you, no matter what. I may not have all the answers, but I'll give you whatever I have … always," he whispered.

She nodded. She appreciated River for helping her and was beginning to feel like he was a true friend, though she didn't like to think of the bond he mentioned. As long as they stayed just friends, she could live with that. As she thought about that, she realized his friendship could be something great. He worried for her safety, answered her questions, and wanted to be there for her. As long as he didn't expect anything romantic, then she was all for his friendship, knowing he had the potential to be very special to her.

"So what do we do now?"

He looked down and reached for her hand. "We live our lives the way we want to."

And she knew as he said those words that she could definitely do that.

Chapter
11

"What do you mean you have to be in the Fourth of July parade?" Legacy asked Calli while they were testing out shades of blush at the mall.

"Our squad is doing a float, so I'll be cheering and throwing out candy. But I still want you to come and watch. Zach's going to be there. You can meet him," she said and winked at Legacy.

"Fine." She didn't want to go and watch a parade by herself, but Calli was her best friend. She could suck it up for one afternoon.

"When the parade's over, we can get a funnel cake and play some of the games until the fireworks display."

"No, I'll leave after the parade. I don't want to be a third wheel."

"You don't have to be a third wheel. You can ask Adin to come with you." She said as she tested more blush.

"I don't know about that."

"Legacy, come on! You are *dating* Adin. There's nothing wrong with you asking him to go with you to the Independence Day Celebration."

"I'll think about it." But she really didn't want to think about asking him out. She liked it better knowing Adin was doing all the asking at this point.

Calli wiped colors of blush on the backs of each of Legacy's hands.

"Wow. You have one hot hand and one cold hand," she said, amused. "Which color do you like best?"

"I was holding my iced latte in my right hand," she explained, "and it's a million degrees outside." She looked at the samples. "I like the one on the left."

Calli looked around for an attendant, so she figured this was as good a time as any to bring up yesterday's events.

"I talked to River yesterday at work."

"What about?" she asked, but her attention was directed elsewhere. "Excuse me, can I get these two shades, please?" she asked the girl behind the makeup counter. "I like them both."

"About his family and my family."

"What did he say?"

She explained the entire conversation. Even the detail about how protective he was of her. Calli paid for her products, and they were back in her car by the time she finished with the story.

"What do you think about all that?"

"From everything we've learned, he makes sense."

"It seems weird, though, that he didn't want you telling

anyone about this. I mean, I get what he said about his family, but still, you have a right to tell whoever you want."

"I know. I don't think he meant it that way. I just think he was worried what people would say about him."

"People like Lissa."

"And people like Adin."

"Adin?" She frowned.

"Yes. Adin told me his family didn't get along with River's family."

"Why? You don't think Adin is like you and River, do you?"

"No. River called him mortal. Besides, there's that whole prophecy thing. Apparently, gods can be destroyed, but the way River talked about Adin being the key player, he sounded as if Adin was an innocent bystander, unaware of his involvement in this. If I'm with River, then Adin can live a blissful life without me. If Adin dies, then River and I can't be together. It doesn't make sense to me. River thinks Adin is the link, but that *that* is the extent of his involvement."

"So why does Adin's family not like the Gorgos family?"

"I don't know. Adin thinks they're evil. But there are many evil people in this world that are not part of Greek god ancestry. Maybe they were wronged in some way. It's possible since Ms. Gorgos is controlling. There's no way Adin's family could connect that evil behavior to her being a descendant of monsters created by Greek gods," she said, shaking her head.

"Really? That's the first thing I would've thought," Calli teased. "So are you going to keep this from Adin?"

"I don't want to. He came over last night after I got home from work, and I wanted to tell him. But after the way he acted the last time we talked about River, I think I should wait until everything makes sense to me before I try to explain it to him."

"So when are you seeing Adin again?"

"Tomorrow. He's taking me to his house to meet his mom. She's finally back in town again."

"Wow. That's a big step."

"Not really. I've already met her, but I think he wants to introduce me to her as his girlfriend. Besides, he's already met Lissa. I mean, since we've started dating."

"Your mom's priestess," she laughed.

She stuck her tongue out at her. "It's not like we can put off this introduction. I have already been to his house, so I guess it *is* appropriate."

"I guess you're right. I haven't met Zach's parents yet, but I haven't been to his house either. Maybe he'll kiss you tomorrow. You know, a big, sloppy kiss." Calli wagged her eyebrows as she pulled into Legacy's driveway.

"He'll do that when he's ready. Right now, I'm really enjoying the little kisses his gives me."

After Calli dropped her off at home, Legacy stayed inside the rest of the afternoon. The weather was hot and sticky, and the next morning, it was still just as hot and miserable. Morning time did not bring a break from the sweltering heat.

She got up and got ready for her day with Adin. She was nervous about seeing his mom, so she looked for something nice to wear that would keep her cool. She didn't need to be sweating bullets because of the heat *and* nerves. She settled on a coral skirt and white top. Jeans would have been way too hot, and shorts were a little too casual to wear for this encounter. This would be the second skirt that Adin would see her in. Hopefully, he'd be able to contain his desires a little more successfully than the last time. She giggled to herself as she got dressed. She really didn't want his mom to see him like that.

She fixed her hair in a loose up-do. If she'd left it down,

it would've frizzed up before she even got to Adin's house.

She slipped on some flat shoes and accessories and headed down to the living room. She heard Adin pull in the driveway and didn't wait for him to come to get her.

She opened the door, saw his car, and stepped onto the porch. She turned to face the door to lock it since Lissa and Olive had left to run errands.

"What are you doing?" Adin said, and she jumped.

"You scared me!" She turned around, and he was walking up the porch steps.

He laughed. "I'm sorry. I didn't mean to scare you." He put his arms around her waist and hugged her while watching her eyes. "You should have waited for me to come get you," he said, raising his eyebrows.

"Don't be silly, I heard you pull in." She shrugged and turned back to the door to make sure it was locked.

"But it could have been someone else."

"I saw your car. I knew it was you," she said as she turned back to him.

"Next time, will you please wait for me to come to you if you're here alone?" he asked, his eyes concerned. He was obviously bothered by the fact that she was home alone.

"Fine," she conceded.

He took both her hands in his. "You look ravishing. That color is beautiful on you," he said and bent his head down to kiss her cheek.

"Are you sure I look okay? I am in a skirt." She laughed.

"You can wear a skirt every day. I promise, I won't mind at all," he said as the corners of his mouth twitched, fighting a smile.

She rolled her eyes. "Let's go," she ordered, dropping one of his hands and keeping the other.

He followed her to his car, letting her in first and then getting in the driver's side. She leaned facing him with her knees together — the left one higher than the other since she was leaning toward her left — slanting toward the gearshift. She rested her arm casually on the middle console, so he could hold her hand if he wanted without having to reach for it on her bare legs. She wanted to make sure he didn't have a reaction like the last time. Even though he did recover by the end of that date, she knew they didn't have time to wait out his reaction before she would see his mother today.

Her preparations weren't necessary. Adin didn't grab her hand. After he pulled out of her driveway, he reached over and put his hand on her left knee. She suppressed a gasp, but she couldn't do anything about her racing heart. Her breathing sped as she looked down at his big, strong hand resting gently on her knee. He moved it softly from side-to-side, stroking her skin, and it felt absolutely wonderful. Her leg tingled at his touch, and her mouth fell open for the air to come more easily. She was breathing much too fast at this point, unable to concentrate.

She was worried about his reaction to the skirt, but she was the one falling to pieces! She needed to pull herself together. She took a deep breath and looked up at him. He looked smug.

Smug? Fine, two could play this game.

Adin had on light tan shorts and a white shirt. His shorts were loose and longer than her skirt, almost covering his knee, but that wouldn't stop her. She shifted slightly so that her weight was off her arm on the console.

Adin kept his eyes on the road while she set her plan into motion, but she decided she should first distract him in case he suspected her plot. She lifted her hand and stroked his arm that rested across the console to get to her knee. She kept her eyes on Adin, and he sighed at her touch, but his smug expression didn't completely dissipate.

She rubbed his arm a few more times, and then she was

ready to make her move. She slipped her hand from his arm, moved it over to his right knee, and pushed back his shorts so that her hand was on his bare leg. His shorts fell back over her hand, which was now only partly exposed. She gently stroked the inside of his thigh with her fingertips.

Adin's expression went from smug to tense. She could tell he hadn't expected her to touch his leg. Good. His breathing picked up, and it looked like he was trying hard to concentrate on something. A distraction, she guessed.

She didn't realize at first—since she was enjoying her little victory—that her breathing had, too, expedited again. She found herself caressing the inside of his leg more than she originally had planned. It felt so good. It obviously felt good to Adin too. He tried to control his reaction, but this time, he was letting himself enjoy the touch a little rather than trying to ignore it all together.

She kept her eyes on him, watching his expression. His mouth was open, and she could hear the quick breaths he was taking in. Every now and then, when he exhaled, he'd shut his eyes in a long blink. Just watching how he reacted made her heart pound in her chest. She felt flush all over, and even though the air conditioner was on in his car, it was beginning to feel very stuffy.

She couldn't feel his hand on her knee anymore. He was now stroking higher up on her leg, and she could feel him inching a little more toward the hem of her skirt. She relaxed into her seat and glanced at his hand. He didn't stop. He kept moving his hand back and forth and side-to-side. His hand felt hot against her leg, like he was burning to touch her, and her leg was the only relief his burning hand would get.

She knew she was still stroking the side of his leg. She wanted to look at his face, but she couldn't trust what her eyes would show him since she was enjoying his hand on her leg way too much. She kept her gaze down as she looked in his direction. To her surprise, she noticed her hand was no longer visible on his leg. Without the confines of tight clothing and because of the relaxed angle she was now in, she hadn't realized how far her hand had slid up under his shorts. Her eyes shot up to his face, and he was no longer controlling his expression. His eyes were burning.

Adin stopped the car suddenly and looked at her. She felt like the heat of her face was radiating off her. Her ears burned and throbbed. He stared at her intently for several seconds. He was breathing so hard that she could smell his sweet breath as it brushed against her face.

She wanted him to kiss her, passionately, and she wondered if he thought about it. He had never kissed her like that before. She wanted to know what he tasted like and hoped she was about to find out.

She realized that she was still stroking his leg and that she needed to stop. But Adin's intense gaze was making it very difficult for her to think clearly. She grasped the side of his leg to keep from moving her fingers. His breath caught, and his eyes shut. When he finally exhaled, he spoke.

"Legacy, we should probably go inside," he whispered.

"What?" She turned to look out the windshield. She was so caught up in the moment that she hadn't realized where they were. At his house. "Oh. Okay." She slipped her hand away from him, and he took his hand off her leg to turn off the car. She didn't wait for him to come around to her door. She needed the fresh air. She hoped it would help clear her head because she needed to collect herself, quickly. She opened the door and stood up, stretching and taking a few deep breaths. Adin took his time coming over to her side. She figured he was trying to get himself together, too, before he took her in to see his mom.

When he got to her side, he didn't even comment about

her opening her own door. He just shut the door and put his arm around her to lead her into the house.

They stopped at the front door, and she turned to look at Adin. "How do I look?" she asked breathlessly. She still hadn't pulled herself together.

"Like an angel," he whispered, closing his eyes. Great, he hadn't pulled himself together either.

She took a deep breath and turned back to the door. There was no point in putting this off. Adin turned the knob and stepped in, holding it open for her. She walked in, and she could smell food cooking in the kitchen.

"Mom?" Adin called out. His voice cracked. He grimaced and then cleared his throat.

"In here, honey."

He took Legacy's hand and led her to the kitchen. His mom walked out, wiping her hands on an apron. She stuck out her hand toward Legacy, and she shook it.

"Mom, you remember Legacy. Legacy, this is my mom, Myrha Sheppard."

"It's a pleasure to see you, Legacy," she said, shaking her hand.

"It's a pleasure to see you, too, Ms. Sheppard," she responded, letting go of her hand.

"Please call me Myrha."

"Myrha," she corrected.

"You should hear the things that Adin says about you."

"All good, I hope."

"Of course," Myrha said, looking at Adin. "I'm going to finish cooking lunch. You kids should go have fun, and I'll call you when it's ready."

"Are you sure you don't need any help?" she asked.

"No, thank you." Myrha smiled at her.

Adin led Legacy to the living room, and they sat on the couch right beside each other — their sides and bare legs touching. He turned on the television as a distraction, and she turned her head to face him.

"Does your mom know I've been here before?" she whispered.

He turned his head to look and her and nodded.

"How does she feel about that? That you brought over a girl when she wasn't home?"

"She doesn't care." He shrugged. "I explained to her what happened."

"Okay," she said, turning to face the TV. But Adin put his lips to her ear.

"Technically, I'm an adult now," he murmured, "so what could she say about it?" He laughed, and his hot breath tickled and caused a slight shiver to shoot through her. He didn't turn away, and she could tell from the increased speed of his breath that his teasing tone was gone. "You smell so good," he whispered, not making a move to turn his head back away.

She figured she should joke with him rather than let herself fall completely into this moment like she had in the car. His mom was in the other room and could walk in any minute.

She turned to face Adin, his face just inches from hers. "Do you want me to put my hand on your leg again?" she dared, raising one eyebrow.

He sighed. "Maybe right now isn't the best time for that," he said with a half-smile.

"Then quit whispering in my ear," she said, smiling back at him.

"Am I making you uneasy?" he teased.

"Yes. So if you don't stop, I'm going to find great pleasure in making you squirm. We both know I can handle you touching me," she said, putting her hand on her chest, "more than you can handle me touching you." She took her hand off her chest and placed it onto his.

"Hmm, I don't know if I agree with that completely." Adin lifted his hand and stroked her cheek.

It felt wonderful, but she knew what he was doing, and she wasn't falling for it. She stared at him with an even expression. She was up to this challenge. She slid her hand up from his chest, along his neck, and to his left ear. She stroked his ear gently between her fingers. His eyes fluttered shut and his head leaned back a little.

"That's ... not ... fair," he panted softly.

Adin's eyes were still shut, so as she caressed his left ear, she leaned her cheek against his so that her lips were at his right. "I know," she whispered, dragging out the last word so that her breath blew into his ear.

He groaned.

"Are you going to behave?" she asked very slowly, still blowing the words into his ear.

He nodded and tried to say, "Yes," but the word didn't completely come out.

She moved so that her lips were now against Adin's ear. "That's a very good boy," she said as she traced her lips down his ear and then kissed his earlobe.

He gasped and then suddenly took her face into his hands and pulled her back to look into her eyes.

She looked at him with her eyebrows raised, waiting for him to say something.

"Okay. You're right. You can handle me touching you better than I can handle you touching me."

"See, I told you," she said, laughing.

Adin dropped his hands from her face and took one of her hands in both of his. "Yes, but *I'm* not touching you the way you're touching me. We're supposed to be taking things slowly, so what you're doing really isn't fair." He laughed.

"Maybe that's true. Maybe I don't want to take things as

slowly as we have been."

He stopped laughing and stared at her with intense eyes again.

It was true. They had gone out several times, and Adin hadn't tried anything beyond chaste kisses and hugs. And she wanted him to *kiss her* kiss her already. What was his hold up?

"Lunch is ready," Adin's mom called from the kitchen.

Adin glanced toward the kitchen, releasing her from his gaze. She sighed and looked down to get up off the couch.

He stood up beside her and put his arm around her waist to lead her into the kitchen.

The food smelled wonderful. Myrha made salad and lasagna. And from everything that was on the countertops, she could tell it wasn't the frozen kind.

"What have you kids been doing?" she asked as Adin pulled out a chair for her.

She looked at Adin as she sat down. She didn't want to answer *that* question. What was she going to say? The truth? *Oh, I've been teasing your son in inappropriate ways…* Not!

"We were watching TV," Adin said smoothly.

"Anything interesting?" she asked.

"No, not on TV," Adin said as he sat down, and his eyes flashed to Legacy to make sure she caught the real meaning of his answer.

"This looks wonderful," she said quickly to get the conversation off what Adin and she had been doing in the living room.

"It's a family recipe," Myrha responded.

They sat and ate, but it was difficult to eat her lunch quickly. Most of the conversation was centered on her with Myrha asking her open-ended questions that required long answers. A few times, she caught Adin giving his mom an exasperated look. She tried to maintain eye contact with

Myrha, but she looked at Adin when she could. He was trying to pace himself so that he didn't finish his meal before she could. Even though that was such a little thing, it still made her smile, and he caught her.

"What?" he mouthed.

She shook her head and looked down at her plate. He realized what she was smiling about and shrugged, keeping his expression playful.

She continued eating and answering questions until she was finished. Adin did finish before her, but just barely.

The conversation was painless. It was really easy talking to Myrha. But the last question she asked threw Legacy off her game.

"Did Adin tell you his dad is moving to Texas?" Myrha asked as they all cleared the table.

Shocked, she looked at Adin. But he didn't look at her. He looked at his mom through narrowed eyes.

"Um, no, he hasn't mentioned it yet," she said, trying to keep her voice even. What did this mean? Why was she telling her this?

"I was going to talk to her about it tonight," Adin muttered.

"Oh, I'm sorry," she said, but turned to look at Legacy, not Adin.

She smiled and shrugged her shoulders. She didn't trust her voice to speak. For some reason, she felt this topic had been very deliberate, and she didn't want to think of the reason why. She continued clearing the table, hoping no one could read the fear in her eyes.

But Adin did.

He walked over to her, but looked up at his mom. "Will you excuse us?" he asked her, and it sounded like he was trying hard to be polite.

"Sure, honey," she said as she continued to cover up the

leftovers, not looking at him.

Adin turned her shoulders so that she was facing the door and pushed her forward. She felt like she weighed a ton, and her legs did not want to work. He helped her through the kitchen, up the stairs, and into his room. She was too shocked to feel nervous about being in his room when he sat her down on his bed. He sat beside her and took both her hands in his.

"Legacy," Adin said softly. "I'm really sorry about that. I really did plan on talking to you about this tonight."

She just nodded, staring past him at his wall. She felt the moisture in her eyes and didn't even care if the tears spilled over.

"Sweetheart, look at me, please."

She was not too shocked to get butterflies in her stomach at his term of endearment. She shut her eyes to force her gaze to his and tears leaked over before she opened her eyes.

Adin reached up to brush her tears away. "My dad got offered a promotion if he transferred to a new office," he started slowly. "Now that I'm eighteen, there really isn't a need for him to live in the same town as my mom. I'm old enough to live wherever I want, regardless of where my parents live."

She just stared at him. She still wasn't sure if she could talk without breaking down. What he said made sense. But for some reason, this didn't feel right.

"He called me last night. He wants me to come over for a couple of days while he looks at houses. I'm supposed to leave in the morning, but will be back Friday night."

"Why..." she started, but her voice cracked. She looked down, cleared her throat and tried again, leaving her eyes on their hands. "Why did your mom bring it up?"

Adin sighed. "Because my dad wants me to go to school out there," he said solemnly.

Her head snapped up, and she looked at Adin with pleading eyes, shaking her head. She felt like someone had just punched her in the stomach.

He released one of his hands and held her face. "That's why I've decided to go tomorrow," he whispered. "I need to explain to him why I want to stay here, and I need to do that in person."

She took a jagged breath and nodded. "But he thinks you're going out there to help pick out a house … because he thinks you'll be living with him."

"He knows I want to stay here, but I'm sure he's hoping I'll change my mind. He's already registered me for the fall term — just in case."

"But you're staying *here*, right?" Gods, she hated sounding this pathetic, but the thought of Adin leaving…

"Yes. I don't want to leave. I want to stay here. With you."

She nodded again, and leaned her head against Adin's shoulder. She felt exhausted. The stress of this knowledge was almost too much for her to bear. He put his arms around her and squeezed tightly. "So you'll be back by Saturday, then?" she asked.

"Yes."

"That's the Fourth of July."

"I know," he said, rubbing her back.

She remembered telling Calli she didn't want to ask Adin to the parade, but after this, those silly fears disappeared. "Calli is in the parade, so she asked me to come and watch her and then hang out afterward. She'll have a date, though, so she suggested I ask you to come with me."

"I'd love to go to the parade with you," he whispered.

"Good," she breathed into his chest.

"In fact, on Sunday, I'm having a party over here. I'll be cooking out on the grill, and everyone will be eating, swimming, and playing games. I'd like for you to come."

"That sounds like fun."

"Is that a yes?" Adin asked softly.

"Of course," she said with a half-smile.

He held her for several more minutes. "Are you okay?"

She didn't know how to answer that question. She wasn't sure if she was okay. "I will be."

"I hate it that you were upset," he whispered. "I never want to see you like that."

"I just got a bad feeling when your mom mentioned it. I don't like the thought of you leaving," she murmured as she lifted her head to look at him.

"Please don't be sad. I couldn't bear it if I thought you were still upset while I'm away."

Adin misunderstood what she meant about not liking the thought of him leaving. She meant leaving for good, not for two days, though she knew she'd still miss him while he was on his trip.

"Don't worry. I'll be fine." she tried to reassure him.

"I'm going to worry anyway. There's nothing I can do about that. But it'll make my trip easier if I know you're okay."

She smiled up at him. "I promise. I'll be fine. Let's not talk about this anymore."

"Sounds good to me," he whispered as he swept a strand of hair out of her face.

They spent the rest of the day enjoying each other's company. Myrha had left to do some shopping, so Adin and she had the house to themselves. It was too hot to really do anything outside, so they stayed in.

They got comfortable on the couch while they watched a couple of movies. They took off their shoes. Adin had his feet on the coffee table; she had hers on the couch beside her. She leaned into his side with her knees pushed against his leg. While she snuggled into Adin's side, she put her hand on his leg — on top of his shorts. He put his arm around her shoulders and put his other hand on her knees, holding them in place. He was touching her bare skin, but it didn't faze him, not visually anyway.

The day was beautiful, and she wasn't thinking about the weather. It really didn't matter to her what was going on outside this house. All that mattered to her was that they were spending time together.

And as the day came to an end, she knew her feelings for Adin were solidified.

She was in love with him.

Chapter 12

Two days without Adin. He'd been such a regular presence in Legacy's life that she felt a little lost. At least she had to work this morning. It'd make day number one go by faster. She had no idea what she would do on Friday. Adin would be back that night, but he expected to be in really late, too late to come over.

Last night, she'd dreamed her familiar dreams of storms, snakes, tornados, but Adin was in this dream again. He'd told her to be careful like last time. She assumed his appearance was due to her spending all day with him the day before. Plus, he was gone to his dad's. The girl wasn't in her dream, so she couldn't ask any questions about what everything meant.

She'd woken up to rain—but not storms. The day felt dreary. She guessed Ms. Gorgos wasn't looking forward to her working today. That was fine with her. She didn't feel like being in a good mood anyway.

While she got ready for work, she thought about Adin and his dad. She wondered if his dad would accept Adin's reasons for staying here, or if he'd keep trying to persuade him to transfer to the university out there. Thinking about that only made her more miserable, so she tried not to think about it … much.

At work, the dreariness continued. Everyone was in a somber mood, and the rain drizzled all day. She and Yale took turns working the cash register while they both worked on inventory. River was there, but he wasn't really working. He'd been running errands for his mom. Legacy figured Ms. Gorgos intentionally kept him out of the store as much as she could since she was scheduled to work today.

Whenever River was in the store, he smiled at her, but it felt forced. His mood was also sad, but it was as if he were only smiling at her in an effort to lift her out of her bad mood. She knew he wondered why she was feeling down, and she was so wrapped up in her own sad feelings that she didn't really think about why he was moping.

While River was out on one of his errands, Ms. Gorgos came out into the lobby.

"Ladies, I need to run to the bank. I was trying to wait for the rain to stop, but I can't wait any more. I should be back in about an hour."

She seemed pleasant. If Legacy hadn't known any better, she wouldn't think there was anything wrong with the woman. She was sure that Yale thought Ms. Gorgos was the nicest woman in the world.

About ten minutes after Ms. Gorgos left, River came

back. "Where's my mom?" he asked Yale since she was at the register. "Her car is gone."

"She went to the bank. Said she'd be back in about an hour."

Legacy heard their conversation, but she wasn't really paying attention. She had her back to them as she organized the magazines on the display rack for the hundredth time today. Even though she was doing the task, her mind was on Adin. She was trying to think of good feelings—his touch, their dates, the flowers—anything but why he was gone. She was so absorbed that she hadn't heard River walk up behind her.

"Legacy, can I talk to you?" he asked, startling her.

She turned around to face him. "Sure," she said, and followed him into the break room.

Once they were alone, River turned to face her. "What's wrong?"

"What do you mean?" she stalled. She knew she looked sad, but she really didn't want to tell him why. He was sad already and hearing her talk about Adin would probably make that worse.

"I can tell something's bothering you."

"Well, you don't look very enthused today either."

"I'm not, but we're not talking about me."

"I'll tell you why I'm sad if you tell me what's wrong with you first."

"I can't do that."

"Why?"

"Because I promised to keep this on a friendship level."

"What does *that* mean?" she asked as she folded her arms.

"It means that I'm sad for reasons you don't want to hear about."

That response only irritated her. Now, she really didn't

care if he knew the reason why she was sad.

"Fine," she snapped. "I'm sad because Adin is out of town, and I *miss* him."

River flinched like her words physically slapped him. He grabbed the back of the chair he was standing behind to brace himself. He then took a deep breath and looked her calmly in the eyes. "Do you want to talk about it?" He was serious, though she could tell he didn't want to know. He only asked because he wanted her to feel better, so she started to feel guilty for hurting his feelings.

"Not really," she answered politely, sitting down in the chair beside her. She really didn't want to talk about it. It wouldn't make her feel better, and she knew it wouldn't make River feel better either.

"Are you sure? You know you can talk to me about anything," he said as he sat down.

"And you said you couldn't deny me anything, yet you won't tell me what's bothering you."

"That's because I know you don't want to hear about it," he said, shutting his eyes and shaking his head.

"But if we're friends, we should be able to speak freely about things," she said, leaning toward him.

"Okay, if I tell you what's bothering me, will you promise to talk to me about your feelings? I know I'm the reason why you don't want to talk about it, and I don't want you to worry about that."

"Fine."

"I-I'm..." River paused and looked down at the table. "I'm *sad* because you're sad."

"You were already down when I saw you."

"I heard you come in, and I could tell from your tone that you were upset. I knew my mom planned on keeping me out of the store, so I wouldn't get a chance to talk to you. Not being able to console you made me feel even worse."

At least he was honest. Now, it was her turn. "Adin's dad is moving to Texas, and he wants Adin to go to school out there. Adin's visiting him now."

"Oh." She was sure River liked this news, but he didn't show any happiness. "When will he be back?"

"Tomorrow night."

She could see the curiosity building in his eyes. "Is he … um … where is Adin going to school?"

"He's going to school here," she said, looking River straight in the eyes. "But his dad registered him out there too." She shrugged.

"Do you think his dad will persuade him?"

"No." But for some reason, her voice didn't sound as sure as she was.

"I see."

"I just miss him, that's all." She tried to sound nonchalant.

"I understand. It's hard going a couple of days without seeing that special someone," he murmured, and she knew he wasn't talking about her not seeing Adin.

She stood up. "I should get back to work."

"No. Wait," River said as he got out of his chair and grabbed her arm.

She turned around to face him. "What?"

He stared at her without saying anything, and she heard his breathing accelerate.

"I can't do this right now," she whispered to him.

He dropped her arm. "I'm sorry. I'm trying. It may not seem like it to you, but really, I am. I'll get better at this. I promise."

"I'm sorry this is so difficult for you. I really do like you being my friend."

"You don't know how much that means to me," River whispered.

"I need to get back in the lobby before your mom gets

here."

He let her escape to the lobby, though a haven it was not. She worked the rest of her shift in the same mood she'd started it in and went straight home after she got off of work. She went to bed as soon as she could without it being too obvious she was a little depressed.

That night, she had another dream. It had some of the same characteristics as previous ones, but instead of actual snakes, she saw the three snake holes again, which she was standing in the middle of. It still had a storm brewing, and she knew a tornado was inevitable. But other than the similar things she dreamed about before, this dream was different. She wasn't running from the tornado. She was standing under the storm clouds waiting for the tornado to form. She wasn't scared of it. She wanted it to come. She needed it to come.

She saw the same girl as before, but she was across the field. She watched her in horror as she stood under the storm clouds. She started to run toward Legacy, and she turned to face the girl. She extended her arm in her direction with her palm out.

"No." Legacy didn't yell. She said it calmly, but with finality.

The girl rocked back on her heels. She wanted to come to Legacy, but her order stopped her in her tracks.

Legacy knew she was dreaming, and she knew she wanted to ask her questions the next time she dreamed about her. But in this moment, it didn't matter. She didn't need her answers because she was aware of all the answers. Her conscious self didn't know, but her mind knew.

She looked back at the clouds, waiting for the tornado to form, and the girl screamed.

Legacy looked at her, and she was crying. "You have to run!" she screamed. "It's coming for you!"

"No!" Legacy yelled to her so forcefully that the ground shook below her feet. Her eyes shot up to the sky, and she yelled, "No!" again.

The black storm clouds faded to a light gray color and parted, forming a circle of beautiful blue sky. A voice, a female voice, spoke.

"You have no choice." It was so soothing that it felt like a trap.

"Who are you?" she demanded.

"I'm everything. I'm everywhere. You can't stop me. You have no choice."

Then the storm clouds went furiously black again, and she woke up.

It was early in the morning, and she knew Lissa would still be home. She decided it was time to come clean with her. She wanted to tell her about the dreams she was having and maybe even tell her about everything else. If Lissa knew what Legacy knew, maybe she'd tell her more about what was going on.

She ran downstairs and to the kitchen where her guardian was eating breakfast.

"Legacy? What are you doing up already?"

"I had a dream. I've been having weird dreams ever since you told me about my mom."

Lissa looked away.

"You said my mom would be contacting me, but you didn't know when or how." She paused. "I think she's contacting me through my dreams."

"Legacy, that's absurd," she said, shaking her head, but she sounded panicked.

"I don't think it is." Legacy ground her teeth, unable to hold back her hurt. "You're a priestess, aren't you? All the priestesses have the title of Melissae, which has to be where your name came from. I can't believe you never told me you were on the family payroll."

She shook her head, not as an answer, but in disbelief. "It's not like that—"

"My heritage is linked to Zeus. That's why you're here— why I was left with you. Why focus on telling me about my mother and not my father?"

Lissa gaped at her. "How do you know all this?"

"I figured it out," she lied.

"How? Your dreams?"

"Yes." River had helped more, but the dreams had been helpful too. "I feel like I'm on the verge of learning something, like I know all the answers in my dreams, but they don't stay with me while I'm awake."

"Look, I am not on the *payroll* as you say. But I cannot discuss Zeus with you. Don't look at me like that. He is the ruler of all the gods. Let's just say any discussion about him is above my pay grade. Regardless of what you're thinking right now, I do love you, and I'll help you in any way I can, but he is off limits." When Legacy gave her a dubious look, Lissa went on. "All I can say is I'm sorry. Nothing I do or don't tell you isn't out of malice."

Legacy sighed. Lissa looked sincere and she couldn't help but believe her.

"How have you been feeling?" Lissa asked when the tension eased. "Anything strange going on?"

"Er." Sad that Adin was gone and hopeful he'd give her a big kiss when he returned. But Legacy was certain Lissa was being more specific about feelings. "I don't really feel any different. There've been a couple of times I'd gotten an eerie feeling, like being watched or something."

"What? What the hell are you talking about?" Any expression Lissa had quickly morphed into concern.

Uh-oh. She'd have to confess about her little snooping expedition. "Well, okay, don't get mad." Legacy lifted her hands in surrender. She was totally toast after this. Could a pre-goddess be grounded? "After you told me about Mom, I did some snooping around. In your room. I'm sorry. I know it was wrong, but I found a box under your bed. I had trouble opening it." Oh gods, was she blushing? "But when it popped open, I felt a strange breeze and had a sense of … I don't know … foreboding? I guess."

Lissa jumped up from the table and ran into her room. Legacy was right on her heels. She looked under the bed and then looked back at her.

"There's nothing here," she said.

Legacy dropped to her knees, looked. And saw nothing. Lissa was right.

"Where did you put it?" Legacy demanded.

"Legacy, I have no idea what you're talking about. I did not have a box under my bed. What did it look like?"

"It was a wooden box. It had some word carved at the bottom of it on the inside. *Elpis*, I think."

Lissa gasped. "Oh, no. No, no, no, no, no." She started pacing and chewing on her fingernails.

"I take it that means something."

Lissa glanced at her quickly as she continued to create tracks in the rug.

"Do you think my mom had something to do with it?"

"I-I don't know."

Legacy wasn't sure she believed her. Maybe she should tell Lissa more. Like about the prophecy, but she felt as if she needed to protect River for some reason.

"Hmm… It could have just as easily been a trick. You have to tell me everything you've experienced. I need to make sure someone isn't interfering with your change."

"What do *you* know?" Legacy asked, using this new leverage to gain more information.

"This isn't a game, Legacy."

"Then quit toying with *me*. I get the feeling you're purposely keeping things from me. For all I know you could've been the one who set this whole mess into motion by telling me."

"I know you're confused." Lissa sighed. "I'm sorry. I need to discuss this new development with, er, some people." And then Lissa left with Legacy staring after her.

What the hell did her change have to do with a wooden box?

Well, if Lissa was off to get answers, Legacy was going to run to her source.

She didn't want to call him from the house phone, so she grabbed her cell phone and ran outside before calling River, not sure if the mysterious box or whatever force had shown it to her had some kind of listening powers.

"Hello?" River asked on the other end.

"Hey, it's Legacy."

"Um, hi." He sounded distracted. "What's up?"

"Can you talk right now?"

"No," he said casually. She assumed he was in earshot of his nosey mother.

"Is your mom around?"

"Yes," he said just as indifferently.

Crap. That meant he definitely couldn't talk. She wondered if he could get away from the apparently wretched hag.

"Can we meet later?"

"Sure. I'm getting ready to leave now to go play football at the park."

"Can we meet there?"

"Yes."

Sweet. "I'll see you at the field."

"No. I can't do that."

What was he trying to say? "Do you want to meet

somewhere else?"

"That's it," he agreed.

"How about behind the rocket slide?"

"Sounds like a plan."

"I'm heading that way now," she said.

"Okay, bye."

She jumped in her car and went straight to the rendezvous point. River was already there, dressed for playing football.

"Hi," she said to him as she walked up.

"Hey, sorry about that. I didn't want Mom to think I was talking to you."

"That's fine."

"I saved your number under an assumed name, so I'll know it's you when you call again and can make sure I'm away from my mom next time."

"Don't worry about it. I'm glad you came."

"Of course," he said softly.

"So are you really here to play football?"

"Not anymore." He smiled. "I was supposed to, but I sent texts to the other guys and cancelled after you called. I didn't want to meet you at the field since they're still playing."

"Oh." She felt bad for taking him away from his plans. "We could have met later."

"Don't be silly. You need to talk, and I want to be here for you." He was sincere, but he was keeping it friendly.

They walked behind the slide to a picnic table away from where the neighborhood kids were playing.

"So what do you want to talk about?" he asked after they both sat down.

"I was talking to Lissa earlier and she asked me if I've experienced anything out of the ordinary. I told her about sneaking around in her room and opening a box under her bed."

River chuckled. "If there was some kind of personal toy in it, I don't want to know about it." Then he paused and smiled crookedly at her. "Unless you are curious as to why a woman would have—"

"Ew. Gross. No." She shook her head. "That's just it, though. There was nothing in it. I told her I got a weird sensation when I opened it. It had a bunch of carvings on the outside, but on the inside there was just *Elpis* carved at the bottom. She freaked and left."

The smirk on River's face slowly fell, and his expression turned blank. "I'm sorry. Did you say *Elpis*?

"Yes."

"Are you sure?"

"Yeah, why? What does it mean?"

River cursed under his breath and shut his eyes. "Literally," he started, "it means hope."

"Um, okay. So what's the big deal? Hope is a good thing, right?"

"Technically, yes."

"Okay, stop with the literally and technically crap and spit it out!"

River's fists slammed onto the table, making her jump. "Give me a minute," he gritted through his teeth. He rubbed his forehead for several seconds while she waited, not-so-patiently, but quietly. "Sorry," he sighed, then opened his eyes. "I've still been researching your family, and this kinda confirms one of my theories. According to one of the myths, Zeus created a woman named Anesidora and he gave her a beautiful container she was never to open. Her curiosity got the best of her. When she opened it, the evil contained within spread across the earth. She quickly closed it, but the only thing left in the box was the spirit of hope."

"And you think this container was the one I found under Lissa's bed?"

River nodded slowly.

"Um, okay, but what does Anesidora have to do with my family?"

"There are some versions of myths that connect Gaia by way of Demeter to Anesidora. Some say they are the same person, just different interpretations."

"Hmm ... and my mother's name is Dora. That's a very good guess."

River looked grim. "That's not all. Anesidora has another name she is sometimes referred to." He looked directly into her eyes. "Some call her Pandora."

"Pandora?" She gasped. "Pandora's Box?" As in *the* Pandora's Box? The symbol of actions that may seem minor but end up having major consequences. No way. "Are you telling me I opened Pandora's Box?"

"Yes."

"It actually exists? I just thought that was —"

"A myth?" River smirked. "Isn't that what we've been dealing with, darlin'?"

He had a point. Then she frowned. "What does it mean?"

River's jaw ticked. "That we're in some serious trouble."

Why couldn't changing into a goddess be easy?

Chapter

13

She hardly slept last night. Not because she had bad
dreams, tried to cope with her new understanding about
herself, what Pandora's Box had to do with anything, or was
too excited about seeing Adin—though she was giddy at
that thought. She couldn't sleep because of all the fireworks
being prematurely shot. Unfortunately, she couldn't expect
any better sleep tonight since today was the Fourth.

The parade started at nine o'clock this morning, so she
knew Adin would be here early. She got out of bed and
quickly got ready. She wore cute shorts and a tank top. This
was the most skin that Adin would've ever seen, but it was
hot. Not to mention the fact that this outfit could be a nice

little stepping-stone for tomorrow, but she wasn't sure if anything could prepare him for the bikini.

She pulled her hair up off her neck so that she could stay as cool as possible—the rain from the last two days would make it steamy outside in the heat of the sun. She put on some makeup, hoping it wouldn't melt off by the end of the day, and then she was ready.

Lissa was off for the holiday, but they weren't exactly speaking, so she stayed upstairs until she heard the roar of Adin's Camaro. She ran downstairs and waited patiently by the door until he knocked. She only let him finish one knock before she swung the door open.

He stood there, startled, with his fist in the air to knock on the door again.

"Hi," she said, and he dropped his hand and laughed. "I waited for you to come to me."

"Yes, you did," he said, still tickled.

He was wearing shorts and a light-colored shirt, also prepared for the summer heat.

He looked her up and down and smiled widely.

"You look beautiful!" She knew she wasn't dressed up, so he must have really missed her as much as she missed him.

He threw his arms around her and hugged her tightly. She put her arms around his neck and kissed him under his jaw.

"I missed you so much," he whispered in her hair.

"I missed you more," she teased.

"No way. I missed you more than anyone has ever missed a person before in the history of the world."

She couldn't think of a comeback, so she just laughed.

Adin pulled away and took both her hands in his. "Are you ready? Calli's probably already there. We need to hurry if you want to talk to her before the parade." He was still very excited.

"Okay," she said, smiling.

He walked her to his car and then got in. She had her left ankle resting on her right knee. He put his right hand on the side of her left knee. She guessed taking things slowly was working. After he got over the initial shock of a touch, he seemed to handle subsequent times much better.

"How did everything go with your dad?"

Adin rubbed her leg and looked at her. "Fine. Everything's sorted out."

"Good," she said, looking back at him.

"So what did you do while I was away?"

"Hmm … nothing too exciting. I worked Thursday and didn't do too much yesterday."

"I wanted to call you so badly last night when I got in, but I didn't want to wake you," he confessed.

"Well, I was probably awake. Our neighbors were shooting fireworks at all hours last night. I hardly got any sleep at all."

"Oh, I'm sorry. I hate that your sleep was disturbed," Adin said, sounding concerned. Then he got a devilish look in his eyes. "Though if I'd known you *were* awake, I probably would have come over, scaled a tree, and climbed in your window." He glanced over at her with a smirk.

She snorted. He was definitely full of himself, but it was very adorable.

They got to the park and over to where the floats were gathered for the parade. Adin held her hand as he guided her through the crowds. They found the Oak Grove High School cheerleader's float, and made their way to it.

"Hey, Calli!" she yelled to get her attention.

Calli turned around and grinned at the sight of Adin and Legacy holding hands.

"Hi, you two," she said, smiling.

"Hi, Calli," Adin responded.

"Where's Zach?" Legacy asked.

"He's sitting in the stands with some friends of his. I'll introduce you after the parade."

"Looks like you got some inspiration for your float," Adin noted.

She looked it over, and it looked surprisingly familiar.

"Yeah, so we stole some ideas from the senior float. I don't think too many people will notice," Calli confessed.

"Calli!" Legacy chided.

"Oh, please! Like no one has ever used a muse before. It just so happened our muse was their float," Calli said as she pointed to Adin.

They all laughed.

"We're going to go find a seat. Good luck."

"Thanks, Legacy."

Adin held her hand and weaved her through the crowd again to get to the stands. She scanned the bleachers, wondering which guy was Zach, but she had no way of knowing. They sat in the middle and waited for the parade to start. The sun was already beating down on them.

"Crap, I forgot the sunscreen," Adin said. "I'm going back to the car to get it. Do you want me to get you something to drink while I'm gone?"

"No, don't worry about that," she said, shaking her head.

Adin frowned at her response. "I'll be walking right by the concession area."

"Okay, some water would be great."

While Adin was gone, Ellen and Kate walked up. *Great.* She should have known they'd make an appearance for Calli's benefit.

"Hi, Legacy," Kate said.

"Hey," Ellen said, less enthused.

"Hi, girls. Did you come to watch Calli too?"

Ellen shrugged and Kate said, "Yes."

They sat down on the bleacher right in front of her, and several minutes of silence passed.

"Where's Thad and Seth?" she finally asked.

"Around." Kate shrugged. "Probably breaking up a fight between Alex and Laos again," she mumbled.

Legacy looked around the bleachers again for any sign of a guy looking in Calli's direction, but there were just too many people. She was turning back around when Adin started up the bleachers.

"Looks who's here!" Ellen whispered to Kate, and Legacy fought a smile.

"Oh no. He's walking this way," Kate said in disbelief.

"Hi, Kate. Hi, Ellen," Adin said as he stepped on the bleacher beside them.

"Hi," they said in unison, and watched as he stepped past them and took his seat next to Legacy. Both of their jaws dropped.

Adin opened the sunscreen, took Legacy's hand, and squirted some in her palm. He put some in his hand, too, and they both started rubbing the lotion on their own legs.

"It looks like it's about to start," Adin said as he finished.

"Uh-huh," she mumbled as she kept rubbing the lotion all around her legs. She kept her head down because she knew if she looked up, she wouldn't be able to keep from looking at Ellen and Kate.

When she finished, she glanced at them as she lifted her head. They both looked shocked, and she half-smiled. Adin had the bottle of lotion ready to squirt more into her palm—he was waiting for her before he continued putting it on himself.

They did their arms next, and Adin finished with his face. Her makeup had sunscreen in it, so she left it alone, but put a little on her ears. Since she was in a low-cut tank top, she put the remaining lotion on her exposed chest, neck, and shoulders.

"You should probably put some on your ears," she said to Adin while she finished rubbing the lotion on her chest.

"Um, okay," he said, looking away from her to grab the bottle. He wasn't sly enough not to get caught glancing at where her hands were. Poor thing. Tomorrow would be difficult for him.

When he finished, he put his hand on her knee and turned to face her.

"There're some stages set up for bands playing this afternoon. Do you want to walk down and watch them?"

She turned to look at him. "Sure."

She noticed Adin had left a little lotion on his ear, so she reached up and gently started rubbing it in. "What kind of bands are playing?" she asked.

Adin squeezed her knee. "Um ... rock, country, and adult contemporary," he said, but his voice sounded strangled.

She was watching what she was doing on his ear, but the sound of his tone made her look at his face. Oh. He was enjoying her rubbing the lotion in. She hadn't really thought about it like that. She chuckled.

"Sorry, I was just trying to rub it in for you," she said, shrugging and dropping her hand.

"No need to be sorry," he said with a smile.

The parade had started, but she could tell Ellen and Kate's attention was directed behind them rather than at the parade. They watched as Calli's float passed, and she skillfully threw candy right at all of them. Legacy watched the rest of the crowd to see who else her BFF specifically threw candy to, but there was no hope. Everyone loved candy, so everyone stood as the float passed.

When it was over, Adin took her hand and helped her

down the bleachers. Once they were free from the crowd, he put his hand around her back, and they went in search of Calli. They didn't have to look long.

"Hey guys, I need to go change, and I'll be ready. Meet you at the concession area?" she asked.

"Sounds good."

Adin and she headed that way, but he left her in front of the food vendors to go put the lotion back in his car. Of course Ellen and Kate would find her there alone.

"What's the story?" Ellen asked as she walked up to her, leaving Kate trailing behind. So *now* she wanted to speak to her.

"We're dating."

"How long?"

"He asked me out after my birthday."

Ellen was about to bark another question when her eyes focused behind her. Legacy assumed Adin was walking up.

It was him, because when he reached them, he kissed the back of Legacy's neck and moved his lips around to her ear as he stepped beside her. She smiled crookedly at Ellen.

"Sorry it took me so long," he murmured.

Still smiling, she turned to look at him. "That's okay. I've been chatting with Ellen and Kate."

He flashed his eyes at them and smiled, then he looked back at her. "Are you hungry?" he asked as he wrapped his arms around her waist.

"No, I'm fine."

"Well, I am. Do you want to come with me to get a snack?"

"Of course," she said to him, and then turned to Ellen and Kate—who both had their mouths open. "I'll see you guys later."

Adin decided what he wanted to eat, so they got in line at the corndog vendor. "I really don't care for Ellen," he said while they were waiting.

"Yeah, I can't stand her."

He looked at her incredulously. "Then why are you friends with her?"

"I'm not. Not really. Ellen wants to be Calli's friend, so she tolerates her. Kate's not as bad, though. Why don't you like Ellen? Not that I care. I'm just curious."

"She's superficial."

"And?" That wasn't a big news flash.

"And I don't like the way she looks at you."

"I'm a big girl."

He looked at her with raised his eyebrows. "Yes, you are."

And the Ellen and Kate conversation was dropped.

They got Adin's corndog and found Calli. Zach was already with her. He was very good-looking, and Calli was simply glowing. They did all the introductions and walked around the park. The guys hit it off and played some of the vendor games while she and Calli talked—but not about their dates; the guys were always in earshot. They ate all kinds of junk food, played miniature golf, and enjoyed each other's company. It was a great day. But very hot.

That afternoon, they walked by all the stages, taking in the different types of music. Legacy liked the rock band best, but Calli was a country music fan. The guys stayed neutral, but she was sure they would've sided with their respective dates if it came down to it.

When Calli wanted Legacy to go with her to the ladies room, the guys walked them over and stood outside, which Legacy thought was very sweet of them.

"So what do you think about Zach?" she asked when they got into the restroom.

"I think he's great. He's nice, charming, and so very handsome. You picked a great guy, really."

"He kissed me last night!" she squealed. "I've been dying to tell you all day."

"What?" She was happy for her but a little jealous. Calli hadn't been seeing Zach as long as she'd been seeing Adin, and Adin hadn't kissed her yet. Well, not in the way she was waiting for.

"I know. I couldn't believe it. Legacy, oh my gosh, he is the best kisser! We made out for what seemed like forever."

"Wow. I'm really happy for you."

"So is Adin a good kisser?"

"I don't know," she mumbled as she washed her hands.

"He hasn't kissed you yet?"

"Not like that, no. But I think maybe he might kiss me tomorrow. He's having a pool party at his house, and I'm hoping my little bikini will push him over that edge." She giggled.

"I wouldn't worry about it. I'm sure he'll kiss you when he's ready. He's obviously very taken with you. You should see the way he looks at you."

"I know. I really like him too." More than like.

"I think it's more than that," Calli said as she fixed her hair.

"It is," she confessed, not looking at her.

"C'mon. Let's get back to the guys." Legacy was thankful Calli wasn't going to push for more info.

Adin and Zach were chatting by a tree, waiting on them when they came out. They all went to find a seat for the fireworks display.

Adin and Legacy sat on a slight hill, but Zach and Calli went farther back, hoping to get a better view. She was glad because now they could enjoy the show alone.

"Are you having fun?" Adin whispered.

"I'm having a great time," she said, looking at him.

He reached up and stroked her cheek. "Good, I'm glad

you're enjoying yourself," he murmured.

"Are you having a nice time?"

"I'm always having a nice time when I'm with you."

Adin stared at her with intense eyes, and her heart started racing. She reached up and gently wiped a bead of sweat from his forehead. She did it to distract herself from his gaze, but his lips parted when she touched him, and he started breathing heavily.

The sound of the first firework exploding in the sky distracted her from his glorious face, so she looked up to watch the first several explosions of brilliant colors.

"Wow," she whispered, and turned to Adin to share this with him.

Adin was staring at her. She wasn't sure if he'd ever looked away. She stayed locked on his gaze, his face glowing with the vibrant colors shooting in the sky. But the sounds of the explosions became muffled by the sound of her heart crashing.

Adin reached up and gently stroked her face. They were both breathing hard. He leaned in slightly, glanced at her lips, and flashed his gaze back at hers.

The voice in her head screamed in excitement. He was finally going to kiss her. *Kiss her*, kiss her. There was no doubt in her mind. It was already hot out here, but now her body felt overheated as her blood rushed all over in anticipation.

Adin slid his hand from her face to the side of her head, his fingers reaching her hair. He put his other hand on her other cheek, still leaning in. She wet her lips, leaving them parted. He kept his gaze on hers as he moved closer and then slowly closed them as their lips touched.

She could no longer hear the fireworks that she knew were exploding all around them. Adin kissed her so very softly at first, barely touching his tongue to hers. She could feel his hot breath in her mouth, and she tingled all over.

As the kiss slowly became more intense, they both started gasping for air; his breath washed over her. She reached up, grabbed his arms, and clutched him closer to her. He tilted his head to the other side, kissing her passionately.

He tasted so good. There was no fantasy that could top this reality. All that mattered to her was that Adin was kissing her, and it was the best experience of her life.

The last firework must have gone off because people were clapping around them.

The intensity of their kiss slowed, though their breathing did not. He gently pulled his lips away and leaned his forehead against hers, leaving his hands on her face. They sat there for several seconds waiting for their breathing to return to normal. She was still clinging to his arms. She felt as if she would fall back if she let go of him. Her body felt so feeble in his gentle embrace.

"Definitely wow," he whispered.

She had forgotten the last thing she said was *wow* about the fireworks. She wanted to say something now, but she was still breathing too heavily. She just nodded gently. She slowly released her hands from his arms and took a deep breath to try and steady herself. Adin pulled his head back to look her in the eyes.

"You are so beautiful," he murmured.

She tried to smile, but her lips were shaking. She realized now that she was slightly shaking all over, and she hoped he wouldn't notice.

People were walking around, leaving the park, and she knew Calli must be nearby. She glanced to the side, and yep, there she was. She and Zach were standing about twenty feet away, giving them some privacy. But her BFF knew what they were doing because when she saw Legacy, she grinned.

Adin was watching Legacy, but when she sighed, he

followed her gaze. "I guess they're waiting on us."

"Yeah," she breathed.

He helped her up, and they walked over to Calli and Zach.

"Did you two enjoy the show?" she asked teasingly.

"It was magical," Adin said, and she could feel his gaze on her.

Legacy just nodded at Calli.

"Zach's taking me home. We'll talk later."

"Bye," she said evenly.

Adin and Zach did that fist bump thing guys do before they left. Then Adin took her hand and walked her to his car. She was still dazed. On the way home, he held her hand and stroked the back of it with his thumb. Every now and then, he'd lift their joined hands and kiss the back of hers. It was amazing.

"What time do you want to come over tomorrow? The party starts at one o'clock, but I need to set up everything."

She'd been so wrapped up in their kiss that she'd totally forgotten about the party tomorrow. She looked at him and opened her mouth to answer, but her gaze drifted to his very kissable lips.

He chuckled. "How does eleven sound?"

She blushed and looked away. Caught lusting after his lips. She tried to clear her head and focus on what he was talking about. Party. Right. Heck, she could drive herself over to the party tomorrow and save him the trip, but she said, "Eleven's good." She didn't think her brain could handle a deeper discussion than that.

When they got to her house, Adin walked her to her door and she struggled to find her voice.

"Thank you for going with me today," she said, looking into his eyes.

"Thank you for asking me. I had a wonderful time."

He stepped closer to her and rubbed her arm.

Bye-bye, voice.

Adin put both his arms around her waist, pulling her against him. She stretched up on her toes and put her arms around his neck, playing with his hair. Okay, so her voice did not want to cooperate, but her body was jumping at the chance for a repeat. Adin shivered at her touch, released a low moan, and then kissed her again.

Gods, but this man could kiss!

"I have to go," he finally said, breaking away.

She whimpered, wanting to keep his mouth on hers, but she wasn't going to push for more.

He groaned. "I'll be here in the morning."

Obviously, he didn't want to stop either, but he found the strength to turn and walk to his car. At least one of them had willpower. It was definitely not an ability she had. She watched Adin drive away before going back into the house. She closed the front door and leaned against it with a sigh.

No, she had no willpower at all.

Chapter

14

The next morning, she showered and ate breakfast before she took her time getting ready. She didn't want to be sitting around waiting for him to arrive, so there was no point in hurrying. Though she couldn't stop thinking about Adin, the night had helped her brain learn to function again. She left her hair down since it'd be getting wet anyway, and put on a little waterproof makeup. She painted her toenails to match her bronze swimsuit and sandals. She put on a pair of jean shorts and a white, sheer top with exposed sides so that her bikini top could be seen. She threw her sunglasses in her hair, and she was ready. Mentally and physically.

Adin showed up promptly at eleven o'clock. When

she opened the door, his eyes popped, and he gasped. He definitely liked what he saw. He put his hand on the doorjamb as he tried to compose himself, but he seemed to be at a loss for words. At least she hadn't been the only one lately to lose the ability to control mental functions. She held back her smirk of triumph.

Legacy wasn't so distracted by his reaction to her outfit not to notice how he looked. He had on his swimming trunks with a fitted T-shirt. Adin may not be a god like River was going to be, but he sure did look like one.

Neither of them said much on the way to Adin's house, but they both smiled a lot. Oh yeah, they'd definitely rounded a new corner in their relationship.

When they got to his house, she helped set up for the party.

"So who all's going to be here?" she asked as she put out some of the food.

"Just some friends."

"Do you have any family coming over?"

"Nope. My mom's spending the day shopping with my grandma. She left after making all the side dishes."

"So what's the occasion?" The Fourth was over, and it wasn't like it was his birthday.

"This is the first Saturday we were all able to get together. Several of the guys are going away to school, so this is like their farewell."

"I see."

They finished setting up just as Adin's guests started to arrive. She stayed by his side as he introduced her—as his girlfriend, sweet!—to all his friends. She recognized the ones from school, but many of his friends didn't go to their school, and most of them brought dates. They all seemed very nice. Of course, several of the guys were rowdy, but she expected as much.

Adin left the front door open so new guests could come right in, and they headed for the backyard, which was full of people whose names she didn't remember. Even though most of the ladies came as dates, there were a few single girls. Legacy stayed by Adin as he cooked the burgers and hot dogs. Sure, she didn't really know anyone, but she also didn't want any of the single girls to get any ideas. Adin was *her* boyfriend. Boyfriend? Did she just giggle?

"Well, look who's here," Adin said, and Legacy turned toward the backdoor, where she saw Calli walking out.

"Calli? What are you doing here?" As she asked, she saw Zach walking out behind her.

"Adin invited us."

She turned to Adin, and he was smiling. "I said friends were coming. Your friends are my friends," he said as he leaned down and kissed her forehead.

She reached up and stroked his arm and smiled. He was treating her as if they were a real couple. She knew how she felt about him, but getting all these reinforced signals from him felt good.

Zach walked over to chat with Adin, and she walked over to Calli and hugged her. "Why didn't you tell me you were coming?"

"I didn't have a chance. Adin talked to Zach while we were in the restroom last night. Then after the fireworks show, you were too *tongue-tied* to speak."

They walked over to one of the side tables and visited while Zach helped Adin finish cooking. A couple of Adin's friends who came in late walked over and struck up a conversation with Legacy and Calli. She thought it was really nice of them to try and include them with the rest of the crowd since they obviously didn't know anyone else besides the two guys manning the grill.

Until the tenor of the conversation changed and Legacy

realized they were being hit on. She was too shocked to put a stop to it, so Calli was the one to break it to them.

"You two seem like really nice guys, but we already have boyfriends." She tried to let them down easy.

"Nobody said anything about boyfriends," the muscular one said.

The girls were speechless at the change in his tone.

"Besides," the taller one added, "even if you really do have boyfriends, they're not here right now. I know just about everyone here, so I'd know if either of you were already taken."

He was obviously mistaken, but she didn't know how to correct him. She was still too shocked to speak.

"I think you'd like to take a swim with me," the muscular one said as he took hold of Legacy's arm and tried pulling her out of her chair.

Her shock wore off, and she turned to glare at him. She found her voice now. "You're wrong, asshole," she snapped, yanking her arm back.

Out of nowhere, Adin was at her side.

"What's going on, Dave?" he asked the one who'd grabbed her. From the look in his eyes, he was about to knock out this Dave guy. Legacy was surprised he was showing this much control. She, on the other hand, wanted to deck the jerk.

"Take it easy, Adin. Mike and I were just trying to make new friends," Dave said. Mike must be the tall one. From the look Adin shot him, Mike was going to be kissing the concrete with Dave ... without Legacy's help.

"Yeah," Mike agreed, touching Calli's shoulder.

Zach pushed him off her.

"What's your problem, dude?" Mike puffed out his chest like a freaking caveman, but compared to Zach ... well, Zach could definitely take him.

Legacy couldn't let this get out of hand, so she needed to bust up the testosterone fest. She jumped out of her seat to try and do just that, but Adin shoved her behind his back.

"Wait," she said to Adin, and looked over at Dave and Mike from behind the safety of Adin's back. "We haven't been properly introduced," she said quickly to the two idiots. "I'm Legacy, Adin's girlfriend." Mike and Dave immediately relaxed their stances and looked at Adin apologetically. "And this is my best friend, Calli, and her boyfriend, Zach."

Dave and Mike tried to mumble apologies to Adin, but he just shook his head at them, not wanting to hear it. He turned around to look at her. "Are you okay?"

"I'm completely fine. That wasn't the first time I've been hit on by some self-centered punk."

"I'm sorry," he whispered, and then kissed her briefly.

"It's not your fault."

Adin mumbled something unintelligible and then scanned his backyard. Seeking out Mike and Dave, she supposed. She grabbed his face and turned his head back in her direction to distract him from seeking out a fight.

"Is it time to eat?"

Adin sighed. "Yes."

"Good. I'm starving."

He walked her over to the table on the covered patio and fixed her plate. Calli and Zach ate with them. Everyone else was eating, swimming, or throwing a football around. When they finished eating, Calli and Zach jumped in the pool, and they immediately started kissing each other. She was delighted to see Calli so happy.

Legacy stayed out of the pool to help Adin clean up some of the mess. As the time passed, though, she noticed Adin wasn't making a move to the pool. She realized a little late that the reason was probably related to her having to take off her clothes and walk around in a bikini in front of all his friends—two friends in particular. She wasn't going to let Dave or Mike ruin her fun.

"It's really hot," she said, leaning toward Adin and moving her shirt back-and-forth like she was fanning herself.

He smiled crookedly at her, but didn't say anything.

"I think I need to jump in your pool so I can cool off."

"I need to throw out the potato salad. It's been sitting out awhile, so it's probably not any good. I have some more in the refrigerator we can bring out."

"Nobody's eating right now. It can wait."

"It'll just take a minute."

Ugh. This wasn't working. She'd just have to be direct.

"Well, okay. You can join me when you get finished," she said as she stood up and started to take off her top.

Adin stood up and took both her hands in his, stopping her from removing her clothes. He didn't say anything—his panicked eyes revealed his concern. She stared back at him and then slipped her hands out of his. He just stood there watching her, so she grabbed the sides of his shirt instead, and with a smile on her face, she started pulling it up. He finally relaxed a little and pulled off his shirt for her.

She rubbed her hand on his bare chest, and he smiled.

"I think this is my favorite outfit that I've seen you in," she joked. Seriously, he was stunning ... absolutely gorgeous ... but she was trying to stay focused on lifting him out of his mood.

Adin laughed lightly and then sighed. "I'm sorry. I know I need to chill. I was just really bothered by—"

"Stop," she whispered, shaking her head. "The best way for you to chill is by jumping in a nice cool swimming pool."

He laughed louder at her corny joke. "Okay. But let's get some sunscreen on first."

Adin grabbed the bottle, but she took it out of his hand and squirted some in her own palm this time. Then she started to rub the lotion on him. He squirmed at first, and she wasn't sure what to make of that. But she continued to rub the lotion all over his chest, back, and shoulders, trying not to think about what she was actually doing.

Then she took off her clothes before he could protest again and left them in the chair she was sitting in. She could tell when Adin saw her in nothing but her bikini that he briefly considered dealing with the potato salad again, which she would be forced to assist with, so she acted quickly.

"Will you put some on my back?" she asked as she squirted some lotion in her palm again before handing it to him.

He hesitated, so she started rubbing the lotion she had in her hand onto her stomach and chest. She watched him while she rubbed the lotion on herself, but he was watching her hands.

"If you don't want to put it on my back, I can ask Calli. If she's busy, I'm sure I can find someone willing," she teased as she stepped away from him, pretending to leave.

Adin grabbed her arm and smirked. "Turn around."

She did, and he gently rubbed the lotion on her back and shoulders while she worked on her stomach. As Adin rubbed the lotion down her sides to her hips, she flinched, and he stopped, not moving his hands from her hips. He stepped up against her back and put his lips to her ear.

"What's wrong?" he whispered.

"Er, nothing." She shrugged and started rubbing the lotion on her stomach again.

"Legacy?"

"I'm, umm, I'm just ticklish." Even though he did accidentally tickle her, having him rub lotion on her was not an unpleasant experience, to say the least. It was easier for her to rub lotion on him because she didn't have to think about what she was doing, but it was impossible to ignore Adin rubbing it on her, feeling him touch her so gently. Especially when he grazed a ticklish spot.

"Oh." Adin chuckled against her ear. "That's need-to-know information."

She shifted her weight, trying to distract herself because she knew there were a lot of people around them. But as she did, she heard his breathing spike, which did not help her.

She slid her hands from her stomach to on top of his at her sides and intertwined their fingers together. Then she pulled his hands around her stomach so his arms were wrapped around her. Adin leaned down and kissed her shoulder.

"I taste like lotion," she warned.

"You taste like heaven," he murmured.

Her heart raced, and she knew that she needed to do something fast before she tackled him right here, right now. She slipped her right hand from Adin's and leaned over to grab the bottle. She squirted some lotion in his hand and slid out from his arms to take a seat next to him. She looked up at him while she squirted lotion into her own palm and then looked down to rub it onto her legs.

Adin took a seat and rubbed his lotion on his legs too. It took her longer to finish, but he obviously didn't mind. His gaze lingered on her hands until she was done.

"Let's go swimming," she said eagerly. She grabbed his hand and dragged him out by the pool, and then she dove in.

By the time she swam to the shallow end, Adin was already there. If he looked stunning before, he was downright sexy now. His wet hair looked darker, and his eyes looked bluer than the water, which was glistening off his hard body. She stared in awe, partly because of his beauty and partly because he stared at her with the same awed expression.

"You beat me," she teased.

"I cheated." He shrugged, smiling.

He reached out and pulled her up to him, and they made their way to the deeper water. She put her arms around his neck and pulled herself up, wrapping her legs around his waist. Gods, he felt so good against her. He put his hands on her back and looked up at her while she stared down at him.

"See this isn't *so* bad," she said with a hint of a smile.

Adin laughed while he rubbed his hands up and down her back.

"I'm glad to see you two finally in here," she heard Calli say from behind her.

Adin turned them to the side so that they both could see Calli and Zach. Those two were standing side-by-side with their arms around each other.

Adin slid his hands down, thinking Legacy was going to unwind herself. He was wrong. She squeezed her arms around his neck, and he put his hands back where they belonged.

"We were busy." Not entirely true, but she didn't need to go into the real reason why they hadn't been in the pool.

Adin let out a short laugh, but didn't correct her.

"We're going to leave soon. We have plans for tonight, and I need to get ready," Calli said.

"Oh, okay. Well, thanks for coming," she said.

Adin slipped one hand off her back and stretched out his arm toward Zach, hand fisted. "Thanks for coming, man."

"No problem," Zach said, and fist-bumped him.

The rest of the guests were pretty much preoccupied with doing their own things. Adin and she chatted with them periodically and were in and out of the pool the rest of the day. Each time they swam, she wound her legs around him, and he held her up. He was more relaxed with each swim that they took.

By early evening, most of the guests had left, and Adin and Legacy had started cleaning up the mess. After they were finished and the last person left, Adin put his arms around her.

"Would you like to swim one more time before I take you home?"

She *liked* this idea. "Sure."

They walked outside and into the pool from the shallow end. Once in the pool, she dunked under the water to wet her hair. As she came back up, she smoothed it back.

"You are so beautiful," Adin whispered as he stepped toward her. He said that a lot and she liked it. More than liked it.

She reached up and put her arms around his neck and her legs around his waist like she had been doing all day. Adin gently walked them to the side of the pool and into slightly deeper water. When her back hit one of the pool's walls, she gasped, and he slid his hands down to her waist. She twisted her fingers in his hair, trying to anchor herself while she looked down at him. She could tell from the intense look in his eyes that he wanted to kiss her, but at this angle, she knew he wouldn't be able to reach without her bringing her head down. Her heart was racing, and oh yeah, she wanted to kiss him. But she wasn't going to make that move. If he wanted to kiss her, he'd have to figure out a way to make it happen.

He did. He grasped her waist and pulled her down so that her face was at his. That quick move sent a shock through her system. The man who wanted to go slowly was replaced by one that was hard and demanding before her.

His lips found hers, and they kissed for a while. She loved it. Gods, she loved the way this man owned her.

Adin groaned and pulled away from her suddenly. He looked heaven bound with his hands on top of his head. She panted while she watched him, wishing he'd just come back to her. He took a deep breath, and then brought her body back up against him, but he didn't pin her against the wall again. Adin moved them around the pool, away from the temptation of cornering her against the wall, so she let him. He'd only just kissed her for the first time—really kissed her—yesterday. He was still at war with taking things slowly.

A few minutes later, he was splashing water at her, being playful. Now that they were alone in the pool for the first time today, she felt a little playful herself. But in a different way. The little escapade a few minutes ago gave her a taste of the Adin she'd longed for, dreamed about for years. She put her lips to his ear and kissed it gently.

"I really like your shirt being off," she whispered in his ear and then kissed it again while she rubbed her hand down his chest.

She felt Adin shiver and heard his breathing pick up. She wondered if it was her kissing his ear or rubbing his bare chest that stirred that reaction. It could have been a combination, but she wanted to see. She put her hand back around his neck, but kept her lips at his ear.

"Do you like having your shirt off in front of me?" she asked right in his ear, and then kissed his earlobe, savoring the taste of him.

A shudder rocked through Adin, and he put one of his hands in her hair, holding her head to his ear. He moaned and shifted his weight, breaking the water around them.

"Yeah," he said, sounding strangled.

The ear. Definitely the ear. She giggled right into it, and

her hot breath against his skin was apparently too much for him to bear. He started kissing her neck, and her playfulness vanished.

"Do I still taste like lotion?" she panted.

"No," he groaned as he kissed up her neck and to her ear. "You taste like heaven," he breathed into her ear before kissing her there.

It felt so good that she wanted his lips back on hers. She weaved her fingers in his hair and pulled his face over so she could kiss him again. He was more than willing.

It seemed like her life was getting better and better. She knew she had problems dealing with the news of her mother and her destiny at first, but now, she was getting used to it. Honestly, she really didn't care about what was going to happen to her at eighteen.

She felt like Adin was her life, and she knew she wanted to spend the rest of her life with him.

No matter how short, or different, that life might be.

Chapter
15

The rest of July had gone by way too fast. Adin and Legacy had spent every free moment they had together. He'd taken her out, visited her at home, brought her to his house. It didn't matter what they'd done, as long as they'd been together. And things between them had gotten hot and heavy. Well, in the PG-13 sense.

As the summer progressed, the days just kept getting hotter and hotter. She didn't think it was possible to be this hot already when it wasn't even August yet. And the heat wasn't like normal. The humidity was almost nonexistent. It was so dry that there were burn bans all over the state, and Calli often commented about her parents' irritation that their beautiful pond was slowly evaporating.

When she'd slept, she'd dreamed, so now she was dreaming every night. Her dreams were always variations of the same nightmares. She either saw the tornado or knew it was coming, but she was never scared of it. The little girl in her dreams was always scared enough for the both of them. Either she saw the snakes, which seemed to accumulate, or the three snake holes. Every now and then, she'd dream of the bright vivid sky with the confetti of lightning bolts falling like rain, and they always disappeared before reaching her.

One new characteristic was present, though. Her hands were always different temperatures. One was always hot and the other was always cold. She didn't think much of this in her dreams, so she hadn't paid much attention to that detail when she'd been awake either.

Working became annoying because that was just less time she got to spend with Adin. But she needed the money, so she went, grudgingly. Ms. Gorgos had stopped using excuses to keep River from the store when she was there. Either the woman had accepted their friendship, or she was picking her battles more wisely. Legacy figured it was the latter.

River and Legacy talked all the time at work, but he properly kept his feelings in check. She hadn't called him after that first time. There wasn't a need, and she didn't want to lead him on. Besides, when she wasn't at work, she was usually with Adin anyway.

But as time went on, she was beginning to feel guilty about keeping her friendship with River a secret from Adin. She felt as if she needed to tell him everything. Not only did she want to be honest with him, but she wanted him to know.

She hadn't told River about her plans. He'd only try to talk her out of it. She knew Adin was only human and wouldn't completely understand this mythical life she was part of, but she wanted to be with Adin for the rest of his life, so she needed him to know ... to understand.

Adin was leaving tomorrow to go to his dad's for the weekend, which only solidified her resolve to tell him now. That'd give him the weekend to deal, and she could get this out before she lost her nerve. If that made her a chicken, then she'd wear her feathers proudly.

Adin's mom was out of town, so he'd asked her over to his house so he could cook her dinner the night before he left. At least if he got mad at her about River—and her silence—no one would be around to hear him yelling.

When he picked her up, he complimented her on her outfit, though she knew he never really cared about the clothes she had on—he was complimenting *her*. When they arrived at his house, he held her hand in the car and put his arms around her several times while he finished up dinner.

They ate out on one of his porches. It was hot, but breezy. The food was very delicious. He made grilled fish and sautéed vegetables, and she ate everything. They were past the stage where she would pretend she wasn't hungry and not eat much, thank heavens.

Throughout the evening, she didn't talk much. She was going over her speech about River and her mom and her dreams, trying to decide how best to start. She knew he wouldn't like any of this, and she hated thinking that he may be leaving tomorrow upset with her. By the time they finished eating, she couldn't stop obsessing about what she was going to say to him.

She was so deep in thought that she barely noticed Adin clearing the table. She stayed outside on the porch while he put the dishes in the kitchen. When he came back, he took the seat right next to her, instead of the one he sat in across from her when they'd been eating.

Adin brushed his hand across her forehead and tucked her hair behind her ear.

"What are you thinking about?" he asked softly.

She wasn't ready for this! How in the world was she going to get this all out without him getting mad? She didn't want him to be upset with her, even though he had every right to be. Everything had been so perfect, and she was going to ruin it.

She shook her head faintly and felt her eyes moisten. She couldn't look at him.

He saw the expression on her face and became alarmed. "Please, Legacy. Tell me what's wrong." Adin stroked her face between his hands and gently turned her head toward him.

She looked at him briefly and then shut her eyes so he couldn't see them. Tears fell down her cheeks.

"Is this about me leaving? Don't worry. Please don't worry. My dad's not going to change his mind about school. You know I'm just going down there to help him unpack."

He'd jumped to the wrong conclusion, but she understood why. The last time he'd gone to see his dad, she'd been upset too.

She shook her head without opening her eyes. "It's not that," she said, her voice thick with sadness.

She heard Adin catch his breath, and he dropped his hands. She opened her eyes at the sudden change in his demeanor and looked at him. He looked like he was bracing himself for an impact, but his face looked *pained*.

She started crying and threw her hands up to cover her face. "I need … to talk to you … about something, and I-I don't know *how* to do it," she said through sobs.

He sat there quietly while she took a few deep breaths, trying to calm herself. He wasn't talking or trying to console her, but she could clearly hear his fast breathing.

She finally dropped her hands and looked at him. His mouth was open, eyes wide, face gravely pale. His body still braced for the impact.

"What?" he asked, barely a whisper.

"Please, please … don't be mad at me," she begged, shaking her head, but watching his eyes.

He just sat there. His expression unchanged. Gods, he was going to be pissed!

"I've been talking to River … about my mom," she said cautiously.

Adin's eyebrows furrowed briefly. Then his whole body relaxed and hunched over. He slowly put his hands on her wrists, moving them up her arms as if he were struggling to climb a mountain. He reached the tops of her shoulders, put his arms loosely around her neck, and leaned his head on her shoulder. It felt like he could barely hold himself up. "Oh," he breathed into her neck.

That wasn't quite the response she'd been expecting. She sat there for a minute, waiting for Adin's jagged breath to return back to normal.

It didn't. But he found his strength again, and his loose arms tightened around her. One hand slid to her back to press her to him while the other twisted into her hair, clutching her head.

She put her arms around him, but she wasn't sure what was going on. "Um, this wasn't a reaction I'd considered," she whispered. "I thought you were going to be furious with me."

He sighed. "I just need a minute."

He was still obviously disturbed, but at least he was seeking solace in her rather than screaming at her.

"I thought you were breaking up with me," he whispered into her ear.

Her body tensed up, and she grabbed him tighter. "No,"

she whispered. "Never."

She felt him nod his head as though he couldn't talk.

They held each other for a long while. Then he lifted his head and kissed her. This kiss felt urgent, and because she was already so emotional, more tears spilled over. She realized the thought of being without her caused him all this pain, so now she was hurting for needlessly doing this to him. She pulled away. "I'm sorry. I didn't mean to…"

"Shh…" Adin shook his head and crushed his lips to hers again.

When they finished kissing, they held each other. She knew she still needed to talk to him about River, but Adin was obviously not ready. After several more minutes, he finally pulled away and looked at her. His eyes were a little red, like he'd been fighting tears. But nowhere near the color of red her eyes had to be. She could feel how swollen and wet they were.

Adin took a deep breath and exhaled slowly, watching her eyes. "So you talked to River about your mom?"

Great. He felt better, but she still felt horrible.

"Yes," she said, looking down.

"You can tell me," he said sincerely. "I won't get mad."

She needed to tell him, so she figured she should just get this over with now. At least he wouldn't yell at her. Not after thinking he was losing her.

"Do you remember talking about the whole Greek mythology thing?"

"Yes, River told you something about descending from the mythical gods."

"Right. Well, we've talked a lot about his family and mine. He confirmed what Lissa told me about how the gods descend. He mentioned a goddess named Anesidora after noting the similarity of my mom's name. There are some versions of myths that connect Gaia through Demeter to

Anesidora. Some say they are the same person, just different interpretations. Regardless, Demeter is Persephone's mother and there is some connection to Anesidora." She waited to make sure he was following her, making the connection to what they'd already discussed about her connection to Persephone through her last name Kore.

"Go on."

"According to one of the myths, Zeus created Anesidora and gave her a beautiful container she was never to open. Her curiosity got the best of her. When she opened it, the evil contained within spread across the earth. She quickly closed it, but the only thing left in the box was the spirit of hope." Legacy sighed. Gods, this was all so weird. "This Anesidora is also known as Pandora."

Adin sighed and shook his head.

"The night you asked me out, I found a box in Lissa's room. When I opened it, it had the word *Elpis* carved in the bottom. That words means hope. Do you see how this is adding up?"

"You think that container is Pandora's Box?" Legacy couldn't decipher Adin's expression, so she slowly nodded. "And I take it River agreed with this."

Okay, so Adin wasn't very happy. It would be downhill from here.

"Yes. He also confirmed some of my research where I discovered Demeter and Zeus created Persephone. Demeter hid her from several gods who wanted her, but then she was abducted by Hades and taken to the underworld. I asked River about his theories, and he thinks there are a couple of possibilities."

Adin's expression was hardening, but he was staying calm. "What did he say?"

"Either Demeter created Dora, who created me, or the original Demeter, Anesidora, whatever, is my mother, and

I'm actually Persephone. Either I am her or a likeness of her."

"That doesn't make any sense."

"I know. When I asked him why gods would create a similar god, he said something about changing destiny. So he thinks if I am Persephone or like her, then my mom, whichever one she is, created me to stop the abduction. That's why my mom left when I was a baby. Not because she was in danger, but because I was."

Adin's eyes softened. "Nothing is going to happen to you."

"I know this sounds weird. I had a really tough time believing it myself. But you have to look at all the connections. If I am a goddess, I'll reach my full power by my eighteenth birthday. If I make it until then."

"What are you talking about?"

"Besides the threat of Hades, I think it's River's family that's after me. His mom specifically. He said he thinks my mom created a powerful god with a pure ability—me. Most gods don't know how powerful a new god is until that god reaches maturity. But that there are some who know, and if that knowledge gets into the hands of a vengeful god, then that god may try to destroy the new god. The weather has been acting weird this summer, and River thinks it's his mom's doing. Ms. Gorgos is powerful. If she can destroy me before I turn eighteen, then she'd assume my powers on top of the ones she already has. Plus, she doesn't like my mom, so killing me is just another incentive. One of many."

"What does that mean?"

Crap. "You're really not going to like this."

"I'm sure you're right." He sighed.

"Just don't get mad, please."

Adin looked at her calmly. "Legacy, I won't get mad at you, I promise."

She nodded and took a big breath. *Here goes nothing.* "River said the night Lissa told me about my mom he also found out about a prophecy, and it's the same night you showed up at my birthday party."

"Me?" Adin looked confused.

"Yes. River said the three of us are bonded together through a prophecy. Which is that I would end up with River as long as *you* were alive. He thinks that's why you finally asked me out after being friends all these years. Maybe my turning seventeen triggered the prophecy."

"That's absurd! No one knows what the future holds. Asking you out had nothing to do with a freaking prophecy. He probably just likes you and wants to be with you."

"He does like me," she said, looking down because she actually believed River's feelings were stronger than that. "He said he already feels attached to me. That's why he's told me all of this. He said he wasn't supposed to, and he's fought with his mom over it. But he couldn't deny me anything, so he gave me what I wanted," she whispered.

"I-I don't know what to say," Adin said, leaning back in his chair and putting his hands on his head.

"I asked River what his part in all this was. He wasn't sure, but he thinks he was created out of the likeness of one of the gods that originally pursued Persephone before she was abducted. He's that god's attempt at a real chance with her ... with me."

Adin shook his head. He probably couldn't trust himself to open his mouth without yelling.

"River said he thinks you're the link in the prophecy, since whether you live or die will determine if he and I will be together. His mom doesn't like me, so River thinks she may come after you. Killing you would keep me from being with him. Plus, it would destroy me emotionally before she could destroy me physically. He wanted me to warn you ...

somehow."

"I—" He stopped, shook his head. "Do you believe any of this?"

"I believe parts of it. I think River is trying to help me. When I talked to Lissa, she didn't deny any of it. In fact, Demeter also had priestesses who were titled Melissae. I came right out and asked her if that's what she was." She looked at Adin. "You even mentioned it was odd that she didn't go out with my mom the night of her supposed death if they were such great friends."

"What did Lissa say?" he asked cautiously.

"She was shocked, but when I mentioned the box in her room, she freaked out and ran to her bedroom, but it was no longer there. From the way she and River acted about the box, it can't be anything good."

"So what parts do you believe, specifically?"

"I think I am like Persephone. I think my mom left me here in Lissa's care to keep Hades, or his likeness, from coming after me, so I could have a better destiny than Persephone did. I think my dreams are trying to warn me or help me—I'm not sure which one yet. I think Ms. Gorgos is going to try to kill me, and I think River is in love with me," she whispered.

Adin's eyes turned sad. "How do you feel about him?"

"I think he's nice, and I consider him a friend." She looked down at the table. Gods, this was hard. "I feel like I can talk to him without being judged, and I feel like I need to protect him from people who'd want to hurt him for being open with me." She glanced at Adin, who looked confused. "I don't feel about him the way he feels about me. He knows how I feel about you, and it hurts him, but I've been very honest with him about that fact. He knows I want to be with you, and he's okay with just being friends."

"It doesn't work that way, Legacy," Adin said. "If he

feels only half as strongly as I do for you, I know he won't stop until he finds a way into your heart. I know this because that's what I'd do. That's what any man in that position would do."

"I told him if he couldn't keep his feelings in line, then we couldn't even be friends. He couldn't stand the thought of not being friends, so he agreed. I think it was hard for him at first, but he's been doing pretty well lately. I think, for him, the prophecy doesn't necessarily mean *now*. He believes we'll be together someday, but he's not sure when that'll happen. Until then he's okay staying friends."

"What do you think about the prophecy?"

"I don't know what to think. I can understand if his family was responsible for your death how I would despise him and not want to be his friend at all, much less anything more. So I can totally see that part. But I don't understand how I could not be with you if you were alive." She looked down at her hands on the table. "I already feel like we were meant to be together. Forever."

Adin lifted her head to meet his gaze. "I feel that way too," he murmured. "And I felt that way long before the night of your birthday party."

She smiled at him, but it wasn't a happy one. "I don't understand how everything else can make so much sense, but I can't accept what he said about the prophecy. I mean, I know you care about me, and I know River does too. So I can see how River thinks we're all bonded. He feels bonded to me, and I feel bonded to you…"

"We are bonded to each other," Adin corrected. "River isn't part of that."

"I know. But he's still my friend."

Adin took her hands in his and looked down at them. "I don't want you to be friends with him."

"Why?"

"Legacy, I don't trust him. I know you think he's helping you with your mom, and he might be. But his intentions are not, um, honorable." Adin's jaw ticked.

"What do you mean?"

"Whether or not he's telling you the truth, he's helping you in order to gain your trust. Once he has that, there's no telling what he will do. He could turn on you and help his mother and you wouldn't see it coming. Or," Adin paused, "he could use that trust to get into your heart. I'll be in college while he's there with you every day at school. He has an ulterior motive, Legacy."

"I wouldn't let that happen, and I don't think he'd purposely try to take me from you. He knows that would hurt me, and he doesn't want to do that. Besides, why would he want me to warn you about his mother?"

"Because he wants me left alone since that's apparently the only way he'll get you," Adin snapped.

"But even when I was upset about you being at your dad's, he wanted me to talk to him about it even though I could tell it hurt him to hear me talk about you like that. He wants what makes me happy, and he knows that's you. He wants my happiness no matter what it costs him."

"Of course he does. If you go crying on his shoulder, he gets to be the one to console you. Then you'll always turn to him when you need support. Legacy, he has an agenda."

She took a deep breath and looked away. She felt like she wasn't getting anywhere with Adin. She wanted him to know *and* understand.

"Legacy," Adin whispered, and she looked at him. "You said something earlier that bothers me."

"What's that?"

"When I asked you how you felt about River, you said you feel like he doesn't judge you."

"Yes."

"Do you think I judge you?"

"No." She shook her head, but she wasn't entirely sure if she was being truthful. "I think you don't understand. I want you to understand. That's why I told you. I was really upset at the thought of making you angry, but I needed you to know. If any of this is true, then I wanted you to know about it because I want you to know about me."

Adin looked deep into her eyes. "You can always, always come to me. I will always be here for you. I will always listen to what you have to say. You have no idea how much I care about you. I will always try to understand whatever it is you want to tell me. But because I … because of how I feel about you, I will always, *always* try to protect you. Even though I will do whatever it takes to protect you, that does not mean I don't understand."

She nodded, and he wrapped his arms around her.

"I just told you that you can always come to me," he whispered in her ear. "Now, I want to ask you to do just that. Please, Legacy. Please come to me whenever you need to, whenever you want to, whatever the reason. I want to be the one you turn to. Always. Forever," he breathed.

"That's what I want too," she whispered.

Adin held her in his arms, rocking her gently. Even though this hadn't been easy, she was glad to have it all out in the open.

What seemed like an eternity later, Adin finally spoke again, but did not let her go. "What about your dreams? Are you still having them?"

"Yeah."

"Are they always the same?" he asked, stroking her hair.

"No. Parts of them are, but I've been dreaming about my hands too. They're always different temperatures."

"And?" He seemed like he was waiting for her to say more.

"And it's odd. I've never dreamed about that before."

"But your hands are always different temperatures, Legacy."

She yanked away from him, startled. "What?"

"Er, your hands. One is always hotter than the other." He stared at her like he didn't understand why she was shocked about that.

She pulled her hands away from him, touching each one to the other arm to feel the difference. Her right one was freezing, and her left one was blazing hot. Even looking at them, she could tell the fingers on her left hand had a red tint to them.

She grimaced. She didn't know what to say.

"You didn't know this, did you?"

"No," she said, shaking her head. "How long have you noticed this?"

"Um, I don't know for sure, but when I held your hands the night of your birthday party, I noticed it then. I guess I've noticed it ever since. I can't say for sure if I noticed before your birthday. Before then I tried not to be too obvious about my feelings, so I tried not to touch you too much."

"Hmm..." She wondered if this was relevant.

"Do you think it means something?"

"I don't know. It's interesting, though."

She sat in silence while she pondered it. It had to mean something, but what? She couldn't figure out what her hands had to do with anything. Unless this was part of the changes she was going through.

"River said there are no coincidences. I wonder what this means." She rubbed her hands together.

"No coincidences," Adin mumbled.

She looked over at him to read his expression, but it was unfathomable. He flashed his gaze at her and smiled. Then he lifted his hand and rubbed her arm.

"If the different hand temperatures are new, then maybe that has something to do with the changes Lissa mentioned."

She smiled back at Adin. He was trying and that meant a lot to her. "Possibly."

"What are you smiling about?" he asked, his lip twitching.

"I'm just happy that you're trying to understand this. I know you don't like River, but you're making an effort and that makes her happy."

"I don't like River for many reasons, one of which is the fact that he seriously thinks he'll take you away from me. Any man would feel threatened by that. But this isn't about River. He may be a source of information for you, but to me, that's all he is. This is about you, not him."

"Thank you," she whispered, and leaned in to kiss his neck.

Adin put his arms around her again and held her for a while. "Will you please do something for me while I'm gone?"

"Of course."

"Stay safe. I'm going to be worried enough about you as it is. I'm not going to ask you to stay away from River because I know you can't. Just be aware that even though there may be no *coincidences*, not everything is always as it seems either. So please be careful. For me."

He said it again. Be careful. This time, they were on the exact porch that they were on in her dream.

So was that a coincidence, or something that wasn't as it seemed? Gods, she didn't know. But in Adin's arms, she knew either way it didn't really matter.

Chapter

16

Legacy pulled into Calli's driveway on another dreary day. Dreary because Adin had left to go to his dad's house. At least he'd be back tomorrow, and early enough this time that they'd made plans to go out when he returned. But she was going to use part of this time away from him to be productive ... well, help Calli be productive.

They had a summer English assignment—a paper on *Hamlet*—so of course Calli had waited until they only had a few weeks left of summer before she started on it. Adin helped Legacy with hers last month, so she was already finished. She'd found a copy of Kenneth Branagh's movie version of the play and brought it with her to Calli's house.

At least they could watch the movie and follow along in the book.

Once she was inside, she got down to business. She put in the movie, and Calli popped some popcorn. They sat quietly while they both watched, and Calli followed along with the play. When it was finally over, she got out her laptop and they started on her paper. Legacy couldn't remember the last time she had so little fun spending the day with Calli. The movie was great, but no one liked homework during summer break.

"How are things with you and Zach?" she asked as Calli saved the final version of her paper.

"So far, so good."

"Do you want to double when Adin gets back? We can go see the new movie that comes out next week."

"Ah, that sounds like fun. I'll talk to Zach about it."

"I talked to Adin about River," she said timidly, now that the dreaded homework was finished.

"Really? What did he say?"

"Nothing I didn't really expect. He doesn't trust River, but he understands why I talk to him. He wants me to come to him, though, if I ever need to talk. He thinks River has an agenda."

"Is that what you think?"

"I don't know. Maybe."

"Does it matter if he does? I mean, he *is* helping you."

"I know. And I've told River how I feel about Adin. I don't want to lead him on—even if he is helping me."

"Hopefully, Adin understands that."

"I think he does. Actually, he helped me too. I told him about the latest entry in my dream catalog, and he was the one who pointed out the reality."

"What's new in your dreams?" she asked as she printed out her paper.

"My hands are different temperatures. One is hot and the other is cold. Adin told me my hands are always like that. I asked when he noticed, and he said he did the night of my party. He couldn't tell me if my hands were like that before that night since he was trying to control his feelings back then. But that night seems to be when all this craziness started."

"Well, I've known you for years, too, but I haven't been trying not to touch you," she said, laughing. "I've never noticed your hands like that before. In fact, the first time I did notice it was when we were at the mall, and you said it was because of your iced latte."

"Yeah, I remember." Interesting.

"What do you think it means?"

"I don't know, Calli. But I think it means something. Maybe it's part of the changes I'm going through."

"That's what I think too. Are you going to talk to River about it?"

"No. He knows too much already."

She decided to stay the night at Calli's house since spending time with Calli was better than sulking about Adin at home in her bedroom.

After a day of work, it was fun spending the evening doing girly stuff. They did makeovers, painted toenails, and talked about their boyfriends.

Before they turned in for the night, Calli had to feed the dogs, so Legacy went outside with her. Once they were outside, they noticed the gate had not shut completely when Legacy pulled in, and one of the dogs was missing. They grabbed some flashlights and started walking down the road.

"Spike," Calli called out. "I hope we find him before I have to go wake up my parents."

As they passed River's house, Legacy glanced over

there in search of the dog. Great. He was outside, and he had to have heard them and seen the lights flashing. Just what she needed, River to see her in her pajamas. *Not*. He walked over to them.

"What are you two doing out here in the dark?"

"We're looking for one of my dogs," Calli said.

"Have you checked with security? Maybe someone saw him and called."

They were in a gated community with security, so surely the dog hadn't gone far.

"No. I didn't think about that."

"I'll keep looking while you go call," Legacy told her.

"Okay," Calli said, and ran back to her house.

Legacy kept walking down the street, but she could hear River walking behind her. She so didn't want to deal with him right now. She barely had any clothes on. She turned around and glared at him. "What?" she asked, flashing the light in his face.

He raised his hand to block the light. "I'm helping you look for the dog."

"I can manage," she said as she shifted the light away from his face.

"I know you can, but two pairs of eyes are better than one."

"Well, the second pair will be back out right after she calls security," she said, putting her hand on her hip.

River stood there staring at her. "I don't want you out here alone," he muttered.

"We're in a gated community. What can happen to me here?"

"Did you forget my mom lives right there?" He pointed to his house.

Crap. "I guess you have a point. I'll go wait at Calli's house."

"No, I can walk with you."

He wasn't getting the hint, so she'd just have to come out and say it. "I don't want you walking with me."

He walked up closer to her. "Why?"

"Because it's late. I'm tired. I'm in my pajamas, and it's not appropriate."

"Calli has seen you in your pajamas. Think of me as a friend like she is." He smiled.

"But I haven't known you as long as I've known her."

River knew she had him with that, so he was more direct. "I'm not letting you out of my sight until you are safely back indoors."

Ugh! "Hmph." Stupid prophecy. She turned and walked away from him. "Spike! Come here, boy!"

She stomped down the street with her stalker in tow. She could tell he was still right behind her. She wanted to turn around and give him a piece of her mind, but she wasn't sure if she'd be able to keep calm.

They walked down to the next street where a new estate was being built. She walked around the shell of the house, swinging her flashlight in every direction. Her foot caught some of the construction debris and she tripped. River grabbed her arm and pulled her to him. She looked at his face, only to find he was watching the ground, making sure she had her footing before letting her go.

"Are you hurt?" he asked, concerned.

"No, I'm fine. Thanks."

Even though he let go of her arm, he was still standing right up against her. She thought he was going to step back, but he didn't. She looked at his face again, and his eyes were shut. She stepped away from him, and he opened them.

"Sorry," he whispered, but he was breathing heavily.

She didn't say anything. She just turned and walked to the side of the house where the woods were. She flashed the light in the trees and called the dog again. She didn't hear anything, but she thought she saw movement. She couldn't be sure. It was dark, and she was moving a light around. Her eyes could have very easily been playing tricks on her.

She started to step into the trees, but River grabbed her arm. She looked back at him.

"Don't go in there."

"Why?"

"Please, Legacy. I don't want you to get hurt." He looked at her with a wistful expression, but she couldn't understand it. She wasn't sure if he was just worried about the woods, or if there was a deeper meaning in his expression. "Look out!" he yelled, and pulled her to the side.

She saw a rustling on the ground and jumped anyway. *Eeek!* It was a rattlesnake! She started to move. She had to get away before it struck.

"Don't," River whispered, halting her escape. He reached over, picked up a piece of scrap lumber, and crushed the snake. "Let's go." He grabbed her by the arm, and they walked quickly down the street and back toward the house. They saw Calli walking toward them.

"Where have you been?" she asked Legacy as she got closer.

"I was out looking for the dog."

"I got him already. Security had him."

"Oh. Good. Okay." She looked at River's face, and then looked at his hand that was still locked tightly around her arm. He dropped it.

"I'll see you at work tomorrow," she said as she walked away from him.

"Sweet dreams," he murmured.

There was nothing sweet about her dreams that night. She guessed her encounter with a real snake wasn't enough; she dreamed about them all night. When she finally woke up, she was relieved to be back in reality. Even better, Adin would be back today.

She got dressed and headed to work. Calli stayed in bed. Ahh, the life of a debutante.

River was already there when she arrived. She guessed he was so giddy from seeing her unexpectedly last night that he rushed up here to see her as soon as possible. *Stupid* prophecy.

"Good morning," she said as she walked in the door.

"Good morning," River responded, but he didn't sound as cheerful as she thought he'd be. Maybe he'd taken last night for what it had actually been and didn't obsess about it all night. That'd be a big relief.

"Where's everybody at?" she asked as she walked to the back to put up her purse. She didn't have to turn around to see if he was following her. She knew.

"Yale called in and my mom stayed home. We have family visiting from out of town."

Nice … it would just be the two of them then.

"Hopefully, it won't be too busy," she said as she locked up her purse and headed back out the door.

It was slow all day, but she stayed in front by the register just in case anyone came in. River spent most of the morning in the back, but came out at lunchtime.

"What do you want to eat?"

"Don't worry about it. I can go get something."

"Don't be silly. My mom buys us all lunch all the time."

"I don't care. Whatever you want is fine with me."

"How about we just order a pizza?"

"That sounds good."

He walked over to where she was standing and gently stroked her arm. "What kind do you want?"

She stepped to the side so he couldn't reach her. The touch felt too intimate for just friends. "Pepperoni's fine."

River smiled as he called and ordered the pizza. "It'll be here in thirty minutes," he said once he got off the phone.

She shrugged, but he didn't go back to work. Maybe she needed to be verbal about it. "Okay," she said with her eyebrows raised.

But he kept standing there, staring at her. She stared right back. Then he moved back over to her and stroked her arm again. "Why did you step away from me?" he asked softly.

"Because I didn't want you touching me." She shoved her shoulder in an attempt to knock off his hand, but he kept it there.

"Is it because you like me touching you and you don't know how to deal with that?"

"Er, no. What gave you that crazy idea?"

"Just a hunch."

"You're wrong."

He stepped to the side again, so now, he was standing right in front of her. She took a step back and realized she was backed up against a wall. He put his other hand on her other arm.

"I think you do like me. More than you're willing to admit."

Why was she in the pits of hell?

"Look, River, I don't want to hurt your feelings." She tried being nice, but as she spoke, he took another step. Now he was uncomfortably close. "You're right," she whispered, and River's eyes popped open. "I do like you. But I don't feel about you the way I feel about Adin."

He flinched at that acknowledgement. "You *will* love me. One day."

"Not this day, and not ever if I have anything to do about it."

"Well, I'm tired of sitting by and watching you grow

closer to Adin. You're supposed to be growing closer to me," he whispered.

He asked for it. "I love the way Adin makes me feel. The way he talks to me, holds me, hugs me, kisses me. There's nothing in the world that can top that."

River dropped his arms and huffed angrily. "I can't do this anymore. I tried being your friend like you wanted, but I'm done. I want to be with you. From here on out, I'm going to be pursuing you like any other man would do in this situation."

So Adin was right about River.

"Right, because there are so many men out there pinning their hopes on a *prophecy!*"

"Touchy much?" He smirked and stepped right up against her, their bodies touching. "I think you're putting up a fight because you're afraid of the temptation."

"You have completely lost your mind." She put her hands on his chest and shoved him back. "I don't want to be with you. I want Adin!"

"There's nothing wrong with giving him a little competition. He's going to mess up, and I'll be the one you'll turn to."

"No." She shook her head and glared at him.

"Legacy, you *will* be mine. I'm going to be the one who'll be there for you in the end."

"No! You're going to be nothing to me. You *are* nothing!"

"Baby, I'm everything. I'm everywhere. You can't stop me. You have no choice."

She slumped back on the wall and threw her hand up over her mouth. She shook her head, staring at him in disbelief. His words had been in her dream. The one where she stood under the tornado, daring it to come for her. She wanted it to come. She needed it to come. She yelled, "No!" up to the sky like she just did to River, and the words that

River just spoke were the words from that female voice.

The sudden change in her expression softened his stance. Now, he looked concerned. "What's wrong?"

"Nothing." She stepped aside, intending to walk away from him, but she found herself running for the restroom.

She burst through the door and ran to the sink. She splashed water on her face, hoping the cold water would make her numb. It didn't. She could clearly feel one hot hand and one cold hand on her cheeks. There was no escaping her reality.

Why was this happening to her? Everything had to fit together. With each new experience, she was more certain about that. But if everything kept making sense, then how did this prophecy fit in? She truly felt like she belonged to Adin. She wasn't just telling herself this. She felt it with every fiber of her being.

But River felt the exact same way about her. She couldn't be mad at him when she thought of the pain that caused him. Because if she couldn't be with Adin, she knew she would be hurting too.

River knocked on the bathroom door. "Are you okay?"

She didn't want to talk to him. She felt sorry for him, but that didn't excuse his behavior. If he was going to be actively pursuing her, she would have to be on guard. This was the first time she was actually looking forward to school starting and this job ending.

"Legacy?"

"I'll be out in a minute."

She took a few deep breaths and wiped the water from her face. Then she walked out of the restroom. River was standing right there.

"I'm sorry. I didn't mean to say all that."

"Apology accepted," she said as she stepped around him and walked back to the register.

River followed her. "I'm not saying what I said wasn't true," he muttered. "But I shouldn't have been a dick about it."

"I understand," she said, looking down, fidgeting with some papers.

"I think about you all the time," he breathed. "I just don't know how to do this anymore. I can't sit by and watch you fall in love with *him*."

She looked up at River, and he was looking at his feet. "I get it." And she did. He wanted her, and he was through pretending that he didn't.

He looked up and met her gaze. "You don't know what I've been going through. When I saw you unexpectedly last night, it made my day. Just seeing you. But when you tripped, and I caught you ... with you so *close*..." He sighed, shutting his eyes. "You have no idea."

"I said I understand, but that doesn't mean I'm going to change my mind."

He opened his eyes. "I know how you feel, which is why I've tried to be a good friend to you. I wish I could continue being that friend. But that's not who I am. I'll still be there for you, and I'll still help you whenever you need it. But I just can't deny my feelings anymore. I know that's what you want, and it's killing me that I can't do that for you."

"I know you can't change your feelings, but neither can I. I really don't want you to be hurting, but I can't be what you want."

This was such a mess. River's confession just added to her list of crapola she had to deal with. His longing looks spoke volumes. He wasn't hiding his feelings anymore because he wasn't pretending anymore, and it would make working with him brutal.

By the gods, if she got through this with her sanity intact, it'd be a friggin' miracle.

Chapter 17

Legacy couldn't wait to see Adin. She had already missed him so much before she went to work. Now, she was aching to see him.

The knock on the door made her heart flutter. She opened it, and Adin was standing there with roses. She didn't even take them from him. She threw her arms around his neck and squeezed him to her. He put his arms around her and held her tightly. She was where she belonged. *He* was where she belonged.

"I missed you so, so much," she breathed into his chest.

"Me too." He kissed the top of her head.

She didn't want to let go of him, but they couldn't

stand here in the doorway all night. She took a deep breath, breathing in his luscious scent, and let go.

"These are for you," he said, handing her the flowers.

She took them from him and reached up and kissed him softly. Then he put his forehead on hers and stroked her face.

"I really, really missed you," he whispered.

She nodded and stepped away again. "I'll be right back." She went into the kitchen to put the flowers up and met him again at the front door.

Once they were in the car, she held Adin's hand in her lap and took her other hand and held his arm. If she didn't have her seatbelt on, she would have leaned up against him, but she still tried.

"When did you get back?" she wondered.

"About thirty minutes ago. I took a quick shower and came right over. I couldn't wait to see you," he said, gazing into her eyes.

She reached up with her free hand and felt his hair. "Your hair's still a little wet." It felt so good to touch him.

"I was in a hurry," he said with a laugh.

"What are we doing tonight?"

"I was thinking we'd get some takeout and watch the sunset again. We haven't done that since our first date."

"That sounds wonderful." It sounded perfect.

Adin was glowing. He looked even better than before he'd left. She couldn't keep her gaze off him.

"How was your trip this time?"

"Better. No arguing, just a lot of unpacking."

"Arguing?"

Adin's smile faded a little, and he glanced at her. He looked like he didn't want to tell her what he meant by that, but surely he could see the concern building.

"When I was there before, my dad had a hard time

understanding why I wanted to stay here," he said slowly.

"What did he say?"

"Umm, I don't really remember all the specifics of it." Adin looked out his side window. He had to be hiding something.

"You can tell me," she whispered.

"I don't want it to upset you."

"Will it upset me?"

"Yes."

"Were you arguing about me?" Did his dad hate her or something?

"Legacy," he murmured, shaking his head.

"Please, Adin."

"You came up, yes. But the arguing was directed more toward me and my life."

"Did you talk about me this time too?"

"Of course." He stroked her hand.

"But you didn't argue this time?"

"No. He understands what I want, and he's not going to press it anymore. He knew he needed to speak his mind last time, and he did that. We argued, and then he understood how strongly I felt about everything."

She nodded. It still felt like he was leaving a lot out, but as long as he was staying, she really didn't care. If it took a fight with his dad to make sure he stayed here, then she was all for that. Yeah, she was being selfish.

"How was your weekend?" Adin asked while she was mulling over his fight with his dad.

She really didn't want to talk about what happened while Adin was away. She had every intention of telling him everything about her weekend—just not right now. But since he'd asked, she couldn't put it off.

"Um, well, I went to Calli's Saturday and helped her with her *Hamlet* paper."

"She hadn't started it yet?" Adin asked incredulously.

"Nope." Legacy laughed. "But I spent the day with her, and she got it done."

"Good. How was everything else?"

She sighed. She knew what he was getting at. He wanted to know about River.

"I stayed the night with Calli." She frowned. Time to find her big-girl panties and fess up. "When Calli went outside to feed the dogs, she noticed that one was missing. We grabbed some flashlights and started walking the neighborhood to find him. We left in a hurry, not bothering to change out of our pajamas."

Adin's happy expression was changing. He knew where this story was going.

"River was outside and he saw us. He came over, and Calli told him what happened. He suggested she contact security. She left, and I kept walking."

Adin sighed. "You went searching alone?"

She let go of Adin's arm and put that hand on top of their joined hands in her lap. "Not exactly. River followed me. I asked him what he was doing, and he fed me some crap about two pairs of eyes being better than one. I didn't buy that, so I tried to brush him off. He wasn't going to let me walk alone, so I stormed off, ignoring him. He kept following me, and when I walked around a new house, I tripped on some lumber, and he caught me." She looked down at her hands holding his. "Um, he let go but didn't move. When I looked up at him, he had his eyes closed. I was already uncomfortable because I was in my pajamas, so the fact that he was right beside me made me feel extremely uncomfortable, so I stepped away. When I did, he apologized." She looked back up at Adin, and his expression was harder. "Anyway, I started to go into the woods, and he grabbed my arm. He didn't want me walking around in the woods. When I started to leave, he saw a snake beside me and killed it. We got back to the main road, and Calli was walking down. Security did have the dog."

"And?" His expression was still hard, but controlled.

"That night, I dreamed about snakes. You know, for obvious reasons. Then this morning, I had to work. Yale called in, and River's mom stayed home with houseguests. River and I were the only ones there, and it was really slow. He left me alone most of the morning, but he came out at lunchtime and asked me what I wanted to eat. I told him I could fend for myself, but he insisted and decided on pizza. When he asked me what kind I wanted..." She paused and glanced at Adin, his hard expression unchanged. "River stepped over and rubbed my arm. I walked away from him, but after he ordered the pizza, he walked back up to me. I was trapped up against a wall." She looked at Adin again, and he was gripping the steering wheel as tightly as he was gritting his teeth. She let go of his hand and rubbed both her hands on her legs while Adin took the hand that she had been holding and locked it to the steering wheel like his other. She took a deep breath. "I don't know if you want to hear the rest of this," she muttered as she exhaled.

"Yes, I do," Adin said through his teeth.

"You're not going to like it," she said, shaking her head.

He laughed sarcastically. "I already don't like it."

That much was obvious. "Okay. After I was trapped, he put both hands on my arms and asked why I stepped away from him. I told him I didn't want him touching me. He said some nonsense about me actually liking him and just not knowing how to deal with it. He stepped right up against me, and I pushed him off. Then we fought. He said he was through being just my friend. He was tired of sitting back watching me grow close to you because I was supposed to be growing closer to him. He said from here on out he's not going to deny his feelings anymore and that he's going to be pursuing me. We were yelling at each other, and he said something that I'd heard in my dream the other night, so I freaked out and ran to the bathroom. When I came out, he was apologetic for his behavior, but he was still resolved."

"What did he say that you heard in your dream?" Adin asked in an eerily even tone.

"His exact words were 'Baby, I'm everything. I'm everywhere. You can't stop me. You have no choice.' All but the *baby* part was in my dream."

"He said you can't stop him?" Adin roared. There went his carefully controlled expression.

"Yes," she whispered.

"I can stop him! I will."

"Adin," she whispered, shaking her head. "He was just yelling at me because I was yelling at him. He didn't mean it like that. He apologized."

"Legacy, you can't expect me to ignore this. He has no right to talk to you like that, and he sure as hell has no right to touch you like that!"

"What's done is done. I was going to tell you about this, but I didn't want to bring it up tonight. I knew you wouldn't be happy about this—"

"I'm pissed!"

She sighed. "I know, but I've missed you. I didn't want to spend this night talking about River. I had a horrible night and an even worse day because I had to deal with him. I want to enjoy this night with you and not think about him."

Adin sat quietly for several minutes, she guessed trying to calm his nerves. Then he sighed. "You're right. We don't need to talk about this right now. Let's just focus on us."

"I'd like that," she said softly. "I've missed you so much."

He reached over and took her hand in his. He kissed the

back of it and put their hands in his lap. She watched his face to make sure he was putting the conversation behind him. His face seemed relaxed, but his eyes stayed narrowed until they reached the restaurant.

They ordered some pasta and breadsticks. By the time their dinner was ready, Adin seemed more at ease. He was trying to be calm for her, and she knew it wasn't easy for him. As they drove up the winding hill to their picnic spot, Adin seemed to put the River conversation behind him — for now.

They reached the place where Adin used to go to think and watch the sunset alone. Now he liked sharing this with her. It was their spot, and she hadn't realized how much she'd missed it until now.

"It is so nice up here," she said as Adin helped her out of his car.

"It's peaceful," he murmured.

She put her arms around his back and pulled him to her. He wrapped his arms around her, put his head in her hair, and kissed her head. They stood there for several minutes, holding each other.

"Our dinner is going to get cold," Adin said with a small laugh.

"Okay." She groaned, and he chuckled.

Adin brought a blanket, and they spread it over the grass where they'd eaten that first night. While they enjoyed their dinner, they talked some, but not much. They were both so happy to be with each other that they mostly stared and smiled while they ate.

When they finished, she shifted her position so that she was sitting between Adin's legs with her back leaning against his chest, hands resting on his legs. Adin had his arms wrapped around her stomach and put his chin on her shoulder. They sat like this while they watched the sunset, which was magnificent. The sky was a rainbow of colors cascading off the horizon.

While she gently caressed Adin's legs with her fingers, he lifted one of his hands and brushed her hair around to her opposite shoulder. He put his chin back down, but continued to stroke her hair on the other side. His touch was so soothing.

"Legacy," he whispered in her ear.

"Mmm…"

"I love you," he said so gingerly.

Her heart swelled, and she could feel it beating harder. It was radiating throughout her body. She reached her hand up and stroked the side of his face. He told her that he loved her!

"I love you too," she murmured.

And she did. She knew she was in love with Adin. There was no doubt in her mind or in her heart. Her heart would always belong to him. Before, she had a very hard time believing that this magnificent creature wanted her … that he was hers. But now she knew he loved her too, and that feeling was overwhelming. He belonged to her. His heart, his soul.

Adin held her a little tighter and pressed his lips into her neck while she ran her fingers through his hair. After he kissed her neck, he rested his chin on her shoulder and kept stroking her hair.

In this moment, there wasn't anything else to say. She knew if she tried to say something, she would cry. She felt a lump in her throat just thinking about the words he'd just said to her. The words that changed everything for her. Even though she already knew she loved him, his love for her meant more than anything else.

They sat unmoving until it started to get dark. Adin loosened his arm that was around her and leaned back. She twisted to the side to watch him.

"We should probably leave before the mosquitoes eat us alive." He chuckled.

"You're probably right," she said, leaning to the side so she could get up.

Adin got up first and helped her to her feet. Once she was upright, she stretched, and Adin laughed again.

"What?"

"You're just very beautiful."

"I'm glad you think so."

"I know so," he said as he wrapped his arms around her waist.

She stretched up on her toes and put her hands on his face, stroking it lightly while she stared into his eyes. He was incredibly handsome, but he was so much more than good-looking. He was beautiful inside and out. She stared at him in awe.

As her fingers caressed his face, he reached up and put his hand on top of her right hand, holding it to his face.

"Your hand is cold," he said as he shut his eyes.

"It doesn't feel that way to me. Right now, it just feels *right* against you," she murmured.

Adin sighed and opened his eyes, staring into the depths of hers. "I love you so much," he breathed. "I've loved you for a very long time. I wanted to wait until the end of summer to confess my feelings since we were taking things slowly, but after the last time we were together— when there was a brief moment that I thought you were breaking up with me—I realized I wasn't going to make it until the end of summer. I almost told you that night, but I wanted the first time to be special, so I decided to bring you back here, to where we had our first date."

He didn't give her an opportunity to respond. He leaned down and gently pressed his lips to hers instead. While he was kissing her, her breathing was jagged. It was only then that she realized the lump in her throat was no longer contained. She was crying.

She would always need Adin as he would always need her. She knew that after tonight, she would never be the same. She had changed.

Chapter 18

"Calli, what time is Zach picking you up?"

"He'll be here in about an hour. Then we'll head to your house."

"Okay, bye." Legacy hung up the phone and continued getting ready.

Tonight was the double date that she and Calli had planned last week. Zach and Adin got along fine, so that was a bonus. They didn't seem like the type of guys that would be friends on their own, but since she and Calli brought them together, they were more than cordial. She figured when Calli and Zach broke up that Adin would probably stay friends with Zach. She didn't expect a breakup soon, but their relationship didn't seem as serious as her relationship with Adin was.

And their relationship was serious. They were now spending every free second together, and when they weren't together, they were on the phone. They talked about everything. She told him about her dreams and her theories, and he was always attentive and insightful. She didn't think he really believed she was going to be a goddess — other than his own personal goddess — but he was never negative about it. He knew that was what she thought, and he was there for her.

River was his new distant self. He didn't talk to her unless she spoke to him first, but he was always staring. Always longing from afar. If he was close to her, he used it as an opportunity to touch her, which she ignored, and he hated. A few times he'd overheard her talking to Yale about her dates with Adin, and that would either put him in a funkier mood or make him more presumptuous. She didn't like him hurting, but she wasn't going to entertain his behavior. She knew her indifference hurt him more than anything, though.

The weather hadn't changed. Since it hadn't rained in weeks, there were still burn bans everywhere, and it was blistering hot. Too hot to do much of anything outside during the peak hours of the day. The spring flowers were dried up and dead, as was the grass and everything else that was supposed to be green or colorful. But the scorching weather outside made a movie night ideal, so that was what they were all going to do tonight. Since Zach had an SUV, they were riding with him. After Zach and Calli picked her up, they were going to get Adin.

She had so busy picking out a sexy outfit that she was running late when Calli and Zach arrived, so she threw her hair up and ran outside. When they reached Adin's house, she got out and went to his door, but he came out before she got there.

"You should have waited for me to come and get you," she teased.

Adin laughed and shook his head. "I didn't want you out in this heat." He grabbed her waist. "But you do look hot!"

She shrugged her shoulders. "I know," she said a little arrogantly while she twisted out of his embrace and grabbed his hand.

They got in the car and headed to the movies. It was the first time she and Adin had been in a car together without him driving. It wasn't dark yet, so she and Adin could stare at each other without any intrusions. Well, *almost* any intrusions.

"What are you two doing back there?" Calli asked as she turned to look.

"Nothing," Legacy said sarcastically.

"You're being awfully quiet," her BFF teased.

"And you're not," she said, unable to suppress a laugh.

Calli turned back around and messed with the radio. Legacy went back to staring at Adin, but he had a playful look in his eyes.

She raised an eyebrow, wondering what he was thinking, but he just grinned bigger. Then he leaned over and kissed her. She realized he was doing this to irritate Calli, but Legacy had gotten so into it that she eventually forgot they weren't alone. She held him tightly to her, drinking in his hot kisses, losing herself in his exploring mouth.

Calli cleared her throat. "You two should get a room!" she chided jokingly.

Adin pulled away laughing, but Legacy was too flustered to find her friend's interruption funny.

It didn't matter because they were pulling into the

parking lot at the movie theater. Adin got out of the car, and she slid out the same door. He put his arm around her and guided her into the theater while Calli and Zach went in hand-in-hand.

When they got inside, Adin handed her some money. "Why don't you and Calli get in line at the concession stand?" It was a good idea. That line was already long.

The guys waited to buy their tickets while she and Calli stood in line to get some popcorn and drinks. While they were waiting, she heard a familiar voice coming in.

And Legacy froze.

The voice wasn't as somber as it had been recently. There was laughing and joking coming from it. She didn't even want to turn around and look. She knew it was River.

She turned to Calli to see if she'd heard him, but she was trying to look around the people in front of them to see the candy selection.

"Calli?" Legacy whispered.

"Huh?" she asked, not looking at her.

Legacy gently tugged her arm, and she turned to look at her. "River is here."

Calli's eyes got really big, and she started to speak. Legacy shook her head quickly. She didn't want her friend opening her mouth since she had no idea where he was.

Calli glanced around causally, like she was bored with standing in line. When she finished, she leaned toward Legacy. "He saw me," she murmured.

Legacy growled under her breath. This could not be happening! She and Adin hadn't talked about River since the night Adin had gotten back from his dad's. From the sound of it that night, Adin wasn't dropping the conversation, but there really hadn't been a point in bringing it back up. Until now.

It was their turn at the counter, so they quickly got their

popcorn and sodas and stepped to the side to wait for their dates.

"Where are Adin and Zach?" she asked Calli when she realized neither of them was in line at the ticket counter.

"Er, I don't know. Maybe they went to the restroom."

Not thinking, Legacy scanned the crowd to try and find Adin. Mistake. River was staring right at her, waiting for her to look for him. Their gazes met for half a second, and he started to smile, but she kept scanning the room, looking for Adin. She couldn't find him. And she sure as hell wasn't going to entertain River undressing her with his eyes.

"River just saw me," she whispered to Calli. "I was looking for Adin, so River probably thinks you told me you saw him and that I tried to find him."

"Don't be silly, Legacy."

"Calli, I told you about what happened. If Adin knows that River is here, he's going to flip!"

"Well, River does look hot. And that guy he's with, talk about ridiculous! They must be related."

Leave it to Calli to focus on their looks. "He said something about family being in from out of town," she mumbled, still looking for Adin.

"Hi, Legacy," she heard from behind, but that voice so did not belong to the man she was looking for.

Calli jumped and spun around.

Legacy slowly turned. "Hi, River."

"Wow. You look gorgeous," River said, staring at her, the longing look front and center.

"Thanks."

River shut his eyes and shook his head. "Umm..." He opened his eyes again. "This is my cousin, Paul," he introduced.

"It's nice to meet you," she said as she went back to scanning the room.

"What are you looking for?" River asked.

"Hmm?" She was still scanning the room, avoiding looking at River.

"Hey," she heard Adin say, coming from the side.

She twirled around to face him. He had a half-smile on his face, and Zach was laughing.

"He just beat me playing air hockey," Zach said as they approached. "No one's ever beaten me before."

"Really?" Legacy asked nervously. How could she get Adin away without seeing the guy beside her?

Adin noticed the tone in her voice and furrowed his eyebrows. As he stepped up to her, he finally saw River and Paul standing behind Legacy and Calli.

"Looks like every time we leave you two alone, men hit on you," Zach said as he put his arm around Calli.

"Hi, I'm River Rysaor." River introduced himself, sticking his hand out to Zach. "I live next door to Calli."

She was watching Adin's face as she heard River's voice. His expression turned to stone right in front of her. He clenched his teeth and narrowed his eyes. This was not going to be good.

"Don't," she mouthed to Adin without speaking. "Please."

He walked up to her and put his hand on her side to move her around him so that now Adin was standing in front of River.

"Oh, well, it's nice to meet you then," Zach responded.

Adin stuck his hand out to River, and she watched from behind. "Adin Sheppard," he said in a grave tone. River's eyes opened slightly wider, then narrowed.

"River Rysaor."

The two of them glared at each other and shook hands purposefully. While they were sizing each other up, Zach and Paul watched in confusion.

Adin stepped right up to River, and Legacy closed her eyes. This was not going to end well. River would be in the hospital, and they were all going to jail.

"If you don't start showing her some respect, I'm going to tear you apart," Adin said as calmly as he could manage.

"If you don't back off, you'll get your chance sooner rather than later." River wasn't calm.

Adin laughed without any humor. "It's not so much fun having someone in your face that you don't want there, is it?" He paused. "*This* is your *only* warning," he growled. He dropped River's hand and turned to her. He put his arm around her waist and kissed her forehead. He had started to lead her off when River spoke again.

"It was a pleasure meeting you," River said with heavy sarcasm.

They kept walking, but Adin turned to look at him. "The pleasure's going to be *all* mine."

Legacy was sure she wasn't the only one who caught all the meanings in that phrase! The pleasure Adin would have when he killed him. The pleasure he would have from her being all his. But at least he didn't beat River to a pulp.

They got into the movie and took their seats.

"Are you okay?" she asked Adin.

"Me? Why?" He sounded puzzled.

"Because you looked like you were about to kill River."

"I'm fine." He shrugged. "Are you okay?"

"I guess so."

"That's all that matters to me. Besides, I'm not going to let him ruin our date."

She smiled at him, and he leaned down and kissed her.

Once the movie started, it was very dark in the theater. She and Adin had their hands on each other's legs, stroking them. She couldn't say what the movie was about because she was enjoying watching his hand on her leg. By about halfway through the movie, their touches had become too much for either of them to bear. She leaned back in her seat and looked at Adin while she breathed heavily. He stared right back for a few seconds, but then he obviously couldn't take it anymore. He moved his other hand to her face and kissed her.

And they did just that throughout the rest of the movie.

When it was finally over, they stood up to leave, and at the back of the room, River and Paul were sitting there. He couldn't have had a clear view of Adin and her during the movie, but he would've had enough of a view to make out their actions. She glanced at Adin to see if he'd noticed. And because he had a smug look on his face, she knew he had. Surprisingly, River sitting back there didn't bother her. He needed a reality check.

She and Adin went to the car, but Calli stayed with Zach while he was getting a refill on his drink.

Legacy leaned against the car, staring at Adin. He put both his hands against the car on either side of her face, pressing against her. He kissed her neck and made his way up to her ear.

"I've had a wonderful time with you this evening," he whispered.

She put her hands on his waist and panted, "Me too."

Adin chuckled. He was enjoying her response more than his own actions. She couldn't allow *that*.

She turned her face so that it was right up against his, pretending she was going to kiss him. He leaned in, willing, but she leaned back. She turned her head to the other side and tilted it toward him like she was going to kiss him from a different angle. He leaned in more quickly, but she leaned back again. She grabbed his head and feigned another attempt. He tried more forcefully to follow through with it, but she grasped his head within an inch of her lips. He groaned.

"I'm going to have to separate you two," Calli said as she approached them.

Adin sighed heavily and bowed his head in defeat. Legacy giggled.

On the ride back, they all talked, though no one brought up the movie itself or the encounter with River. When they got to Adin's house, she got out with him. He wanted to take her home, so they said their goodbyes to Calli and Zach and got in Adin's car.

"Do you want to go hiking tomorrow?" Adin asked once they were on the road.

"Sure. What time?"

"Early. I want to get back before it gets too hot. I'll pick you up after breakfast."

"Okay."

Adin was quiet for several more minutes before he spoke again. "I have to go to orientation in a couple of weeks. I'll probably be at school all that week."

"All week?"

"Yeah, they have these seminars scheduled. They'll show us around campus, meet with the parents, have a banquet for the entering freshmen … those kinds of things."

"Oh. Well, I guess that's good then."

Adin glanced over at her. "I'm going to miss you. I don't like the thought of being away from you for an entire week. I hated going on vacation earlier this summer."

"I know," she whispered.

They pulled into her driveway, but Adin didn't get out of the car. He leaned over to her and put his hand on her face. His mouth twitched like he was fighting a smile.

"If I lean in to kiss you, are you going to tease me again?"

He was trying to distract her from him leaving. It was working. She smiled.

"We both know you're much better at teasing me than I am at teasing you. If Calli hadn't walked up when she did..." He paused, shaking his head.

"If Calli hadn't walked up when she did, I would have kept on teasing you until you couldn't stand it anymore." She smirked.

"I was already at that point when she walked up."

"I don't know, I think you could have taken a little more." She reached up and stroked his chest. "I think you like it when I tease you."

He didn't say anything. He just leaned over and kissed her, and she giggled into his mouth.

"I'm going to have to get better at this," he said between kisses.

"I love you just the way you are," she whispered.

Then he kissed her more sincerely.

After Adin left, she went upstairs and got ready for bed. That night, all her dreams converged. The storm clouds were there, and the snakes were all around her. She stood in the middle of the three snake holes. Adin stood at one hole, River stood at another hole, and a faceless man stood at the other. The girl stood to the side screaming at her to run, but she wanted the tornado to come for her. As it formed and almost consumed her, she yelled, "No!" and it dissipated. After it cleared, the sky turned bright pink, and lightning bolts floated down from the sky, but disappeared before they reached her.

Then a new dream started. She was in Florida at the beach, and the red warning flags were out while the storm brewed in the Gulf. Adin was with her, and he wanted them to evacuate before the hurricane hit. As they started to run, a woman appeared in front of them. She had wavy blonde hair, just like her mom, but she had a red-colored, strong-smelling kipper in her hand. She stared at them before speaking.

"Everything isn't always as it seems."

Then her wavy hair turned into snakes, falling all around her. The snakes started to come for them just as the hurricane made landfall. As the hurricane hit, it turned into River. River threw himself in front of the snakes.

"No!" he yelled, and the woman screamed so loudly that the ground trembled.

River turned to Adin and yelled, "I will tear you apart!" Then River turned back into a hurricane and started charging at Adin.

She woke up to the sound of the phone ringing. She was completely dazed by her dreams. All the old ones coming together in one, and the new dream she hadn't had before.

With her old dreams, she realized the three holes weren't literally snake holes. They represented three men. Two of which she understood. The third one, well, she had no idea who he was, but she felt like this was a love triangle. And she was wrong about wanting the tornado to come. She still wasn't scared of it, but it felt like she needed to stop it.

The new dream was so vivid because Adin had been there during a tropical storm. The red warning flags were sending her a warning, but not just about the hurricane. They were warning her about the woman. The woman looked motherly, but then turned evil. And she couldn't understand why she was holding a fish. A kipper. A herring. She gasped. A *red herring*. Something really wasn't as it seemed. But what? And why was River a hurricane? At least he wanted to stop this woman from hurting her. She understood why he wanted to protect her, but then he turned on Adin. He wanted to kill him. If he killed Adin, then she and River couldn't be together. Why would River attack Adin with deadly intentions when he believed so strongly in the prophecy?

Legacy grabbed the phone as it rang again, irritated with the disruption while she was finally getting somewhere with her dreams. "Hello?"

"Legacy, it's River."

What? He'd better have a good reason for calling her this early. Then she got even more irritated that he'd been the one to wake her up from that new dream.

"I need you to come in today. Yale had a family emergency and my mom's out of town."

Ugh. She had plans with Adin. She didn't want to cancel on him to help River. But this was her job, and she needed to keep it for a few more weeks.

"Fine. I'll be there."

"Thanks. I'm really sorry."

"It's no problem."

She hung up the phone and called Adin. Luckily, he was already awake.

"Hey, I can't go today."

"Why?"

"Because I have to work after all."

Adin was quiet for a moment. "Okay." He sounded a little sad, but at least he understood.

"I'll call you when I get off. Maybe we can do something later." She hoped that thought would cheer him up.

"I can't. I'm going out to dinner with my mom and grandma."

"Oh." They wouldn't get to see each other at all today.

"Call me when you get off work anyway, okay?"

"Sure."

She got off the phone and got ready for work. It was raining outside. The first time it had actually rained in weeks. That was good because they really needed it. But it felt prosaic, which was symbolic of her emotional state. She found out yesterday that Adin would be going away for a week, and now she wouldn't get to see him today. At least they couldn't have gone hiking in the rain anyway.

When she got to work, River was storming around the store. It looked as if he was trying to take care of something, but he was clearly irritated.

"What's going on?" she asked after putting up her stuff.

"The roof is leaking again," he mumbled as he walked past her with a ladder.

Thunder rolled outside.

"I'll go get a mop."

"No. I've already cleaned it up."

River walked up the ladder and took down the ceiling tiles. More water spilled out, and he uttered several curse words.

She went to the supply closet, got the mop, and started cleaning up the water while River examined the roof. She was looking up at River, making sure he didn't fall, and not paying attention to the mess she was cleaning. She was slinging the mop around quickly, but she was standing in the new puddle of water.

River yelled another curse word. "The handyman didn't do this right! I'm going to have to call a roofer."

The thunder got louder outside.

He climbed down and made the call while she continued cleaning up the water, stopping every few minutes to wring out the mop.

After he got off the phone, he started preparing the register for the store to open since she hadn't done it—she was still busy with the mess.

"Did you have fun last night?" he asked curtly.

Thunder crashed.

She didn't want to talk to River about that. It was none of his business. "Yes."

"I was really happy to see you until I realized who you

were with."

"You should have known," she hissed.

The rain was pounding on the roof and leaking through the ceiling back onto the floor. She continued to mop it up, but it was coming in faster than she could dry it. And River was trying to talk about Adin?

"I didn't like seeing you with him that way."

"Were you watching us?" she screeched, turning toward him.

Lightning flashed through the windows.

"It was hard not to when he was all over you like that!"

"*You* could have left!"

"*I* was entertaining family. *You* should have been more wary of your surroundings. And he thinks I need to treat you with more respect? What a joke!"

"What the hell does that mean?" she demanded.

"It means he should follow his own advice and not treat you like a conquest."

"Ugh!" she screamed.

Thunder crashed and lightning glared violently outside.

"You have no idea what my relationship with Adin is like! You're just jealous."

She was slinging the mop, sloshing the water around.

"Of course I am, but I'm not the one who's afraid to admit how I feel. That's you, baby!"

"Oh! Don't you baby *me!* I'm not your baby!"

"I guess it's a good thing I called you in today. You couldn't have gone hiking in *this* weather." He smirked.

"What? How did you know about that?" She was too mad to be as shocked as she should have been.

"I know everything," he said, glaring at her.

Oh no he didn't. "Did you set this up so I'd have to cancel my date?" she screamed.

She slung the mop into the base of some metal shelving

right when lightning struck the building.

She felt a jolt and slumped over.

She could feel water all over her face as she sprawled, unmoving, on the floor.

"Legacy?" she heard River ask frantically as she felt him pulling on her. "Legacy, please answer me."

River kept tugging her on her arm until he managed to gently turn her over. She felt his hands on her face, opening her mouth.

"Oh no ... you're not breathing. Legacy, baby, please, please."

She wasn't breathing? Then how could she hear everything he was saying to her and how could she feel the cold, wet rainwater soaking her clothes?

She felt River's lips on hers, and he forced air into her lungs. It hurt going in. Then she felt his hands on her chest, compressing against her heart. He continued to go back and forth while she heard the beeping of his cell phone.

"I need an ambulance." His voice was breaking. He was crying? He rattled off the address to the store, and then she heard his phone beep again.

"Legacy, they'll be here in a few minutes," she heard him say as he was doing chest compressions. "Damn you, Mother!" he yelled, but Legacy didn't feel the force of his words on her face, so he must be looking away from her. "I'll kill you if she dies, Medusa! Do you fucking hear me, Mom?"

As he worked to keep Legacy alive, her mind was reeling. She knew 1887 was dangerous. Adin wanted her to be careful when he told her this number in her dream, which turned out to be the address of the store. But what she hadn't thought to ask was about River's mother. Nor had she researched her specifically, but the woman was part of the Greek myths. Medusa was a monster. Legacy remembered seeing emblems with her image, but instead of hair, she had snakes around her.

As she thought of the woman in her dream, another piece of the puzzle came together. The woman in her dream last night was Ms. Gorgos. River told her there were monsters in his lineage, and she knew River's mom wanted to kill her. His words just identified that his mom was Medusa, which meant *Medusa* wanted to kill her.

And it was apparent she'd just tried.

Chapter 19

Legacy was rushed to the hospital and put in intensive care. Her life was hanging on by a thread, but she could hear and feel everything. It was as if she were completely aware of what was going on, except she was paralyzed and couldn't speak.

She heard River at her side, crying and holding her hand. From the weight of his words, she could tell he was in so much pain.

"I'm so sorry," he kept repeating over and over again.

She wanted to comfort him and tell him that everything was going to be all right, but she couldn't. And she didn't really know if everything *was* going to be all right. She didn't know if she was going to live through this. Medusa tried to kill her. She was sure of it.

She wondered where Lissa was. Surely the hospital would have contacted her. She also wondered if she'd contact Adin. Legacy knew River wouldn't. Not out of malice, but because he wouldn't leave her side. The bond he'd always talked about, she was beginning to feel it. It had always been there. When she didn't want to hurt his feelings, it was because of the bond. He was right. She was fighting it. She knew she'd have to continue fighting it because she didn't want to be with him like that. But she could no longer pretend it didn't exist.

While she lay in the hospital bed, she started to drift. She felt as if she were falling asleep, but couldn't really tell since her eyes were already shut. The voices in the room — River was one and the others were probably nurses and doctors — faded. Then she began to panic. What if she was dying?

"*You're not dying,*" a beautiful voice said. "*You are part of this earth, like me. You are changing, my beautiful Legacy. Every season is your legacy. That's why I named you that.*"

"*Mom?*" she thought to herself since she could not move her lips.

"*Yes. You will be fine. But you will need to be careful, my beautiful Legacy. River and Adin do not understand, but they will. You must be patient with them.*"

"*What do you mean?*"

"*You are changing. In some ways, you have already changed. They will not understand how you feel about the other, but fate has a plan. They will both be there for you in the end. Medusa will try to interfere with your change, but I will try to stop her. Your greatest fear is Hades. He knows. He has a plan. If he gets his way, you will not be with River or Adin. I don't want that to happen to you again.*"

"*Again?*" she wondered.

"*Yes, you are my beautiful Persephone. Not the original one because Hades drove her to the afterlife. But you are a reincarnation of her. You are a new body but an old soul. I am called many things, but I am Demeter, the goddess of nature. As you will be. When you are ready, we will watch over the seasons together.*"

"*Why can't I see you?*"

"*Because you don't remember what I really look like. You have no true memory of me. You've seen photographs, but you've seen the photographs that I wanted you to see.*"

Wow. She was really talking to her mom. Well, sort of. But she needed to try and get all the answers to the questions she had while she finally had this opportunity. "*What about my dreams?*"

"*That's your old soul trying to help you cope with everything. The little girl in your dreams is you. That's why you wanted to protect her in the beginning and that's why she was scared. You wanted to protect yourself from the unknown, and you were scared of what was coming.*"

Legacy hesitated, but her need for clarification pushed her to ask, "*Are you Pandora? You said you are Demeter.*

"*Yes. I am all things Mother Nature. What I am called is irrelevant.*

"*Did I open Pandora's Box?*"

"*Yes. It was there for a reason, and it has served its purpose. However, you should focus on what is to come and not how events started. Understand your destiny is not yet decided, but your actions will decide it for you. If you are not careful, you will repeat your original destiny and your legacy will not be fulfilled.*"

"*The prophecy? Why would I stay with River if Adin lives? I want to be with Adin.*"

"*I know, my darling. Stay strong, and you will have what you want. No matter whom you want in the end. If you do not stay strong, you will have neither. Embrace this life and live your legacy.*"

The beautiful voice faded into the blackness of her mind. It was surreal to hear her mother's voice, but hearing it helped. She knew everything she'd been told and what she'd discovered had put her on the right path. As she felt the rightness of it all settle, she could hear River's weeping more clearly now. He was alone with her, and she was okay with that.

"Legacy?" she heard Lissa call after a few minutes. She must be here now.

"She still hasn't…" River started to say, but he cried.

"Legacy, it's Lissa." Her voice was right by her, and she felt another hand on her.

"I'm Lissa Borne. I don't think we've met."

"Um, I'm River Rysaor. Legacy works at my mom's store."

"Of course."

She couldn't comprehend her tone, but her voice had definitely changed.

"Have you called her friend Calli?" Lissa asked River in a regular voice.

"No, ma'am," he choked.

Lissa seemed very calm for what was happening. Legacy figured she knew she was going to be okay, but couldn't really come out and say this to anyone. Or Lissa hoped she would be and didn't want any negative feelings to cloud those hopes.

"I'm going to call her," she said.

Legacy heard Lissa leave the room.

"Baby, can you hear me?" River whispered in her ear, stroking her face. Then she felt his head lean down onto the side of her face, and he cried into her ear. "Please … wake up."

"She's on her way," Lissa said as she heard the door open to her room.

She heard a chair pull up beside her bed next to where River was sitting.

"You have to stay positive," Lissa whispered, but not to her.

"I-I-I don't know how to be positive. I love her so much. It's hard enough not being with her, but I-I..." He starting crying again, and Legacy was shocked to hear him say that he loved her. She knew he cared about her, but this went way beyond that. River took a deep breath. "I don't want her to be hurt. I'd rather never have her and she keep on living without me than to ever see her hurting."

"You know who's responsible for this." Lissa said. It wasn't a question. Lissa knew it was River's mom.

"Yes," he hissed. "I know. She doesn't understand."

"It doesn't matter. She's not going to allow it to happen. You know that. I know you know that."

"I know. I can stop her."

"You already failed."

River started crying again. "I didn't expect it to be so soon. I thought she'd wait until Legacy got stronger."

"Your mom doesn't need to wait. In her mind, she has less than a year to take down a god, defying other gods in the process. This isn't going to be easy. She's going to take every chance she can get."

River kept stroking Legacy's hand in his. "Why does this have to be so hard?"

"Because you're not a regular human. Regular humans wouldn't be able to handle this. You're changing too. She is linked to your change. You may not realize it, but she was helping you when you thought you were helping her."

"What do you mean?" His hand stopped moving.

"I mean you have both been helping each other cope with the changes in your lives. I can't tell you if she will love you in the end. Only she will know the answer to that, and she doesn't know that answer yet. You'll have to be patient with her."

That was what Mom just told her. That she'd have to be patient with Adin and River. Apparently, they'd all have to embrace that virtue.

"I don't even want her around Adin, much less in love with him," River muttered.

"She can't stop the way she feels just like you can't. He's not your enemy. You both want Legacy safe and happy. He may not see that yet, but now you do."

She heard the door open.

"Lissa?"

It was Calli's voice.

"Oh no! Legacy?" She heard Calli run to her side, and she felt her rub her arm. "What happened?"

"She got electrocuted," River whispered.

Calli gasped, but she could tell it wasn't from the news. She must have seen River's face.

"Um, I called Adin," she said gravely. "He should be here any minute."

"Good," Lissa said. "She needs to hear his voice."

River sobbed, holding her hand up to the side of his face. "I can't leave her."

"No one's asking you to leave," Lissa said calmly.

She heard the door swing open, and the person's breath caught. No one said anything, but she heard footsteps coming around to the other side of her where no one else sat.

She felt a familiar hand on her face. It was Adin. He leaned down and put his lips to her ear. "Legacy? Sweetheart, can you hear me?" His breathing was jagged. He must have been crying before he even got here. "Please…" he cried.

Adin reached over and took her free hand. Now, he was holding one, and River was holding the other. She heard

Adin sigh. He put her hand on his face and held it there.

"Your hand is so cold," he whispered, but he was taking comfort in that. He leaned down and put his forehead onto hers. His momentary comfort disappeared.

"Legacy, please wake up," Adin pleaded through tears. "I love you so much. I need you more than anything. You *have* to be okay." After several minutes of Adin crying with his head down on hers, he finally spoke to the others, but he didn't move from his position. "What happened?"

"She was electrocuted," River whispered.

"How?"

"The storm."

"She thinks your mother controls things like that."

"I know."

"Do you think that?"

"Yes."

Even though they were being short with each other, they were keeping their voices low and trying to be civil for her.

"She should have tried to kill me instead," Adin whispered. "Not her … not her," he cried.

It seemed like the two men in the room where the only ones crying. Lissa and Calli must be sitting there watching the two of them fall apart.

She wanted to console them. Her love and her friend. They were all bonded together. But Adin wasn't the link.

She was.

If she hurt, they all hurt. If one of them was hurt, she'd be the only one suffering. It was her all along.

"She no longer works for you," Adin whispered, his head still down. It wasn't a request. It was an order.

River didn't say anything. She was sure he agreed with Adin on this.

"Excuse me, we need to examine the patient," she heard a male voice say as he entered the room. "Only her family can stay in here while they do that. It'll only take a minute."

She felt River's hand slip from hers, but Adin didn't move.

"I love you," Adin whispered in her ear, and she wanted to tell him that she loved him too. She wanted him to stay. She didn't want him to let go of her. He lifted his head from hers and placed her hand back at her side. He started to release it, but she squeezed his fingers.

"Legacy?" Adin asked frantically. "She just squeezed her hand," he said quickly, talking away from her.

"Adin…" she barely breathed, not sure if he could hear her.

He was right back at her ear. "Yes, Legacy, I'm here. We're all here."

"Don't go…"

"I'm not going anywhere," he cried, but she could hear a hint of relief in his voice.

"Adin, I'm hurting."

She heard several people gasp. Now that she was able to speak and move a little, she realized she was in excruciating pain.

"Where are you hurting, sweetheart?" Adin was panicked.

"Everywhere."

She lost the grip she had on his hand. She could no longer speak or move.

"Legacy? *Legacy!*"

"Everybody out," someone ordered.

"I'm *not* leaving!" Adin said, and from the tone of his voice, no one was going to argue with him.

"He can stay," Lissa mumbled. Since she had asked him not to go, Lissa wasn't going to make him leave. Thank the gods.

"C'mon, River," she heard Calli say.

She heard River's breathing spike, and she knew he wanted to stay too. But he left quietly.

She felt hands all over her. Adin let go of her hand, but he was right by her head, talking to her, letting her know he was right there with her.

"Why is she in pain?" he asked angrily.

"This is normal. It's actually good that she's in pain. It means she can feel. Now, we need to treat her pain. We're giving her some morphine. She'll be asleep for awhile."

The voice turned away from her, she guessed to talk to Lissa. "Now that she woke up, we're treating her pain, but the medication she'll be on will cause her to be out of it for a few days. She'll wake up here and there, but only briefly. The medication will help her pain while her body heals itself." He lowered his voice and said, "Because of who she is, it's the best way."

"Okay," Lissa murmured, and she realized the doctor was in on the family secret.

When he spoke again, he used a regular tone. "After a few days, we'll start to taper her off the medication to see where she's at in the healing process. If she's in a great deal of pain, we'll start all over again. Hopefully, her pain will be less, and we'll be able to manage it while keeping her conscious."

"So how is she?" Lissa asked.

"All her vitals are good. Her blood pressure is up, but that's probably because of the pain."

They must have given her more morphine because the next thing she remembered hearing were monitors beeping. She heard some voices in the room, and she could feel both her hands being held. She tried to open her eyes, but she couldn't.

"Ouch," she mumbled.

"Legacy?" she heard Adin ask. "Get the doctor," he

muttered.

The other person dropped her other hand and left.

She moaned again, trying to move her body.

"He's on his way," she heard River say, and he held her hand again. "Lissa's on her way back up too."

The pain was building slowly, getting more intense. "I'm really hurting."

"The doctor will be in here in a minute," Adin whispered. "Your pain medication is wearing off, and they need to check on your healing progress."

She started crying. "It hurts. It's getting worse." Was she on fire? Flames licked her all over.

"I'm sorry, sweetheart."

She felt Adin's hands on her face and River's hand stroking her arm.

Then she started screaming. The pain was unbelievable. She was burning alive.

River dropped her hand, and she heard the door open. He must have left to find out why it was taking the doctor so long.

"Legacy? You have to calm down," she heard an older man's voice say as he walked to her bed.

She tried, but she was hysterical. She just cried and cried.

"Can you open your eyes?"

She did, but they were blurry from the tears.

"Why am I hurting? It hurts all over. Adin!" she screamed, turning toward the hand he was holding again.

He put his free arm around her neck and put his head to hers. She cried uncontrollably.

"Shhhh." Adin tried to soothe her. "What are you waiting for? Please just give her the medication."

"I just did. I was afraid of this. We'll give it another try in a few days."

She whined softly as the pain lessened and she wondered

if her skin was charred.

"Try to relax, sweetheart." Adin had his hand on her face, stroking it.

Then the pain disappeared, and she fell right back to sleep.

Sometime later, she heard the monitors clearly, but didn't hear any voices again. She didn't hear anybody talking to her or each other. She didn't even hear anybody breathing.

"Hello?" she tried to say, but she couldn't even hear it herself.

She felt something in her hand. It was the same hand Adin had held, but in it was something hard, cold. She grasped it, trying to figure out what it was, but she couldn't tell.

Then she heard the door open.

"Legacy, I'm your nurse. Can you hear me?"

She mumbled.

"Good. You're under medication. There's nothing to be scared about. I'm going to call Lissa. She's here. She just stepped out for a minute. The beds aren't very comfortable."

"What-what time is it?" she whispered.

"It's two in the morning."

"Adin?"

"He left when visiting hours were over. He's been here every day, all day. So has your other friend. You have quite the little fan club." She chuckled. "I wish my boyfriend looked like either one of them, and girl, they both think you hung the moon."

She wanted Adin here. She missed his hand in hers, anchoring her to reality.

"She's awake," she heard the nurse say. "Legacy, Lissa is on her way up."

"'Ka-a-ay.'"

She felt like she was falling back to sleep, but she heard

the door open again. "Legacy?"

"Hmm?"

"It's Lissa. How are you feeling?"

"Tired."

"That's good. You need your rest."

"I want Adin."

"I know, honey. He's been here, and he'll be back in the morning."

"No … call him, please."

"I'm doing that now. He asked me to call if you woke up."

She started to fall back asleep, but she heard Lissa mumble on the phone.

"She's awake, and she's asking for you." A pause. "Yes." She walked back over and put her hand on Legacy's. "Legacy, he's coming up here right now. You can go back to sleep."

She must have because the next thing she felt was Adin's hand in hers.

"Adin?"

"Yes, sweetheart. I'm here."

"What time is it?"

"It's about ten in the morning."

"Did you come?" He obviously had come at some point, but several hours had felt like seconds to her.

"I've been here since Lissa called me last night."

She tried to lift the hand he wasn't holding so she could touch his face, but someone else had it.

"Who's over there?"

"River. He's been here every day, too. So have Calli and Lissa. Olive has visited you, too, and so did my mom. Everyone's been so worried about you."

"Every day? How long?" She wanted to ask how long she'd been here, but she didn't have the strength to finish.

"You've been here six days. They did two rounds of heavy medication. This is the second time they've tried weaning you off. Do you remember the first time?"

"I remember hurting, and I remember screaming."

"You did," Adin whispered. "You were in a lot of pain. It was very hard for me — for us — to watch you hurting like that. Are you in any pain now?" he asked softly.

"A little. I still feel very tired."

She felt Adin move and fidget with something on her bed. Then she heard the intercom.

"Yes?"

"She's awake and hurting. Can you send in the doctor?" Adin asked.

"He'll be right in."

"You need to rest," Adin said to her. "Your body is healing, but you seem to be doing much better this time. They'll give you some more medicine after the doctor examines you, but it won't be as much as before."

"Okay," she said, a little strangled.

"How do you feel?" Adin asked while River stroked her arm.

"Like I got hit by a train." She grimaced.

She heard the door open. Her eyes were still closed.

"Legacy, I'm Dr. Sutherland. How are you feeling?"

"Not good. It hurts to move."

"We're going to put you on a morphine pump now, so you can disburse the medicine when you need it. You're still going to feel pretty tired. I want you to sleep as much as you want today, but when you're awake, try to stretch out in the bed. Tomorrow, we're going to try and get you up and around. Depending on how well you do tomorrow, you may be able to go home in the afternoon."

"Okay."

"Can you open your eyes for me?"

She opened them slowly, but squinted. The light in the room was too bright. The doctor turned off the overhead light, and she was able to open her eyes a little more. Then he took his light and looked into each of her eyes. Her eyes felt puffy and sore, like she'd spent the day watching sad movies.

He continued examining her, so she turned her head and looked at Adin for the first time. His eyes were red and swollen too. But he looked like he had been crying for days. He looked so tired and weak.

"You look sad," she whispered to Adin as she faintly rubbed her thumb on the side of his hand.

He sighed, and fresh tears formed. "It's been a long week," he breathed.

She tried to smile at him. "I'm sorry you had to go through this." And she was sorry. She didn't want him hurting, no matter how much pain she was in.

He smiled, but his eyes were still gloomy. "I'm sorry I couldn't take your place." His tears spilled over.

The doctor rubbed her shoulder and that hurt. "Do you know what happened to you?"

"Um, I remember being at work. The roof was leaking, and I was mopping." She turned her head to look at River. He looked just as bad as Adin did. She sighed and looked at the doctor. "Then I remember being here and screaming."

She remembered more than that. She remembered everything, but she didn't want River to hurt anymore than he should. She could tell he had beaten himself up enough already over their fight and his mother's involvement. And Adin was apparently trying to be understanding of River and let him stay, so she didn't want Adin to know about the fight she and River had been having when the lightning struck. Adin's leniency would vanish, and even though he looked as if he could barely stand, he'd probably find enough strength to throw River right out of the room with his bare hands.

"You were struck by lightning. You're very lucky," the doctor continued.

She nodded slowly.

"Hit the call button if you need anything," the doctor said as he and the nurse vacated.

She yawned.

"You should try to go back to sleep," Adin whispered.

And she did. She slept peacefully with both her hands being held. She didn't dream or feel any pain. She was happy to have both Adin and River there with her. She didn't like the fact that she wanted River there, but she didn't argue with herself. She didn't have the strength to fight off the bond that was there. She was just glad Adin swallowed his pride and allowed River to comfort her too. She woke up sometime later and heard Adin and River whispering.

"I'm not saying I don't believe you," Adin said. "What I am saying is you're done."

"I won't allow that."

"You don't have a choice."

"Neither does she."

She heard enough to understand what the topic of their conversation was — her.

"Stop fighting," she breathed as she turned her head to Adin and opened her eyes.

He straightened in his chair, stroked her head, and looked at her apologetically. "I'm sorry. We didn't mean to wake you."

"You didn't." She looked over at River. "Be nice."

"I'm sorry," he mumbled.

She looked at the ceiling and slipped both her hands from theirs.

"What are you doing?" Adin asked.

She didn't say anything, she just stretched her arms over her head, stretching her back and pointing her toes. She winced.

"Okay, that's good," Adin said.

"No." She shook her head. "How do I get the bed up?"

"Here're the controls. This one's up, and this one's down. Just be careful."

Adin and River both stood up and watched her face as she set the bed in a more upright position, leaving it slightly reclined. She winced a few times, and they both put hands on her shoulders. She took a deep breath.

"Adin, I can barely lift my legs."

"That's because you're still sedated. You're not supposed to get up right now."

"I'm not trying to get up. Can you just move my legs around for me?"

"Sure," he whispered.

Adin stuck his hands under her blanket and lightly grabbed her ankle with one hand and put his other hand under her knee. He moved her leg back and forth and around in circles. Then he did the other leg. "Is that good?"

"Yes, thank you." She yawned and blinked, but didn't open her eyes again.

"Legacy?" River asked.

She heard him, but didn't have the strength to answer.

"Don't," Adin said. "Let her sleep."

"Do you think we should put the bed back down?"

She wanted to stay just like this. She felt like she hadn't moved since she'd been here, and this new position was wonderful.

"No. Just leave her be," Adin told him.

Good. Adin knew what she wanted. Then she fell completely under.

The next day came quickly. As she opened her eyes,

Adin and River were there with Lissa and Calli. She was asleep every time Lissa and Calli had been in yesterday, so she was happy they were there when she woke up this time.

She saw Lissa standing beside Adin with a determined look in her eyes. Right. She remembered she had to get out of bed today, and it seemed as if Lissa was thinking there was no time like the present.

"Legacy, how do you feel?" Lissa asked.

"Better."

"Good. We need to get you up and move you around. Are you ready to try?"

"Sure."

The bed was still in the same position she put it in yesterday, so she only had to move a little to sit up completely. Adin and River had their hands behind her shoulders in case she slipped back. Adin put the arm rail down so she could slide out.

"Calli, make sure I'm not flashing everyone. Okay?" she tried to joke, but was too weak to laugh.

"Of course," she said with a smile. She came to her side and made sure her gown was securely fastened. Adin wasn't watching her, and she knew River wouldn't watch either.

After she was done, Adin stood right in front of her. He put one arm around her back and the other on her waist, and he gently pulled her out of the bed while she struggled to push. Once her feet were on the floor, she held onto his arms. She felt woozy, but tried to take a step. She stumbled slightly, and Adin grasped her tighter. She heard someone rushing around the bed.

"I've got her," Adin said curtly.

She looked over, and River looked panicked.

"I'm fine," she assured him. "I'm just dizzy."

River nodded and sadly stepped away. He didn't go back to his spot, though. He stayed far enough away to give her some privacy, but close enough he could probably reach her if Adin's grip slipped.

Calli followed them with the I.V. stand while she took the first few steps. After a few more steps, she was doing better. She had been watching her feet, but she felt comfortable enough to lift her head. She looked at Adin's face, and he was watching her feet as she walked. They started to make a circle back to the bed, and he glanced at her face, probably to make sure she wasn't hiding any pain. When his gaze met hers, she smiled.

"Does this count as dancing?" she joked.

Adin almost laughed, but with the condition she was in, he wasn't going to. "I'd be holding you much closer if we were dancing," he murmured.

She loosened her grip on his arms and slid her hands up to the tops of his shoulders. She wanted to wrap them around his neck, but she knew she couldn't stretch up on her toes, and there was too much space between them for her to reach anyway.

As they circled the room, she saw a lot of flowers. One table had many different arrangements, and another table had several different vases filled with a dozen roses in each. There wasn't just one color of roses either. Each of the rose arrangements contained a dozen roses dedicated to just one color. There were a dozen red roses, a dozen white roses, and several other dozens of other colors. She smiled and sighed.

Adin froze and looked at her face. When he saw that she didn't sigh in pain, he relaxed. "What are you smiling about?"

"All the flowers."

"Oh." He smiled back, and they started walking again.

"Who are they from?" she wondered. Though, she had a pretty good idea who brought the roses.

"Everybody in here. My mom, Lissa's co-workers, and Ellen and Kate sent you some too."

She glanced over at Calli, and she shrugged. Legacy should have known Ellen would use her near-death experience as an opportunity to kiss up.

"How many roses are over there?" she whispered. She didn't want to include everyone in the room. It felt too personal.

"Seven dozen," Adin whispered. "One for each day. I didn't want to throw out the old ones. I remembered the last time I tried to do that."

She chuckled, and he smiled.

"I remember when you gave me a bouquet of colorful roses. Do you know what each of these colors represents?" she asked, glancing back at the full table.

"Umm, yeah." He looked at the table and described them from left to right. "Peach is for innocence and purity. Pink is for elegance and grace. The purple ones identify love at first sight. Yellow is for familiar love and everlasting joy. White is for everlasting love. Orange represents the fire of passion and desire. And red is for true love—those are my favorite to give to you," Adin murmured.

"Wow," she whispered. "I'm not sure if I can remember all that."

"You don't have to. I explained each one in the cards attached to them," he said, glancing back at her. He smiled, but it didn't reach his eyes.

Once they made the circle back to the bed, she hesitated.

"I think that's good," Adin said.

He stepped closer to her to help her back in the bed, and she slid her hands off his shoulders to the tops of his arms. But instead of taking her hands off him to grasp the mattress, she wrapped her arms around him, laid her head on his chest, and weakly hugged him. His breathing changed as he gently wrapped his arms around her back and barely squeezed. He held her gingerly for several seconds before kissing her on top of her head.

"I love you," he murmured.

And she knew that his love was all she would ever need.

Chapter
20

Since Lissa's SUV was too tall for her to comfortably climb into, Adin drove her home from the hospital that night. He held her hand and watched her more than he watched the road. He didn't speak. She figured he was hoping she'd sleep since he'd walked her all around the hospital before she was released.

She didn't sleep, though. She thought about everything that had happened over the week. How she'd gotten hurt and the things she'd heard in the hospital—things from her mom, Lissa, and River. She needed to tell Adin, but she was worried how he'd take everything. Mainly, she was concerned about his reaction to River. Adin seemed civil in the hospital, but now that she was out, she wasn't sure if he'd tolerate River coming around.

Once they got to her house, Adin walked her in and up to her bedroom. Lissa had already arrived and turned down her bed. She was in the kitchen on the phone giving someone an update on Legacy's condition.

Adin helped her into bed and tucked the covers around her—she was glad Lissa had brought pajamas for her to come home in. He pulled her desk chair up to her bed and sat right by her, holding her hand. She felt as if she was about to fall asleep, but Adin looked almost zombielike.

"You don't look like you've slept at all over the last week," she mumbled.

"I haven't really," he whispered, rubbing the back of his other hand on her cheek.

"You can't watch me twenty-four hours a day."

"Don't worry about me. I'll be fine."

"You need to get some sleep."

"I'm not leaving you. Please don't ask me to do that."

"I'm not." She hesitated. "Why don't you lie down with me?"

Adin caught his breath and stared at her. "Um, I don't want to hurt you. I'll be fine."

"You won't hurt me. I want you to get some sleep, and I'll sleep better with you beside me. Please?" she breathed, shutting her eyes and feeling some tears starting to form.

Adin tilted his head and rubbed the back of his neck, deciding. Then he let go of her hand and walked around her bed. He climbed in and, staying on top of the covers, propped himself up on his side to face her. It felt like he was being very careful not to touch her. She turned her head to face him and he smiled.

"Now, go to sleep, please," Adin insisted.

She took the arm that was pinned to his side and pulled

it over to rest on her waist. Adin relaxed and scooted over so that he was right up against her side. She lifted her head while she reached over and grabbed the arm his head was propped up on and slid it under her head. Now his arms were around her, his head on the pillow, and his face right in front of hers.

"That's better," she whispered. "I've missed you."

Adin's breathing became hitched, and he began to cry. Once he started crying, he looked away and took some breaths to try to stop, but his tears flowed. "I ... was ... so ... scared," he said very slowly and gently hugged her closer.

"I know." She reached up and stroked his face while the tears that formed in her eyes started to spill over. He was hurting because she was hurting, and now she was hurting because he was.

Adin took a deep breath, but it was jagged. "Please try to go to sleep." His voice was still thick with sadness as he leaned his forehead against hers.

They needed to comfort each other before either of them would fall asleep, and she knew how she wanted to do that.

"Will you kiss me goodnight?"

Adin's eyes opened wider as he stared into hers. She guessed he was trying to read her to see if that was what she really wanted. If so, he got the answer he was looking for. He leaned his head over and gently touched his lips to hers.

Adin kissed her softly, but it was too much. She started to cry, and he tried to pull away. She assumed he thought he was hurting her. He wasn't. She turned on her side so she was completely facing him — not just her head — threw her arm around his back, and clutched him to her as strongly as she could, though she was still weak.

He kissed her passionately, but they both cried. She knew he'd been so upset, so worried over the last week, but he tried to stay strong for her. Now that she was safely home, he could let himself grieve for what she'd gone through, for what he'd gone through with her.

They fell asleep in each other's arms, and it was the best she'd ever slept. She didn't dream. She didn't toss or turn. She woke up in the same position she'd been in when she fell asleep.

When Legacy opened her eyes, she saw a blanket covering Adin. She figured Lissa covered him up after they'd fallen asleep. She was glad Lissa hadn't made him get up. She was probably pleased, too, that he was sleeping.

Legacy wasn't sure if Adin was still asleep when she woke, so she shifted slightly — trying not to disturb him — to see how much pain she was in today. When she did, Adin lifted the arm he had wrapped over her, and she looked up.

"How long have you been awake?" she asked.

"About fifteen minutes."

"How did you sleep?"

"I got to hold you all night," he whispered while he stroked her hair. "It was the first time in my life that I've ever felt whole. I'm sad because of the circumstances, but it was still wonderful to be able to be with you like that."

He looked better, so he wasn't just saying that. He looked like he'd slept all night too. After an emotional week, they both needed last night to heal their souls.

"How are you feeling?" he asked.

"A little sore. Kinda achy. But the stabbing pain seems to be gone."

"Good." Adin smiled. "We need to get you up and around."

"Yeah, I need to brush my teeth," she said, making a face.

Adin chuckled. That was the first time she'd heard him laugh since their double date. It put a smile on her face.

He helped her to the bathroom, and she gave him one

of the spare toothbrushes from the dentist's office. He kept one arm around her while they brushed their teeth. He obviously didn't want to take any chances with her falling.

Then she realized it wasn't just her teeth that needed cleaning.

"Can you see if Lissa is here?"

"We can walk down together and see."

"I know, but I want to take a shower. It has been a week, and I feel sort of gross."

"Lissa and Calli took care of you in the hospital."

"But I'll feel better after showering."

"I don't think that's a good idea," Adin said softly while stroking her cheek. "You don't need to be standing alone in a slippery bathtub."

"Lissa can stay in here while I shower."

Adin shook his head slowly and frowned. "I think it's too dangerous in your condition."

"Well, I can take a bath then. I can't fall if I'm already sitting down."

"I guess that's true," he said reluctantly. "I'll see if she's here. Do you want to stay in here, or do you want me to help you back to your bedroom?"

"Here."

She stepped over to the bathtub, and Adin helped her ease onto the side of it. He went downstairs, and a minute later she heard two sets of footsteps coming back up the stairs. She figured Lissa must be here, so Legacy turned on the water so that it could start to get warm. Then she heard someone running up the stairs.

"Legacy!"

The bathroom door was open, so Adin ran in.

"What?"

He saw her sitting on the bathtub where he left her, but with her hand under the water faucet, gauging the temperature.

He shook his head but sighed. She guessed he thought she was going to try to get in without any help.

"How are you feeling, Legacy?" Lissa asked as she walked into the bathroom.

"Better. I'm still sore, and I want to take a shower." She saw Adin's face and corrected herself. "I mean a bath."

"Okay. Take one of these, so it can get into your system." Lissa handed her a pain pill. "I'll go get you a change of clothes." She left, and Legacy took the pill.

Adin stood against the counter watching her. "Please be very careful while you're in there."

She wasn't so out of it that she'd completely lost her playfulness. "Hmm … you wouldn't let me get hurt. You could always take one with me."

Adin chuckled, which was what she was hoping for. "You should have suggested that *before* I got Lissa."

She laughed, and it felt good.

"What are you two laughing about?" Lissa asked as she came back into the bathroom with some clean pajamas.

"Oh, nothing," Legacy said.

Adin left her alone with Lissa while she bathed, but she did turn the shower on while she washed her hair. No way was she washing it with dirty bath water.

Once she was out and dressed, Adin came back in and helped her get down the stairs. He already had some pillows and blankets ready on the couch. By the time she got comfortable, her medicine had kicked in.

She fell asleep and was out at least a couple of hours. When she opened her eyes, Adin was sitting at the foot of the couch with her feet in his lap. He was in different clothes.

"Did you leave?"

"Yeah, I went to my grandma's and showered after you fell back asleep and before Lissa went to work. She knew I'd be staying here all day, so she went to the office to catch up on a few things. She made some muffins before she left. Are you hungry?"

"A little."

Adin went to the kitchen and brought them back some muffins and milk.

"I talked to Calli. She'll be over here in about an hour."

"Okay," she said as she took a bite of her muffin.

"River is probably coming with her," he mumbled.

She wondered if she should talk to Adin about River now. She had a lot to say about him and her mom. She figured she should start out slow and see how it went from there.

"Was he there the whole time?" she asked, looking down at her food.

"Most of the time. Yes. We were both there all day during visiting hours. We had to leave at night, but Lissa stayed with you. It was very hard for me to leave you at night, but Lissa promised me she'd call if you woke up or if there were any problems."

"But they let you in when she called you that night I woke up."

"Yes. They didn't have a choice." And from the sound of his voice, she knew he was right. He wasn't going to let anyone keep him from her when she asked for him.

"What all was said when I was unconscious?" she asked as she finished her muffin.

Adin sighed. "Um, I asked River what happened, and he said you were mopping when you got electrocuted."

She knew this already. "What did you two say about me?"

Adin exhaled heavily and looked up at the ceiling. "I told him you no longer work at the store." He paused and looked at her. "You don't."

She nodded. She heard the order when he originally gave it. "I meant what was said after I woke up and they gave me the medicine." When she was asleep and didn't actually hear the conversations going on.

"We talked about a lot of things. After you woke up on that first day and they sedated you," Adin hesitated and then whispered, "I could tell River wasn't going to leave. I was too distraught to force him out of there. He just wanted you to be well, so I let him stay."

"Thank you for not asking him to leave," she mumbled.

"I didn't want him there. I didn't want him holding your hand and touching you. But I knew it wasn't about me. It was about you and doing whatever was necessary for you to feel comforted."

"What else was said?"

Adin sighed and took her plate from her to set it on the table. When he sat back down, he gently rubbed her feet while he spoke.

"We talked about my feelings for you, his feelings for you, and his mother."

She could tell Adin didn't want to go into the specifics, so she just nodded. She knew she needed to come clean.

"Adin, did River tell you anything else besides the fact that I was mopping when I got hurt?"

"No. Why?" Adin looked concerned, not suspicious.

"Because I remember everything up until the doctors knocked me out."

"What do you mean?" ·

"I could hear voices and feel touches, but my body didn't recognize any pain until I woke up in the hospital. I remember hearing River freak out. He said I wasn't breathing. He performed CPR and called for an ambulance. I remember him sitting with me, crying," she whispered. "I heard Lissa come in, then Calli, then you. I heard what you whispered in my ear. I felt your head on my head and heard you ask what happened to me. Then the doctors came in and asked everyone to leave, but I didn't want you to go," she mumbled. "So I was finally able to break through that state I was in and squeeze your fingers."

"Legacy!" Adin looked shocked. "Do you remember anything else?"

"Yes. My mom came to me and talked to me." She told Adin everything her mother said, even the stuff about River.

"Wow. I don't know what to say."

"I understand if you don't believe me."

"It's not that I don't believe you, Legacy. This is just a lot to take in."

"Yeah, I'm going to have to be careful like you told me."

"So your mom thinks you're bonded to River too?" Adin asked softly.

"I *am* bonded to him," she murmured, looking down. "He once told me that the three of us were bonded together, and he thought you were that link since the prophecy is dependent on your life. But I think he's wrong. I think I'm the link that bonds us all together. When I was in the hospital bed with the two of you holding my hands, I could feel how much pain you two were in. I wanted to comfort you both."

"He's in love with you."

"I know. He's just a friend to me, but I can't deny the fact we're connected."

Adin's eyes looked sad, and she hated being the reason for that. Then he looked puzzled. "Why did you ask me if River told me anything else about your electrocution?"

Uh-oh. "I'll tell you if you promise me you'll try to stay calm."

"What did he do?" Adin asked, saying each word distinctly.

"We were fighting when I got hurt."

"That's why he kept apologizing. After he confessed about his mom, I assumed he was apologizing for her. What were you two fighting about?"

"You."

"What about me?"

"Well, River was angry when I got to work, and I thought it was because the roof was leaking again. He was short with me up until he called a roofer. Then he asked me about our double date. He didn't like seeing us together."

"He doesn't have to like it," Adin spat.

"I know, and I told him something to that effect. He said you had some nerve telling him to respect me when you treat me like a *conquest*."

"Hmph! Our relationship is *none* of his business."

"I agree. We were yelling about all this when it was storming, and then he said something about the weather wasn't good for hiking anyway. I knew I hadn't said anything to him about our plans, so I asked him how he knew about that. He said he knew everything. I screamed at him, asking if he'd called me in to ruin my plans with you, and that was when lightning hit the building."

"He told me about bringing up our hiking plans with you. He said he'd heard about it from his mother. He was worried she would try to attack you in the woods, so he got away and called Yale to give her the day off. But after your accident, I think he feels like that was his mother's plan all along … that she purposely fed him that information to get you to the store."

"Oh." Knowing he did it to protect her made her feel better than thinking he did it to keep her away from Adin. Even if River's plan had backfired.

"But he did *not* tell me you two were fighting when this came up. Nor did he tell me he was angry with you because of our relationship."

"Don't be mad at him. You saw him at the hospital. He has suffered enough."

"Legacy, I'm not tolerating him. It's one thing if he's a friend of yours who's looking out for your best interest. It's a completely different thing if he's a guy trying to befriend you so that he can be with you."

"I know. I understand how you feel, and I'll agree to not working at the store and to taking other steps you feel are necessary for my safety. But River isn't out to hurt me, and I don't want to treat him like he is."

"You may think he's not out to hurt you, but he *is* out to hurt me. That's what'll happen if he succeeds in taking you away. You letting him stay in your life is just inviting that possibility."

"Adin, I want to be with you. I don't have any romantic feelings for him at all."

"Not yet," he whispered.

"I *need* him in my life."

Adin sighed and shut his eyes. "You know I really don't like this."

"I know, and I know my friendship with him hurts you. I'm sorry about that. I wish it didn't. I wish you understood my connection with him just like I wish he understood my connection with you. You are my love; he is my friend. But I need you both."

"I'll do this. For you. I'm not going to like it, and I'm not going to pretend that I do. I don't want him to be a constant focus of our lives. If he steps over the line, then I'm going to put him in his place."

"I can live with that." She smiled.

The doorbell rang, and Adin got up to go get it. It was Calli and River. They both came in and sat in the living room across from her and Adin. They all talked, but Adin and River's conversations were strained. Neither one liked the other being there. She'd have to get used to this. But first, she needed to clear the air with River.

"Adin, can you and Calli excuse us for a minute? I'd like to have a word alone with River."

Adin flashed narrowed eyes at River and looked quickly at her. "Of course," he murmured. Then he got up and kissed her forehead. River started to get up, and Adin shot him a look.

"You're fine over there," Adin said brusquely.

River glared at him but sat back down. Once she and River were alone, his eyes softened. "I've been so worried about you."

"I know, and I know you feel guilty for what happened to me, but it wasn't your fault. I don't want you carrying the blame for this."

"That's easier said than done," he whispered.

"River, I talked to Adin. I told him what happened at the store. Of course he doesn't want us to be friends. Last I heard from you on the topic of friendship was that you didn't want to be my friend anymore either."

"Legacy..."

"No, let me finish. I know you've been hurting because of my relationship with Adin, and I am sorry about that. But I am in love with him. You have to understand that. If you can understand that *and* respect my decision, then I'd really like it if we could be friends again." She looked down at her hands. "I'm not going to deny that we're bonded together. If you weren't my friend, that'd be very painful for me," she whispered.

River's breath caught. "I-I can try. That's all I can promise."

"That's all I can ask for," she said, hesitating. "Adin understands the need I have to be your friend, and he's not going to interfere with my choice. But he's also not going to stand by and watch you try to take me away from him. You have to understand that too."

"I do. I would feel the same way."

"If you understand the boundaries, then I think he'll play nice. But you have to show him *you* can play nice first. You haven't done a good job of that so far."

"I know. I'll try. It's just very hard because—"

"You don't have to say it," she interrupted. "I know how you feel," she murmured.

River took a deep breath. "Okay."

They sat quietly for a while, staring at each other from across the room. River looked like he wanted to say something, but she couldn't be sure. He shifted in his seat and ran his hand through his unkempt hair before clasping his hands together in front of him.

"Legacy, I am so sorry," he said, gazing into her eyes.

"I told you it wasn't your fault. I don't want you carrying around the blame for what happened to me."

"But I am sorry. I'm sorry about my mom. I've tried to explain to her, but she doesn't understand. And I'm so very sorry about fighting with you."

"River, what did you tell Adin about your mom?"

"The truth. I told him everything I've told you."

"But you haven't told me everything. You never mentioned she's Medusa."

River's mouth opened wide, and he gasped while he shook his head. "How did you find out?"

"I heard you cursing her to the fiery pits of hell when calling the paramedics."

"What do you mean you heard me calling the paramedics?"

"I was able to hear and feel touches, but I couldn't feel the pain until I woke up at the hospital. I'm not sure why, but I heard everything you said to me at the store and in the hospital up until that point." She paused, and he stared at her. She didn't want to go into the details, so she finished her previous thought. "Anyway, besides the colorful words you used, I remembered you saying something about monsters in your family, and you warned me that your mother was evil."

"I didn't want you to know who she was," he said sheepishly.

"Well, next time, make sure I'm unconscious." He gave her an incredulous look, and she smirked. "But is she really Medusa or a likeness of her?"

"She's Medusa, but not the original one. She has most of *the* Medusa's original qualities with some added abilities, but since she was the first new god to be so close to the original, she was bequeathed the original name. The first Medusa was beheaded and had two children with Poseidon. Pegasus and Chrysaor."

"Chrysaor?" That sounded just like his last name.

"Yes. I'm of his likeness. My mom created me with Poseidon, like the original Medusa did to create Chrysaor because Poseidon shares power over the world with Zeus and Hades. Zeus rules the sky and air. Hades rules the underworld. Poseidon rules the waters."

"I had a dream you turned into a hurricane," she mumbled. At least that part now made sense.

River became somber. "I guess now you know everything about me," he said sadly. He obviously didn't want her to know his mother was a real monster. He looked depressed, ashamed, and she wanted to console her friend.

"Can you do one thing for me?"

"What is it?" he asked, looking down.

"Can you give me a hug?"

"I'd love to," he whispered. Then he walked over to her,

dropped to his knees, and wrapped his arms around her.

She held him for a few seconds before she spoke.

"I don't think you're a monster," she whispered.

"I can't be so sure. I feel like I'm turning into one, and I don't know how to stop it," he breathed into her hair.

"I'll help you. We have to help each other."

River squeezed her tightly. "I love you," he whispered.

"I know," she said as she rubbed his back. Then she recalled part of her conversation with her mother that she should tell him about. "I have to tell you something about Hades," she whispered.

River pulled away. "What about him?" His tone was fierce.

"He knows. My mom came to me while I was in the hospital … when I was unconscious. She told me Hades knew about me, and he has a plan."

"I will *not* let him get to you!"

"I know you won't." And in that moment, she honestly believed she had both River and Adin to watch over and protect her.

But as she looked into River's eyes, she had a feeling Hades and Medusa weren't the only things she was going to need protection from.

Chapter 21

After a week of house rest, Legacy was back to her old self. Well, she would never be the same after her hospital stay, but at least now she could get around without hands being all over her. And that was a good thing. Adin's orientation was coming up, and he was using her as his excuse not to go. This discussion was the cause of their first argument since she'd gotten home from the hospital.

"I can skip it," he insisted.

She didn't want him to go, but she knew he needed to. At least he couldn't use her condition as an excuse to stay. "You can't. You have to go. I'll be fine."

"No. I'm not leaving you!"

"Adin, you have to get ready for your classes. You need to go." She'd have to try a different angle since this one wasn't working. "Calli and I will be shopping most of the time anyway. You *know* she wants to get the latest fashion for the start of her senior year." She chuckled, but he didn't laugh.

"Legacy, please don't argue with me on this."

"Adin, I know you're scared to leave me. But you're going to have to get ready for college. I'm going to be worried about you, too, so if you don't go and get prepared, I'll just be more worried than I'll already be."

He groaned, shaking his head in irritation. "Fine. I'll go, but I'm only participating in what I have to. I'll try to come back some of the evenings, but even if I can't, I'll get to come back early since I don't have to go to the freshmen banquet."

"Are you sure you don't want to go to that. You might meet some new friends." She looked down. "You could always take your girlfriend with you."

Adin put his finger under her chin and lifted her head until she met his gaze. His eyes were bright. "Do you want to go?"

"Yes. We haven't gone out since before I got hurt. It'd be nice to get dressed up for you again."

He wrapped his arms around her and kissed her. It was settled.

After Adin left for orientation, Calli's attention went into overdrive. She was with her practically every day and every night. She'd stayed over with Legacy since Adin didn't want her by River's house. He used the excuse of River's mom, but she knew that wasn't the *only* reason.

Since it was raining most of the week, they stayed inside most of the time. If they went out, it was to go shopping, so they were still technically indoors.

She and Calli had talked about a lot of things. Legacy

had brought her up to speed on the conversation with her mother, and Calli had been supportive. They'd also talked about Zach. Calli felt as if their relationship had stalled, but she still enjoyed hanging out with him.

Calli had even talked her into going to the Summer Set Festival. Their town had a celebration every year at the end of summer. Legacy didn't really feel like going because Adin wouldn't be back in time, but she reluctantly agreed.

During the few times Calli hadn't monopolized her time, River had come over to visit. He tried to be the friend he was in the beginning. He wasn't letting his feelings for her overpower him like he had been doing before her accident. It was nice to be able to talk to him again without worrying about playing defense to his offensive maneuvers.

On Thursday, River came over and they watched a movie.

"Calli wants me to go to the festival tomorrow," she said with a shrug.

"That's a good idea. You need to get out of the house."

"Yeah. If you're not doing anything, you should come too."

His eyes sparkled. "I'm not doing anything."

"Good." She smiled.

They went back to watching the movie and chatting during the boring parts. River stayed until Calli came over. It was beginning to feel like Legacy was being babysat, but she *did* enjoy the company.

Calli spent the night again, but this night was different than the ones she'd had over the last couple of weeks.

Ever since she'd gotten hurt, she hadn't had another dream. Not even an inkling of one that she just couldn't remember. But tonight, she dreamed the same dreams she'd had the night of her double date. All her old dreams were merged into one. The tornado was coming. She yelled at it, but wasn't scared. The girl was there ... that was her. She stood in the triangle of holes, and then she and Adin were on the beach, standing in front of Medusa holding a red herring. Finally, River came charging toward her as a hurricane. Nothing new. All the elements were exactly the same as that night.

She woke up wondering why she dreamed again after all this time and why that dream was exactly the same. She had no answers, but she was obviously missing something.

Calli woke up and saw her sitting in the bed.

"What are you doing?"

"I had another dream," she said, looking at her.

"What about?"

Legacy told her every detail of the dream while she listened and watched her expressions in silence. She explained to Calli who River was so she would understand the significance of the hurricane. She'd already told her about Medusa when she explained the conversation she'd had with her mother.

"That's really weird."

"Yep. I'm not sure what to make of it." She shrugged.

After they contemplated it for a while, they got dressed and headed to the festival. It was still raining outside, but they went anyway. River met them there, and they walked around and ate junk food and played games under the tarps, staying dry. It was nice being there with her two best friends. River was definitely a best friend to her now. He was the one who helped her through all her questions and confusions. She knew she could turn to him for anything. Just like she could with Calli. She was happy to have him as a friend and very happy he was trying to be that friend to her.

After she downed several lemonades, River walked them to the restroom. Calli, being the female best friend, knew it was her obligation to come along.

"Where's Zach?" Legacy asked once they were alone. She wondered why he hadn't come along, but she didn't want to ask in front of River. Even though they were both her best friends, they were still getting to know each other.

"He's been out of town. He'll be back later today, so we'll meet up later," she said as they dried their hands.

"Oh, okay."

They walked out of the restroom just as it started to thunder and headed toward the bench where they'd left River. He wasn't there.

"Um, where'd River go?" Calli asked as more thunder sounded.

"I don't know. Maybe he went to the restroom too."

They waited a few minutes, but he still didn't show. They started walking away from the restroom, and then they saw him.

He was with Adin.

She felt a thrill run through her since she hadn't expected Adin to be back until tomorrow. She walked faster toward him.

But as they neared, it was apparent by their stances that River and Adin were fighting. As Legacy and Calli got closer, she could make out what they were saying.

"You shouldn't have told her!" Adin growled.

"It doesn't matter to you. It's really none of *your* business," River retorted.

"*She* is my business."

"Then maybe *you* should be honest with her!"

They finally made it over to Adin and River. "What the hell is going on?" she demanded.

They both looked shocked that she'd caught them.

"We're just having a disagreement," Adin said, walking over to put his arms around her.

She pushed him back. "No! Tell me what you were talking about."

"Legacy, we can discuss this later."

She knew Adin didn't want to talk to her about this in front of River. "Then what are you doing back already?" She was happy to see him, but her question came out as an accusation.

"We finished up early," Adin whispered. "I found out yesterday that we'd only have one seminar this morning and I'd be free to come home, so I wanted to surprise you. When you weren't home, I called Lissa and she said you'd come here."

His words softened her anger, and the original thrill was back. She put her arms around him and hugged him tightly. "I'm sorry. I've missed you so much."

"I missed you too," Adin said as he kissed the top of her head.

After Adin released her, keeping one hand, River stepped over to her. "I'm going to go ahead and leave."

"No, River. You can stay."

River glanced at Adin. "I can't." He turned and walked away from her.

"River, wait!" she called for him, but he didn't turn around.

She let go of Adin's hand and started to follow him, but Adin grabbed her arm. "Legacy, what are you doing?"

"I'm going to talk to him. I'll be right back."

Adin dropped her arm, and she ran to catch up to River. By the time she reached him, Adin could still see them, but they were too far away for him to hear.

"River?"

River turned around and faced her. "What?"

"Why are you leaving?"

"Because it's for the best. You want me to be your friend,

and this is me being that friend."

"I don't want you to go," she whispered.

River shut his eyes. "I know," he breathed, and it felt like there was more meaning behind his answer than what she understood.

"What were you two talking about?" she asked River, and he opened his eyes.

"I think you should ask him."

"I'm asking you."

"You know I love you, and I'll do anything for you. But this is something you need to talk to him about. Wait until you're alone with him, and don't let him get out of telling you. I'll be here for you if you have any questions."

River put his arms around her and hugged her. He held on a little longer than normal, but it didn't really feel like he was holding onto her for his benefit. It felt as if he were giving her support.

He let go of her and stared into her eyes. "I like it when your eyes are green," he murmured. "They match mine. It makes me feel like we're on the right track."

She smiled at him, and he smiled back before walking away.

Legacy walked back to Adin and Calli, but didn't talk about what River had said. They spent the rest of the day together, and by that evening, Zach had joined them. She knew Calli was happy to see him, but it made her sad that Adin and River didn't get along as well as Adin and Zach did. She remembered thinking Adin and Zach wouldn't have been friends if it weren't for their girlfriends. She wished there was some way to make Adin and River become friends for her benefit. She'd have to figure that out somehow.

Adin took her home from the festival, and it was the first time they'd been alone together all day. She knew she needed to ask him about his argument with River, but there wasn't a tactful way to do it. She figured she should wait until they were in her house before she started. She wanted to be able to watch his face, not him watch the road. So instead, she held his hand and rubbed his arm, knowing he could feel the two different temperatures of her hands.

When they got to her house, Lissa was there. She didn't want an audience for this conversation. They'd have to go someplace where they wouldn't be interrupted.

"Come upstairs with me for a minute," she said to Adin as she pulled on his arm. She figured her bedroom was the safest place to talk about this.

Once inside her room, she shut the door. She turned around to start her interrogation, but Adin was standing right in front of her with desire burning in his eyes. He pushed himself up against her, which shoved her against the door, and he locked his lips onto hers.

She was caught off guard by his reaction, but it slowly made sense. They hadn't seen each other in days, and she practically dragged him up to the privacy of her bedroom. Of course he would mistake why she wanted to be alone with him.

After the first few seconds of realization, her resolve wavered, and she threw her arms around him. She kissed him back with as much intensity as he was kissing her. She felt his hands slide down her sides, but his right hand left her body. She heard him fumble with the doorknob, and she realized he was locking it.

The sound of him locking the door made her shudder slightly. Even though they'd been alone in her bedroom before—and he had slept in her bed with her the night he brought her home from the hospital—they'd never been alone like *this* in either of their bedrooms. She was excited and nervous.

Adin broke away from their kiss suddenly, slid his hand into her hair — grabbing it and tilting her head — and kissed down the side of her neck ... all at the same time. Gods, that felt so good. She was squeezing him up against her as tightly as she could and gasping for air. The sound and feel of her panting against his skin made him moan, and he crushed his lips to hers again. She could feel him all over her, and she wanted more. She started sliding her right leg up and down the side of his, and Adin pressed himself even harder against her.

"Adin," she panted when he moved his lips back to her neck.

"Mmm?" he responded without moving his lips off her.

"I-ahh-I..." She wanted to tell him that she needed to talk to him, but his eager hands felt too good. She couldn't concentrate.

He moved his lips from her neck to her ear, kissing her along that path.

"Yes?" he breathed into her ear. His hot breath sent a powerful shiver through her body, and he liked that. He moved his lips hungrily to right below her ear, kissing her along her neck again.

"We have to talk," she whispered quickly. Adin ripped his face off her neck so that his lips were not on her. He was still holding her tightly, and now he was panting against her. His breathing sounded like groans as he tried to catch his breath.

They stood there until their breathing slowed. Then Adin lifted his head, stepped back one step, and rested his head against the side of hers. He moved his hands off her and onto the door. Their bodies were still touching, but at least they weren't compressed against each other.

"What do you want to talk about?" he finally asked.

She rubbed her hands up and down his waist in an effort

to ease the blow of the topic, but she was too worked up for that kind of touch.

"Umm..." *Forget it!* She squeezed his side and leaned her lips back over to his. He moaned as his opened mouth slowly found hers again, but his hesitation was evidence that he was trying to control his eager behavior. After a few seconds, he stepped back up against her, kissing her harder, and she knew she had to stop this now.

She put her hands on his chest and pushed him away. "Wait." She kept her hands on his chest as she threw her head back against the door and looked up at the ceiling.

"I'm sorry," he muttered.

"Don't be."

He took a few steps back so that they were no longer touching and ran his hands through his disheveled hair. He left his hands on top of his head, and she could feel him watching her. She didn't want to look at him and see the desire still burning in his eyes.

"Maybe you should go sit at the desk," she whispered, still watching the ceiling.

Adin retreated to the desk, and she took several deep breaths. She unlocked the door before she sat on the bed — she hoped *that* would provide them with the incentive to behave. She looked at him, and thankfully, his eyes were calm. They stared at each other for several seconds, and then Adin cracked a smile.

"What?" she asked, smiling back.

"You had a hard time controlling yourself." He smirked.

"Me?" She laughed. "You were the one who threw me against the door."

Adin took a deep breath and started to stare intensely into her eyes. It was way too soon to bring up any specifics of what'd just happened. If she didn't get this conversation going now, he'd find his way to her bed. "Stop," she breathed, shutting her eyes.

"We can't talk in here," Adin said, standing up. "Let's go outside and get some fresh air."

She sighed and nodded.

Adin followed her outside to the backyard and sat at the patio table across from her.

"So what do you want to talk about?"

She took a deep breath before starting. "I want to know what you and River were arguing about."

Adin gritted his teeth and stared at her. Then he shifted in his chair, put his arms on the table, and leaned his head down. "I don't want to talk about that."

"Why?"

"Because it's complicated."

"I have a right to know."

Adin flashed his gaze up to her and leaned back in his chair, folding his arms against his chest. "Fine. I'll tell you what's going on if you promise me you'll hear me out on everything I have to say."

She didn't like the sound of this. "Okay," she said timidly.

"Do you remember when I told you my family didn't get along with the Gorgos family?"

"Yes."

"That's because we already knew everything about them."

"What?"

"We knew they descended from the Greek gods … that they came from Medusa's line."

"W-Why didn't you tell me this?" If he'd told her, she could have avoided that psycho woman from the beginning!

Adin's eyes narrowed, and he took a deep breath. "Just because we knew where they came from doesn't mean we believed they were powerful. I didn't believe River's mother was capable of what she did to you."

"But when I told you about River that first time, you got mad at me for believing him."

"Legacy, I was never, *never* mad at you. I was angry with him for telling you. Once he found out enough information, he was able to make the connection to your mother. It was his way in, and it infuriated me."

She felt the blood fall out of her face, and she shook her head. "You knew who I was," she muttered incredulously.

He watched her eyes carefully. "Yes."

"That wasn't a question," she clarified.

Adin sighed. "My family has known, but I didn't know at first. When I was on vacation, I told my mom that I asked you out, so she told me a little about you. But she was careful not to say too much. Then I realized the possibility of who you really were when you told me about your conversation with River. When I visited my dad that first time, we talked about it. Remember, I told you that we fought? Well, that's why. I told him what you told me, and he confirmed what I suspected. Then he wanted me away from you. That's one of the reasons why he wanted me to go to school in Texas."

"Why did he want you away from me?"

"Because he knows there's a good chance we won't be together," Adin whispered, looking down.

"He believes the prophecy?" Tears started to form in her eyes.

"Yes." He glanced back up. "He believes a lot of things," he muttered sarcastically.

"But why?" She stared at him while he sighed, shaking his head. He was reluctant to continue, and warning bells were going off in her head, signifying they were on the verge of tearing into the heart of River's warning.

Adin sighed and shook his head. "Because we descended from the Greek gods too."

Legacy gaped at him, shaking her head in disbelief. Her knees were wobbling and a cold sensation crawled down her back. She felt as if she was about to faint. "River said you were mortal. You're already eighteen." No way. No way!

"That's another reason why I didn't want him telling you about all this. I've already lived with the expectation of changes, and my eighteenth birthday came and went without an ascension. That's one of the reasons why I never pursued you before. I didn't know how to explain everything. So after I turned eighteen and nothing happened, I realized I put my life on hold for a bunch of silly family stories that amounted to nothing."

"I talked to my mom. She said I would be going through changes. I believe her."

"I believed my parents too. I'm not saying it won't be different for you. I do know there are powerful gods out there. But it may not happen."

"You should have told me this!" she yelled, jumping out of her seat. She shook her head frantically while she backed away from the table, heading toward the house. When she reached the back wall, she leaned against it for support because she felt weak in the knees. Her breathing became hitched as reality sunk in. "It's like you've been lying to me." She started crying, and her head slumped into her hands.

Adin got up, walked to her, and put his hands on her arms. "I haven't lied to you," he whispered. He pulled her hands down to look at her eyes, but she kept them closed. "Please, Legacy. You promised you would hear me out. Please let me finish."

"Fine," she said angrily, opening her eyes and folding her arms against her chest. "Then, what's the other reason?"

"What are you talking about?"

"You said *one* of the reasons you didn't pursue me before

was because you expected to change too. What's the other reason?"

Adin shook his head while he stared at her. Then he shut his eyes before speaking. "I don't want to tell you that."

She started to cry again, which made her even angrier at him, so she pushed him away from her and walked back to the table. "Too bad," she said through her teeth.

Adin kept his gaze on her while he walked to the seat next to her. After sitting down, he stroked her arm while he spoke. "I was also hesitant before because the original god that I was created like already had a companion he was strongly linked to."

What? This was freaking crazy! Just frigging perfect. Not only was she furious with Adin, but now she felt sick for making him put up with River and acknowledging their bonded triangle. She never realized she had competition for Adin! "Which goddess?"

"Legacy, please don't..."

"Which one?" She said each word distinctly.

Adin pursed his lips. "Aphrodite."

Her hands flew to her mouth, and she gaped at him. "The goddess of love? Are you kidding me?" She remembered reading about her, but didn't really do any research because everyone already knew who she was! How was she supposed to compete with a goddess of beauty, sexuality, love, and all the other beautiful qualities that make men madly in love with women?

"Please don't worry about this, sweetheart. I love you. I want to be with you."

"Besides the fact that you are connected to her, how can I compete with a goddess of that stature? With her power over love, she could have any man she wanted. I couldn't stop her if she wanted you."

"If you're worried about repeating the destiny of

our original gods, then there *are* some stories that said the original god who I'm like spent part of his time with Persephone."

"The god that Persephone spent time with was Hades. Are you telling me you were created from him?" She started to cry again. This could not be happening to her. She was in love with Adin. Mom said Hades had a plan. If his plan was for her to fall in love with Adin, then he was already winning. She wanted to be with Adin no matter who he was created from or similar to.

"No! No, I'm not like Hades. He is a real threat to you. I'm not going to take you away from your family, and I'm not going to allow him to do that either."

"So why didn't you just tell me everything?" she demanded.

"I wanted you to find out for yourself. I mean, I wanted to help you—like when I brought up Lissa babysitting you on the night of your parents' accident—but I wanted you to be the one to put the pieces together. I wanted you in control of your destiny."

"We all have our own destinies to fulfill. We don't have to repeat the ones of our creators or the original gods we are like. And even if we are destined to do that to a certain degree, we still have a good chance of being together all the time since our similar gods were together part of the time." She took a deep breath, trying to rein in her anger. "The only other god I remember reading about that was with Persephone was Adonis."

Adin smiled at her.

"Adonis?" she asked incredulously.

"Yes. I'm not the original Adonis. I was created in his likeness, but I didn't ascend to a *godly* status when I turned eighteen."

"And this Aphrodite, have you met her?"

Adin sighed. "No. But she does exist, and that's one of the things my dad and I argued about. But she's with Adonis. They're happy. There's no reason for her to come looking for an alternative."

"Speaking of arguments, I take it you and *River* argued because he found out about you and believed you should've been honest with me. How long has he known the truth?"

Adin's eyes narrowed. He clearly didn't like her bringing up River. "We opened up about what we knew while you were in the hospital. We were alone with you for hours and hours every day, so we had to talk about something. Until then he had no idea that I was a part of his world. I probably wouldn't have said anything then, but I was too upset to think clearly. Obviously, if I had been in my right mind, I would have thrown him out of your room as soon as I got there. He *cannot* be trusted."

And she wouldn't have known to confront Adin. "How can you say that? He hasn't lied to me!"

"Legacy, I have *not* lied to you! I love you, so I did what I thought was best for you, not what I thought was best for me, and River is a selfish bastard who's only looking out for himself!"

She stood, stepping away from the table. "I think you should leave."

Adin's jaw dropped, and her heart ached to see the pain that formed on his face. "Sweetheart, please," he whispered, standing up.

"I heard what you had to say, and I'm having a hard time wrapping my head around the fact you kept this from me and discouraged me from getting information from River when you knew the truth all along." Her breathing hitched as tears leaked down her face.

He stepped forward. "I'm sorry," he breathed. "I thought I was doing the right thing for you."

She looked down, not able to stare at his watery eyes. "I know. I just need time to think."

And mend her heart.

Chapter

22

She woke up on the last Saturday of summer vacation thinking about everything, and she started with the most recent event—her fight with Adin.

She'd spent two days lost in her thoughts, trying not to cry at feeling betrayed by Adin. At times, she'd understood what he said, but at others, she'd felt let down by his not confiding in her. He'd called her several times, but she wasn't ready to talk. His messages had professed his sorrow and love, which made her a little too emotional to deal directly with him just yet.

Calli had brought over chocolate ice cream, and Legacy had cried on her shoulder. She couldn't discuss this mess with her other best friend. Legacy knew River meant well encouraging her to talk to Adin about this, but talking to River would just keep open the wound she was trying to close.

She knew she needed to wrap up this unfinished business with Adin since his banquet was coming up. She'd finally accepted the truth, which was Adin had no idea the Gorgos family was in town or that she'd confided in River about anything until long after the fact, so he wasn't the only one who hadn't been forthcoming with information.

With River and his mom out of town, Legacy could run by the store to get her last check. It didn't take long for her to get dressed and get to the store. She parked and ran in for probably the last time.

"Hey, Legacy. What are you doing here?" Yale asked.

"Came to get my check."

"Oh. It's in the break room by your timecard. C'mon."

Legacy followed her while Yale chattered on about the things she'd missed, which hadn't been much, and about Legacy's accident and time in the hospital.

"And Ms. Gorgos got the ceiling fixed fast. I think she was worried you'd sue her for your accident. I mean, I don't think you can do that since it wasn't her fault. It was an act of God, you know."

Oh, it was an act of a higher power, all right, but this power had been evil.

"That storm was nasty. Good thing you didn't get stuck hiking in it," Yale went on.

Legacy felt her scalp prickle, the hairs on the back of her neck standing. "I never told you that."

Yale turned around with an innocent expression. "Never told me what?"

"About hiking," Legacy said slowly.

Yale's innocent expression morphed to a cocky one.

"Oops."

It was her only warning. She lunged for Legacy as the ground started to shake. She tried to fight Yale off, but she was strong. Legacy didn't even have time to contemplate what was really happening. Other than she was fighting for her life.

Yale grabbed her hair and banged her head against the wall. Legacy saw stars and tried to stay conscious, the metallic taste of blood turning her stomach.

"I never think before I speak," Yale sneered.

Legacy elbowed Yale in the gut, straining to create enough momentum to knock the deranged chick off her feet. She wasn't completely successful, but Yale stumbled back enough for Legacy to grab hold of something. She looked to the side to see what she'd grasped.

A chair. Thank the gods!

Yale drew back her fist to punch Legacy when she flung the chair at her attacker.

"What's wrong with you?" Legacy screamed as Yale dodged her attempt at retaliation. Legacy swung it at her again, but Yale eluded her blow.

"Oh, come now … you know if I kill you, I'll get your powers."

Legacy charged her with nervous energy. Yale was apparently a part of the myths, but she couldn't think about that now.

"You can do better than that," Yale said, laughing as she flipped over Legacy and landed behind her. She grabbed Legacy's hair, yanked her head back with one hand, and wrapped an arm around her with another. Legacy was trapped. "You opened that box," Yale whispered, dangerously calm. "Before, your ascension would've been difficult. Now, it will be impossible. You set us free, and soon we will take your hope too."

Legacy elbowed Yale in the gut as hard as she could while she stomped on her foot. Yale screeched and slightly loosened her grip on Legacy's hair. She steeled herself against the coming pain and whipped her body around, hair ripping from her scalp. But she was free. She ran around the table and grabbed a letter opener that had been left from the day she and River had shredded all those documents. She wielded it like a sword. "Who are you?" Legacy panted.

"Euryale." But the word hadn't come from Yale's lips. Yale jerked her head up, looking for the source of the sound. Then she glared at Legacy.

"This is only the beginning!" she screeched. Then Yale's body dissolved into a bunch of snakes that slithered away.

What the hell?

Legacy didn't stand around figuring it out. She ran for her car, using her shirt to wipe the blood from her busted lip as the ground tremors stopped. Was Yale even real? Was she Medusa's pawn the whole time? She had to get out of here. First, the lightning strike, now the attack. Medusa was really gunning for her. She felt too rattled to explain what happened, but she knew she needed to call Adin. After not talking to her in two days, he answered on the first ring.

"Legacy? Sweetheart, I'm so—"

"Yale just tried to kill me," she screamed into the phone as she tried to contain her sobs.

"Son of a... Are you okay? Where are you?" She heard him rustling with his keys.

"I—I'm in my car, heading home."

"I'm across town, sweetheart. I'll be there as soon as I can."

Legacy screeched to a stop in her driveway and flew through the front door, right into Lissa. She grabbed Legacy's arms to stabilize her, staring at her face while Legacy rattled off the details of her attack, her voice getting louder, and by the end, she was screaming mad.

As she yelled, thunder crashed outside, and she gasped, looking around the room with nervous energy coursing through her. Had Medusa just tried to kill her through Yale? Was Medusa trying to kill her now with another storm? Legacy was borderline hysterical.

"Legacy, you need to calm down before you hurt yourself again!"

She frowned at Lissa, momentarily stunned by her words. "Again?"

All her dreams flashed through her mind while Lissa stared at her, waiting for the final piece of the puzzle to fall into place.

"Medusa?" Legacy couldn't even finish the question. She couldn't even finish the thought because she didn't know what she was trying to ask.

Lissa shook her head, watching her eyes.

Why was she thinking about her dreams? She already knew why she was having them. She was standing under the tornado. She wasn't scared of it, but she didn't want it to come. When she'd yelled *no* up at it, she thought she was yelling at the person responsible, which she later discovered was Medusa.

Legacy gasped, her dreams connecting to form a beautifully completed puzzle.

She'd been wrong. That was why she'd had that new dream again. She hadn't figured everything out like she'd thought.

"Medusa isn't causing the weather problems?" Legacy asked blankly.

"Not all of them."

"Who?"

"You know who."

"Me," she whispered. She knew, but she didn't

understand.

"Legacy, were you angry when you got hit by lightning?"

"I was fighting with River about Adin." Legacy exhaled slowly. "I hurt myself by accident because I was mad?"

"Yes. When you've been here and the weather's been beautiful, you've been happy —"

"And when I've been sad, it's been rainy or gloomy," she finished.

Lissa nodded.

"But what about the tropical storm in Florida when Adin was there?"

"That wasn't you. I believe that was Medusa's doing. Either she tricked Poseidon into doing that, or River did it."

"Why would River do that?"

"To get back at Adin for asking you out. I don't know for sure. And if he did do it, he might not have consciously done it. He may not know what he's capable of. Just like you didn't know you could control the weather, he probably doesn't realize his emotions are manifesting into his abilities."

Legacy stared at Lissa, a sense of understanding washing over her. "I can control the weather."

"Not yet, not really. You have to learn how to control your emotions, or the earth will suffer. If the earth suffers, everyone suffers. This is the change you are going through. You need to accept this and learn to deal with your emotions properly. If you are unable to control yourself, the consequences could be devastating. And not just for you."

Everything was clicking now. "That's why Medusa had the red herring in my dream. She was distracting me from the truth that it was me all along causing the weather here, not her."

"Right. And she'll keep messing with you, Legacy. You said you heard the word 'Euryale' when you asked who

Yale was. That's the name of one of Medusa's immortal sisters. This has Medusa's handiwork written all over it. She wants your powers, and she wants revenge against Poseidon. He is the reason the original Medusa was killed. Demeter and Poseidon are siblings, of sorts, and they both have earthly abilities. If she kills you, it would devastate Demeter, which will sadden Poseidon. Plus, she'll gain some of those abilities when she destroys you, making her more powerful than Demeter. I think that's what she's really after. The revenge angle is an emotional reason. She's a monster. She's incapable of true emotion."

"But why would this new Medusa create River with Poseidon if she wants revenge against him?"

"Because she's a monster, Legacy. You're looking for logic from an entity incapable of being reasonable. But from an outside perspective, I would think that maybe she wanted to cover all her angles of attack against you and your mother. Poseidon probably hoped the new Medusa had more heart than the original one, and she used his kindness against him."

Since Poseidon and Demeter were siblings, that'd make River her cousin. "Why would there be a prophecy involving cousins being together? I know this is the south and all, but that's gross."

Lissa chuckled as they finally sat down. "I said they were *like* siblings. When gods create new gods together, it isn't always a romantic creation. I'm sure you've read some of the stories on Greek mythology. A god doesn't even need another god to create a new god."

That made sense. Now that she didn't have to worry about being romantically bonded to a type of cousin, she needed other answers. "Why did you tell River when I was in the hospital that Medusa hurt me when she hadn't?"

"Because my job is to help you, and it was what he

needed to hear. He needs to be strong for you because he's your best ally when it comes to stopping Medusa. He's going to be powerful soon."

"So you know River is going to be powerful, but what about Adin? He told me he descended from the gods too. That he was created in the likeness of Adonis. His parents told him he'd ascend, but when he turned eighteen, nothing happened."

"Everything isn't always as it seems."

Hmm, Adin had told her the same thing. "Okay, what about Hades? Mom said he knows, and he has a plan."

"Hades is a real threat to you. He's always been, though. He may now have a plan to take you away, but that doesn't mean he hasn't tried before. I don't want you consumed with fear. Adin and River will protect you. You just have to be careful with them."

"Why do I need to be careful with them? Shouldn't I be careful about Hades?"

"That's not what I meant. Obviously you need to be wary of Hades. But Adin and River both have very strong feelings for you. Your safety is their main objective, and I don't want their feelings to cloud their judgment. They both want to be with you, but you can only be with one of them. One will get hurt." She paused and stared directly at Legacy. "There is *no* way around that. But if they let their emotions get the best of them and Hades gets to you, then both will get hurt. I think you knowing this—how much River and Adin are hurting—will be what ultimately destroys you if captured. They can love you, but they cannot lose sight of what's really important. You have to be careful with their emotions, Legacy."

That made sense, but she suddenly realized that Lissa always talked about her mom, never her dad. "When you told me my mom was alive, why didn't you tell me my dad was too?"

"I am your mother's priestess. I was created to serve her."

Okay. As Legacy internalized that bit of information, she thought about her dreams again, searching for answers, completing the rest of the puzzle. "The lightning in my dreams." And it clicked right there. She smiled. "It's not real lightning. It falls from the sky like confetti and glitters, but it never reaches me. Why is that?"

"Why do you think that is?" Lissa smiled too, apparently knowing where Legacy was going with this.

"Because my dad is Zeus. The lightning bolt is his symbol, and in my dreams, the lightning symbolized him. It fell from the sky and glittered down as a gesture. It was as if he were showering me with his love." There was no doubt in her mind that this was the reason.

"Very good," Lissa whispered.

"So I inherited the lightning ability from him."

Lissa nodded cautiously. She obviously knew more, but wasn't going to elaborate. At this point, it didn't really matter. She'd been attacked not fifteen minutes ago, and here she was relishing in understanding.

Lissa took Legacy's hands in hers. "You have been given a great gift, Legacy. Not the abilities or the chance of eternal life. You have an opportunity to live out *your* legacy."

"What happens when the legacy I seek isn't the one I'm destined to have?"

"For now, just know that it's your free will to live your life the way you choose. You can develop a relationship with Adin or River and seek that happily ever after."

"I have relationships with both of them." She immediately felt defensive.

"And that's your decision, but Legacy, you're going to have to make a choice before someone makes it for you."

"I've already decided." Legacy pulled her hands away from Lissa and rubbed her aching face. She needed some Tylenol. And her scalp was on fire. "Any insight as to what happens now?"

"You keep changing. You'll get stronger, and with the help of the people who love you, you'll get more controlled the closer you get to eighteen. You'll be experiencing things you may have no idea how to accept. At times, it'll be very difficult for you to understand what is happening, but you'll need to learn how to harness your abilities."

"Then what happens … when I turn eighteen?"

"You haven't chosen the path you wish to take in your life, Legacy. You may know what you want now, but other circumstances haven't come into play. Until they do and you and the others decide on those circumstances, your destiny, your *legacy* is unclear."

Legacy was grateful for Lissa's help, and she realized her guardian had been helping her all along by letting her discover these truths with River and Adin. She must have known Legacy needed to embrace the bond she had with the two of them on her own terms. If Lissa had told her this in the beginning, Legacy wouldn't have believed her. She had been so disbelieving that she hadn't even listened to herself, her old soul.

The roar of Adin's engine blaring down the road and the squeal of tires as he slammed on the brakes jolted her from the couch. He was running through the door before she reached it.

"Oh, sweetheart." He grabbed her face, gaping at her injuries. "Come here." He pulled her into his arms, dragging her into the bathroom.

He retrieved a washcloth and gently wiped her face once he'd wet it, without speaking. He looked all over her face, making sure he inspected and treated every abrasion.

He looked everywhere ... except her eyes. They had fought about Adin not telling her everything he knew, and now he seemed to be walking on eggshells. This was not how she'd pictured their reunion.

"Why did Yale attack you?" he murmured while brushing her hair aside, looking at her busted lip.

"It was Medusa's doing. She turned into snakes after working me over. I heard the name Euryale, so she was either Medusa or some manifestation of her or her sister."

Adin sighed, resting his forehead against hers, shaking his head, the sound of a tortured animal escaping his lips, and she knew it was the guilt—that he hadn't believed River's mother was capable of harming her like that— causing it. "I'm sorry," he barely said.

He finally took a deep breath, squatting in front of her and making eye contact for the first time since they'd entered the room. "I love you so much, Legacy," he whispered.

"I love you t-too." She did not want to cry, but his sincerity tore her up.

"I'm so sorry about everything. I have felt horrible ever since we fought. It feels like I've failed you, and I never wanted to do that."

Legacy didn't want to rehash their discussion from last night because she knew she couldn't take the emotional drain, but Adin was in so much pain that she wanted to make him feel better. "I understand why you kept quiet. I honestly do."

"I promise you I will try to tell you everything from here on out. No matter how hard it may be for me to talk about things that could hurt you."

Legacy didn't want him making that kind of promise. She wasn't sure he could keep it. "I'm going to trust your judgment," she said as she stroked his cheek, hoping he understood she meant that.

He put his arms around her waist and pulled her into his lap as he sat fully on the floor. He buried his face in her hair, holding her to him. "Can I finish telling you what I know?" he whispered. Legacy nodded and he squeezed her tighter. "My dad explained to me that after I was created like Adonis, Demeter decided to recreate Persephone."

"Me?"

"Yes, sweetheart. When Demeter was successful, she needed to hide you from Hades. She left you here in Lissa's care, so you could live your life in peace and have a chance to make your own decisions. That's what I know. Now, what I think is that our families decided to have us grow up together to see if we'd have more control over our destinies. I don't know for sure, but that's my guess."

"They wanted us to be together?"

"I don't think they planned it like that—hoped is a better word. I think they wanted to give us the free will to choose, but I'm sure my grandma lives next door to you for a reason." He chuckled.

"But then the Gorgos family moved here."

He pulled back, clasping his hands on her cheek to stare into her eyes. "My theory is that Medusa wants revenge against your mother, so she wants to destroy you. If she destroys you, then she gains your powers in the process—if you have any. Plus, it'll keep River from being with you. The possibility of you and River forming a relationship is a chance she's willing to take. I'm sure she thinks if that happens, she'll use it against you. I'm also certain she thinks she can control River. I'm worried he'll end up doing her dirty work for her. Your accident is proof that's possible, sweetheart."

But he didn't know what she'd just learned. She told him about her conversation with Lissa, telling him the truth about everything. He was shocked to hear about her weather abilities, but he believed her.

"You know I love you. I'll love you no matter what happens to you when you turn eighteen. But you have to know I'll protect you from Hades and Medusa, which in my mind, means River too."

She knew Adin would protect her at all costs. As for the River battle, well, they'd save that for another day.

Adin continued to rock Legacy, caressing her side, her hair, touching her and kissing her while she thought back over everything that'd happened. Over the last few months, she'd found out about her mom, fell in love, found a new best friend, and believed in the mythically impossible. It was amazing how different her life was now. She had changed. There was no doubt about that. Whether these changes were the ones that Lissa had told her about on her birthday or a byproduct of experience, Legacy didn't have a clue. But she liked these changes just the same.

After realizing this, she now understood consciously what her subconscious self had been trying to tell her all along. She could control the weather and possibly other things. But more importantly, she was a powerful goddess.

Well, at least she was going to be.

Epilogue

Adin was taking her to his freshmen banquet tonight at his new school. She started getting ready with a manicure and pedicure at the salon, and Calli tagged along. They talked about her conversation with Lissa and her life in general. She could always count on her to listen when she needed and change the subject when she was through venting. And she did just that.

"So what are you wearing tonight?"

"I want to look perfect for Adin, so I'm going to wear the red silk dress that Lissa gave me on my birthday. I was saving it for a special occasion, and tonight will be perfect. And it goes great with the red shoes that you gave me, of course." She chuckled.

"You are going to look hot!"

"That's the idea," she said, and they both laughed.

"Well, since we're at the salon, you might as well have one of the stylists do your hair."

"That's a good idea. One less thing for me to have to do when I get home."

When she and Calli finished with their nails, Calli had a hairdresser style Legacy's hair into a loose side bun. Then Legacy went back home to finish getting ready. She fixed her makeup for an evening look and put on some dangly earrings that accentuated her hairdo. She put on the red silk dress and the red stilettos. She also wore the watch that Adin had given her, though she wore it every day. Lastly, she clasped the platinum necklace that her mother had sent her.

After she put on the necklace, she lifted the pendant, the meaning finally dawning on her. It wasn't just an abstract design of a triangle formed with platinum wire and sprinkled with diamonds like she had originally thought. It wasn't abstract at all—it was a tornado.

She stood in front of the mirror and saw how beautiful she was. She was never one to be vain, but she had to admit she looked like a goddess. She shrugged it off by thinking it was the professional help she'd received in her attempt to be beautiful for Adin, but at least she *was* beautiful.

She waited downstairs for Adin to arrive. Even though they'd been dating all summer, she felt strangely nervous. She figured it was probably because this was the first time they'd gone out like this—they would be meeting a lot of new people, and she was naturally a shy person. Plus, so much had happened in the last twenty-four hours. They had fought about Adin not telling her everything he knew, and he confessed that he'd continue to make those types of judgment calls for her benefit. And she also discovered her abilities while talking to Lissa. A very eventful twenty-four hours indeed.

When she heard the knocks on the door, she felt the butterflies in her stomach like she had felt on that first date. She smiled at herself because she knew it was silly to feel this way. She got up and took a deep breath before getting the door.

When she opened it, there stood Adin, her own personal Adonis, literally. He was astonishingly handsome. He had his hair gelled and fixed perfectly, and his blue eyes gleamed like the sky on the clearest of days. He was wearing a black suit with a white shirt and a red silk tie. She reached over, lifted the tie, and looked at him with her eyebrows raised.

"I talked to Calli," Adin said, glowing like he was looking at his own personal goddess. And she was just that—his.

"Of course." She smiled.

Adin stepped closer. "You look…" He stopped and sighed. "You look so very beautiful. A vision of true beauty." Then he pulled his right hand out from behind his back and handed her a dozen red roses. "These are for you."

She smiled and took them from him. "Thank you. You look very handsome yourself. I think I'm going to have to change my favorite outfit that I've seen you in. The swimming trunks with no shirt just dropped to second place," she said with a laugh.

He laughed too, and then she took his hand and led him into the house so she could put the flowers in water. When she finished with that, Adin leaned down and kissed her before leading her to his car. She used the ride to his new school as an opportunity to tell him her latest theory.

"You know, if everything isn't always as it seems, then maybe the prophecy isn't real. River has helped me by telling me about Greek mythology. Maybe he wouldn't have done that if he didn't believe he would be with me. Plus, he's helped me by bringing out some strong emotions. When I was happy with you, the weather was beautiful. Then as our relationship heated up, so to speak" — she blushed at the thought — "so did the weather. When you were gone, I was sad, and the weather was rainy. But these are typical characteristics of summer in the south. The anger River brought out of me ignited my fierce reaction, which triggered the lightning. I probably wanted to hit him, so my aim must be off." She laughed.

"True." Adin chuckled.

"So maybe there's a reason behind the prophecy — that it was meant to bring me and River together to help us with our emotions during our changes, and it isn't really literal."

"That's an interesting thought," Adin said, nodding. "I'd like that very much."

"I'm sure you would." She stroked his leg. "I just wish I understood why Lissa said I may already know who I want, but that there were other factors to be considered. Factors that haven't presented themselves yet, and once those elements are considered, my destiny will become clear."

For that, Adin didn't have an answer.

When they pulled into the full parking lot, her butterflies from earlier reappeared. "I wonder why I'm so nervous."

"You're probably just worried about making a good impression."

"Maybe." He was probably right. She and Adin had gone out many times, but this was the first time he'd be showing her off.

They walked into the hall, and everyone was dressed up. Adin introduced her to the dean and the faculty that he remembered from his orientation. There were sororities and fraternities present trying to recruit new freshmen. She figured even though they were not of true Greek descent, Adin might embrace their ancestry and pledge to one. Though, most who joined did it for the parties. She wasn't an idiot.

As they watched the crowd, she noticed all the beautiful women. There were a lot of them, and she caught several of them eyeing the man on her arm. Seeing all these beautiful strangers reminded her of something from long ago.

"There are a lot of beautiful people here," she murmured. She thought it best to stay generic and not say beautiful *women*.

"Hmm? I guess so." Adin shrugged.

"Some of them are eyeing you," she said, looking down.

"They are probably wondering how I ended up with the most beautiful woman in the world."

She chuckled. He was trying to make her feel better, and it was working. "I remembered you used to come to dances with beautiful girls, and you never brought the same girl twice." There was no doubt he could have any woman he wanted.

Adin laughed. "It's not what you think."

She looked at him with an eyebrow raised.

"Those girls were family."

"What? You could have asked anyone you wanted. Why did you bring family?"

"Because by the time I got to high school, I knew who I wanted to be with." Adin smiled and slid his fingers along her cheek. "But she wasn't ready. Since I couldn't ask you, I didn't want to bring the same cousin to all the dances — you'd think I was taken if I'd done that." He laughed again.

"You are taken," she whispered, and leaned over to kiss him.

"Yes, I am."

They spent the rest of the banquet shaking a lot of hands

and meeting a lot of the entering freshmen. She couldn't remember anyone's name, but Adin was doing a better job at remembering some of them.

The evening went really well, so she felt kind of silly for getting the butterflies earlier. As it drew to a close, she stepped away from Adin to use the restroom before they left. When she stood in the bathroom, she couldn't help looking at her face. She was glowing. She was happy. She was complete as long as she was with her Adin.

As she walked out of the restroom, she saw Adin talking to one of the women they had spoken to earlier, but she couldn't remember her name. She was stunningly beautiful, though. She had long, thick hair and a body so curvy that it'd make even the most committed man do a double take. She guessed the woman grabbed the first opportunity to speak to him alone. Adin looked like he was being polite, but that woman seemed a little domineering. She was laughing and touching his arm. It was obvious to Legacy that she was flirting with him, so Legacy wasn't going to sit back and let her have her fun. She was going to walk up there and put a stop to it.

As Legacy walked over, Adin spotted her and smiled. She smiled back, and he put his arm around her when she reached him.

"Legacy, you remember Venus."

"Sure." She was glad Adin threw her name out there.

"Apparently, we have several classes together."

Venus stuck her hand out to Legacy and she shook it. "It was a pleasure meeting you tonight," she offered.

"Likewise. Adin is going to love this school. My parents went here, and they brag all the time about how much fun they had here with each other."

The woman seemed very polite, and Legacy felt silly again for the initial reaction she had to her flirting with

Adin. But still, it was good for that chick to see he was not available for her to have fun with.

She turned to face Adin. "Are you going to pledge?"

"I haven't decided." He shrugged his shoulders.

"I am. My parents are *legacies*, so I don't really have a choice. They're really into the mythical stuff."

The way Venus stressed the word "legacies" made Legacy's spine prickle. She made a noncommittal sound and nodded at the woman. Why did she feel very uneasy all of a sudden?

"That's why they named me Venus. My last name is Dionne, which means most beautiful, and Venus is the very definition of beauty, love, and sex. She is, after all, the Roman form of Aphrodite."

Legacy took in a quick breath, trying not to gasp. She felt weak in the knees, but she also had a sense that she needed to run. Adin flashed his gaze over to her and tightened his grip around her waist. She was sure he'd caught the same thing she had.

After everything Legacy had learned this summer, she knew what this meant. Adin said Aphrodite was happy and not looking for an alternative. And she believed him. She still did. Venus wasn't Aphrodite, the goddess of love. She was Aphrodite's likeness. Just like Adin was Adonis's likeness. Venus came here to get Adin. Legacy knew it. She was positive.

She was sure because she knew the one rule that seemed to be constant in her mind since the beginning of summer.

There were no coincidences.

The End

About the Author

Mandy Harbin is an award-winning, bestselling author of several books across multiple romance genres ranging from contemporary to paranormal erotic romance. She is also the number one bestselling author in teen romance under the pen name M.W. Muse with her popular Goddess Series. She is a Superstar Award recipient, Reader's Crown and RWA Passionate Plume finalist, and has received Night Owl Reviews Top Pick distinction many times. She studied writing at the University of Arkansas at Little Rock, earned several degrees, and even pursued an MBA until she realized becoming an author did not have to remain an unfulfilled dream. Mandy is a PAN member of the RWA and lives in a small Arkansas town with her non-traditional family, and although she is a direct descendant of British royalty, they refuse to call her princess. When she's not penning her latest book, you can find her hanging out online where she loves to connect with fellow readers or stalking Mickey Mouse at Disney World.

www.MandyHarbin.com
www.MWMuse.com

Author's Note

Want to stay up to date on all the latest info? Sign up for my Newsletter! I do giveaways and stuff.

Need more? My website has details on the next release. You can also like me on Facebook. I don't mind. I'm kinda likable.

Finally, I want to thank you for reading this book! If you enjoyed it, I would be very grateful for a review. If you didn't like it, leave a review anyway... as long as it's honest, that's all that matters.

And cake. Cake matters, too.